THE PIRATE QUEEN OF RUIN

A SINS OF THE FLESH NOVEL

ASH RAVEN

Copyright © 2023 by Ash Raven

All rights reserved.

No part of this publication may be reproduced, stored or transmitted in any form or by any means, electronic, mechanical, photocopying, recording, scanning, or otherwise without written permission from the publisher. It is illegal to copy this book, post it to a website, or distribute it by any other means without permission.

This novel is entirely a work of fiction. The names, characters and incidents portrayed in it are the work of the author's imagination. Any resemblance to actual persons, living or dead, events or localities is entirely coincidental.

Map designed using Inkarnate

Sensitivity Read by Nemosyne Digital

Edited by Lunar Rose Editing Services

Cover art by Rowan Woodcock

No part of this book was created using AI (Artificial Intelligence)

Violence can be the answer, even if it's fictional

Contents

Thank you for picking up the second book in my soft, dark Monster Romance series, Sins of The Flesh. This is an adult Sapphic romance featuring an Eldritch Tentacle God, their Pirate Captain, and the human heiress that binds them. Please read through the warning below to prepare yourself, and know that this is not an exhaustive list.

CONTENT TAGS:

Throuple power, murder as a love language, ovipositing for power, rejected mates, arranged marriage gone wrong, yo-ho pirates, a sexy sword fight, my body is literally a temple, grovelling, the eldritch horror plays matchmaker, everybody fucks everybody

TRIGGER WARNINGS:

Sexual assault (on page, semi graphic), physical assault, child abuse (historic, semi graphic), drugging, trauma responses, fatphobia (not MCs), parental abuse (emotional), violence, gore, necromancy, body horror blood, torture, mention of human trafficking, murder, humans as a source of power

SEX RELATED KINKS:

Ovipositing (no pregnancy), tentacles, stuffing, aphrodisiac, knife play, light bondage, spanking (pussy and ass), traffic light system safe words, praise kink, captain kink, voyeurism, orgy, light degradation (not MCs), ass play, spitting, power exchange dynamics, edging and orgasm denial

If you think a warning was missing here, please send me an email at: ash@authorashraven.com

Founding & Notable Members

Augustine Ravenscroft (he/they)

Deg'Doriel 'Father Doug' (he/him)

Ramón Lagarto (he/him)

Orthia Moore (she/her)

Kragnash 'Nash' Hawthorn (he/him)

Nora Birch (she/her)

Arlo O'Shea (he/it)

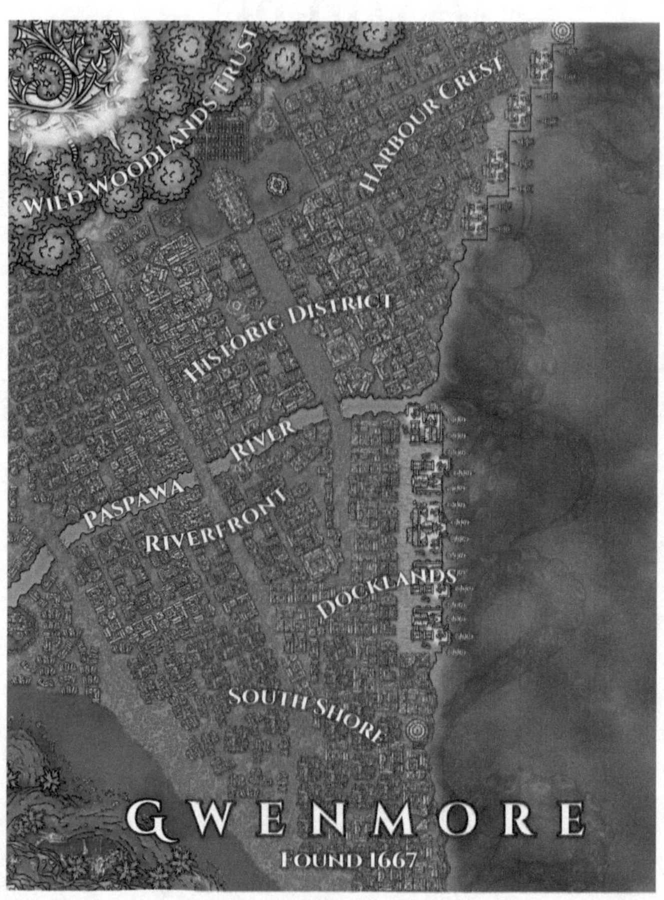

WILD WOODLANDS TRUST
HARBOUR CREST
HISTORIC DISTRICT
RIVER
PASPAWA
RIVERFRONT
DOCKLANDS
SOUTH SHORE
GWENMORE
FOUND 1667

PROLOGUE
ORTHIA

Screams erupt from the temple. My sisters scatter across the busy streets of Moorcri to escape the advances of the king's men. Since my brother has taken the throne, they don't fear the wrath of the goddess as they should. Our vows to her are sacred, yet these men think to make light of such things.

I am not scared of them. As it is neither a holy day nor one for tribute, they have no right to enter our sacred place. Their presence has disrupted the prayers of my sisters, the ones who entreat the goddess to continue our blessings of prosperity. The cloaks they wear over their armour mean nothing to me, and I won't remain silent under such an attack to our priestesses.

"Soldiers," I shout, rushing through the temple to find three of them have cornered one of the women. "How dare—"

"Ah, Princess." The captain of the guard swings around, the smile on his face as foul as a pig's. "Just the maiden we are looking for."

Before I began the rites to become a priestess for our goddess, the captain of the guard had attempted to court me. He was my father's best soldier, my brother's advisor in war, both statuses that should have allowed him marriage to me. But I could never be with a man, let alone one as foul as him.

"Unhand her before I have your heads," I demand. "I should have your honours striped and your backs flogged for even stepping foot in here."

"I see you have passed the second rites then." He eyes my newly shaved head. "Pity. The King wishes to speak with you," the captain sneers.

"Then leave this place," I say, matching him look for look.

He stares me down for a moment, a hatred for me in his eyes. "Men, take your leave."

I watch them exit the temple. There is no trusting these guards, not since my brother was crowned. I peer over to the priestess before I cross the boundary. She nods at me, and then I am off to the palace to speak with my brother.

The men surrounding my brother's throne all stand and make way when they see me approach. My fury must be palpable. To have their guards distress the holy women who serve our kingdom is unspeakable. I won't stand for such a thing.

"Ah, sister, there you are."

The king's smile is cruel when he finally graces me with his attention. My brother has always been ruthless about getting what he wants. I know the servants still whisper about how our eldest brother passed under such distressing circumstances. My eldest brother always respected the gods, respected our temple, and prayed to the goddess as he should.

Devotion is something our father demanded of us. For the goddess will always protect us. Before his death on the field of battle, he encouraged me to make my vows to the goddess, to join the temple, and to be her servant. I have promised myself, my maidenhood, and my soul to the goddess, and on the full moon I will place my offerings before her altar to complete the rites. Then, I will have only one mission in my life: to serve our goddess and spread her story.

"Your majesty." I dip my head as his title demands of me. "Is there a reason you have sent your men into the temple without cause?"

"Your sharp tongue will not do you well," he scowls. My brother steps off his dais, and there is a glint in his eye as he stares down at me. "Maybe I should simply remove it. I'm sure your new husband won't care if you can speak. He's given me quite a lot of warriors for your maidenhood."

"You despicable-"

The clap rings out around the halls of the palace as he backhands me hard enough that I tumble to the floor. I move to cover my face and find blood on my lips. His precious rings have cut me. My body shakes with anger, unrepentant and violent. I stand up again, ready to fight the king, to kill my own brother if I must.

There isn't time to strike or shout before ladies I have never met before rush to my side. I fight them, watching my brother as they drag me from the hall. Strangers scrub my body with foul-smelling oils and coarse brushes and ignore my struggle before dressing me in a long robe. They are staff of the man my brother has sentenced me to marry. They don't know me or care about me. My body trembles with each yank of my arm, each forceful action these women bend me into until they are shoving me through the halls of my own palace.

My hands are bound in delicate ribbons, a beautified prisoner for a stranger. There is a ceremony performed by my brother, an act of disobedience to our goddess, the sole being capable of blessing such a marriage, and he has the audacity to smile. Next to him, the captain of the guard smirks, as if he knows something he shouldn't. I refuse to say the words, and they move on without me. My choice in the matter means nothing to them.

I can't look my new husband in the eye. I can't bear the sight of him, or my brother. Those disgusting men have been conspiring since the ceremony ended, discussing plans to join our nations. We are two small islands in this great world. Not even our combined forces could stop the neighbouring northern islands from sending us all to Hades. This is not about peace or a united front against our enemies. My brother is a greedy king, hungry for all the power he can get his hands on. He is using me to get more.

"Princess," my husband calls out, waving his goblet from the far side of the room where I am doing my best to pretend that today has never happened. "It's time we take to our beds. Tomorrow will be a long journey for us."

My blood, which had been thrumming from the copious amounts of wine I've consumed, turns to ice. The female servants around me rise to usher me to the room where we are to complete our marriage rites. The feasts have been conducted, and now it is time for this. Walking through the palace is a blur, yet I can't think clearly enough to remind the women where my rooms are. They push me hard into the arms of a guard and I don't understand what is happening. Before I can reprimand them or demand the guard unhand me, a cloth is tied around my mouth. Furious tears drip down my cheeks as I struggle.

The captain of the guard comes into view.

"His majesty said to throw her on his ship. If there is anything left of her in the morning, he'll behead her himself."

My body shivers uncontrollably in the chill of the early morning. I am numb to the pain, the feeling of hands grabbing, pushing, choking. There is no part of me that is left untouched. My screams and tears do not affect these monsters, nor do they move the gods to grant me the mercy of death.

The sun crests over the water and blinds me from my position tied to the railing of the ship. My wrists have stopped bleeding; the rope is crusted around my flesh now. Other fluids have caked across my body. The blood between my thighs is still damp. I stare off at the sea until a slap across my face steers my focus away from the despair I feel for my existence.

"Oh, looky here," a sailor shouts. "Bitch is still alive. You looking for a second round, princess?"

I would rather peel my flesh from my bone before I let another man touch me. My mouth opens to hurl some form of abuse at the cretin, but I have no voice. A rasping sound leaves me, and that is it. He laughs at me, and more of the crew join in. They all stare at me now, some grabbing hold of their crotches.

"Clean 'er up," another man announces, a sneer so vile spreading across his lips that my stomach rolls. "She's ta be presented back to her husband."

A crowd cheers as I am dragged, naked and bound, from the docks up to the cliff where the palace stands tall above all else. My childhood home overlooks our island and our ocean. It's all ruined now. As we pass by the many shops that line the market, bodies are strewn among the burnt buildings. Shops along the market have been looted and proprietors executed. Outside the temple, naked and broken, my sisters kneel, forced to watch my demise as well.

We are barely past them when cheering erupts, and I know they have been slain. May they rest in peace as they deserve. May their stories echo across the underworld for all to hear. The gods have abandoned us.

Overlooking the sea in a courtyard of the palace, there is a small altar made of the purest stone our people could find when they first came to be on this island. It is a holy place to make sacrificial offerings to our goddess, and my brother's head lies next to it. The scrapes against my torso now as I am bent over it, next in line to die.

Then comes the rustling of leather and metal as the guards who stand for this new king gather around and watch. The captain of the guard stands proud in front of them all, the same smirk on his face from the ceremony. The pig.

"Today, we put an end to a cursed line of rulers, ones who wish to keep you in the dark, ones who deprive you of the real message." The traitorous man I was forced to marry addresses the crowd.

A heavy blade is placed along my neck. There is no fear left in my body, no humanity. I snarl and kick out like a wild animal. Whips lash across my skin, but I don't stop. These traitors will know that I will not go out without a fight.

"This is the end of an era of lies," he continues, the sword lifting off my neck. The last thing I hear is a whistle of iron slicing through the air, yet I try one last time to voice my rage.

"Suff-"

Water surrounds me, crushes me, swallows me whole until I have become one with it. How I am alive again, I don't know. There is no light, only darkness and fury. My body burns, and a fire courses through my broken limbs even as the water tries to extinguish it. Nothing will cure me of this rage.

A ripple in the water causes me to snarl. I bare my teeth, all that is left in my mouth, as if that will frighten off the creatures of the deep. My pain is the only thing keeping my mind clear of the fog that is threatening to take over me.

The goddess did not protect me, did not save me from the hell I was forced into. Her brutal inaction as I wailed for it all to end, I will remember it for the rest of my days. The gods do not care for us mortals because we are not worth saving. A chaotic and evil creation that only causes suffering.

How I would make those who cause harm shudder in fear. How I would burn cities to the ground to strike terror into all those who think to take away another choice. I will ruin any king or man who crosses my path. I will ruin the world until there is nothing left and I can start a new one to prove to all how wrong they were.

I will not be an absent god.

The water surrounding me suddenly evaporates and I am lying on the floor, gasping for air.

"Who calls to us from the depths?"

The voices that erupt in the darkness with such force bring tears to my eyes. As terror and rage war within me, I can't find mine to answer. There is a flicker of light, like a flint striking stone to create fire. It doesn't catch though.

Instead I am left in the dark, unseeing as the ground beneath me morphs into something softer, something slick that writhes against my bleeding flesh. A humming surrounds me until my muscles have turned soft and I believe I will melt into nothing.

Still I can't speak. My lips part, but not even a sound comes out.

"Hush," the voices rasp and the floor begins to envelop me.

My body is too weak to panic, whatever spell this creature has cast upon me is set. As it absorbs me, finally reaching my end, I want for nothing but revenge. Regret that I shall never have it turns my stomach.

The pain of my body that kept my thoughts clear lessens and a fog rolls in. It douses my thoughts until the rage inside me cools, but I crave vengeance.

"Yes, you shall be our heart."

Tentacles surround me, engulfing my senses. There is no light, only the scent of pomegranates in the air, like the blossoms of the trees in spring and the ripe fruit mix together as I gasp for air. My body is still even as I demand it move. I must move, because I have no other course of action but to ruin those who sought to hurt me and my family. Even if they were my blood once, they are no longer.

"To have what you seek, you must give up your past, give up your false gods."

"Th-" My voice finally cracks and the sound echoes in the vastness of the dark. "There are no gods."

The appendages move me, lifting and anchoring me until I dangle in the air. The flint strikes again and a pink light burns softly. Tentacles the colour of the ocean on a summer's day cover every place I look. They pile on top of each other and move in masses. Suddenly eyes blink open, creating spots in the fleshy walls of this prison.

"Our heart," the voices hum a soothing vibration. *"There is a god, and it is we."*

Fear and terror should be running through my veins. My body should tremble at such a sight, but I find that I can't bring myself to such a pitiful act. There is nothing I worship now, nothing I will ever feel but hatred for my humanity and those people.

"Give yourself over to us, our heart. Allow us your temple and we shall enact a great violence. We shall bring about a new world order, and give you what you seek— revenge." Their voices soothe and stoke the burning anger in me all at once.

A tentacle rises towards my face, the soft glow hypnotising me as it presses into my forehead. Before my eyes, a pink light ruptures and the image before me is one of destruction. I stand in the throne room of the palace, my body dripping with the blood of my enemies. Tentacles slip in and out of my body as I raise the head of my husband high in offering.

The pink light flashes again and the vision changes. I am surrounded by creatures the likes of which I have never seen before. These monsters caress each other with care and love. My body sings with a new feeling as I watch them find pleasure and peace within the arms of their sisters. It's only when they part that I see a figure emerge.

She is a goddess, her brown skin and eyes glistening as she approaches me. Her soft, round figure melds with the water, distorting her from me. Is that a hand reaching for me, or is it a tentacle? I want to hold onto both. The mirage before me ripples between that of a woman and that of tentacles until I can't decipher which is more real, until I believe they are all the same being.

"Come to us, Orthia," she pleads from the water. "Find me."

"The missing part of our soul calls for you, Princess Orthia of Moorcri. She floats through the cosmos, waiting for the time we can rise from the abyss and be whole again. She waits for you to claim her as our soul's mate so we three may be in one union. But first you must protect our power within your temple, use our abilities to gather the essences of beings to give us strength."

If they wish for such a broken harbinger, then they shall have it if that is what it will take to get my revenge. I will gather their strength and do whatever it takes to bring them to our world.

"How will I know she is the one?" I ask.

"From this day forth, only the touch of your soulmates will bring comfort and pleasure."

"Then so be it."

The flint strikes again, this time burning brighter, and the pink light explodes. The tentacles around me quiver and press to my flesh. It is only then I feel the meat of my body, the broken skin and bones begin to meld together. As tentacles stitch me together again, I feel their own sharp edges mar my skin, etching into me the mark of this new beginning.

"When you strike, strike for us, our heart. Feed us and we shall grow."

My body shakes with each step I take up to the palace. The bodies of guards still litter the hard-to-reach areas, and blood stains the mosaic beneath my bare feet. There are men shouting ahead of me, barking commands as someone softly cries out. My nostrils flare as I allow the rage into my lungs. I grab an abandoned sword from the ground and let the heavy tip drag across the floor until I reach the crowd of soldiers, unafraid of them, of death.

In the centre of the circle is an abused child, covered in lashes and bruises. He covers his face to protect himself, but the short whip still connects.

"You." My voice wobbles like I have forgotten how to form the words. They turn at the wretched sound of my voice, and they all blanch with fear. "May you suffer in the afterlife."

Unable to wield the sword properly, tentacles crawl from under my skin, down my arm, and wrap around the hilt of the sword as I swing against the first guard.

I've never done this before. The pink glow coming from my skin is nearly blinding as I lash out at these despicable people. Every time they swing at me, the pain only makes my fury hotter. My blood sings with each screech, when my blade sinks into their necks and a surge of power crashes through my body like a great wave. With each kill, it feels like I am absorbing their life force.

Only when there is just the child and I left, do the tentacles ease into my body once more. Brutalised remains surround us, staining our skin until we appear like red monsters. I stumble to the child and realise he is praying.

"There are no gods," I say, bundling them into my chest. He cries out and thrashes against my hold, but I don't let him go even as chills wrack my body.

"There is only Love," the ancient beast's voice rumbles in my head. Tears spill down my cheek as my being vibrates.

"There is only Love," I repeat, carrying the boy down to the docks with me.

There are no people along the way. No one is at the market today, yet I feel them, eyes watching and shadows shifting. I settle us into a merchant ship, the men aboard scattering as I begin to pull up the ropes and loosen the sail. The boy lies curled up at the mast. It is only once we are far out at sea that I help him clean himself.

Salty water burns the skin, but it cleans the wounds. I don't recognise him from the palace, but I am not sure I would have. His eyes are a startling shade of blue, his hair dark. It is a face I will never forget now.

We dress in clothes meant for trading with a nearby island, and I tuck him into a bedroll below deck. I stare off into the setting sun, the island I have called home my whole life before me, growing smaller the further we sail.

"Devour it," I command, calling forth all the power I have collected on my rampage.

The world shakes, and the water beneath the ship jitters. Giant teal tentacles burst from the ocean and attack. There is no scent of blood now, no screaming for mercy, simply the soft destruction of a home that ruined me. The pink glow of Love's power mixes with that of the horizon. It's a beautiful sight as my world blurs and I collapse.

342 Days

It is always the cannon fire, the smoke, the damned splintering of a ship's mast that sailors talk about if they survive a fight at sea. Shaken and weary, they will make port and head straight for the nearest tavern to drown their emotions in cheap alcohol. They never talk about the silence that follows, how normal the waves sound lapping up the sides of the victor's vessel. If they survived, they certainly don't talk about the whimpering men who beg for their lives.

That is the sweet siren song to my ears that I crave before I feed my Love.

"Don't tease us, our heart," they rumble, their voices echoing through my mediation.

I can think of nothing more satisfying right now. It's certainly better than slogging through another boring meeting at Our Lady of Mercy. I could be in my quarters on the ship, grinding on Love's slick tentacles while they tease me. They could take me into their abyss and wrap their tentacle around me until there is no part of me visible. There I could suck and worship them as they choose.

"She is still alive, but unaware of it."

No sooner are the words out of the pretentious sandbag's mouth, do I lose my meditative state. The pleasure of my Love is yanked from my grasp, and I'm brought back to this horrid present. This group, this network of monsters, surrounds me and I want nothing but the waters of the Paspawa River to rise up and wash me away from this grotesque basement.

Augustine Ravenscroft is a founding member, a dream-eating monster many wouldn't dare to question or even look at the wrong way. He is controlling, overly fancy, and fucking nosy. While I stay clear of nearly everyone outside of these meetings, he knows more about my life than most. He knows where my moral compass points and that these meetings are nothing but a formality for me. I show up to keep the others away from my docks and to keep their noses from sniffing around more of my business than necessary.

For the first time in months, my focus lasers in on the conversation happening around me. Last time Ravenscroft did anything even worthy of note was seven years ago when he finally snapped at some creature obsessed with Milson Bushwhipper. Sandy ripped the guy to shreds and a new door had to be fitted in that precious library. That had been a meeting filled with shouting and demands for his expulsion from the city. He hadn't exposed his true nature to any humans though, so he simply got away with it and earned a further reputation for being one of our deadliest members.

His words make my insides quake and writhe until I'm moving without my control. The tentacles beneath my skin squirm and threaten to burst out. Love swallows my consciousness, swallows my rage, and feasts on it until they can take control of my body. I hear the words they speak, and it soothes me.

"What do you mean unaware?"

Lights flicker. Their voice shakes the tiled ceiling. Pleasure swells in me at the sight of so many creatures scattering like ants afraid of being squashed. *Cower, you so-called monsters.* Run from the thing that will truly end all of you. Words, muted as if by the sound of the ocean crashing against the shore, filter through me. *Ritual, control, ichor, forever.* Augustine has claimed a woman without her knowledge.

An innocent monster is unaware that anything has changed. He has taken away her choice.

The rage that burns in my dead heart swells. My fists shake, and suddenly, I am back in my body. There has been no feeding. We have followed the rules and have waited for Love's insatiable hunger to reach a peak before hunting for more souls. Now, I don't possess the strength to bring forth my Love to ruin this gluttonous twat.

The others sit in silence, the weaker monsters huddling in fear. Nora, the member of this group I am closest with, looks ready to play the peacemaking queen she is. The Fae haven't been to war in centuries because of her family's lineage. But I will not be placated by platitudes now.

Augustine looks as if he has more to say to me, but I can't listen. Before my body betrays me more than I can allow it, I storm out of the parish centre, the courtyard of Our Lady of Mercy, and through the main streets of Gwenmore. I'm not worried about others following me. They know that to intercept me outside of that basement means blood. In there, we are safe from each other, but out here, they make the wrong move against a fellow monster, which is a death sentence.

If I can't have that pile of sand, I will find another scumbag. I will hunt them down for my Love, for my own twisted pleasure. The burn of power that comes with a hunt is what I crave now more than anything. A ghost of Love's tentacles settles around my shoulder, a familiar weight that doesn't slow me down but steers me in the right direction.

I will kill any man who thinks to harm another. And for one of our own to take away the choice of a woman, there is nothing lower. A plan begins to form in my head of all the ways I shall ruin Augustine Ravenscroft. It will take time, and the power I need to feed Love will take a long while to gather. But it will be oh so worth it.

This bar is way too nice.

My outfit doesn't necessarily meet the dress code here, as my usual hunting grounds on the south side of the river are less savoury. Greasy overalls and steel toes don't mix with the white-collar crowds. Heavy bass music pumps through the sound system as people push their way to and from the bar. There is an even mix of university students and older office workers here. The board outside the bar had proudly displayed a two-for-one on shooters and free entry for ladies. Tuesday night was the night to be here, I suppose.

Then again, the Northbank would have a thriving nightlife even if the oceans had dried and the sun fell to the earth. I watch the crowd. My eyes move from loud frat bros absorbed in a drinking contest, to a booth of women dressed in Pancake Parlour polos, to a pair of girls just down the bar from me. A man in a plain suit approaches them and the hunt begins.

There is a pattern in men, human or monster, that can be picked up the longer they are studied as prey, rather than as predators. The way they prepare for their own hunt, the way their body language portrays their true intentions, it is all predictable. He leans into one of the girls, making sure he buys them both expensive cocktails while they giggle at some bullshit he said. He moves with a practised ease that comes from having done this before and that's how I know. If they had turned him down for a drink, he'd have moved on to the next prey he spotted until he found one he could take.

It's a disgusting exchange that I have seen happen for centuries. Men are all the same when they believe they are the apex predators. Bars may have changed styles and gotten fancier with alcohol, but they are all the same. I take a sip of the gin and tonic the barkeep served me an hour ago and wait for him to make his final move, the one where he chooses a girl and she is somehow convinced to leave her friend behind.

Bad personal safety. There is a reason women are taught to travel in groups, and he is undoubtedly one of them. It takes two more rounds of cocktails, both girls giggling without concern. One shift in the music has one of them shimming and running off to the dance floor. Fate has decided which girl he will prey upon tonight.

If only he knew.

They leave the bar quickly after that. One brush of his hand on her exposed thigh and a whisper in her ear has her nodding along. Whatever he promised her will be a lie. A good man wouldn't get a woman drunk and try to initiate such contact. But good men don't exist, not really, not since they realised that pregnancy wasn't magic from the gods.

I follow them out of the bar. He is barely able to drag her down a side street before he shoves her against one of the trees that line the pavement. They are supposed to help keep the air clean and lower street noise, but in the dark of the night, these trees are nothing except hiding spots for real monsters.

"No." I hear her say the words loud and clear, but he ignores them.

The final nail in his coffin has been hammered in. I dig into the pocket of my overalls and pull out an old, short pocket knife that a crew member gave me before she left to travel west at the turn of the twentieth century to dig for gold. This is less ostentatious than carrying my old dagger strapped to my torso. I flick the blade open before grabbing the man's shoulder. Both of them jump when they realise they aren't alone, but it is too late for him. Chills race up my arm as I hold onto him. He tries to fight me when I rip him away from her, but even as short as I am, I am stronger than he could ever dream of being. When I kick in the back of his knees, he crumbles like they all do.

"Look, I don't have money or a phone." He starts, hand presented and visible. In what fucking reality do adults not have a phone?

"You're lying," I say, pressing my blade into his gullet. "Are you okay?"

The girl looks at me when she realises I am speaking to her. She nods slowly.

"Go back to the bar and ask the bouncer to phone you a cab. Go home and forget about tonight," I command.

I don't have to say another word. Sober as a judge now, she sprints off down the street and back in the direction of the bar. Once we are truly alone, I let myself slip. Tentacles emerge from under my skin, stretching the material of my thermal as they wind their way around the prey at my feet. His shriek is cut off by the press of my blade, but the scent of piss rises in the air.

"Please, don't."

"Begging," I grunt, tentacles grappling with the man until his chest is displayed. "Makes me want to hurt you more."

He doesn't get another word out. We are exposed here on the street, and I find that sour smell too off-putting. Before he can finish his next inhale, my mind focuses on the anger and pain of centuries of seeing men like him succeed and dig my knife into his chest. Love's power burns through me, searing away the chill and filling me with a righteous euphoria that I chase. The calming pink glow of their light fades slowly, like the man in my tentacles refuses to die.

But they all do.

Now dead, when I lift the man, I feel nothing but his weight. I re-pocket my knife and adjust him on my shoulders. Tentacles slip beneath my skin again as though I am their ocean. They are hidden in the depths of my body. A home for Love's power when we first became one. They are my guide and I am their heart. We are one.

Being on the Northbank makes disposing of the man simple. While the Riverfront area is more residential these days, the old warehouses and factories have transformed into luxury loft apartments. This side is full of bars, restaurants, and anything the city council could think of that would build commerce and further encourage tourism. The Northbank connects to the Harbour Crest Pier and into the high-end wharf where the city elite stores their planet-killing yachts.

A night on the Northbank is safe.

It also means that the Gwenmore PD doesn't give a shit about patrolling this part of the city on a quiet Tuesday night. The Paspawa River is in low tide; the stairs that lead down to the silted bed of the river are wet but exposed. I clomp down them without care. It's a short walk to a bridge, and the older mooring points the city used when it was still young. The heavy, rotted wooden posts are covered in algae and muck, but they do the job in a pinch.

Taking my knife back out once more, I shred the man's suit jacket and tie the strips together in a makeshift rope. The label says it's a cotton-poly blend, which means as long as my knots hold out, this guy will be fine for a while down here hidden amongst the moors and long disused fishing traps.

I look out at the river as I walk along the bank towards home, towards *The Princess's Despair*. The wind blows softly, creating ripples and guiding me back to the bay. Light bounces off the water, and for a moment, I am transported. Memories flash through my mind, like historical re-enactments or old documentaries. Fires and salty waves, the pressure of the sea trying to crush my half-formed body as I dive to save the creature whose rage called out to Love.

Once again, hopelessness is hard to bear. This injured soul doesn't fit with my twisted mess of a soul. She isn't the one promised to me by my Love. I hold onto her as she weeps in anger, her tears like blades of ice through the hollow place that has formed in my chest. The best I can offer her is revenge, knowing those who have wronged her shall never see an afterlife of peace.

I blink hard to clear the memory. I have long since given up on the idea of soulmates. Love's promise will ring in my ear for all of time, but I no longer search for my other half. They may exist, but I can't be what they truly need, not any more. They deserve a normal life, far from anyone that I may offer.

Neither human nor monster, I am determined to stay away from both.

Chapter Two
Delphini

There are few things in this world that I wouldn't give up for my parents. Evening with friends, trips to Greece to visit my *yiayia*, my whole ass life.

Pink is not one of them, though. No matter what the echelons of the Harbour Crest Country Club members say, no matter how they look at me, they will have to pry this baby pink tennis outfit from my cold, dead hands. This outfit is the best flotation device a girl could ask for when said girl is drowning in the deep end of the old money society. The verdant golf course, emerald tennis courts, and lush croquette greens surrounding the club are dotted with people dressed in all-white outfits.

I don't care that I am the odd one out. I have been my whole life. This part of me— the one that is hyper-feminine, pinks, peaches, and rouge—will never be silenced. It is a part of my being, like my thick curly hair and the stretch marks that cover my thighs and chest. There isn't a shade of pink that doesn't fit a formal occasion.

Even my wedding dress is a blush shade of pink if simply to piss off my fake ass fiancé.

My shoulder aches as I put my whole body into the forward swing of my tennis racket. Sweat drips down my face and neck as I try to keep up with the match. Across the court, my so-called fiancé, Miles Bradshaw, returns the ball too hard in my direction. Before I can pull to the side, I take the neon bullet to the stomach. A cackling laugh echoes around us on the sidelines as the morning sun beats down on my bent-over form.

Audrey Paine was the first woman I met in Gwenmore who wasn't a Bradshaw. At my first party in the city, she hung off Miles's arm like he was the son of God. Her pouty lips were so close to his ear that she might as well have shoved her whole tongue into it. It didn't take long to learn that her attraction to Miles wasn't simply for his looks but also his drug connections.

His hand groping her ass nearly the whole night was enough for me. I snapped one picture of it and sent it to my parents as proof that he would not be the reformed playboy his family claimed he was.

All I got in return was a conference call to explain how that isn't evidence of infidelity or a breach of contract. Having our smarmy lawyer infidelity is the highlight of my holiday season.

"Your picture shows two people who are friendly, Miss Fields. Examples of infidelity, as listed in the premarital agreement you signed before moving to Gwenmore, are lewd acts with another person, sexual congress with another person, online relationships involving the sharing of sexually explicit images or videos, and public declarations of love for another person."

"Stefan, he was clearly-"

"Thank you, Stefan. We'll speak to you again in the new year about the post-marital agreement we need drafted." My father, Brackston, cut the lawyer from the line and immediately moved to video call.

That is his go-to move for long-term intimidation. A phone call doesn't suffice. He wants me to see the disappointment on his face. I rearrange my phone set up quickly to make sure I look more professional before answering the call.

The Fields family are a vicious lot. They have fought for everything they have ever had and will keep fighting. They will cut anyone down to get it as well. It meant the environment I grew up in was hostile and demanding, but it also meant people didn't play games with me. Like when girls at prep school tried to bully me, it wasn't a surprise a week later I had them wholly ostracised by the male student body. A simple rumour, a little slip of the tongue to a few boys on the swim team, and those girls were outcasts.

That viciousness is turned on me now.

My mother, Marietta, is also on the call. They are a picture-perfect pair dressed impeccably and powerful as they sit in their high-rise office in Chicago. Brackston removes his glasses, and the dark eyes that match mine are piercing. He is analysing every pixel on the screen in front of him before he goes in for the attack.

"Have you forgotten what you did?" He asks.

As if I could forget, as if they would let me forget the tiny incident that started it all. They are punishing me after what happened at the last Paris Fashion Week. I had been photographed "shoving" a designer that my mother loves. His whole show was the exact same heroin-chic white woman. I can't stand that shit, and I told him. The shove that all tabloids used was nothing more than a friendly farewell gesture. But he told the world something else and ensured everyone knew they shouldn't work with me... or my family.

"No," I answer, feeling misplaced guilt rise in my throat.

"Then why are you bothering us at Christmas for something so stupid?"

"I wasn't thinking," I lie, acquiescing to them rather than having an argument.

Nobody denies Marietta access to her luxuries. My mother has clawed her way up from struggling Greek skincare to running the most exclusive spas in the world. She will do whatever it takes to get what she believes is hers.

My father is no different, Brackston Fields, grew up knowing he would run an empire one day. Our family might not have been the first Black-owned hotel in Chicago, but we would be the greatest. Nothing has stopped him, slowed him down. The hotels and resorts in the Fields conglomerate are the best because of his ruthless business tactics. He will remove every obstacle in his way by whatever means necessary. He will take any shortcut or loophole and work it until he has all the advantages he needs.

I used to think my parents were inspirations—people I wanted to emulate, to be like when I became an adult.

However, I've learned that I am just a pawn in both of their grand schemes for wealth and power. While I would do anything for them, they would do anything with me to get what they wanted.

"This is your chance to finally help the family, Delphini," Mom purses her lips. "The only way you get out of this arrangement is if he dies."

Miles stares at me with the same hatred I have for him. Since that phone call, I have been doing my own scheming, plotting, and planning. It has come down to the wire, and my window for getting out of this sham of an arranged marriage is closing faster and faster. The wedding is this weekend. Our rehearsal dinner is tonight. All the evidence I have gathered in the months of sharing an apartment together will be for nothing if there isn't footage of Audrey and Miles together. The setup is ready, I just have to execute it.

"Jesus, you get worse every time we play, Phi," Miles says as Audrey hops over to him with a towel.

"Say that to me on the piste with foils," I sneer, righting my posture with grit teeth. "Then I can-"

"Phi-phi!"

Before my threat is finished, someone shouts my name across the short distance from the club patio to the tennis courts. Even from here, I can see Lottie leaning over the railing and waving. Her white linen trousers are blindingly bright and her sweater is expertly draped over her shoulder.

"I'm done," I tell them. "I'll see you at the party later."

Without a backwards glance, I grab my belongings and leave the court. When I walk up the steps to the patio, I see Lottie at the table we have sat at since we became friends. My usual iced coconut matcha latte is already there and waiting for me.

"Lottie," I smile and kiss her cheeks when I arrive at the table. "Going sailing?"

"Of course. Marcus and I can't stay off the water when the weather is this gorgeous."

Charlotte Ford-Astor is the daughter-in-law to the club's president. The Astors are one of the founding families of Gwenmore. I am not sure exactly where their money has come from, but it's old. Her family is from Maine, and their money comes from timber. Charlotte is their golden child with a master's degree in economics that she will never use because she married her college sweetheart last summer.

Marcus Astor, her husband, has one vice, and it's old books.

A weird one, but when he drops $137,000 on a book about fishing, only to find out it is a fake, it falls under the category of vices. When your money is centuries old, I suppose it's easy to brush off a stupid mistake like that. I only know about the incident because Lottie called me sobbing about her inability to get the Hermes Birken she wanted because Marcus had spent that month's 'treat' allowance on a fake book. She had been downright distraught about how she wasn't sure if she could handle the shame of knowing her husband had been duped. The whole thing was sorted a few weeks later and I was invited to brunch so I could see the new Birken.

"How's the back swinging coming along?" she asks, a slight cringe in her features.

I take a sip of my latte. "One day, I will hit Miles right upside the head with my racket."

I hate tennis. I always have. My parents dragged me to Wimbledon summer after summer to sit in the sweltering English heat as if watching professionals would help me pick up the sport. All I did was celebrity watch, making little mental notes of who was with whom and what they discussed between matches. What happens in a VIP section never truly stays there.

While I was still in school, I enjoyed fencing, but outside sports were never something that could hold my attention. I don't like being out in the sweltering heat if it isn't for the purpose of lounging by the sea or people-watching. There is certainly no reason for me to be working up a sweat.

She laughs at my joke anyway. Her sleek hair shining in the sun as her head tips back. This is why I like Lottie; she actually laughs. She may sometimes be vapid, but at least she has a sense of humour.

"I know you hate it, but all the work will pay off." Her eyes dip down from my face, and I know she is thinking about that first time I played tennis here with Miles. That was an absolutely shameful display that I staunchly shove to the back of my mind. "Anyway, best not to work too hard when we are going to have a lovely evening tonight. I love a yacht party. Honestly, it is the best way to have a celebration."

"I would beg to differ." I roll my eyes.

My summers may have been spent in Greece with my mother's family; I am not a sea-faring kind of gal. Even though they are usually stable, the moving water beneath my shoes always makes my stomach roll. I can't get over the rocking motion, even if I simply imagine it. I tried to argue against the party being on the boat, saying my parents would be more than happy to pay for a venue, but they wouldn't hear any of it.

I know why.

The Bradshaw's yacht, *The Platinum Signal*, is nice, luxuriously furnished and completely decked out in gadgets to make holidaying on the open water enjoyable. However, it is also the only fully furnished thing they own at the moment. Their house, ski lodge, and summer home are all empty, nearly gutted to scrape together enough money to keep saving face with the public. My parents and I are the only outsiders who know about their troubles, and a part of the engagement contract we signed included an NDA about finances... or the lack thereof.

Exclusive luxury spas really are the most incredible way to dig through the elite's dirty laundry while they are being scrubbed clean. After a brush at a charity gala, Marietta issued an invitation to our New York spa, and everything came to light. At the same time, the Bradshaw matriarchy steamed all the vodka martinis out of her system. She will have used that knowledge to negotiate this whole shambles of a marriage, because the only thing worse than being attached to new money is no money at all.

Another part of our agreement is that neither of us is to cause a public scene, such as excessive drug use. Otherwise, the contract is null and void. My parents refused to be involved in such a scandal, especially after Paris. Miles has a long history in the party scene and has made tabloid headlines on multiple occasions. The man is as subtle as a bull in a China shop with his vices, yet he is still viewed as a boon to my reputation and status among the wealth of America.

"Please, Phi, it will be a great time. Everyone will drink until they are messy, someone will break the ice sculpture, and tomorrow, the papers will be screaming about what an absolute bash it was," Lottie says as a waiter drops off sparkling water for her. Condensation drips down the glass bottle, and I get lost in the rivulet, slowly soaking the table.

"You're right," I sigh, forcing a weak smile. "Plus, what's the point of having a new dress if I don't have a party to show it off at?"

She squeals and does a little dance in her seat. Discussion of the party is easily pushed aside for a more important topic– fashion.

On the whole, I am damn conscious of everything I wear. Not only because I am a plus-size woman but because I need my brands to be as exceptional as I am. Tonight, my dress is from an up-and-coming designer based in New York who had the most diverse and body-inclusive show I have ever seen. It was all the rage, so I commissioned them for an evening dress then and there. It took an age to nail their schedule down, but the custom dress is mine. They were a doll to work with, selecting fabrics and cuts that made me feel as beautiful as I am.

I pull up a photo of the dress on my phone. Charlotte gasps so loudly that several other women enjoying a liquid brunch turn to us. They look at us, and just as they are about to say something, one of the women recognises me. The sheepish smiles and apologetic shrugs tell me they don't want to risk their chance of getting an invite to one of our exclusive spas. I'm drawn back to our table when she rips my phone from my hand and starts pinching and moving around the screen.

"One, I need the details for this designer. Two, you look stunning. Show-stopping. Iconic," she gushes, but doesn't stop inspecting the picture.

That had been a good weekend, all on my own. A train ride up to New York, meeting a few of my fellow influencers and friends for brunch, followed by the fitting of a lifetime. And trust me, I have had my fair share of fittings in my short life.

For the party, I have gone with a sleeveless, fuchsia dress, with draped panelling reminiscent of my mother's Greek heritage. The silk is fine and smooth and flows ethereally with every step I take in it. A portion is nipped at my waist and accents the flare of my hip, showing off my hourglass figure. I have never felt more like a goddess than I do when I have that dress on.

All the better, Miles hates it.

Chapter Three
Delphini

Nights in Gwenmore are cold. Maybe all of the East Coast is like this, but here? A thick fog rolls in like an old lover, and the breeze finds all your personal warm spots to freeze over. In Chicago, you expect it. There were days when the lake would be near frozen, beautiful shards of ice creaking and knocking together as the wind kept pushing you closer and closer to the edge like it wanted you to fall into the icy depths of Lake Michigan.

Here, it feels different.

Looking out at the water, the champagne glass in my hand near full still while my stomach riots, there is no wind calling me to the bay. The waves of the Atlantic are enough. The sounds of the party directly behind me fades in and out of focus as *The Platinum Signal* slices through the water, until we are a decent distance from the harbour. I can feel it slowing down, the anchors weighing the ship so we don't float off, and still, the pre-party granola bar I had while diffusing my hair threatens to go overboard.

The boat is still, but I can feel the waves. The rocking, the motions of the tide sinking. That sounds ridiculous. It is ridiculous, I tell myself. It's a silly fear of the open water that a lot of people have. I swallow the thick lump in my throat and return to the party full of people I don't know.

Lottie and Marcus are here, of course. She is dangling on his arm like he is god's gift to mankind. Gone is the linen, replaced with delicate lace, a navy colour that reminds me of the seas near my *yiayia's* villa in Paxos.

I'm envious of them, jealous beyond belief now that I really think about it. Before I was thrust into the marriage of convenience, soulmates, and true love, the whole romance seemed pointless. My life was scheduled and organised down to the last second before everything happened. There wasn't an ounce of fiction that could convince me that romance was what I needed in my life. But after months of seeing Marcus look at her like he'd walk over hot coals just for her to spit in his direction has changed me. I want to be a part of something like that. Their love is fucking palpable, and Miles?

Miles is surrounded by a flock of girls who look even younger than me. As I am already a burden to my parents at the ripe old age of twenty-seven, that man whore is what I deserve. Except I have prospects and money beyond imagination that should have saved me from all this. My parents are too greedy.

My future mother-in-law is insect-like as she walks over to me. She's deathly pale, unlike quite a few of the other women here, and downright fucking mean. She reminds me of the overly secure rich girls I went to prep school with. I guess it's proof that some people don't grow out of being a bully.

"Delphini, darling, I thought Miles said he spoke to you about that dress?" Her gaze shifts down my body and I get a bit happier knowing I've pissed her off, but she can't do anything too heinous to me about it. She's dead fucking broke; she needs me and my family's wealth to keep up this lavish lifestyle. "You're practically glowing in the dark compared to everyone else."

This is a black-tie event. All the men are dressed in subtly different versions of the exact same black suit, and nearly all the women are wearing some dark-shaded evening dress. I am the only one in something bright. I am the only one dressed like I'm not going to a royal funeral.

"Miles even went so far as to try and rip the dress out of my hands, Evelyn," I say with a smile. One of the photography team members walks by, and his camera flash is discombobulating. "But you will see me dead before I stop wearing my signature pink."

"Oh would you look at the Vanderburgs, I have to speak with them about our Sunday tee time."

Evelyn Bradshaw doesn't scowl, too much Botox if I had to guess, but the chill that washes over me at her last look at me is terrifying enough. My fiancé makes eye contact with his mother and then turns his death glare right on me. I raise my glass of champagne and take a delicate sip, unbothered and unfazed by his pathetic attempt at intimidation.

I learned from the best. He will have to try harder.

Lottie sees our exchange and is over by my side instantly. All those pilates classes she says she does have her moving through the crowd in a blur of lace. She snags two small caviar canapés and hands me one.

"Hangry or trouble in paradise?" she asks before stuffing the other in her mouth. She has no idea what kind of lie I am living, and it's growing harder and harder to keep secrets from her.

I keep my smile plastered on as I eat the food she's given me. "Hangry. There could never be trouble when I know Miles is about to come whisk me away for a private rendezvous."

"Mm," she eyes me as I take a larger sip of my drink and let the soft fizz tickle my tongue before I swallow. "Well, if Miles ever needs any help in the grovelling department, Marcus spends plenty of time on his knees for me."

My cheeks heat at that. Not because I feel scandalised or because half a glass of champagne loosens me up, but because I can picture it. Vividly, gloriously. In the short time I have known Lottie and, by proxy, her husband, I have thought that if they were ever to ask me for a threesome, I would jump at the occasion. If only to watch how their love intertwines with their sex life, to see that passion up close. Now I have a clearer picture of what that would be like.

The mega-wealthy, in my experience, falls into two categories: prudes or deviants. Evelyn? Clearly a prude. Me? Well, I happen to fall into the latter category. Lottie has given the impression she does too with how openly she speaks to me about her relationship in and out of the bedroom. Marcus is an eager submissive. And God would I happily get on my knees for her, too.

I polish off my glass before I let that thought go any further. Not only is my dry spell clearly rotting my brain, but it doesn't matter, even if they did invite me to a little scene. My engagement contract with the red-faced man trying to push through the crowd of well-wishers says no infidelity. I am tying myself to one man. Forever.

"Charlotte, I think Marcus wanted to speak to you about some kind of book auction?" Miles says before he even comes to a stop in front of us.

She blinks for a moment, like she is debating whether she believes his blatant lie, but then winks at me. "Like training a puppy."

Miles waits only a moment before he grabs me, his hand gripping my free one until my knuckles hurt. It takes everything in me not to flinch, not react. Thoughts that I have had over and over again for months come swimming to the surface.

Why am I putting up with this? Why wasn't this fucking behaviour a part of the engagement contract? The petty digs about my weight, the way I style my makeup or hair on any given day; it's all bullshit I have heard time and time again. From my parents to major design labels, while I am unique enough, smart enough, and attractive enough, I'm not the right kind of pretty.

But being the right kind of pretty isn't going to save my fucking shoulder as Miles yanks me from the bridge deck where the party is officially happening down to the owner's deck into the private living room space. The heavily glossed wood floors shine, and the white leather sectional in front of us is ostentatious. No doubt the yacht will have cost the Fields family a small mint to have cleaned and decorated. Every floor is on display and has to show the people directly above us that the Bradshaws are not in dire straits.

"Let go of me right now," I hiss, pulling to get my hand back. We are alone, and I don't want this fuck touching me.

Miles releases his grip and looks around. We are well and truly the only people on this deck. The full-service bar is upstairs. The catering staff use the elevator that leads directly to the kitchens. There aren't even some cheeky guests down here having a joint. It is just the two of us.

"Why the fuck are you wearing that dress? I told you not to."

"You don't get to decide what I wear-"

"The hell I don't. You may think that because your family has money, it means shit. But it doesn't. Not here. Without me, you are nothing. Do you think the Fords or the Astors would look twice at you? Without that fucking ring on your fat finger, you are nothing." He points at the glass in my hand, the large diamond on it weighing me down like a lead weight. "If I tell you to do something, you do it."

"Excuse me?" I protest, rage bubbling up. My limbs feel lighter than air all of a sudden, like I could strike with such speed and strength I could knock him right off the yacht.

We get into this argument once a week. He tries to assert some kind of fucked up dominance and toxic masculinity shit, and I tell him to go fuck himself. He isn't the physical type. The only time I have seen Miles Bradshaw do any sort of exercise is when he forces me to play tennis with him. The trips to the gym are more of an excuse to take suggestive pictures of himself.

Not once have I been scared of this idiot getting physically violent with me, if only because it would leave evidence behind. Grabbing my hand too hard, throwing a vase of flowers at my feet, belittling every ounce of me? The list of offences doesn't leave enough evidence to be in violation of our contract.

"Do you know who is fucking paying for this party? Me. It isn't you. It isn't mommy-fucking-dearest upstairs. It is Delphini Fucking Fields. You don't get to speak to me that way." I point my perfectly manicured finger back at him, taking a step forward, ready to fight. "You worthless-"

It's the first time I've seen this look on him. Red in the face from anger or alcohol is a typical look on Miles, but the colour has drained this time. His pale skin isn't even flushed, but his eyes make me stop. There is something terrifying about blue eyes, a coldness in them that makes me shiver at first glance. Miles' blue eyes are lifeless when he smiles at me. I'm frozen right on the spot, my insult trapped behind my lips as I look at this sinister face he reveals to me.

I'm scared, and I should be. I am alone with a man who has been nothing but abusive and toxic as shit since we met.

When Miles grabs me this time, I flinch. My whole body jumps right out of my skin as he grips my bare arm and twists. He jerks us around until he has me bent over the back of the sofa. His crotch pushes against my ass as he presses his whole body into my bent arm and back. Air bursts from my lungs in short pants, and my hair falls across my face.

I can't move. I should be able to push him off. The exact manoeuvre for this rolls through my head like one of those 80s fitness tapes my mom used to put on for us to do together, but my body won't do anything. Whatever anger I had, that fight in me, twists into something worse. Fear. Miles twists my arm back farther until I cry out.

"I am tired of your goddamn attitude," he whispers, his hips rolling into mine, and fear as I have blessedly never known drips down my spine. The slick fabric of my dress shifts, rising higher up my legs. "My dick hasn't gotten wet in six months, Phi, but that ends tonight."

"No," I croak, my voice wobbling. It's not the voice of a strong person. The thought that I am in over my head makes my chest tighten, and my mouth dry up. I need help.

"Yes." He thrusts against me. "Remember, you are nothing except a means to an end."

Miles pulls away from me. The weight of him is off me and my balance falters. I faceplant into the leather sofa, but I can't bring myself to get up. Not yet, not while he is still there watching me. I don't care that I've ruined my makeup or creased my dress beyond repair. He doesn't get to see the tears in my eyes.

"Get cleaned up," he sneers. "You look like a fucking middle-class whore."

His footsteps are light as he leaves the owner's deck. Blood rushes through my ears as the silence descends around me. My body moves without my direct acknowledgement, without thinking I should be doing anything in particular. Slowly, I walk towards the primary cabin where our belongings are. My heels echo against the floor and walls, too loud. They are too loud. Like the thumping of my pulse in my ears.

My phone presses to my ear and rings before I think better of it. It can't be that late here yet, but the time difference means it's closer to one o'clock in the morning in Greece. It rings though, like it has since I memorised the number when I was still a kid. It keeps ringing until the dulcet soft tones of my *yiayia's* Greek come through the line.

"Hello, this is Sotiriou. Leave your name and number, or I won't call you back."

I clear my throat, trying to keep the tears from falling and further ruining my makeup. "Hi, *Yiayia*. It's Del."

My words hang there for a moment. I am not sure what I am saying or what I should say next.

"I'm sorry I'm not there with you. I-" My voice cracks, and I slip into Greek as if that will comfort me while she is so far away. *"I miss you. I promise to come see you soon and tell you everything. I love you."*

I end the call, my phone slips down my dress and I lose sight of it as tears finally pour free. Before they can fall onto my dress, I dab them away with the back of my hand. A homesickness like I haven't felt before settles in me. The weight of my engagement ring feels more like a chain around my finger, anchoring me to this reality. I have wanted for nothing my entire life, but I am in need now. I need to get away. I need to escape this hell. I need to get out of this engagement contract.

The bland-patterned wallpaper lulls me into a weak trance as I practise measured breathing to calm myself. The shivering stops, my nose clears up, and the cage I've built inside myself, which seals away any soft feelings, is locked up tight again. If I knew how to throw away that key, I would. I'd toss it into a pile of keys, so even if I felt the urge to unlock that cage, I'd never be able to find the right one.

I open the closet doors until I find the one that Miles so graciously assigned to me. There are two garment bags inside, an empty one that my pink dress came in and one that contains a dress he found suitable for this evening. Carefully, I slip off mine. I don't think about the creases in the silk, the slight wet spots from where tears landed on it. I pull out his dress and stare at the ivory, beige, ruched mess.

One battle lost does not mean this war is over.

My go bag is tucked under the bathroom sink like I asked. Fuck knows how much time I spent in a daze since Miles left me, so I don't spend any more than necessary fixing my makeup. I pick the roots of my curls out to make them look fuller since some of my definition is gone and call it good enough. I still look good.

I am good.

The dress I slide on now is clearly not designed for a plus-size body, maybe even the average body. Honestly, this would look hideous on anyone. It barely fits over my hips, the ruching doing the opposite of what it should. The silk fabric is taut and exposes more of my belly line than I'm usually comfortable with. There is no shame in having a pronounced stomach, but I show it off when I want to. Not because this shit bag I am supposed to marry tells me to.

I pull the zip up with a bit of manoeuvring and slide my pink strappy heels back on. The steps for my plan are already in motion. I will not let a threat from Miles ruin the rest of my life. Nor will I allow anyone else to use me as a means to an end.

It's like I was never even gone. The party is exactly like I left it. Members of the catering crew scurry about with trays laden with caviar and empty glasses as party-goers sip champagne and talk about nothing. I don't see Miles among the crowd and am glad for it. His mother is still talking to the Vanderburgs, though I doubt about tee times or anything to do with the country club for that matter. That family is trying to unseat the current mayor as if their life depends on it, and party-goers will want a piece of that influential pie.

Finally, I let out the anxious breath I locked in my chest.

It's surreal looking around the bridge deck and realising no one noticed I was gone. Why was no one concerned that I wasn't there? Anger bubbles up inside of me at being ignored by these people. I am the bride-to-be. Did Miles tell everyone a lie about where I was or what I was doing? My stomach turns, and I'm not sure if it's because of the boat rocking or the fear still trying to break me. I have a plan; Miles's threat will not stop me.

I make a beeline for the bar with every intent to get a glass of something bubbly to settle my stomach, but I'm quickly pulled to the side by someone I barely know to talk about my *yiayia* and her skincare company. My grandmother's family has been in the business of lotions and potions for as long as anyone can remember. It wasn't until my mother met my father that they gained international renown as a luxury skincare brand that you could only find in the most exclusive spas. Yiayia has never cared about that; her only concern is providing her family a better life. Honestly, everything I tell them can be found on her website or the brand's social media page, but hearing it from me leaves an impression.

Once I promised to have a PR package sent to this woman with "a huge following," they finally let me leave the conversation. I don't even make it two steps before Lottie grabs my hand. She looks at my face and a sly smirk graces her lips.

"Looks like you've had quite the rendezvous, Phi-phi."

"Yes," I agree immediately, refusing to admit an ounce of weakness. "Now, let's get a strong drink."

That isn't a part of the Delphini Fields brand. The downside to making my life, and my personality, my job is that I am always on. There are no breaks, no time for tears. There is no being angry in public. No one can know what I've been through to get to this point in my life unless it is candy-coated and beautifully humble. Everything about me is my brand.

"So, will you tell me all the spicy details?" she asks.

"No." I plaster on my own smirk, if only to prove her assumption it was an illicit meeting true. She eyes my dress, and I wonder if she is going to comment on what a crime against fashion it is. Or will she compliment it regardless, because, like everyone else, she enjoys whites and neutral tones as much as the next elitist?

"You weren't gone for a very long time. Doesn't seem like he spent much time on his knees."

"Now, that I can agree with." We're talking about two different sorts of being on your knees here, but I don't care. Lottie tolerates Miles the way everyone who isn't licking his boot does. It doesn't matter what her real feelings are when the Bradshaw name can move mountains up and down the East Coast.

"Next time," I promise, subtly eyeing the crowd for my target.

We each take a glass of champagne and we toast to men on their knees. While Lottie takes a delicate sip, I drink the glass in one long gulp. This isn't what I wanted. Fine champagne like this one doesn't fizz or tickle my nose. It easily slides down my throat, and I want to feel the burn. I want to feel anything to justify the burning in my gut that is desperate to be unleashed. Raising a perfectly manicured finger, I signal for the bartender.

"Martini, extra cold, three olives." It's rude, but I barely look at him. Like everyone else here, I assume my drink will be made as requested. Life is a show;

everything is a performance, and I am about to give the most important one of my life. The one of the happy, in-love fiancé who could think of nowhere better to be than on this stupid fucking yacht.

Lottie takes another sip of her champagne and skims me over again.

"Now, I know it is symbolic for the bride-to-be to wear white, but why are you dressed like a used condom?"

I choke. My cheeks heat and I fan myself to keep from crying through my fresh makeup. She's right. I look like a fucking used condom because of that dickwad. I laugh so hard I snort, and that causes Lottie to choke on her champagne. A genuine smile, one that makes the corners of my eye crinkle and my heart warm, settles on my lips. A few guests look at us, like they are ready to sneer, but then they see who is being louder than the rest of the crowd and turn away.

"Miles, or I suppose more specifically Evelyn, chose this dress," I say.

"Well, hopefully, your good fashion sense will rub off on them sooner rather than later."

As she says the words, my drink is placed in front of me and the bartender is gone before I can even say thanks. I raise my glass to Lottie before taking a large sip. Amongst all the grey-haired and red-faced people, only a few stand out. It takes a few sweeps, but finally, my eyes settle on one woman. She's tall, reed-thin, and has cheekbones that could cut diamonds.

I'm going to convince her to fuck Miles on this boat.

Honestly this part of my plan is pathetically simple. Martini in hand, I leave Lottie at the bar and walk over to her. As I approach, I make eye contact with the photographer tilting my head to the side to get them to come along with me. The smile plastered on her face is obviously fake, but I don't care. I am filled with the righteous sort of indignation for my own vendetta. I am determined to see my fiancé fuck someone who isn't me tonight so I don't have to deal with him for the rest of my life.

"Audrey, Miles is looking for you. He has something for you in the primary cabin," I say, ghosting a hand over her bare arm. The camera flashes and now we've been pictured together. Me dressed in this condom, and her in a slinky, near sheer floor length slip dress that future tabloids will say is overly suggestive for a rehearsal dinner. I try not to think about what the papers will say about my dress come the morning. She waits for the photographer to leave before she speaks to me.

"Well," she says heavily, as if speaking with me is the most immense burden she's ever carried in her life. "I shouldn't keep him waiting, should I?"

Like a greyhound preparing to chase the rabbit, Audrey Paine is on point. She cranes her elegant neck and looks over the crowd before setting off in the opposite direction towards the owner's deck.

Now for step two. I do another once-over of the crowd, looking for the man I need to speak to next. With a name that only old money could support, Teddy Bushwhipper is the be-all and end-all for Gwenmore gossip. I have given him more skincare than I care to admit, but he is the man to go to when a girl needs information.

I take the final sip of my martini and place the glass on a passing waiter's tray then grab two glasses of champagne. If I have learned anything in my short time of being acquainted with Teddy, it is to never arrive empty-handed. When he sees me approach, he smiles big enough to show all his teeth. Teddy pushes his glasses up his nose and tucks his phone into his jacket pocket with urgency. My eyes catch on the silver chain around his neck that clips to his tie with a decorative pendant. I've never seen a piece of jewellery like that, but the oddity of it suits him.

"Phi-phi, doll, this is going to be the party of the year," he greets with a faux kiss on each cheek. "And where did you scurry off to with the fiancé half an hour ago?"

I hold in my eye-roll and hand over the glass of champagne. While I'm not surprised Teddy noticed this disappearance of mine, I am annoyed he's brought it up.

"A lady never kisses and tells, Teddy." I smirk.

Something akin to disgust rolls through me as if a large wave struck the side of the yacht. My throat clogs, and my chest tightens as I think about even the possibility that Miles would force me to do that. I don't want that man anywhere near me, in body or spirit. But this is an act, and I am the lead, so I keep my perfectly plastered smirk on my lips as I take a sip from my glass. It settles like mud in my stomach.

"Take all the fun out of my evening, why don't you, Delphini Fields?"

"Teddy, I do believe I'm about to make your decade." This immediately grabs his attention, and he looks around cautiously. He takes a step closer to me. "I heard someone in catering whispering about Miles and Audrey in the primary cabin. While I don't want to believe the rumours, we've all seen the way she hangs on to Miles. My heart couldn't bear it if I were the one to walk in on them, but I need someone I can trust to tell me the truth if they were to find out about an affair."

His gaze turns scrutinising as he looks at me again with renewed interest. The hand not holding his glass goes to his tie and he fiddles with the pendant there for a moment while he thinks. I stare back at him with matching intensity. I will not show weakness. Suddenly, his brow softens.

"You know, if something," he rolls the word around on his tongue before he says, "unsavoury happened downstairs, I can keep a secret."

"Nothing I couldn't handle."

"Alright, alright," he placates, raising his arms slightly in defeat. It's on the tip of his tongue to comment on my dress. I can see it in his eyes, but I fold my arms across my chest and give him a look that dares him to say it. "I'm always happy to help with a scheme if it means getting to nose around someone else's yacht."

"And we love you for it, Teddy."

We part ways, and I make a point of chatting with each and every single guest at the party, making sure the photographer catches me with all of them in this hideous dress. With each lap I take around the deck, I make sure to grab a glass of water from the bar. I'm not a lightweight by any means with the Fields' European approach to alcohol, but all the champagne is making me woozy. When I am standing still the world continues to sway. At first, I excuse it as the water being a bit choppy and the boat rocking, but it is smooth when I peer out across the ocean. There isn't even a breeze.

The moon is half full. The decorative lights around the yacht are glowing so bright I see stars. The wine is strong, but I am stronger. Every time I end a conversation, I look for Teddy but can't find him. I push through more conversations, doing my best to focus. Words keep rolling together in their mouths though, accents twisting syllables until I have to ask them repeatedly what they have said.

"Phi, are you okay?" Lottie pulls me away from an older man whose name I can't even remember now. "Have you eaten anything?"

"I-" I'm fine. The words nearly come out of my mouth, but for a brief moment, all the murkiness clears from my head, and I see the evident concern written on her face. "I'm feeling a bit seasick."

It must be that. I have never been good on boats of any size. I knew this would happen, going so far as to take something for motion sickness before I stepped on *The Platinum Signal* hours ago. It must have worn off, or the alcohol cancelled it.

"Do you need help getting below deck?"

My ankles are wobbly in my heels, but I am still standing. It would be an embarrassment to have to be escorted below deck like some kind of lush. I look around me, not really seeing the faces of guests any more, just pools of colour floating on top of evening wear. My throat struggles to swallow the rising bile.

"I am going to lie down. The night is still young and I want to see that ice sculpture crack." I force a smile, and Lottie grips my arm.

Her eyebrows furrow for a moment when she touches me, but she pulls back quickly and smiles.

Marcus appears in a blink, and I think I have a decent conversation with him for long enough that the photographer gets a better picture of us.

I don't know.

And the harder I think about the fact that I don't know, terrifies me. Nothing explains why the fuck I am feeling this way, why every thought in my head is dipping in and out of my consciousness until even a basic inkling has my neck giving out and my head lulling to the side. I am cold in this dress. My dress, which I commissioned for this party, had a cape that would have kept me warm.

A shiver tracks down my spine and I grip the railing of the stairs for dear life as I make my way down to the owner's deck. My foot is not even on the last step when I hear the voices. Murmurs and giggles coming from the living room space. The two of them stick out like sore thumbs in their dark outfits on the stupid white couch.

"Phi, it took you fucking long enough," Miles says, tie askew and hair rumbled, like someone has been running their fingers through it.

Elation rolls through me, but I can't figure out why. Why is this a good thing? Miles has been a hot mess the entire time I have known, but why is it important right now?

"I told you the fat bitch would need an extra pill."

Audrey Paine.

Yes! This is it. She is why this is a good thing. Infidelity, contract broken, Delphini is free to go to Greece. My knee buckles as I step towards them, not even registering the scene before me. It's all spinning and I think I am going to throw up. Maybe that will help me feel better and help me see more clearly what is happening in the lounge, so when I go to the lawyer's first thing tomorrow, I can show them the pictures Teddy took.

Where is Teddy?

"Oh darling, look at her. She thinks she's won." Audrey coos so sinisterly I recoil as they come near me.

"Grab her," Miles says, and suddenly, hands are on me.

I don't like this. I don't want to be touched right now, but I can't get my arms free. They snake around me and drag me down more stairs. The back of my heels knocks against each step, finally waking me up enough to fight. I jerk my elbow as hard as I can into the guy holding me.

He drops me and I realise I've fucked up more than ever. I fall down the last few stairs and crumble onto the floor of the main deck.

The world doesn't go black. I can feel the pain radiating from my wrist and I can tell I am only wearing one shoe, but I don't know where I am. Miles and Audrey are still talking, directing the three, no two, men who carried me away from the owner's deck.

The music from the party sounds louder down here, where the lights don't reach. A flash goes off, and I'm manipulated again. A breeze tunnels down here, strong gushes of it turning me to ice. I can't feel my fingers.

A hand shoves my underwear aside. Tears leak down my cheek when I realise what's actually happening. The men holding me up, assaulting me, are doing so at Miles's whim.

"Tricked me." I swallow the sob that threatens to come out with my accusation.

"You can't beat me in a race when you are three laps behind," Miles explains, loosely waving his wrist about. "I've known for months what you've been planning, Phi. I'm just better at your own game, and I won't leave any evidence behind."

As suddenly as the hands are on me, they are gone. I collapse onto the floor with a whimper. The heavily waxed wood panels are so slick with sea mist I can't get a grip to stand up again. This isn't how tonight is supposed to play out. I can't let those photos get out. They will ruin everything.

When something touches my leg, I kick out, terrified of what it could be. Terrified they will grab me again. Another gust of wind rushes over my body and I realise the top of my dress is pulled down to my waist. My arms go to cover my chest, but as I shift my weight to one wrist, my elbow gives out and I crash into the floor again, hitting my head.

"Stay fucking still, stupid bitch," Miles grunts, yanking my ankles together.

I catch sight of the neon rope, the fibres practically glowing in the dark. Each time he twists and knots it, it pinches me. Another yank, my shoulders protesting and pleading for mercy, and I am upright again. My back is pressed to the metal railing.

Audrey grunts, and there is a large crash behind me that causes water to spray my back. I gasp at the bitter cold.

"What're you doing?" I demand.

My words slur together so hard I am not even sure I said them in the correct order. Miles ignores me. There is more shuffling, and they keep yanking me.

Yank, yank, yank.

"Enjoy the swim." Audrey pats my cheek condescendingly.

Then I am upside down. My body smashes against the railing before I smack against the surface of the water and I am dragged under. I want to believe I struggled, fought harder against them, and that I was strong enough to stay above the surface. Surely I can survive being thrown overboard? But I'm scared to open my eyes, to see nothing but darkness, and know I will never see the sunshine again.

Chapter Four
Delphini

It's warm. Like the sun is high in the sky, and I am laying on a sun bed on the stretch of private beach outside of *Yiayia's* villa. Waves brush across the sand with ease, barely a breeze in the air. There isn't a single thought swimming through my head. I am at peace.

A sigh, so easy and free, leaves my body and it's like I am weightless. My skin tingles and my eyelids flutter open. I gasp hard enough to choke. Something, someone helps me roll into a recovery position and cough up lungfuls of water.

It's dark. I am still warm, but there is no reason for it. There is no light, no windows, no breeze. I lay on my side in an endless darkness that doesn't cease. My head isn't swimming any more. My skin vibrates, my blood pounding through me until I feel nothing but rage pulsing through my veins. I clench my fist as scattered images and memories crash through my head.

"Yes, sweet one, burn with it," a voice, or many voices, echo in the dark.

My eyes squeeze shut. It isn't Miles or Audrey. The voices sound older and like they are struggling to form the right words as if English isn't their first language. *Fuck.* What sort of situation did I wake up in? What did he do to me? The fear that mixes with my anger only focuses my thoughts until all there is Mile's smug face. I come up on all fours, ready to fight, to kill anyone who gets in my face. As my wrist gives out, something wraps around me.

Thick, glowing appendages steady me, preventing me from face-planting into the black nothing. Suddenly, there are more of them around my wrists and ankles, supporting me until I am being pulled up and floating in the nothing. I jerk in their hold, and they give slightly, allowing me to move a few inches. My arms tingle, the urge to fight rushing through me. My limbs shake with fear and fury, my body winding tighter and tighter, preparing to shout, to die before I give in to whatever hell this is.

"*Now be still,*" the voices whisper in the dark, trying to soothe me.

My teeth grit together. "No."

"*Sweet one, I am here to offer you a choice. You may join us or remain in your watery grave.*"

My blood runs cold at the ultimatum, at the word *remain*. Am I already in my grave? Am I lost in some purgatory and at the whim of this monster? With the energy still rushing through me, my rage twists into terror. Sweat beads across my forehead, and my stomach rolls. I don't want to die. I will not let them kill me. I. Will. Not. Lose.

"Who is 'us'?"

"*We are the dawn, we are the darkness, we are the future.*"

With each pronouncement, lights spark in the dark, like a neon sign coming to life. Rushes of pink illuminate the space around me, the void I am trapped in. Masses of rising thick, blue tentacles surround me. I cannot see an end or beginning to them. I cannot see the body they're attached to, but I see them pulse and twist around one another.

Sets of eyes blink into existence around me and multiply until there are sixteen pairs. The eyes spin and spin around the space until they are a blur and converge into one massive glowing sphere. The rounded iris is a deep shade of blue that reminds me of the Ionian Sea. Comfort and confusion keep my head bobbing, barely staying afloat in this ocean of insanity.

"*We were at the birth of this planet's life, and we will be here when it ends, when there is no land and the water rises until there is nothing but vast oceans.*"

Tentacles wind up my body until I am cocooned in the warm, wet masses of them. I'm blinded by the pink glow. A familiar scent thickens in the air. My chest rises, my breathing harsher and harsher as horror sinks into my bones. I'm going to be crushed to death by some fruity-smelling monster that reminds me of home.

My limbs go numb, and all I can think is attack, thrust, lunge, the fencing mantra beating in my bloodstream like a last-ditch prayer to God. My good hand moves and wriggles until I can grasp onto one of the tentacles. I refuse to give up.

"You are not like the others, and yet you suffer their same pain," the monster whispers.

"And what pain is that? Constriction? Smothering? Being crushed to death by a giant fucking octopus?"

"No, sweet one, the anger inside of you we have not seen for many, many generations. We do not need to encourage, nourish, or guide it into the darkness as we have with your sisters. No, the darkness in you has always been rippling right under the surface, waiting for us to claim you."

My hand tightens around the tentacle, but the ones surrounding me do the same. A shuddering gasp leaves my lips as suckers graze my exposed chest and the hideous dress I'm wearing shifts even lower. The appendages around me freeze. Their grip on me no longer pulses. I look at the great eye before me and snarl as if I am some sort of wild animal as if that will scare it and cover up that noise.

"We offer you a choice, sweet one. Your destiny has split in two. Choose us and accept she who waits, whose soul rages

and longs for yours, or choose death and let those who hurt you win."

"What happens if I choose you?"

"Your soul, your body, your anger, it all becomes ours. We shall be your patron, providing you with boundless power for our mission. You will never know fear again, but you will leave behind everything that you know. You will be transformed into our perfect visage."

"And what mission is that?" I start pushing against the tentacles again, my finger slipping over their smooth skin. I have to get away from this thing. Whatever hallucination this is, I am going to snap out of it. This can't be happening to me.

"Be still." The monster's words rattle my teeth in my skull and tears slip down my cheek.

A tentacle, thinner and glowing much softer than the rest, rises up to my face. I can't lean away from it. My hand bats it away, but it just wraps around my wrist, before touching the centre of my forehead.

Visions flood my mind. Monsters everywhere. Things that I only thought were myths walk through my thoughts like they belong there. Bathed in steam, I can see myself at the centre of them. There is a hungry look on my face as different monsters approach me. I'm not scared when one of them with sharp talons touches my cheek, I'm excited.

She touches the vision of me, and I swear I feel it too. There is danger as she slips her hand down to my throat, but all I feel is the building heat between my thighs. Another monster with green skin begins to kiss my neck. The odd protrusions in her mouth scrape against my warm skin. Thrill zip down my spine at the sensation. Pleasure overwhelms my initial fear, and my body accepts the unnatural and seems to hunger for more of it. The woman kissing my neck directs me to look at something, at someone.

Through the steam, surrounded by tiles and tentacles, sits a woman. Her skin is flushed red from the heat. There are marks on her body, but I can't figure out what they are. I just know they are glowing, calling to me. In the vision, she runs a hand over her shaved head before tracing it down her body. They trace the curls between her legs, and as she spreads her fingers apart, a thick tentacle rises from the water, blocking my view. She moans as it touches her skin.

My breathing turns to panting. *Yes, yes, mine*, my lips form the words, but there is no sound. The woman in steam looks at me like I am her salvation as the tentacle sucks on her clit.

"Come to me, Delphini," she calls.

I blink, and suddenly, there is a different scene. The nude woman from before is dressed but covered in blood. Her clothes cling to her front and I see the defined muscles of her arm as she raises a knife again. She brings it down onto the man kneeling before her. I can't see him. Her body is glowing so brightly; he's just a shadow, but I am enraptured at the sight of her. The brutal, yet precise, force she exerts has my body heating in a different way.

The rage from early returns, the urge to strike, overwhelming my arousal.

I want to kill.

There is an explosion of pink light; tentacles rise around me, consume me, and feed me all at once, and I am whole. Everything in the world is new and correct. I am as I always should have been.

Then, the vision ends.

The neon-lit tentacles around me ripple, like the beast shivers, just as I do when I feel my pulse between my legs. Its pupil dilates, turning from one long slit into an endless dark void like the one I woke up in. I don't see myself in a reflection like I should. Instead, I see her again: the woman with tanned skin and angry eyes staring back at me. Her beauty is soul-deep, yet weary. It's like she has been waiting for a safe place to rest, waiting for me.

There is no explanation why I know she is waiting for me, why I know that she is mine. Deep in the crevices of my soul, there is a rumbling, a clattering behind the cage that holds my heart. More tears pour from my eyes as I am flooded with a sense of longing. I'm open and exposed, yet still surrounded by tentacles. They vibrate and emit a low purr that seduces all feelings away until I simply am.

"*Yes,*" the monster hisses. "*You are the one.*"

"Who was that?" I ask. "How do I know you aren't trying to trick me?"

"*Trust us, Delphini Fields. All you must do is accept us, join in our mission, join with us, and all will be right in the world.*" Tentacles slip around my body more, fluid dripping onto my skin, etching a mark on my chest.

"Join with you?" I gasp, trying to see what they are doing to me. Each dribble tickles the space between my breasts and my nipples harden at the sight of the suction cups pulsing.

"*In time, all will be revealed. First, you must seek your revenge, use your fury to feed us their souls, their power. Our mate waits for you, but will you join our mission?*"

Everything about this could be a lie. This could be hell, but flashes of that woman, my soulmate, keep drawing me back. The ache in her soul, the hunger in her eyes, I know she is real. If she is real, then everything else about this is as well. The monster said my destiny is split in two. This is my chance to seize control and take charge of my choices.

"I accept."

2 Days

Cutting the nylon rope off the woman's ankle is simple enough. My filleting knife snaps the plastic and I collect the woman in one arm and the pathetic gym weight tying her down in the other. The water at this depth is dark and silent– peaceful. If I could remain here forever, I would be tempted to. But I can't let my life's work falter because I want something as simple as peace. Failing my Love isn't an option.

I break the surface of the water and slowly swim back towards the small boat I used to get out this far. A few miles off, a yacht that is lit up like fucking Christmas is partying away. I wonder if she is a part of that group? There are no signs of any other vessel out here, but judging by the state of this one's skin, she's been under the water for a few hours. I'd been ashore, hunting, when Love signalled me.

When I arrived back at *The Princess's Despair*, my quartermaster had the sailboat ready for me. The older Selkie and I have been through this a few times now. She knows this routine well enough to know I don't want assistance. What no one knows is that I'm terrified one day one of these rescues will lead to my soulmate. That I will drag them back into this life and they will be shackled to someone who can't love any more.

Even if she accepts us, returning to this reality is still hard. We don't know what her life was before she was abandoned to the sea.

I throw the weight aboard first, the large disk clattering against the metal. With one arm gripping the side of the boat, I try to haul the woman up. Her once-white dress keeps catching on the edge. I have no choice but to cut the garment off her and push it away from the boat so it doesn't get caught in the motor. This time, I haul the woman up and crawl in behind her.

Once I have my jacket on, I look at her again and try to assess the physical damage to her body. She is bruised, the side of her face scraped and somewhat swollen, and one of her wrists appears to be broken. Love must still be trying to convince her that her revenge is a cause worth fighting for if it isn't fixed yet. Where her appearance isn't marred with bruises, it is a soft, deep terracotta colour that reminds me of the statues of a place I have long cast from my mind. Her figure could have easily been cast and fired by a great artisan, organic and perfect all at the same time. Something ancient people would have left at temples to honour gods and goddesses in hopes they would bring good fortune to the land.

But this woman has been ignored by them, like we all have.

I toss the oversized towel I brought along over her body and crank the motor on. She doesn't flinch as it fires to life. We set course back to the dock. I watch the area around us, looking for anyone who might be out. The Coast Guard is quiet as usual, but now that the weather is turning warm and the tourist season has begun, late-night fishermen and reckless university students abound. The last thing I need is for them to shine a light in our direction and believe I am dumping a dead body.

She still could be a dead body if she doesn't accept.

I probe my thoughts for Love, but they are silent. Doesn't matter, I suppose. If she does wake up in a few hours, it would do no good for anyone if it is on a metal table in the morgue. When I am not searching the dark horizon for potential problems, my gaze drifts back to the woman.

There is no indication of what she is. No fins or scales that say she is of the water. She could be a Selkie whose coat has been stolen. She has the curves of one, but my gut says she is of the land. I have rescued the occasional nymph from a greedy pirate; she is beautiful enough to be one. The dress she wore didn't give me anything besides the fact it looked fancy. Not like one of Lloyd's girls though. She was dumped too close to Harbour Crest to work in one of his clubs, and the snake knows not to throw his accidents in my territory any more.

As we approach the ship, I cut the motor and glide the last few yards into the mooring point. A few crew members are waiting with a blanket, ready to help warm up the new arrival.

"Captain," Aiofe greets me solemnly. The Selkie I made my quartermaster over twenty-five years ago has never been one for smiles. Her demeanour has been curt since the day she cut off the hands of the man who stole her magic coat.

Two girls, Neela and Hamako, tie the boat down while Aiofe helps me bring up the unconscious woman. A chill grips my chest at her touch, but I don't react. Another, Lakelynn, quickly wraps the extra blanket around her and we lift the woman onto the ship. It's late, but the night crew stands watch as we carry the woman down the steps, past the old captain's quarters, and through the door clearly marked "employees only."

The room before us opens into a cavernous, humid space that is neither of this world nor of Love's. It is held in a pocket dimension between worlds, safe for all who are allowed entrance. It was a fucking pain in my ass stealing this magic door from the Fae realm, but what they don't know can't hurt them. The shoddy thing isn't perfect, which is even better for Love. They can partially exist in this dimension without having to work through me. It means they can be freer here.

We take the woman to my quarters and lay her down by the fireplace. I set about lighting it while Aiofe looks at her.

"Do you think she'll join us?" she asks.

"I think so." I strike a match and toss it onto the kindling. The room warms quickly; the soft glow of the lanterns only assists in lighting the space so much.

"She isn't like the usual catch," Aiofe states matter of factly, as if we are so regularly diving for dead bodies in the harbour, rather than once or twice a decade.

I don't answer her; she doesn't need my agreement or disagreement on the matter when it is so plain to see that the being neither dead nor alive in front of my fireplace is different from the rest of the crew. Aiofe touches the heavy coat she has wrapped around her waist. She's nervous.

As she should be. All new recruits are different; some adjust well to our way of life, others fight tooth and nail to return to their old life so they can pretend nothing happened and that bad people, bad men, don't exist. There is something about this woman that tells me she will be trouble.

"Go," I say. "Join the others in the bath. Tomorrow will be a busy day, the start of a busy season, I'm feeling."

"Busy is good." My quartermaster shrugs before looking me over subtly. "You alright? I know you were interrupted this evening."

"You have known me long enough to know nothing truly interrupts my hunt."

Aiofe nods. She doesn't broach the topic of why I have been skipping the Tuesday meetings. It has been a few weeks since I last attended and all the crew have seen my war path since. Night after night, getting further and further from the water in search of those who are guilty of being a vile man. Love is sated, and we are safe. That is all that should matter to her and the rest of the crew.

"Call for me if you need me, captain."

"Aye," I wave her off, going behind the screen in my room to change into a dry pair of trousers and a fresh shirt.

The door closes, and I wait. My heart's steady beat counting the seconds until there is no risk of someone bothering me this evening. I pull the damp cotton scarf from around my neck and rub the soreness from my nape before dragging my hand up through the soft fuzz of my hair. I dig through a drawer at the top of my dresser for a fresh handkerchief and tie it around myself.

The soft fabric on my skin is a coat of armour. Like the rest of my clothes, it is chosen to assert myself in a way that makes others feel fear. Intimidation upon sight is a skill I have honed for centuries. Stained with the blood, the sweat, and the tears of the men I have ruined, the old clothes on my back may be designed for a man larger than me, but they do the job. I dress to strike fear into the hearts of all creatures who wish to harm women. Any soft edge I once had died a long time ago. All that is hidden under these oversized clothes now is a body marked with centuries of wear and anger.

It is nearly dawn when the woman finally stirs. I have sat beside her for hours, staring, waiting. Her wrist clicked back into place an hour ago and her bruises are nearly gone. This is nothing like that first time in the northern sea, and yet I feel as though it is with how my knee bounces and I fidget with my knife. The sheen on the blade in the firelight is a small comfort.

There is no flash of pink light this time, her mark hidden beneath her coverings. I tuck the blade away so as to not frighten her.

"Shit," she groans and rolls onto her side. A shiver, violent and visible, wracks through her before she settles with a defeated sigh. "Where's my phone?"

Her reaction to being alive again isn't what I expected. But she is finally fucking awake. The creature that I've spent hours memorising takes her sweet time to realise she isn't alone. Bad instincts. That doesn't mean I am not lost in the power of her gaze once she finally draws her eyes from my bare feet to my face. The deep brown shade is striking, consuming. Even as this creature stares up at me with unguarded wonder and curiosity, I can tell a single look from her could bring weaker beings to their knees.

Something tickles in my chest and I could swear it was hope.

She swallows audibly and averts her gaze. I watch how her fingers curl tighter around the covers, keeping them close to her chest. *Is she the one?*

"She is home," Love's pleased voice echoes in my head and I sigh with a small touch of relief. They are back to me, the silence no longer so heavy.

"What are you called?" I ask, trying to be gentle in a way that isn't in my nature.

"Delphini."

Her voice is soft, with an accent that tells me she isn't from Gwenmore.

"Do you remember anything from..." I let my voice trail off, allowing the woman in front to fill in the space if she so chooses.

"Some of it, it's- it's blurry." She shrugs her shoulders delicately, and all I can think is this woman won't be able to handle anything.

It will take the whole summer to get her ready for service. Everywhere I look, all I see is a softness that isn't suited to the way of life on this ship, in this job. She may not be crying now, but there is no doubt in my mind she will break. There is a power within us, the crew, that Love bestows upon us to transfer the essence of humans to them. This creature is going to struggle to draw forth the anger required to even summon an ounce of that power.

There is a weakness in her that calls to a long-dead part of me, though. I want to see her in tears of ecstasy. Like a sickness inside me, I want to hear her beg for my command, my touch. I want to be the one she comes to for everything she needs because I am her guide, her protector.

Could she...

"Delphini," I start, standing up abruptly as if pacing the length of my quarters will rid me of this new, rabid energy. "Where are you from?"

Safe starting point. Particular creatures gravitate towards different regions of the world. If she truly is a nymph, she could easily be a Naiad from one of the many national forest regions. Her presence is steady, calming, as she watches me move up and down the room. She could be from the Redwood National Park. It would make complete sense that she is of such a noble and ancient clan. Would people try to steal her to get a ransom?

"Chicago," she murmurs. "Where are you from?"

"Doesn't matter." I brush the notion that I will answer personal questions aside. She doesn't need to know. This conversation is about figuring out what she is without straight up asking her. From what I have gathered through centuries of this work, it would be rude. Creatures are offended when you guess right, and they are offended if you guess wrong. Getting them to tell you is like getting a Fae to speak their true name to you. A minefield. "Is there next of kin we need to contact?"

Her eyes narrow, long lashes touching her cheek. Delphini's whole body language shifts, and the hairs on the back of my neck rise. The ire I feel from her is nearly cutting.

"I can do it myself," she says. "Do you have my phone?"

My patience is generally weak. I am not impulsive and can't be with the life I lead, but I am used to a certain level of respect from the crew and from creatures in the city. They know something is lurking in my depths, another being that is neither human nor monster. They know that a fight with me would end in their demise. This one doesn't have that instinct.

Yet.

"No. Should we be concerned they will be looking for you?" If she is a part of a pack or charm, they will be looking for her and causing a stir. I will not have that on this ship.

"I don't know, maybe." She rolls onto her back again and stares at the ceiling. "I thought I was supposed to leave everything behind for this?"

"You are, but closure is important."

"I'd rather leave it open for now."

Her words make me pause in front of her. Clearly, she wasn't taken from her family then but has been cast aside by them. They could even be the ones who killed her in the first place.

"How many people do you have to...?" I ask, changing the subject away from families if I can.

It takes a moment before she responds, "Four."

That will take some time in this modern era. Between surveillance and forensic technologies, we can't just murder anyone. Well, I do, but I own the docks around here and have centuries of experience. I can harvest the essence of my prey in moments and have it fed to Love before someone even notices I am there.

"Have you been waiting for me?" Delphini asks.

As she moves to sit up, her palm slips on the wooden floor, and I instinctively reach to catch her. My fingers wrap around her bicep harsher than I intend, but my world lights up. Centuries of icy waters and frigidity rush through me, out of me, as I yank my hand back.

I stare at my palm in confusion as something new takes hold of me. Wonder.

Her touch *burns*.

"She's the one." Love's voice is warm as they confirm it.

Delphini is mine, the other half of my broken soul. After centuries of waiting, of convincing myself I didn't need this part of Love's promise, she is here. My soulmate. I fall back into my chair.

"Holy shit," she whispers, staring at my hand and then my face.

I swallow the sudden lump in my throat, "I've been waiting."

This beautiful creature is mine? She is my opposite and my match. Her softness to my hard edges will blend together until we are one. My faith in our mission, in Love, has never wavered. They have always provided and guided me and my crew, but this feels like I have a chance at peace.

"Can I touch you?" she asks.

I lay my hand before her and wait for her to come to me. Her delicate fingers ghost over mine until our palms connect in a burst of heat that radiates up my arm. My whole body heats, and the tentacles of my body beg for freedom to absorb Delphini and all the warmth she has to offer.

"Feels like lying in the hot sun all afternoon," she murmurs, like she doesn't honestly believe it.

"It feels like you are mine," I say, unable to keep the awe from my voice.

"All it took was losing my humanity…" her voice trails off.

"What?" I ask, still marvelling at her touch, still soaking in every bit of warmth from her I can.

"I mean, people don't just get magic and meet tentacle monsters."

"What are you talking about?" I pull my hand back, and immediately goosebumps rise on my flesh and the tentacles holding me together push against my insides to get closer to her. "Nymphs believe in mates, don't they?"

"What?"

She looks at me as if I have grown a second head, and my brows pinch together, trying to think of what else she possibly could be. Only, in the end, I decide being blunt is the best course of action. My soulmate can certainly forget such an offence.

"What creature are you?"

"What, *what* now?" She sits up straighter and my eyes are fixed on the curve of her form, the way the fabric drapes, sinks and rises like rhythmic tides across her body. A thrumming heat swells in my gut and I'm not sure if I've ever felt it with such an intensity before, this lust.

"There's nothing to be worried about." I try to keep an even tone, but the hairs at the back of my neck have risen again. My body is split in two, warring between craving her touch and suspicion. When she doesn't answer, I press harder. "Just spit it out."

"Spit what out?" Her voice wavers as her emotions reveal her aggravation.

If, for an instant, I thought she was reacting to the trauma she had experienced, I would have stepped down. I would feel Love trying to cool my anger before it is misdirected in a disastrous way. However, they are silent, and the daggers this woman is trying to stare into me tell me everything I need to know.

"What are you?"

I rise up from my chair and tower over her now, but she doesn't allow it. As ever, my soulmate would; she stands up and stares me down. Delphini is taller than I am by a few inches, but that doesn't stop me from stepping into her space with purpose. I will make her answer me by forcing her to approach the dying fire. Her anger rises further, her chest heaving, and the fist holding the blanket up clenches so hard I think she might tear holes in it. But she keeps her mouth closed.

"I will ask again." My voice rises the longer she stares, unflinching and brutal. "What monster are you?"

"I'm a fucking human being!" she shouts, and every ounce of annoyance and fight leaves my body. No. It's replaced with fear. "What the fuck else did you expect?"

"No." The word slips from my lips before I can stop it.

Lamp light flickers, and then a voice cracks from the abyss.

"She has chosen us," Love states.

Delphini, even while shaking from the experience of our patron's voice, nods in agreement. She has chosen us. How do they expect me to accept that which I have sworn off? That which has shown us time and time again they aren't worthy? As if there have not been centuries of fury to erase my humanity?

"We do not. Learn to accept her. She wants nothing but to be yours. She accepted her gifts with open arms, with grace, with joy. Learn from her, our heart, or you shall both suffer." Love's voice is a whisper in my ear as they read my thoughts.

The weight of their tentacles caressing my torso and neck doesn't remove the tremor from my clenched fist nor lessen the goosebumps that erupt across my skin.

Delphini is a human.

My mind whirls. She has seen too much of this place already. She can't leave, but I can't let her around the others. The crew will eat her alive, and if the tightening sensation in my chest means anything, it is that Love will be greatly displeased if anyone hurts Delphini. I don't want her to get hurt, but I can't expose her to more of our world. There are rules, consequences, for humans seeing the monster world.

Without another thought, I shove all the fear I had buried deeper into the pit of my chest and grab her arm. She reacts instantly, trying to push me off her. But that's not what has me pausing. It's the warmth of her touch, of her skin on mine. It's such a sweet relief to finally enjoy the touch of another, but it turns my blood to ice just as quickly.

"What are you doing?" she demands.

With a grunt, I have her arm twisted behind her, and she freezes. Her ragged breaths come out in short pants that only get shorter the longer I hold her in place. The line of tension across her shoulders is so tight she's shaking. Or is she shaking from fear?

Good. Be afraid of me. That's the way it should be. This is how it will be for us until I figure out what to do with her. She can't stay here, no matter how much seeing this side of her suddenly causes me pain. She isn't safe. She can't be mine.

"Walk."

The words are harsh on my tongue and tinged with venom. She stumbles but doesn't release the grip on the blanket around her. Outside of my quarters, the crew has begun preparing for the day. All work stops, all friendly chatter and joking quietly as they watch me half drag someone I just rescued down towards the baths on the opposite side of the great hall.

Having the brig next to the bath made sense at the time when it was erected. The marble walls are solid, and only one heavy iron door allows any amount of light through. The brig in this dimension is sound and smell proof. It's mostly clean since it hasn't been used for decades. The original purpose of it was to protect a former crew member during her lunar shifts. A few of the sirens tried to convince the werewolf she'd be fine, they'd be fine, but up until her dying day, she didn't trust herself.

The inch-deep claw marks on the walls prove the werewolf was right.

Delphini pushes back against me as I move to shove her inside. The heat of her body, my own acceptance of that heat, makes me pause for a moment. But I feel the eyes on me. I can't let them know what she is now that she is alive again.

"No, wait," she begs, and it twists something inside of me. "We can talk about this like civil human beings."

"That's just it." I sneer, pressing my cheek near her ear for this last warm caress. "We aren't human."

The door slams shut as she turns around. For the first time, I wonder if I should go against Love. Centuries of being with them, I have never doubted, never faltered, from the core tenets of our relationship. But how could they do this to me? To choose her? We have worked so hard to try and bring them here. Even as hunting has grown harder and harder without exposure to the human world, I haven't stopped trying to bring them here.

A human will only cause chaos and destruction. It's all they know. We can't risk her ruining our plans.

My fist smashes into the iron door. It creaks with force but doesn't dent. The great hall is silent, but I have never been one to downplay my anger or hide these emotions from the crew so they don't see this as the defeat it is.

"Nobody speaks to the prisoner, and nobody fucking touches this door."

"Aye, captain." After watching this display, a chorus of voices call out, some more sure than others. Good, this will keep her safe.

The door leading to the ship's lower deck opens up, and Nargol, an orc gunner on night shift, pops her head through. Thick braids fall across her shoulders and the tentacle etchings that cover her pale green face glow a slight pink colour as she passes the barrier.

"Oh, Aiofe, your gooner is here." Her deep sing-song voice is loud enough to raise the dead.

I close my eyes in frustration. Of course, those fuckers would send that lovesick idiot here this morning. They go weeks without more than a text message, and the first person they think to send is Sampson. I don't know what Aiofe sees in the Dwarven male, but at least he is polite and, as she puts it, "submissive and breedable," unlike his twin, who is a dickhead.

Aiofe leans against the door to her small quarters, toothbrush still between her lips. She nods to Nargol, a slight but knowing smirk on her lips as she slips back into her room. That is the most expressive I've seen her in a while. That is also why I hold my tongue about her relationship with an outsider and a male one at that.

Their happenstance meeting at Our Lady of Mercy is a rare case for the crew here. All of us have suffered at the hands of men, some monsters, and primarily humans. We have been discarded and forgotten by the gods before Love even found us. Unsurprisingly, most of the crew don't venture from the ship or the waters surrounding the Docklands. We have built a haven here.

Grabbing my hat and gear from one of the many hooks by the portal door, I breeze by Nargol and ascend to the main deck. My bare feet don't make a sound as I walk across the deck. The gangplank, bright orange and wide enough to be accessible, is still tucked against the railing. I tie a leather scabbard to my hip and buckle the heavy, studded belt around my waist. It's wide enough to be an under-bust corset, but the hardened material holds more secrets and protects me from a knife to the gut. It's saved me more than once.

"Sampson," I call, leaning over the railing to look down at the dock. "We weren't expecting you."

The Dwarven is shorter than me by a few inches. His dark red hair is greying at the temples and along his thick, full beard. He dressed impeccably as always, a full suit and all that shit. He even has a fucking hat in his hands like this show will impress anyone in this decade. As the morning sun bursts over the horizon, I can see the soft smile he gives me.

"Good morning, Captain Moore. I am glad I can deliver this message to you directly." He clears his throat and breaks eye contact. "Certain beings are concerned about your poor attendance."

"Are they now?" I run my tongue over my teeth and plant my elbows on the sea-weathered rail. This does give me an idea. "What day is it?"

"Thursday," he answers quickly, like I might fling a dagger or something at him if he doesn't. Sensible.

"You can tell your boss I'll see him on Tuesday then." I turn without waiting for a response. Sampson will tell Ray, and that lizard will tell Deg'Doriel. Now I just have to hide the human until then. She can't be my problem, but she can be the human for those buffoons to deal with.

I can't garner a reputation for saving humans, not again. That lad two centuries ago was the last one, a special circumstance.

Aiofe leans against the stair railing. She's wearing the brown leather harness Sampson gifted her a few years ago. She's kept it in excellent knick, and we all know how it fucking delights the Dwarven if her stories of victory are anything to go by.

"You need the afternoon shift?" I ask.

"No one comes between me and the job, captain, you know that," she answers, but doesn't move from her spot. "All good?"

What a weighted question. When have things indeed been good for us? Between the harshness of our existence, our pasts that never truly wash away, and the ever-looming knowledge of what is to come, what does good really mean? We live. Tourist season is starting up, which means more cash in our pockets. After thousands of years of waiting, my promised soulmate has arrived, but I can't accept her.

"Enjoy your walk around the dock, Aiofe."

CHAPTER SIX
DELPHINI

I can't see.

The thin slit of light coming from the door isn't enough to illuminate anything in this space. My hands move across the scarred walls, trying to find anything to give me more light. With each new mark I find on the cold stone, my heart rattles harder in my chest.

Terror swells in me like waves and with each crash my breathing gets harder. I'm trapped. This is where I will die again. Staring into the dark, nothing until I don't wake up again. The pain of my nails cracking against the floor isn't even enough to calm me. Trapped. Caged. Monster.

What the fuck used to be in here?

"Her name was Lyra."

Voices echo deep in my head, and I scream. Once the sound is out of my mouth, I can't stop it. My throat burns as the fear turns to anger at that woman and at myself. I collapse onto the stone floor as my lungs finally empty. The cold digs into my back. *They* are speaking to me.

"Hello?" I call out. "Please, this isn't what you said would happen."

"*Sweet one, no one has ever said this life would be easy.*"

"You said she was my soulmate."

"*As you are the one, so is she,*" they explain. "*But she will not simply bow to fate when it has been so cruel.*"

I don't know if I want to fight her locking me up or hold her until that fear behind her stare melts away. Both would be good, I suppose, thinking harder about her as a whole. The vision of her murdering that shadow surfaces, and I wonder if that was a metaphorical murder or a real one.

She is handsome, either way. Sharp features with a scattering of dark spots from sun damage. My soulmate has led a hard life if the way she paced around her room tells me anything. She hasn't known true peace.

I knew when I woke up that she would be watching over me, waiting for me. They hadn't said anything about being thrown in jail for being fucking honest or how her touch would set my insides ablaze. It was bad enough to wake up naked and then get angry with her, but then she grabbed me like that, and I couldn't... I couldn't...

My chest constricts and tears spring to my eyes. I can't let what Miles and Audrey did haunt me. They think they have beaten me, but they haven't. Crying won't get me revenge, even as my throat constricts anyway.

"Breathe, sweet one. It's only you and us in this room now. You are safe."

"No," I hiss, voice straining for control. "I am trapped in a fucking cage."

"She is doing what she believes is best."

"Best for who?" I demand. "I went through hell, and now she intends to do it again herself."

"She is scared for you." The words slip through the ether with such softness I don't want to believe them. *"She has been waiting centuries for you, but she reacted rashly. Do not think this won't have repercussions."*

I fall back onto the floor and let this harsh, new reality seep into my bones like the cold. Rejected. The one person in the universe that some ancient god decreed would choose me ended up throwing me away. I was assaulted, drugged, sexually assaulted, murdered, and then tossed into some sort of fucking stone cell meant for scary monsters. As if I am the damn monster here.

The fear in her gaze had been so real. The fire in her eyes froze over, and her tiny mouth trembled. My soulmate is terrified of me.

Maybe I am the monster?

I don't even know her name, but already I am desperate to feel her, to witness any emotion she can offer me again. They were so palpable, a raging storm that I am lost in. All the red sirens in my head are screaming that this is dangerous territory, but even from this cell, they only look like a lovely shade of pink.

If only I can find the eye of it, find a way to make her see that I was brought here for a reason.

I force myself to think of other things when I feel more tears drip down into my hair. Thoughts of my family drift through my mind. I don't want *Yiayia* to worry about me, but I don't think I could hold it together over a phone call. Will my parents have seen the pictures? Will they be concerned when I don't answer their phone calls like I always have?

I'm sure Miles shared them with every rag newspaper he could think of. Everyone at the party will have heard the story from Audrey's big mouth about the position she 'caught' me in. My entire reputation has been dragged to the bottom of the ocean like my body.

A shiver courses through me at the thought of those hands, and I wrap the blanket tighter around me.

She will have made sure to spin a great tale, convincing everyone in attendance that once they docked again at the end of the party, that's when she caught me. Maybe she'll be bold and tell them I fled the scene once I realised my secret was out, and seen with more than one man as well. She'll claim I ran off with them.

The Bradshaws will be pleased as punch to start the proceedings to gain my generous trust fund. It is supposed to be my reward for all my hard work for the family. It should never have been in that stupid fucking contract.

Fury, hot and festering in my gut for months, finally takes hold of me. I scream again, until my lungs hurt. There is nothing else I can do.

I did it all for my parents; I did everything for them. My life was nothing but trying to please them and make them acknowledge how good I was. I worked night and day to raise the Field name higher. I never complained and I always did as they asked, even agreeing to that fucking engagement.

Now? It's wasted. All my hard work has been thrown away because of the greed of others.

"Doesn't matter," I murmur the lie to myself in the hopes I will believe it.

For the first time in my life, I am free of the weight of expectation, and I end up in a fucking cell.

"She knows that if the others realise you are human, they may react poorly, sweet one." Their voice is soft in my ear now, a coiling sensation inside me stirs.

"What does that even fucking mean?" I groan, throwing my hands up. "Are they going to eat me?"

"I would never allow it."

I close my eyes and breathe through the frustration. Anger won't fix this. I need to wait and find the weak spot. I've already fucked up once since waking up. I should have lied and just agreed to the first thing she called me.

But what kind of relationship survives when it is born of a lie?

A pathetic smile curls at the corner of my lips. It's vain of me to be happy she called me nymph. She at least thought I was beautiful enough for a moment. I saw the way she stared at my hips, at my mouth. Her gaze was assessing, but she lingered.

Hold on to those, I tell myself.

I can do what I want. No more coy smiles, no more being polite and civil, no more abusive fiancé. Those are good things I can focus on, too. This is my chance to be me without fear of retribution from my parents. They aren't my family any more.

And this me wants that woman to fall in love with me. By whatever means necessary, she is my goal now and her love will be my reward. No more wanting from the sidelines and being detached. A new life means a new way of living.

After I kill the people who did this to me.

"So, how am I supposed to get revenge from here?" I ask.

For the first time, I notice how my voice, now strained and dry, echoes off the walls. It only adds to the level of fear still pumping in my veins. My fingers still shake from the way she yanked me across that giant foyer.

"Do you wish for the power to be free of this place?"

Something tickles inside of me at the question, profound and unsettling.

"What do you want in exchange this time? More murders?"

"A vow, a bond so unbreakable that you will be forever transformed. But power is not gained without something lost."

"So I promise myself to you, and what?" I ask again, my voice barely a whisper.

There isn't anything to really lose. I have already died once, and that somehow got me a soulmate. Making a vow with them doesn't seem to have a risk, and that is what made me hesitate this time.

"There is something inside of you, sweet one, a cavern that is empty, a vessel that is powerful enough to hold the power we are going to bestow you with."

"You want to impregnate me?" Bile rises in my throat.

I have never wanted kids. I've vocally denied any maternal instincts that my own mother tried to instil in me. And, being the sole heir to the Fields dynasty, this has caused nothing but problems in my relationship with them. Maybe they even thought if they forced my hand in this fucked up arranged marriage, that I would fall pregnant by accident.

"Do not debase us with such a vile concept." Their voice rises, and every part of me vibrates. My body freezes in terror at the feeling of falling.

"I'm sorry, I'm sorry." The words rush out of me as a tear slips down my cheek. Why am I crying?

"Close your eyes and open your mind, sweet one. Come to us."

It takes a while. Meditation has never been a skill I possessed. It isn't like I haven't tried. Mom regularly tried to get me to understand her wellness retreats and I know the steps that I am supposed to take to get to the calm, centred state. I get distracted along the way without a proper objective. Without a finish line, I wander off. I need to know what I am striving for, not sit silently while waiting for it to come to me.

There is an objective this time, though, and I focus on that. I visualise *Them*, tentacles and eyes and beautiful pink colouring. My breathing slows and my limbs tingle until I feel myself slip beneath the surface of reality.

Neon lights burst behind my eyes and I shield my face. Blue eyes watch me closely. Appendages writhe and dance before me, deliberately wrapping around me until I am lifted. My skin vibrates with each subtle squeeze from the tentacles. That same fruity smell from before hits my nose, but this time I find it familiar in a different way. I know the scent from a distant memory.

Tentacles recede until all that is holding me up in front of the monster is a single limb around my middle.

"The vessel is different for everyone. In you, this place will never be occupied because that is your choice. Become one with us and let our power fill that place."

Randomly, horrifically, I get flashbacks to that day at the gynaecologist's when I had an IUD inserted. How much it fucking hurt, like my guts were being torn apart from the inside as my uterus adjusted to that demonic little piece of plastic. "A pinch" my fucking ass. That thing lasted for all of two years before I demanded it be removed early.

"Will it hurt?" I set my face, ready for them to say yes, that pain seals the bond or some other crazy fucking shit.

"No, sweet one, you may feel nothing, or you may feel pleasure. We do not cause pain for those who wish to serve us. You will see soon enough."

The safe answer is nothing, to get this bonding over with and with zero feeling, to get out of this as unscathed as possible. I have already been through hell and back in the past 24 hours. But as my fingers slip over the tentacle at my middle, my skin begins to thrum with new life. The rage in me, the simmering in my blood swells inside of me and pulses between my legs at the one base thought.

Release.

From my old life and expectations, from the feeling of hands that don't belong, from the hurt of her sudden rejection. If only for a short while, I want to be free of everything but carnal release.

"Pleasure," I demand, before softly saying. "Just be gentle."

The neon flares before the pink glow outlining the tentacles soften. The eyes converge into six, and suddenly, a form takes shape. Their mass of tentacles becomes curvy, a womanly torso with tentacles for legs and hair. They smooth a human-like hand through the masses and smile. They tower over me with a look that speaks of the pleasure they can bring me.

How is this? Or would..." They trail off, a webbed hand smoothing over their body to reveal a flatter, more masculine chest.

"No." I reach out to them.

While I have nothing against men and have dated a couple, women have always been my preference. How could they not be? Even one as alien to me, with a mass of tentacles, has a form more beautiful than any man. The slick suppleness of their deep teal skin calls to me. My fingers shake as they skate across the expanse of their collarbone. The tip of their clawed finger touches my jaw carefully, deliberately.

"Tenderness," they murmur, trailing their gaze from my lips to my breasts, to my mound. *"For a soft creature as sweet as you, we would offer nothing less."*

"What should I call you?" The tentacle around my middle lifts me higher until I am floating over their mouth.

"When your pleasure peaks and your body opens to us, you may call out the name we have accepted." Their breath ghosts across my skin and I shudder at the warmth. Two more tentacles slide up my legs. They slither across the inside of my thighs until I am spread wide enough to accommodate the size of their head. My legs are swallowed up to my knees by their hair and the tendrils hold me open. The tentacles leave a trail of slick behind that sets my skin alight as they trace the pronounced curves of my body up to my breasts.

My lips part as something latches on to my nipples. The contact makes my body burn. Each breath I draw grows quicker and quicker as they softly suckle at the peaks. They keep their eyes locked on my pussy. I've never had a partner so absorbed in me, in watching the manifestation of my pleasure grow. Only when I am shaking, grinding my hips in the air for friction that isn't there, do they speak again.

"Love."

I scream at the first touch of their tongue on my neglected flesh. They lap the arousal they caused, drink me down like they have never been satisfied in such a way. The tentacles attached to my breasts unlatch and I groan. My nipples are sore, hard brown peaks now slick with Love's juices.

"More," I whimper, my fingers digging into the tentacle wrapped around my middle.

Their eyes meet mine, and then the thinner tentacles are massaging my breasts. The tips flick my nipples in turn and each touch sends a jolt of pleasure straight to my clit. My eyes close and my jaw loosens. Love's sharp teeth tease my flesh as their tongue teases my pussy, thrusting in only to keep licking.

Months spent with just my vibrator have left me hypersensitive to the touch of another and whatever lube is coming off of these tentacles is driving me right to the edge of exploding. My thighs tremble around their head and I am already so close.

"Fuck," I shout when they tease my clit. "Fuck, please."

"*Breathe, sweet one,*" their voice rumbles over my pussy. As I inhale, I feel the coil relax in my core, and I do as they command.

I suck down a shaky breath and my lower muscles relax. Love lazily strokes me with their tongue, each glide sending shocks of pleasure through me that I breathe through. When the tentacle around me tightens I don't even feel it. Pleasure courses so joyously through me that my limbs feel heavy and free.

"There you are," Love's mouth doesn't stop working, but I hear them clear as day. *"Good girl."*

A shiver racks through my body at the simple words and my breath threatens to stay locked inside me. Even the slightest hint of approval that I am performing well sends me rocketing into an orgasm. At that slightest hitch, my exhale brings forth my climax. Staring into their blue eyes, I feel euphoric and light bursts across my vision in pink shards. My body trembles as wave after wave of relief threatens to pull me under a deeper spell.

"Love," I moan.

The tentacles on my breasts are still teasing, still working me up like I didn't have a mind-altering orgasm. My clit throbs in time with my nipples, but I feel empty still. They aren't done with me yet, though.

They move me, masses of tentacles surround me, coat me in slick fluid that makes me feel like an exposed nerve. One touch and I will cum until I pass out from the sensation. Their near human form dissolves and all that is left is masses of tentacles.

They caress my neck, my fingertips, my lips. A single one slides against my teeth and flavours of hot summer days and pomegranate burst on my tongue. I try to suck down more of the addictive juice, but the tentacle moves away. Not a part of me remains untouched and I want that to never change. I want to feel this, feel them forever.

"You are ours, Delphini, your sweet essence is one we shall savour into the new age and beyond."

As they speak, pale pink illuminates my chest. I inhale sharply at the sight, the soft burn of the light on my flesh. My eyes focus enough that I can see the faint design of tentacles curling across my skin. Love touches it, traces their tentacle over my heart even as they continue to play my body so tenderly.

"Are you ready to receive our power?" they ask. A cool whisper across my overheated skin.

"Yes, yes, please, Love."

It begins with a small touch. The tip of a tentacle teases my pussy, wide and soft, rather than hard, until my body relaxes. They press so gently inside of me I sigh with relief. They move slowly with tentative thrusts that push deeper with each stroke. I beg them for more as their tenderness turns to torture.

"Love," I grip onto a tentacle over my head and the sucker kisses my palm, the inside of my wrist. "Please, fill me."

"Shh, sweet one," they whisper again and my whole body shivers. I clench around the tentacle inside of me and they all pulse. *"Be patient."*

More suckers kiss at my skin, while the teasing at my nipples changes once again to suckling. Another moan leaks from my slack lips. I can't keep up, my sense of rise and fall like waves, my body and theirs drift away from me under their constant touch. Their tentacles move inside me with a smooth, aching rhythm. It isn't until there is a hard push against me that the sensation of fullness inside of me overwhelms the other touches.

I'm restrained by pulsing, glowing tentacles and my pussy is stretched beyond anything I have felt before. It isn't too much, though; all I feel is a pressure inside of me that is begging for release. As if hearing my thoughts, a tentacle inside of me twists and I feel the sucker latch onto the wall of my pussy.

My back bows as an orgasm, one so fierce I hear the tiny splash of my release, rips through me. Every part of me shakes as Love's thrusts become more forceful, with each clench of my muscles I feel the change in them. The way the tentacles swell and undulate inside of me.

"You are ready, sweet one. Do you accept this power?"

I'm half out of my mind with pleasure, yet I know I need this. No matter how much I want to drown in this moment, there is more outside of the prison. I need Love's power to prove myself, to her and everyone else, this is where I am meant to be now.

"Yes." My voice is steady, strong despite the fact I am boneless and unable to lift even my neck to look down at my body. "I accept."

Love's light surges, their tentacles shudder underneath me, and something touches deeper than before. It tickles, neither a pinch nor a relief. My brow furrows as my body tries to adjust. Tentacles inside me thrust slowly. Suckers work hard across me and more slime coats me.

"Be a good girl, sweet one, keep breathing."

On my next inhale, I know what's happening. I don't know how I know, although the feeling is so unlike anything I have ever felt before. The pulsing, the swelling– Love is implanting something inside of me. A moan rips through me.

What the fuck is wrong with me? My pussy clenches like it is trying to hold everything inside of it and tears slip down my cheeks. My body burns with a searing pain-pleasure that isn't natural but is so addicting.

"You've done so well, just as we have asked. Take your reward."

A sucker attaches to my clit when I think I can't take any more, when I am too full. Pink shards of light whirl and I explode. My mind separates from my quivering body and I am surrounded by warmth. The pink of the lights lowers to a deep magenta colour that reminds me of the pomegranate my *Yiayia* would pick from her tree. Serenity settles over me.

The brush of Love's tentacles across my skin is the only thing that keeps me anchored in a sea of euphoria.

The cold cell floor is a harsh reality to return to.

Bursting out of my trance is like resurfacing after being caught underwater for too long. I gasp and roll to my side like I've been pulled from the ocean once again, ready to spit up salt water. My hand brushes over my chest and the subtle, curved marking from Love. Etched lines cross with small, raised circles to form a phone-sized knot between my breasts. I flatten my palm to it and feel the warmth.

I sit up and realise I'm the same. No, I feel like I could run a mile without breaking a sweat. I check the rest of myself over and find a large etching on my skin below my belly button. The positioning of it is obvious, but I can't help the chuckle that comes out of me. I'm losing my mind, but at least these tattoos make me look badass.

In the silence, I evaluate myself, physically and mentally. My body is whole. There isn't a feeling of pain anywhere. I'm not sticky from the time I spent with Love. I should be grateful for that. Before all this, my preferred idea of aftercare was a long hot bath, something to ease sore muscles and wash away any traces of my partner or lube. Now, I wish I was a little bit sticky, just to prove I was in a whole other dimension.

Mentally, I would like to think I am handling all this shit really well. I died, was resurrected, and had amazing sex with a tentacle god monster who might as well have laid eggs inside me.

"Love, is something going to fall out of me?"

I wait for them to speak to me, but they don't. The silence in my mind shouldn't feel this wrong, but I don't want to be alone. The walls around me close in more as I continue to wait for them, hoping they can hear me. I'm not pregnant. I know that isn't what happened, but any reassurance that when I stand up my insides will stay where they belong is important.

"I suppose my soulmate is getting a talking to," I say to myself. Hopefully, whatever repercussions Love mentioned aren't going to scare her off of me more. "She hates me already. How much worse can it get?"

With those final last words, I stand up.

Being alone has never been an issue for me. I'm used to it. My parents were always busy when I was growing up and nannies only cared about shoving dinner down my throat so they could send me to bed. Once I entered prep school, the nannies were replaced with coaches. Fencing isn't a team sport. We were a group of students making up a team that would just as soon tear each other to shreds if it meant we would win.

I have the chance to be a part of something now. There is a person out there who is mine. The sting of rejection is surface level. A gut reaction on her part, I tell myself. She needs to get to know me, then she will see.

She will accept me.

I sound fucking crazy, but I only have my vengeance and my soulmate. My promise to Love is simple. Once I am out of this cell, I am going to kill Miles and Audrey and whoever they hired to help them. Nothing is going to keep me from fulfilling that.

I tug the blanket firmly around my chest and roll the top over to secure it. Time to get out of this prison and start proving myself. I am not a quitter, I am a doer.

Feeling around the gauged walls, the iron door makes me jump when my fingers touch the smooth surface. There is no doorknob, and the hinges are on the other side. I tap my broken nails against metal, sending little jolts of discomfort up my fingertips until I get an idea.

When I was thrown in here, she punched the metal so hard I heard it creak. Could I break the door down? I press my palm flat against the metal and push. Nothing happens and I feel stupid. Were there words I needed to speak? Is the power Love gave me different than what they gave to her?

My head is filled with questions and no one to answer them. *Think, Del.* Brute force has never been my style. This is a test of mental fortitude. I pace the length of the dark cell, trying to remember if there is a lock or a latch on the other side of this door.

I think it's just a latch. I'm fucked if there is a whole chain there.

"Does it matter what's there? I can't open the door." I speak through a few scenarios of what I could do but keep returning to the same thought. I need to ram the giant, sturdy metal door on a cell designed to hold a whole-ass werewolf inside.

I psyche myself up and jump on the balls of my feet like I used to before a fencing match. The floor isn't too cracked, so I'm not worried about falling. With each side, I feint a shove motion and decide that sacrificing my left shoulder will be worth it. Love said they gave me the power to get out of here, so that is what I am going to do.

Not even three steps away from the far wall, I fall on my ass. It's like a cartoon: my foot slips on something, and I pinwheel my arms to try and remain steady, only to end up flat on my back. My head doesn't smack the ground, but the wind knocks out of my chest.

I gasp through the pain. This is for the best. It saves me from risking my bones. I lay on the ground for a moment, but then I feel it. Something wet is soaking through my blanket. Irrationally, I think it's my blood. The longer I stay in my spot, the more sure I am that it's not in a puddle of my blood. It's too much. I roll over with a groan and feel for a wet spot.

It's a small puddle, a shallow divot in the stone from long years of wear. Cautiously, I touch it. No immediate burning sensation, and when I sniff my finger, there is nothing. Throwing any self-preservation to the wind now, I swirl my fingers around in it and try to waft towards me like I would a fine wine. Sommelier, I am not, but this water does have a rosy, salty scent.

There is no dropping sound. So in the dark, I brush my fingers around the edges of it and find a barely there trickle. Crawling on my hands and knees, I trace the rivulets of water back to their source. A small crack in the far wall that, when I first felt around this cell, felt like all the others. But now it's wet and...

And I don't know what that means for me.

A groan, deep and guttural, bursts from my chest. This is so fucking typical. My fists clench, and I am reminded again that most of my acrylics have fallen off. I don't even try to stop the waves of anger. I'm alone and hopeless and every part of me wants to fight despite how fruitless it would be to do so right now. My limbs begin to tingle and my body burns. I squeeze my eyes shut to stop the frustrated tears from slipping down.

With each heaving breath I take, more waves crash into my thoughts. Long-buried resentments are unearthed and washing up at the forefront of my mind. My parents, my life, my cold heart.

My fist slams over the crack and the wall shakes.

I open my eyes and see the world illuminated pink. A small area of Love's mark peeks out from my dress, glowing. I do it again. My fist meets the stone wall and it crumbles away. More water dribbles through the crack, but so does a new form of light. It's low and warm, but I can't stop now. I ball my fists together in one clenched form and raise my arms above my head.

The last conversation I had with Dad flashes through my head, how disappointed he was with me and how much I hated him at that moment. For throwing me to the wolves, for abandoning me on the East Coast while he spent time with the one person who ever looked out for me, who cared for me.

Tears drip down my cheeks and I strike the stone one more time. Half the wall crumbles. A kaleidoscope of pinks erupts from the rubble as it disintegrates. The room floods with steam and the scent of salty, floral heat.

"Holy shit," I murmur. "Holy shit!"

I step over a portion of the remaining wall and find pearls scattered across ornate Grecian tiles. Whites, pinks, and deep brown precious gemstones roll across the tiny squares that make up a mosaic design I have only seen in museums that *Yiayia* would take me to as a child. The floor mosaic covers the expanse of a huge bath. In the light, I can see that the wall I smashed through is marble.

"Holy shit."

The words keep coming out of my mouth. This is definitely not what I thought this room would be. A laundry room, perhaps. There were undoubtedly a handful of people around to watch me get dragged across that foyer. They must wash their clothes somewhere.

But this room is a bath.

I look down at the pearls, and for the first time in my life, I wonder if I will need them for cash. I wouldn't even know where to sell these; I just know that good ones cost money, and on the floor in front of me must be about twenty-five grand's worth of pearls. Last week, I wouldn't have batted an eye at dropping that amount of money on anything.

Right now, all I can think about is that that could get me to Greece. Everything at my old apartment was passcodes and biometrics, no key required. My passports are in the fire safe under my bed; *Yiayia's* wedding set is in that safe. I have to get those things.

My next thought makes me pause, the pearls and rubble at my feet rippling into a vision of a possible future.

I'm on the ferry to Paxos, the island in front of me, a fresh start away from all of this. My soulmate grabs my hand, she looks relaxed. There isn't any fear when she looks into my eyes. These pearls would be enough to at least get us there, and I know *Yiayia* would let us stay with her for as long as it took.

It's too perfect, but I grasp onto it with all the control I have in my new life.

New plan ascertained, I scoop up all pearls. The steam in the baths has me dripping sweat just from walking around the pool. There are jars, bottles, and vases in every available spot, but none of them are empty. Each is filled with an oil, herbs, or balm that smells heavenly.

"Another time," I tell myself. I am certainly treating myself to a full-day spa experience here once everything is settled.

Finally, a small terracotta figurine is buried in the far corner behind a chipped vase. The paint on it is nearly rubbed away, but it's solid. When I gently lift the top half off, there is no balm or dried herbs. Not even dust at the bottom. I gently drop the pearls into the base and say a quick thank you to Love for all they have provided me.

There is no telling the purpose of this pot. Too many Saturdays spent in Greek school as a kid have taught me that these figurines could be for anything. It's never a good idea to risk the wrath of a god, and since I pledged my soul to one, it makes sense to offer them thanks.

I set the figurine back as I found it and head towards the slatted wood doors on the opposite side. Steam wafts from the heated pool and clings to me and my makeshift dress. The doors are a set of pocket doors, each slat a twisting of dark and light wood. They are damp from the air and release a sweet, green smell.

Confidence. You are meant to walk out these doors, I tell myself. My chest rises, and on my next breath out, I let the weight of everything go. It's just like any other event. I plaster on an at-ease expression with a soft smile. I am meant to be walking out of the baths and asking for a fresh set of clothes. I don't know anything about the exploded wall behind me.

The doors glide open like magic, and I wander into this massive hotel lobby. That's the only way I can describe this room. Artistically high ceilings, marble walls, more immaculate floor mosaics– it reminds me of the first resort we opened in Greece. Everything feels oddly like home. There is an arch that leads to an impressive dining area, a hall with doors that must lead to private rooms, and more open space beyond that I can't even see.

The only thing missing are windows. Not a touch of natural light in this place. Everything is lit with warm, low lamps that hang from chains attached to the ceiling.

It's ethereal but causes goosebumps to scatter across my arms. As I rub them away, I spot a hulking woman with braids and green skin.

"Hey, newbie," she waves jovially and starts walking over to me. "How ya feelin'? I saw 'em carry you inside during my shift."

"Tired and a little hungry," I admit once she is standing in front of me. Monsters are real, I remind myself, act natural.

"Yeah," she sighs, twisting a small bead in one of her braids. "First day's always... weird. Nargol, by the way."

She thrusts her hand out to me, and I shake it gently. Her palm is massive, encompassing my own easily, but her touch is light. The rough calluses on her hand scrape against mine when she takes her hand back.

"Del," I say.

"Captain just left for the day and didn't give ya no clothes, huh?"

It's my turn to play with my hair. I smooth a section of curls behind my ear and give her a sheepish look. Playing dumb is the best option right now. I don't know what happened after I was tossed in that room. No need to inform this nice monster lady that I haven't been given clothes because I am a prisoner.

"Yeah, when I woke up, I looked for something and got a bit turned around."

"Don't take it personally," she assures me as she turns to start walking away from the baths. "Captain's been... busy lately and not really around if she isn't working."

There is an apparent tone in her explanation that says I should not ask a single question about what the captain has been up to. For whatever reason, I'm not privy to that information.

Yet.

Once I prove to her that we are meant to be and that it's best that she accepts me, there won't be any secrets between us. Any worry, fear, or concern that she has, I want to be able to help her. Whatever is going on with her, I will always support her.

We walk down the long hallway, and I have to force myself not to stare at the mosaic. It is a work of art, one that feels like we shouldn't be stepping on it at all. The geometric pattern from the foyer has twisted into tentacles that remind me of Love. Deep blue tendrils are lined with pink quartz tiles that appear to be glowing as they do. Nargol stops in front of the door and checks me out, openly. It's a bit of a surprise, but I refuse to shy away from the heat of her gaze. Love said my favours were mine, even showing me a heated vision with multiple women, and I have always liked sharing.

She smiles brightly. Broken tusks that frame her lips peek out as she flashes her teeth. Her soft chuckle follows her as she steps into the room. I follow behind her and nearly stumble. The gasp that comes out of me is awe filled.

"You more masc or a femme?"

"Femme," I mumble, "Pink is my favourite colour."

This is the biggest closet I have ever seen. This is like a dream come true. Closet isn't even the right word. This room has the same high ceilings as the foyers, and it is covered in racks on racks of clothes. There are styles of dresses and jackets and trousers I have never seen before. It's like every London Fashion Week of all time uses this room for storage.

I'm snapped out of my daydream when clothes start falling from the sky. My blanket dress slips, and heat floods my cheeks.

"Incoming," Nargol giggles in such a devious way that tells me she is going to be great fun.

There is something to be said about the whiplash of emotions I am going through. It's definitely a trauma response of some kind, it has to be. Up until I was reborn, my sex drive was solely dedicated to my vibrator. I kept all my flirting and sex eyes to myself to keep my end of the contract in pristine condition.

And after my first meeting with Miles, any possible sexual interest I had in him died. The dick.

But now? Wild and free Delphini is ready to go. Another thing to clarify with the captain once I get a chance to speak with her. Does she want to keep our relationship closed or open? I'm getting ahead of myself, missing the biggest steps of the plan to make my soulmate love me.

The clatter of boots in front of me has me nearly jumping out of my skin as Nargol holds up two leather belts for me.

"Sorry," she finally says, handing me the one with a silver buckle. "You're really handlin' this different than the last girl. Lakelynn didn't speak to anyone for a whole month. Not that she really says much now."

I have no frame of reference for who that is, so I focus on the clothes in my arms instead. Billowy white linen shirt with a pink ribbon detail, lacy sleeves, and decent-looking woollen trousers. No bra or panties, though. I look at Nargol and she looks back.

"This feels like something I shouldn't have to ask for."

"I can give you a stay and bloomers for now, but someone will have to order your delicates online later."

I don't know what a stay is, but I am nodding along all the same. The clothes she's handed me aren't for lounging around, and I doubt the captain is the type to relax. The girls and I are going to need at least a little support.

A stringy, pink panelled thing is tossed at me a few minutes later and I don't have long to feel ridiculous about the first thing before thin white fabric slaps me in the face.

"Chemise, bloomers, then stay. The boning in that is minimal, so it should be fine for whatever job the captain assigns you. I imagine you'll get put on the day shift in front of everyone. Too pretty for the night shift."

My cheeks heat again, but Nargol is gone before I can ask her what she means by that or how the fuck I put on a stay. The door slams behind her and I clench my teeth. This is fine. I pull on the clothes, tucking the chemise into the trousers to add extra coverage between me and the array of buttons that close the front flap. The legs are baggier than I like and I have to roll the cuffs up, but they fit my booty well.

Once I have untangled the strings of the stay, it's a bit more obvious how to wear one. It's a soft, blush pink colour with delicate embroidered flowers in dark shades of pink. The entire garment looks hand-stitched and like it came right out of a Jane Austen period film.

It's a whole experience organising my tits in a way that feels comfortable and secure. I tie it up the best I can, making a short bow in front of me so I don't have to stretch to untie it later. Then I adjust the straps on my shoulder, which are longer than necessary and also have ties.

I pull the shirt on, cinching the ribbons at my wrists but opting to leave the top ribbon open to show off the detailed work of the stay. I don't care if it's the right way to wear this thing. My chest is heaving and pink is my confidence colour. It's my armour and I will need that to face the soulmate who rejected me again.

Getting the rest of the clothes on is easy. I refuse to acknowledge how weird it feels to wear old underwear when I step out of the room. Back in the foyer, Nargol is now talking with someone else, and they do not look happy to see me. The woman seems ready to pull the fucking sword strapped to her side on me.

I blanch and scan the room again. There is a door not too far from me.

"Del..." she calls out.

No time to deliberate. I bolt for the door and grab an actual scabbard from the wall hook as I fling the heavy wooden door open. The heaviness of it throws me off, but I can't think too hard about it in the dark. Two steps into the narrow hallway, and I feel it.

The boat rocks on the water, and my knees wobble. How the fuck did I not feel that earlier? How the fuck is there a hotel on this boat?

I stumble towards a set of stairs and grip the railing for dear life as I climb towards the light. Now would be a really great time for Love to reassure me that this is some magic monster shit.

On deck, there is a whole crew of people dressed as pirates working an old-timey sailing ship across the bay. There are rows of benches jam-packed with regularly dressed people as well. What fresh hell is this? My stomach rolls as the boat sways softly.

A woman hanging onto a rope flies above my head and lands in front of the benches like a superhero. She whips off a fancy feathered tricorne to reveal a shaved head.

Fuck. Me.

The captain bows in front of the cheering crowd, and as she begins to speak, her scowling face doesn't once break into a smile as she talks about the history of *The Princess's Despair.* I don't catch a word of it. My eyes are trained on the corset she's wearing under the heavy, adorned jacket swallowing her form. The teal colour is gorgeous on her sun-tanned skin, but the leather has my full attention. It is adorned with knives and perfectly outlines the shape of her breast.

She paces in front of the audience and then suddenly draws a sword from her hip. The crowd erupts into applause as a heavy drumbeat begins a slow cadence somewhere behind me. I can't take my eyes off her to see what's happening. Low and rhythmic singing floats through the air, and my dizziness moves from my stomach to my head. I step towards the audience on wobbly knees and wrap an arm around a mast. Words ripple through my head, and my neck feels heavy. The scabbard still clutched in my fist slips and I pull it into my chest.

I push the hilt up with my thumb and immediately regret it. My finger is sliced open by that very real weapon.

But as my blood blooms, it isn't exactly the right colour. It's not a red red, it's lighter. The deep colour reminds me of the flesh of a dragon fruit. Goosebumps erupt across my skin and the hair at the base of my neck rises. When I look up, there are three pirate women singing directly at me.

The words of the music pierce my thoughts, and sharp pain vibrates over my chest. I drop the scabbard and clutch my bloody hand over the exposed etching. My nostrils flare as I breathe through the pain. I don't take my eyes off the singers.

I won't be intimidated by whatever sort of monster they are. As foolish as that might be.

"Sirens." Love's whispered voice eases the pain, but as I am about to speak with them, they are gone again, slithering away somewhere else.

The monster women in front of me seem to get I'm off the menu. A sigh leaves my lips and I watch as they sing around the hypnotised crowd. They inch closer to the benches, and as the few men in the crowd grab for them, I see it.

Almost invisible, magic flows from their lips as they sing in wispy, pearlescent bars. As the men eat it up, the sirens move between them without being touched.

The women and children look sleepy in comparison. I can't make out what they are doing, and too soon, the drum fades, and the music stops. The captain steps back in front of the crowd, and the crew sets to work doing whatever it is they do on a pirate ship. Ropes go swinging and I shuffle over to the far railing. We are nearly back to the docks, and rows of small commercial fishing boats come into view, along with colossal sea freights that will make port on the South Shore.

I lean over the railing when my stomach rolls again. Not doing it, I am not going to be sick in public. The ship slowly pulls towards the opening of the Paspawa River, and a historic wharf comes into view. Bunting floats around some of the mooring points and I see a few old, motorised boats floating just out of sight under the dock.

Everyone ignores me, which is weird and great. I'm used to being around people who would recognise me. They are people who know who I am, what I am. These families probably don't have a clue that I used to be almost famous.

I also don't know what to do with my hands. At times like this, I usually think about content, write out caption ideas, and review my calendar. My phone was essentially my whole life and now I don't have it. It feels wrong, like my body is unsettled because I don't know what is happening. There is no feed.

That is a good thing, I think. Closing my eyes, I take a deep breath of the surprisingly refreshing sea air. The only thing on socials at the moment is most definitely those pictures. I wrap my arms around myself to cover the shudder that racks through me.

It's fine. Doesn't matter any more.

I'm out of the contract; I'm out of that god-awful fake relationship.

I'm free to act however I want and have a soulmate now.

And I'm going to kill Miles.

My limbs tingle a bit as I think about how I am going to do it. He will fear me, even before he knows I am not dead. Rage swells in my chest at the months I spent in screaming matches about stupid shit. When he suddenly had all the money he could want again at the tip of his finger, it quickly meant nothing to him if it meant he couldn't continue his old life.

A smile spread across my face. I bet he is having the best damn time right now.

And I am going to rip the rug right out from underneath him.

3 Days

How the fuck did she get out? I blink against the sun as it pierces through the sails, highlighting Delphini like she is an offering. She glows under its warmth as she moves from the mast to the railing.

Love is in my head. I sense them, but they refuse to answer me. That explains where they went during the morning. They were with her. Is this how it is to be now? I must share them?

For centuries, monsters of all kinds have come and gone from my crew, but I have always had Love with me. In my thoughts and in reality. When my rage wasn't enough to keep me buoyant, their tentacles held me aloft. They kept me from sinking into a darkness I couldn't return from. They guide me on our mission to return Love to their true power. They are mine. Never has there been a split of their presence in me after a crew member joins up.

Is this because she is mine or because she is human?

I move through the motions of finishing the show. My sword is drawn and I mimic my "famous last battle" on the high seas where I went down with my ship. Lagulla, the gorgon who is dressed up in the heavy British uniform, dances around me to make the crowd giggle. Nonetheless, quickly enough, it all comes to an end when she rests her sword on my shoulder near my neckerchief and the mooring ropes are tossed down onto the dock.

She makes a grand final announcement and the crowd of tourists cheer. It is hard to keep the grimace off my face as they rise to form a queue for a photo opportunity with us. A chill racks my body as the first grubby child places their sticky hand in mine.

This story is a necessary fabrication. Piracy was at an end, and we needed fresher hunting grounds. Too many ships that came into these waters were immigrant ships filled with humans and monsters alike seeking refuge in Gwenmore and further afield. They wanted a new life, a second chance, and that was something we couldn't take away from them.

The best way to create a myth is to die. So, in one final battle with the British, I faked my death. Now, children take photos with me while they hold tiny cardboard swords of their own, their parents commenting on the craftsmanship of this recreation.

They don't know it is my real ship.

Only select monsters in the city know the true story of what happened that day. It's common knowledge that I survived. I am here, after all, day in and day out, performing during the tourist season. What they don't know is why I left the young human boy alive that day to spread the story of my demise. Even now, the memory of his face, those blue eyes, they haunt me. He was the second human I let live after seeing me summon Love.

I have been at peace with my fake life for a long time, content with the rules established by the monstrous founders of the city. They are easy enough to follow. Don't expose the monsters hidden in the shadows and don't form serious relationships with them. Now, it is unravelling before my eyes with the simple presence of a human woman. One that has been gifted to me by the ancient god I have dedicated my life to serving. She leans against the rail and watches the tourists vacate the ship.

Someone has given her clothes.

My eyes travel across what would have been unflattering on most. They are unflattering. They are clothes meant for work, yet she wears them like they were made for her. The wide legs of her trousers cinch around her hips and waist in a way that is hard to look away from. Her curves trace the form of her body like tall waves, rising and falling in tantalising places that have me wondering what they will feel like crashing against my body.

I purse my lips. Another reason she can't be here. She is too beautiful.

Delphini turns around, and all thoughts leave my head. Her shirt is wide open, the thing being worn entirely wrong. Pale pink ribbon frames her heavy cleavage and the matching stay highlights the warm undertones of her brown skin. I can imagine the heat of her under my hands. The warmth of her lips on mine, her touch searing away any shiver or chill that tries to ruin our joining. Her hot-

No. I close my eyes to hide her from my sight. She is going back into that prison until I can present her to the group. Until I can keep her somewhere far away but safe.

"She has chosen us."

And where is my choice in the matter? I have spent centuries searching and even more learning to live without my soulmate. Surely, I am deserving of having my choice now just as much as she did. Love has always been mysterious but fair. None of this makes sense. She is a devastating and ruinous human that can only end in our downfall.

I want nothing to do with her. Her external beauty will mean nothing. She is a human, a being created through ugly violence. Love does not make mistakes;

they are all that is and will be. They are greater than any god, but this must only be a test of my will. Renewal of my devotion to our mission to raise them from the depths that keep them imprisoned.

I look at her again. Delphini smiles at me, and I want to hate her for it. She isn't smug or coy. She seems genuinely pleased to see me despite how our first meeting went. Aoife steps down from the upper deck to take care of her. That is fine, it's how this all should be. I can't want anything to do with her, yet when my quartermaster turns the human by the shoulders to take her below deck once more, my eyes follow the sway of her hips.

There is too much time to dwell on my soulmate. There are more tours of the ship and re-enactments while we sail to and fro across the bay, but I know these routines. Like the etchings that mark my body as Love's, I know every word and step of this dance we concocted decades ago to keep the monstrous appetites at bay. The money these tours make is divided amongst the crew, and the rest is placed aside for when someone leaves. A parting gift to thank them for their service and to help them prosper, to prove that Love is capable of so much more than any other god.

Between each slash of my sword at Lagulla, visions of the past come to mind. Every failed touch at someone new, the chill that would rack my body as they sobbed and screamed. It was inevitable that I grew to hate the touch of others. Any craving I had for comfort, for something more in this life, was chased away with every being we guided to their revenge.

Now, there is someone whose touch doesn't feel like ice in my veins. Yet I refuse it. Her palm against mine felt like salvation, but I know mine are covered in the blood of so many. She would be horrified to learn what her soulmate had done.

Thinking of Delphini now, my mind is in chaos, shattering the careful world I have constructed to be a haven for my crew and for Love while we fight for their cause. It is a fact that a single human can ruin everything.

It is why we don't allow humans to know of our existence. It has been a rule since the founding of the city. The moment one learns of our existence, we extinguish them. For most, that simply means feeding. Even that tremendous pompous sandbag knows that our rules are written in stone. A human who knows that monsters exist is a dead human.

Come Tuesday evening, Delphini will be a dead human again.

My steps falter as I even think of her dying. Sweat drips from my brow and my breath catches. The vision of her lying in front of my fire, broken and refusing to wake up, clouds my eyes with tears. How could such a memory bring me to this reaction? Something in my chest aches for no good reason while Love hisses once again that she has chosen us. That I am to accept her as the gift that she is.

Delphini is our soulmate.

However, Lagulla doesn't miss her step in the show, and instead of slicing through the air, her sword comes down on my shoulder. It cuts through layers of fabric until it meets my skin. The sharpened steel embeds itself in my flesh, but that isn't what concerns me.

As the crowd shrieks and the crew rushes in to control the ensuing panic, the sleeve of my jacket falls to my feet. The length of my arm, etched with tentacles that mark me as Love's, is exposed to the sun. Its warmth kisses my skin, but I can't savour this rare moment. Nobody can see how much I have given for the mission or how much humanity I had to sacrifice to be like them.

"Crew," I holler over the tourist, "Another shanty to steer us home."

Neela and the other sirens begin to sing, their magic lulling the crowd into a stupor. Lagulla pulls her sword from me at last and I shove my hand through the ripped sleeves of my clothing to cover my arm. She stares at me, and there is no telling if it is with disgust or wonder. I run below deck and into our home.

Delphini is still not back in the cell.

I should be more concerned about the blood I am dripping onto the tiles, but my eyes are latched onto her. She is carrying buckets of rubble from the bath to the wheelie bin we use to haul trash onto the dock. Her sleeves are rolled up revealing more soft skin, but her chest is thrust forward. Between her ample cleavage, I can see the etching of Love's mark now. Directly over her heart twists a gathering of tentacles.

What happened for her mark to be placed there?

"Holy shit, what happened to your arm?" She breaks the spell she has cast over my thoughts by screaming.

I sneer at her out of defence and sidestep her. I won't be lulled into any concern of hers or her warmth. Aoife appears a moment later, and I can see the same question ready to form on her lips.

"What is the prisoner doing?" I demand.

"Cleaning up her mess while the cell is useless." Aoife nods her head towards the sliding doors of the bath and I stare at the massive hole in the wall.

My wall.

She blew a hole through my wall.

Pink fills my vision as my tentacles pulse beneath my skin, slipping from my exposed arm until they have covered my wound. I spin on my heels intending to grab hold of that human and shake her for this damage. How dare she destroy a portion of my home?

I never get the chance.

Love materialises from their void, a long teal-coloured tentacle piercing the pink haze clouding my judgement and wrapping itself around me. They pull me deeper into the bath until I am standing at the epicentre of the mess. All around me, chunks of marble and dust will take days to clear and rebuild. It only makes my anger grow, makes the etching on my arms glow with power until there is nothing but blinding light.

"*Our heart, breathe,*" they rumble.

"How dare she?" I seethe. "She has ruined it."

"*Look again. What do you see amongst this marble? How do you think a human was able to do such an act?*"

My chest heaves with each breath I draw, but I do as they ask. I look at the cracked tiled floor of my bath, and amongst the rubble, I see them. Lost between hunks of marble is a spatter of broken pearls. The small gemstones are useless in this state, but I know where Delphini was able to harness the strength to break down the wall.

Love gave her the power.

"Why would you do this?" I ask, my body falling into the tentacle. Any fight I had washes away as I stare at the broken mess at my feet. Betrayal coats my heart, my soul, like fresh snow. Everything is cold and dead.

"*She is the one,*" they state with glorious finality that brings tears to my eyes. "*To protect herself and to declare her as one of us. She has a determined soul.*"

The tone of Love's voice softens, and it sickens me. It is as if they are swimming away from me, diving into a pool I can't follow. They gave a part of themselves to her as if that will make it harder for her to be removed from my ship. My body shakes when I swallow the sickening lump that settles at the back of my throat.

As darkness settles inside of me, my body dips from our dimension.

I am in Love's void. Around me, their eyes float in harmony, and their tentacles slide against one another. The scent of pomegranate in the air is intoxicating. My body relaxes further with every breath I take. A thick tentacle holds me aloft before my true god, my Love.

"We have spent centuries waiting for her, heart, but do not think of us like your gods of old," they admonish me, and heat fills my cheeks. *"You were first to call us Love, and it is a name that we present forth with honour and pride. For to have the greatest of all emotions bestowed upon us is no simple prayer or offering. It is a gift we cherish."*

"Don't leave me." It's all the words I can muster up as I stare into the depths of their dark eyes. My heart beats erratically out of control as I try to maintain some kind of useless facade in front of the one being I have ever loved.

"Your anger awoke us, our heart, but your love for us sustains us. Do not doubt what your devotion means to us."

Tears slip down my cheeks as shame washes over me. How could I? They are my Love, and I am their heart. We are inseparable. Their tentacles encase my body, holding me while sobs wrack through me. They purr in the low light of their void until my mind rests. A small tentacle swipes across my cheeks and under my nose with tender care.

"With you, we shall rise again from the darkness and bring forth the new age together."

As soon as I appear, I blink and the void is gone. The mess of the bath is still at my feet, and Love is still wrapped around me. I sweep my hand over the length of them, collecting the slick that coats their tentacles to rub into my gasping shoulder wound. They are with me, they are mine. The slime warms my skin and I watch how it stitches my flesh back together. The etching on my skin connects once again as though they were never sliced apart.

Finally, I do as I am told and take a deep breath, cycling through them until my world is at my feet once again. The pink clears from my vision and my tentacles slip beneath my skin. There is nothing I cannot handle or fight off.

As Love slips back into their void, the tip of their tentacle catches my cheek as if to kiss it. They are still mine. No one else in the crew has the connection we share. It has been uniquely mine for millennia, until she arrived.

I grab hold of the fallen sleeves, gripping onto it and the blood-stained shoulder of my jacket, before marching out of the bath. The rest of the crew gathers in the main hall by this point. They stand apart from Delphini as she removes the last of her acrylic nails and drops them in the trash.

"Crew, the bath is closed for the weekend." My announcement is met with a chorus of groans. "If any of you lot are artistic enough, it appears we are in need of a new mural. Hamako will handle all the ideas."

Several faces light up at that, but I know what they are more concerned about.

"As for the prisoner, she will remain with us for a while longer." I turn my gaze to her for a moment, and that mistake has certainly given away that my emotions towards this *chosen one* are not as clear cut as they should be. "Aoife, assign her tasks to keep her busy and set her up in a room."

"Captain?" Nargol pointedly looks at where I am holding onto my shoulder. "You need somebody to look at that?"

"No, and I don't want to be interrupted for the rest of the night. Drink a glass to my health at dinner, why don't ya?"

The crew hollers at that as I leave the hall to head towards my quarter. I pass Delphini, and there is a pull to her I can't resist. There is no reason for me to address her directly. I have made my remarks to the crew, and I should spend the rest of my evening doing something fucking worthwhile with my time.

But I can't stop myself from speaking to her.

"You *will* regret your choice."

Chapter Nine
Delphini

While most of the ship's crew are good pirates listening to their captain, a handful have decided I am not a complete loss. At dinner the first night, I stood in line as Aoife directed me to and waited to be handed our evening meal. When the giant woman with tusks and blue-grey skin refused to serve me, acting as if I didn't exist in the line for food, it took a half-bird girl's intervention to get me a plate.

"Give her a plate," she demands.

"Captain's orders-" the woman grumbles.

Her talon-tipped fingers wrapped around the nearest tusk, and she dragged their faces together. "She got here the same way we all did, Cookie. Feeding her won't get you in trouble."

I take my plate and run before she can change her mind.

Nargol, for as much as I probably got her in trouble, sits next to me. She runs through all the crew members names, even waving the shy Lakelynn over to sit with us. It isn't against the rules to sit with me. Just talk to me. When we are officially introduced, Nargol spends the rest of dinner going on and on about damn near everything under the sun. Scheduling issues she was having with Aoife, her plans for her day off on Sunday, the next time the chef, Cookie, is planning on making her famous carrot cake.

The info dump should be overwhelming, and to most I guess it is. But every word that comes out of her mouth takes me one step closer to getting to know the captain, to getting in with the new place I am calling home. Even if Aoife interrupts Nargol's story about Neela, another siren on board, glitter bombing the training room by accident, to tell me I have to go wash all the dishes from supper.

Friday and Saturday are a blur of work. Nobody recognises me, or if they do they keep it to themselves. I'm Del, and everyone who speaks to me wants to know why the captain locked me up. There must have been a reason, but I can't tell them. If they don't know I am human, maybe it is safer that way for now.

My focus is on the captain anytime she walks by, though, and maybe that is telling enough for the crew. I do my best to look presentable, perhaps even cute despite having my hair all shoved into a sleek bun to keep it from touching something gross. I make sure to smile and greet her with every ounce of positivity my body possesses in its exhausted state. For the most part, she just grunts, and I know I am getting to her.

Last night, when I complimented her scarf, she turned bright red.

It's evident to me that she respects the work of her crew greatly, that she is a fair leader to them, and enjoys providing for them. The captain likes to keep everyone on board as happy as possible, given the circumstances of how we all became a member of this crew. She shows it in the way she speaks to them and interacts with them all.

Even if she is a massive grump about literally everything else. All the pieces of her puzzle are coming together in my mind.

Between scrubbing a million dishes and hauling laundry, it hasn't been too hard to pick up on the ins and outs of the ship. If I'm not watching the captain, studying every movement she makes, I listen to the crew speak to each other. There's normal gossip about seeing a tourist pick their nose or someone flirting with a human and then there are the occasional bits of salacious victory stories.

One of the girls on the crew is dating a succubus, so they are all keeping an orgasm raffle going. Seeing how I have nothing of monetary value, excluding the magic pearls I stashed away, I didn't make a bet on Friday night when Joanie strutted out of the main hall to the docks.

"Takin' a walk around the dock is code," Nargol whispers to me. But I recognised the look on Joanie's face as she was leaving, and it was one that screams how ready she is to get laid. Fuck, I probably wear the same expression every time I look at the captain.

Outside of that and one story from Aoife, of all people, I get the impression they don't leave the ship unless they have to. Everyone's whole life is here. Why do they need the outside world?

But that is another mark in my favour. It allows me to be anonymous and test out this new Delphini who openly bares her attraction to a woman who doesn't want her back. Nobody judges me for it either because I'm not the first woman to try and gain her favour.

"Here is the name of that book I mentioned at breakfast," I say, handing her a paper towel I scribbled on.

"Thanks, babes." She smiles, her blunt tusks touching her upper lip. "You doing okay?"

"Eh," I shrug. "I wish the captain would speak to me."

"Captain's always kept to herself," Nargol sighs as she tugs on her boots. I lean against her door frame while she gets ready to work a night security shift on the deck. It's something I've noticed that only the crew who can't pass in the daylight do. "She doesn't like to be touched and from what I've heard, hasn't taken anyone, like ever, to bed. And trust me, many have tried."

"Maybe she doesn't like sex?" I offer. If my soulmate doesn't like sex, that's fine, but I'd wish she'd fucking talk to me about this.

"She likes to watch." The orc woman stands, stretching her muscular frame. "She's in that bath just as much as the rest of us."

"Maybe she's waiting for someone."

Nargol squints at me. "You know more."

"I know that I want the Captain." I flick an exposed string on the pink stay I am still wearing. "And I am used to getting what I want."

The following day, when I arrive at breakfast, I have a moment that catches everyone's attention. While Cookie, the chef, and her girlfriend, Hamako the Harpy, sleep in, breakfast is served a la carte style. Which, in theory, is amazing because it means actually picking what I want to eat instead of accepting a plate of hot somethings. My plate's loaded up with fruits, granola, and Greek yoghurt that is the perfect kind of thick.

But after two days without my regular coconut matcha latte, I'm more on edge than I have ever been in my life. Exhaustion is taking its toll on me. I've been downing the coffee on board, but it's having the opposite effect on my body. Rather than helping keep my energy up, the extra caffeine makes me twitchy, and I'm no less tired.

My hands shake as I reach for the pot of fresh coffee and everything is going fine until it's going horribly wrong.

"Fuck!" I shout, coffee splashing across my hand and down my front.

The skin on my already sore fingers feels like it's going to bubble up and burst in the most grotesque way possible. Tears sting my eyes, but I grit my teeth to keep them in. Do not show weakness in front of everyone. If I start crying now, I am not sure I could stop. Every scary feeling I have been ignoring as wild and free Delphini rushes in as I stare at my hand. I breathe heavily through my nose and I hear my father's voice in my head demanding more from me, telling me I'm not doing enough for the family. *Prove to them you are stronger than some weak sorority-level hazing.*

My food is safe, so I take my plate and return to my room to eat. I can't sit in front of everyone when I feel myself fraying around the edges. I just need a moment alone to collect my thoughts. Nobody laughs, and nobody says anything because I'm invisible per the captain's orders. Every step towards my room increases the trembling in my bottom lip and my burning hand. I'm so close to the privacy of my room, where I can cry to my breakfast before Aoife puts me to work again.

"Delphini." The harsh crack of my name has me stopping in my tracks. The captain is walking down the hall from her quarters. "Where you going with that?"

There is no facade I can keep up in this state. There aren't nice greetings spilling from my mouth when I speak to her.

"To eat," I hiss. "Or does feeding the prisoner go against your orders too?"

"No, what would starving you do? Then you couldn't work." The captain's remark is blunt and straightforward. "Are you crying?"

That question stings worse than the burn on my hand. Something about the way she asks it makes the tears dangerously close to spilling dry up. My plate of food threatens to overturn from my shaking fingers and I know that I'm not going to be able to open my door without serious pain, but I am not weak. She should never be able to ask me that question.

"I'm fine."

She crosses her arms over her chest and I realise she isn't dressed so heavily as she has been. There is no overcoat, knife belt, or boots on her feet. In fact the captain is wearing a pair of busted overalls and skin tight athletic top. I can see the narrow muscles in her arms bulge as she waits for me to do something more.

"You are a prisoner on my ship, I am the captain."

"And?" I ask. She's captain of a tourist ship, that's not exactly a real rank.

"And-" Her voice cuts, and for a moment a freaky milky white coats her eyes, before she blinks it away to look down at my hand. "What happened?"

"Nothing to concern yourself with, *Captain*. I am fully capable of taking care of it."

"For Love's sake," she grumbles, before taking my plate and walking back to her room.

"That's mine!" I shout.

"Then come get it!" She returns, as loud and more annoyed.

The captain leaves the door to her room open and I stand there deliberating whether breakfast is actually worth it. My shirt is still wet and Aoife will come looking for me sooner rather than later.

"Go, sweet one, seize your moment."

A shiver runs down my spine as Love's whisper heats my skin.

I've already died, technically, so whatever argument I was about to have with myself is null and void. Plus, ignoring the captain goes completely against my personal mission of getting her to admit she is my soulmate. I shove all the nurtured instincts I have down and march through the door of the room like it's my own.

The captain's room is all wood. There isn't much of it I remember except the ornate fireplace. It's the only thing in this room that isn't brown. The marble is white with swirls of grey, and is carved to form more tentacle shapes.

Now, I take in the four poster bed with tidy, dark blue bedding, a large privacy screen that doesn't have any sort of design on it, and a wide desk with an old computer that is covered in papers and has my plate sitting on it. Behind the desk there is a huge glass frame with newspaper clippings of all shapes inside.

This room is utterly masculine and impersonal. It might as well be a hotel.

"Sit."

The captain calls from behind the screen, and I follow orders, taking the closest seat possible. Her bed. It's deceptively soft. I sink into the foam and have to force myself to remain upright. The bed I have been sleeping on works, but it definitely is not the quality I am accustomed to. The captain turns the corner around the screen and stops. She stares at me, eyes travelling from my head to boots.

I want her to like what she sees. She has seen me at my literal worst, and what I now consider to be my worst—stained clothes and exhausted body. If she can't stop looking at me like this, it means when I eventually get to look like my usual self, her jaw will hit the floor. I want her eyes on me at all times. I don't want her to look away. The captain has my full attention any chance I can be near, I just want the same.

Something rattles, and I have to tear my eyes away from her. In her hands is an old looking jar and a new bottle of ibuprofen. Her stare has hardened in a blink, her brows deepening and the scowl on her face returning as strong as ever. Anger isn't a look I enjoy on most people, but when I see it on the captain's face, even directed at me, I find that I enjoy it quite a bit.

"Did someone spill their drink on you?" She asks, walking over to me.

For a moment, she stands there. The bed is low to the ground, so I am looking up at the captain for the first time since I woke up in the room. There is no firelight to halo her form, but there is an unmistakable softness about her up close. If my hands were at all steady, I would reach out and smooth the furore from her brow, trace my thumb across her lip. The storm around the captain breaks when we are this close and I wonder if it is some sort of magic soulmate thing that I can utilise to my benefit.

"No, too much caffeine from coffee and not enough sleep are fucking with me," I finally answer. "What is that?"

The jar she opens reeks like old gym socks and bad sushi. Whatever that mess is, I don't want it anywhere near me. She uses three fingers to dig out a scoop of the nasty Vaseline-like mess, and my empty stomach rolls. My breakfast is ruined no matter what happens now.

"It'll fix the burn on your hand and anywhere else you've got one." She pointedly only looks at my face as she explains this, but I am too disgusted by the balm in her hand to care about the fact that she might be insinuating touching my chest.

"That isn't going anywhere near me. My body is a temple." I can't smell like that for the rest of the day. A girl can only take so much.

The captain scoffs some irritated sound of dismissal and then her hand is slapped over mine before I can stop her. There is a flare of pain, the sensitive skin reacting more to the action than the balm. The burning heat recedes too fast to be normal medicine. When she realises I'm not going to resist, she carefully takes my hand in both of hers and works the foul mess into my hand. Her body relaxes into the role like she is more comfortable healing than hurting. The tingling, bubbling tightness of my skin evaporates and all I am left feeling is relaxed, like I am getting a luxury hand massage before a manicure.

A telling sigh leaves my lips as I watch her hands flex around mine.

"All temples require priestesses to care for them," she murmurs. "Do not think I would let anyone here suffer pain when I can easily fix it."

"You could have fooled me," I smirk a little. A comforting warmth is pulsing through me now, threatening to lull me to sleep and bring about wet dreams. It's a dangerous kind of feeling to have when it's just me and my hand.

"Orthia."

"What?" I sit up a bit straighter and look at the captain.

"I am called Orthia, after…"

"The goddess," we both say at the same time.

"Orthia," I whisper her name again as if the addictive heat of her touch has turned my brain soft.

"How do you know that?" she asks.

Her hands are still working mine, turning tendons into noodles and the muscles into jelly. My wrist has gone limp. The only thing keeping it off the bed and ruining her duvet is her.

"My *yiayia*." It's all I can think of to explain that without dumping an ocean's worth of sadness between us. She doesn't know what happened, and the thought of her only knowing what the paper will have reported has a pit forming in my chest. Is she trying to call me back? Has she seen the news?

Orthia nods but doesn't say anything more. I clear my throat, unable to take a big enough breath and she drops my hand. The balm is all dried up. The warmth from her touch is gone. The captain is back in place.

"Get your breakfast and get changed before Aoife puts you to work," she says, leaving before I can even thank her.

I can't breathe without the scent of industrial strength cleaner clearing my sinuses.

The blisters on my right hand ache with every brush of this mop across the cleared floors of the bath, while my left hand still smells bad. I bust through a marble fucking wall with my fists, and there isn't a scratch on me. But a bit of manual labour? Absolute breakdown of my epidermis.

Said wall has now been reformed with some stone stuff that I don't understand and is drying before Hamako can work on the new mosaic feature.

"Not as bad as a rush week," I mutter, dipping the mop in the bucket once again. "Not as bad as Chelsea putting toothpaste in everyone's yoghurt."

With each swipe across the floor, I am getting more aggravated. I didn't know manual labour could even make a person this angry. I thought cleaning was one of those things people do to relax?

The closer to the sliding doors I get with my mop the louder the real action outside becomes. That's what I really want to be a part of today. The grunting and cheering keep me moving faster because I know when I am done, Aoife won't have anything else for me to do until the washing machine is done in forty-five minutes.

With three more swipes, there is a loud cheer. With two more swipes, someone groans so loud even I wince. One more swipe, the screech of metal on metal sets my teeth on edge, and I'm hustling through the bathroom doors and towards the training room.

The facilities are top quality. I don't know who designed them, but they are genuinely impressive. My mom would turn up her nose at the idea of having to share a bath and the lack of Pilates classes, but standing with the twenty or so other women on the crew in this training room watching Orthia and Lagulla train is like watching professional athletes.

The training room is enormous, the equipment a mix of fitness machines and medieval weapons. There are no mirrors either, which is weird and comforting. It also means that I only get one angle of the captain as she deflects a balestra, a complex move in fencing, from Lagulla. The gorgon woman is fast, her footwork is crisp, but her lunge is hesitant. They move to circle one another and I squeeze between people to get nearer the front. Nargol sees me, a large grin spreading across her cheeks as she cocks an eyebrow towards the fight.

"Is that all you've got, Captain?" She calls out.

Orthia takes her gaze off her opponent first to look at Nargol, but then those eyes land on me. There is no telling if the flush on her face is from exertion or from the wink I can't resist teasing her with. The fingers on my left hand flex as she deflects another attack from Lagulla. Her eyes move back to her opponents before she answers the taunt.

"Nargol, if you want to come and fight me, you know where the swords are, and just like last time, you'll end up flat on your ass."

"Can anyone challenge you?" I ask.

"Crew, did you hear something?" Orthia shouts, still parrying every attack Lagulla tries.

"No, captain," is the resounding answer of the room, and it takes everything in me to hold back from rolling my eyes. We are back to this rank thing again.

Even though she's hellbent on the title, Orthia switches from toying with Lagulla to compounding attack after attack until the sword is out of her hand and her snakes are raised in defeat. There is a resounding cheer for the gorgon as she walks over to a small group of women who toss her a bottle of water.

It's now or never to show her what I've got.

I scan the wall of weapons as I weave through the small crowd. The collection is varied enough; I'm certain a sword will resemble a foil I've used before. A sabre type one catches my eye, but it's definitely longer than I am used to and doesn't have a pistol handle. The guard is a polished brass colour with filigree engravings, the handle is moulded for someone who isn't me and my blistered right hand.

It's going to have to do. Even with a smelly, perfectly healed hand, I'm shit left-handed. As long as I don't mutilate myself or the soulmate I am trying to impress, this should all be fine. It's definitely sharp, though. And there are no masks or lame for extra protection. It's time to prove to Orthia that I am more than meets the eye.

"Captain," I sing, turning around to see everyone has their eyes on me. Orthia stands in the centre, a scowl on her face either at my tone or simply because I am challenging her. "I'd like to have a go."

"This isn't playtime, Del," Saphielle cautions. The tall, elven woman steps towards me like she will take the blade away. Her dark skin is marred with burn scars, but her eyes are a supernatural green colour that lures in anyone who looks at her. Her longer fingers are posed, palm open to take it from me. "Don't do something you will regret."

"Saph, if the prisoner wishes to get her ass beat, let her." Orthia's voice is commanding and sure. She hasn't moved from her spot when I peer around the elf. "Comedy is good for morale."

"Trust me," I say, giving her a sure smile.

I'm not actually sure as I walk into the makeshift ring. The crowd is silent, entirely unlike the cheering for Lagulla. I take a deep breath through my nose in an attempt to settle the nerves fluttering about my stomach. When I feel something slide across the back of my sweat-dampened shirt, I shiver.

"You were chosen for a reason, sweet one," Love whispers, their voice echoing around my skull like murmurs in a stadium.

Exactly. Love chose me, I just need her to see it too. Having a real sword fight to prove to my soulmate we are meant to be seems like a great idea. This is what I need to do to reach this goal. Orthia has to know what I am capable of, which means I won't hold back any part of myself from her.

As I take the stance for sabre, right side forward with my blade at the ready, my limbs begin to lighten. The weapon in my hand is heavier and my body is tired, but instinct takes over. My muscles know what should happen now, even though it has been several months. I hadn't found a good sparring partner since I came to Gwenmore, so I am a little rusty. Orthia looks at me for a moment, that serious scowl still set on her face. So I do what comes naturally: I taunt her.

"Ready for my ass whooping." I wink again for added measure.

There is a breath of space, neither of us moving. I know she is sizing me up because I am doing the same to her. Her sword is shorter, the blade wider, and the handle bulkier than mine. It shines in the overhead lighting. Whatever was wrong with her shoulder on Thursday isn't bothering her now. The softness I thought I saw in her this morning is also gone. There is a storm brewing in her features now. Sweat dots her forehead, but she isn't tired. The captain is ready to fight me.

Her first advance is slow, sword relaxed. She feints, either to scare me or to get me off balance. I hold, waiting until I see any sort of twitch in her that will signal an actual attack. Maybe she thinks I will get tired of staying in this position, and she is partly right. My body is thrumming with anticipation, ready to start pumping adrenaline into me so I can win.

Orthia advances, and the rush begins. Her sword crashes against mine with more strength than I expect. My parry nearly fails. She keeps advancing, and I'm trapped in a defensive state, continuing to retreat until I can feel the heat of the women behind me. I have to make an offensive move, but she isn't giving me even a second to do more than block between each cut she makes.

She slashes again, her sword sweeps through the air and I barely block it. The edge of her blade slices down mine until we are hilt to hilt. Orthia isn't even breathing hard. The storm in her eyes darkens her features, but we are so close together I can see how blown her pupils are, the iris a thin circle.

Thoughts of proving my prowess evaporate. I am lost to her this close. Her even breaths tickle my lips, her nose almost touches mine. I want this to be a moment we can remember for the rest of time. Every part of my tired body is screaming *attack. This is your opening*, but I want to kiss her. I want to shove forward until our chests meet, swords dangerously pressed into our skin, and taste her.

Warmth builds between us the longer we are so close without touching. A pull I can't explain is begging me to close the gap. She must feel it, too. She must. A phantom touch, one that I know is Love, pushes us closer and makes my knees bend enough that she can look down at me.

But then she retreats.

We disconnect, and the heat is gone. I swipe my forehead over my shoulder to clear the sweat if only to calm down the desire threatening to burst through me. I lick my lips, salty sweat coating my tongue instead of a taste of Orthia.

"You're better than I expected," she says.

It's not a compliment, but my body reacts like it is. My insides soften, and whatever nerves flutter in me morph into something hungry. A coiling sensation inside me makes me shiver and keeps my pulse racing while I try to calm my arousal.

"I'm good at a lot of things."

Finally, I take my opening and attack. My feet move quickly, lunging forward for my first attack in the few minutes we've been at this. This is where I thrive, where I am best. I can compound attack after attack like this. My sabre clashes against Orthia's with every action I take. The screech of metal echoes around the training room and the hush over the crowd evaporates.

They cheer and chant. I can't make out much, terrified that if my focus falters from this bout, one of us is going to end up bleeding out. But I know they aren't booing; they aren't upset that I am fighting their captain. We come together again, metal slapping off metal. It's frustrating, but rather than my confidence faltering, it grows. I am somehow holding my own against her and it must because of the extra power Love gave me.

She thought this would be easy, a joke, but I am actually surviving the challenge. The goal isn't to win, it is to show her I am capable. It would be nice though. The impossibility of besting someone who has spent centuries fighting isn't lost on me.

"C'mon, *Captain*," I tease between panting breaths. "My ass feels pretty safe right now."

Orthia lunges and pushes me back into a retreat. She doesn't say anything, but I can feel the difference in her swings. She isn't attacking to kill me, but she's shooting to win. Her thrusts are faster. I'm not even parrying them any more. Running away is the closest experience. The razor-sharp edge of her sword comes down over my handguard at my failed block, and I lose my grip.

It's all over. The vibration of the attack sends shooting pain up my arm and the sabre falls to the ground. Around us, the crew is silent, but it doesn't last. They erupt in cheers and rush us. Nargol and Neela are shaking me with excitement, demanding to know how I did that. Orthia gets lost in the swarm of people and it's only when I find her again, do I see the look on her flushed face.

I'm not the only one who was disarmed during that fight.

Chapter Ten
Orthia

7 Day

It has been five days of herculean battles to keep myself away from Delphini, which has only become hard since the training room incident. Aoife has sequestered her to stay within the bounds of our pocket dimension, but that doesn't keep her out of my thoughts when I am on deck or attempting to hunt. Every bar I enter, every club I sneak into, I see her where she is not. Or where I wish she was. I end up leaving before I can find my prey to make sure she is, in fact, where I left her on *The Princess's Despair.*

Every morning, she is amongst the crew as we prepare for another day of performing. She has been given the worst jobs Aoife can think of; dish washing, laundry, and scrubbing the grout between the tiles. Jobs we usually split between us evenly so we aren't working ourselves to the bone.

This is cruel, and it makes something inside of me curdle. When I see how her curls are restrained into a tight bun and her hands, acrylics bitten off, dried from all the detergents, I want to tell her to stop working. She has done more work than any new recruit would have been asked to do.

However, what I want doesn't matter. This is about keeping her busy and away from me, even if she is the most beautiful being I have ever seen thrust a sword into my face. No matter how much her soft smile makes my stomach flutter with elation or how her steady sureness that we are meant to be reminds me of smooth sailing across the Mediterranean.

In the evenings, it's worse. Once our meals are served, she is alone. The crew has been told they aren't to socialise with her, though some still do.

On the first night, since the bath is closed, most take to spending their evening relaxing alone. I catch Delphini staring at the floor mosaics later that night when I am returning from failed hunts. It's easy to get lost in the unguarded way she focuses, but then I feel Love slip from my mind and my anger returns full force.

When everyone is too wound up on the second night, I suggest our evening rituals happen some place drier. I know a few of the girls have learned to pole dance to reclaim some of their bodily autonomy. The crew is more than willing to set up the stage in the dining area for them and anyone else who wants to perform before the night crew has to leave for their shift.

I try to take my usual place amongst the revelry, a place of control where I can enjoy the evening with my sisters, but the erotic dancing, heavenly moans, and slaps of skin don't offer their usual pleasure. I haven't joined them since, opting to hunt or lock myself away in my quarters instead.

I wonder if Delphini would bathe with the crew.

My whetstone slips off my blade as I think about what usually happens in the baths. How those who are so inclined writhe together in tangles of limbs. My blood thrums with the thought of Delphini in those waters. How would she react to Aoife's stern hand? Would she let the sirens sing her into a state of bliss? My clit throbs at the vision of Love's tentacles binding her while everyone has their turn with her.

It has been days of this, too. My thoughts wander as though I am not in control of them. They create such destructive visions that have my body reacting before I can put a stop to them. She is a hurricane in my existence. Sunday afternoon did not help either. Knowing the strength, balance, and coordination hidden under her softness set my pulse racing.

She has me questioning myself, trying to prove things to her that I would have never done before.

It was like yesterday afternoon when the final tour spot had no bookings. A perfunctory exercise more than a necessity, we still practise the performance we put on for tourists. The clash of steel is music to my ear when I am not hunting. It keeps me in check. Yet, with her eyes on me, it caused the opposite. There was a deep part of me that wanted to show her I could kill with one blow. I found myself performing for her, flexing my muscles as though she could see through my costume. I parried harder, and each attack became more aggressive until Love intervened and held my arm. Their slithering tentacle pulled my gaze to hers, to see the heat in her stare.

She wants me like this. It makes her departure all the more critical. I can't risk her being a distraction to our mission to bring Love here. She can fulfil her promise to our patron off my ship and out of my thoughts.

Nargol flirts with Delphini. She has always been one to skirt my authority, but I don't stop her. The human doesn't mind that the large orc woman thinks she is pretty. Who would not think a woman is pretty? Yet I have seen how she reacts; a curl twirled around her finger or a quick, playful rebuff. Either makes me furious that it isn't me she gives such reactions to. Even my own hypocrisy astounds me.

While she has tried to speak to me more since Sunday, to thank me for healing the burn on her left hand, I have done everything in my power not to say a word to her. It's bad enough that I can no longer look at my bed without seeing her there, seeing a future with her spread out across my dark sheets with tears of pleasure in her eyes. However, the way she whispered my birth name, it will haunt me for the rest of time.

I toss my whetstone onto the desk in front of me. What the fuck is wrong with me? Before me is a record of our work. Obituaries of all those sacrificed to Love since they started recording and announcing the deaths of humans. Some are handwritten and in a language I can't read. Others are only just beginning to yellow.

Little mementos to remind me of our mission.

This all ends tonight. It's Tuesday evening, and it is time I show my face in that stupid church basement. Delphini will be spotted for what she is and she will be taken care of. No longer my problem and everything can return to normal.

I flick the blade of my knife closed and place it in the pocket of my overalls. I take off my scarf and wipe the sweat from my brow. There is no reason for me to feel this warm, yet there it is. My body is reacting to something, but I don't know what. While windowless, this pocket has never varied in temperature, no matter what it is outside. It is always magically perfect. Fae bullshit, I suppose.

It's getting hot again. The days are longer, and the nights are humid. The stench of the city rises as beer gardens and bars spill into the streets. Food trucks crowd the Northbank as drunk young people gather to gorge on tacos and dumplings before venturing home. It makes hunting more accessible, but my clothes do not match the season. I can't bring myself to wear seasonally appropriate clothes though, too much exposure.

Tying my scarf back around my neck, I think about the last time I fell ill. It had been the dead of winter, and I decided I wanted to play with the cold dew that covered the ground. Mother was sure I would die. That I wouldn't be able to beat the fever. I swallow hard at the memory and stand up. They have been gone for far too long for me to think of them, but it's better to think of them happy while alive than how they were slaughtered.

I pull my phone from another pocket and check the time. There are notifications from Nora, but I swipe them away. She would not understand this or see the reasoning behind my choices. Every other year or so, she will wander down for Wild Wood Trust, a bottle of the strongest backwater liquor I have ever had under her arm, and demand we discuss *the future*. She is convinced her fated is out there, she just has to find them and drag them back to Gwenmore. I've tried to tell her it is a fruitless hunt, that no good will come of finding your mate.

Bitterness coats my tongue every time I say the words to her. How long had I spent without mine, hoping for my soulmate only to be denied? Centuries spent watching monsters of all kinds join our mission, do what they must and what they want, constantly stumbling upon their mates along the way. The bonds formed between mates skews perspective. You can't see straight when your soulmate is at your side.

And now I feel more right than ever.

It will feel good to rub this in her face.

Deg'Doriel has yet again reminded me that as a founding member of the community, I am required at these meetings in some form, or else. I roll my eyes, but send him a text reminding him that I told his little mob boss I'd be there tonight. There's no reason to get his tail in knots.

My chest heaves as I leave my quarters in search of Delphini. Adrenaline floods my system and makes my stomach roll. These nerves have no place in me, but I can't get rid of them as I walk towards the end of the hall. I am going to see her up close again, and I am going to be in danger of grabbing hold of her and kissing her like I desperately wanted to on Sunday afternoon.

Our proximity to each other is too close as it is. I have heard the pull of a mate described in many ways, and this pull towards her is the same. As we stood nearly chest to chest in the training room, it seemed we were inevitable and I was ready to fall into her. But I can't. I won't. No matter how her soft lips called to me.

The door to her quarters is open, meaning she is still doing dishes after our evening meal. The moans coming from the newly reopened bath wash over me, remind me of all the beings I have given a safe place too, but it doesn't ease me. I picture her enjoying the crew while I sit and watch, begging for my touch to finally satisfy her.

I walk through the mess hall and into the kitchens to escape the noise. She has the sleeves of her sweat-stained shirt pulled up and her hair tied back still. There is an exhaustion in her body that unsettles me. My body is begging me to comfort her, a pull inside me that is the most challenging fight of my life until I see what she is doing.

Delphini is bent over the sink, scrubbing the heavy cast iron pot.

"What are you doing?" I demand, storming over to her and ripping the large cauldron from her hands. Soap drips down my arm, and my nerves morph into fury. "Are you fucking stupid?"

"No." She scowls at me.

"Then why are you fucking ruining my pot with soap?"

"It was disgusting, it needed cleaning."

"Don't fucking touch this again with soap, or I'll cook you in it." I snarl. It's an empty threat, an overreaction, but this is an heirloom. One of our former cooks, a Dwarven woman with a fierce taste for spicy food, had taken this as retribution after she killed her husband. It is a proud mark of honour on this ship.

"I'm trying to do the job given to me, *Captain*."

She calls me that without an ounce of respect behind the title, and yet it sets me ablaze. It makes my blood boil all the more when I think of her moaning it as she begs for release. My scowl deepens as I swing the pot back onto the massive stove. I will have to get Cookie, our resident chef and troll, to preseason this before it rusts.

It takes me a moment to realise Delphini isn't scared. She isn't concerned that I will make good on my threat or that I am tossing a sixty-pound cauldron around as if it were a wooden ladle. She looks too relaxed with her hip resting on the counter and the scrub brush still in her hand. Her gaze is fixed on where my forearm had strained, revealing a small strip of my wrist.

She looks tired, too.

Fuck me. Why do I care that she is tired? I learned the hard way that nobody cares for a tired and poor being. Nothing is given away for nothing. We have to work to keep our heads above water.

I sigh heavily. "We are going out."

"Like *out* out?" she asks, an enthusiasm bubbling in her voice that has me blinking owlishly.

"Sure, whatever the fuck that means."

Delphini drops the brush she is holding into the sink and bolts out of the kitchen. Her bare feet slap against the shining floor mosaics. Well, she at least knows how to clean something. Before my thoughts can wander, I head for the great hall, thinking she will also be there, but I am, in fact, standing in the room alone.

My eyes are drawn to the floors again. The grout between each of the small tiles is pristine, the whitest it has been since we first installed them. Now my mind really does go through a series of hoops, from thinking about her bent over with her ass in the air, to how sore she must be from the work, to how she hasn't complained once. For five days, I have made sure this woman has been put through the wringer just to avoid her.

Although she has made her existence known to me any chance she could, Delphini has proven she doesn't give up. I suppose that can be said for all of us on this ship. We aren't quitters. Life has tried to beat us down and has killed us all once, though even in death, we have refused to give up. We all earn the power and blessings that Love bestows on us.

Doesn't matter. She won't be coming back to the ship after tonight. She is not going to be a problem for us once I hand her over to the others. It will be smooth sailing into the tourist season and I will return to hunting properly to kill Augustine Ravenscroft. Everyone will forget she was ever here.

A few moments later, Delphini returns from her room. She looks fresher– her face is washed of sweat and she has a new dress on instead of the trousers and shirt she has been wearing.

This piece is much more modern than our standard garb. A summer dress meant for this weather that someone a few decades ago will have purchased. Over the top of the shift, she has that damnable pink stay again.

It's *all* pink.

Something about seeing the colour on her centres me. Like she is a beacon I am meant to be heading for, the pale colour lights up when she wears it—a lighthouse in the dark to guide me to safety the way Love has for centuries. I want to grab hold of her and never let go when I see the shade gracing her form. Delphini makes the colour everything it is; feminine, light, calm.

She appears more comfortable with herself in this outfit than in the trousers.

"We're late," I say abruptly, before turning and heading out the door.

I don't look back to see if she is following. The clap of her boots on the wooden steps is enough to tell me she is. Being late is not something I enjoy, although I suppose that is better than refusing to return at all after what that sandbag, Augustine, did. Another thing to add to my list once I am rid of Delphini: find his mate and rescue that creature he has trapped.

This to-do list of mine is getting longer and longer. I throw myself over the rails and land on the docks with ease. Above me, Delphini stares with her lips parted.

"I can't do that."

"Then climb down on the ladder." I point to the narrow wooden planks on the side of the ship.

She eyes them, then flicks her gaze back to me before her shoulders square. A ghost of Love's tentacles touches me, wrapping around my shoulders like a giant python would its owner's neck. The weight of them anchors me on the ground as I watch the human I am charged with grip onto the side of my ship for dear life. Above us, in the crow's nest, I hear a whistle and then Nargol and Hamako are leaning over the railing to watch her struggle.

"Del," the orc starts, but when I glare at her, she shuts her mouth. There is no room for her blatant disregard for my orders to my face. Nargol gives me a look and then slings the fire safety ladder down from the deck. The metal rungs click into the place and Delphini moves onto it. She is on the dock a few seconds later, smoothing her skirt down.

"Thanks, babes." She waves at the watchers and rushes over to me. "Were you just going to let me struggle forever?"

"You need to learn," I lie.

Yes, I was content to wait her out. She would have either fallen onto the dock or gotten over her fear and climbed down.

I buy Delphini a metro ticket and we take the thirty-minute trip to the historic district. Perhaps I should have brought Aoife or Neela with me, but I'm not sure they would support me on this. She is just like the rest of us; we have all made a promise to Love, but I'm rejecting my soulmate. This is the best thing for her rather than an eternity stuck with me.

At this time of night, the trains are mostly empty and Delphini seems relieved that we are the only ones in this car. The rails grind and screech, but otherwise, it's silent. She doesn't try to chitchat or ask where we are going. Her eyes are closed and her head is tilted back. One of her thighs is thrown over the other, exposing the long, thick length of her leg.

She doesn't have a care in the world.

"She knows she is safe with her chosen."

A man sits down across from us and my hackles rise. He is dressed in casual business wear, but I can smell the alcohol coming off of him. I pull one of my boots up to my knee and rest a hand close to the knife I keep there. It's a threat he doesn't see, a way to keep me from getting too anxious on public transport where a blood bath would be less than ideal.

But he isn't looking at me. His eyes are glued to Delphini.

I don't like it. In fact, seeing the disgusting way he looks at her chest down to her thighs makes me want to rip his eyes out. He has no right to look at her at all. The hand that isn't resting on the blade strapped to my ankle grabs hers.

On instinct, I expect to feel a chill, that same visceral reaction I get when anyone touches me. Instead, all I feel is her warmth, a slightly damp palm from the heat of the enclosed train. Her fingers curl around mine and my stomach twists with doubt.

Isn't this what you've always wanted? a small voice whispers in the back of my mind.

"Is it our stop?" Delphini asks, a little sleepy.

"Yes."

Usually, I would go to another stop before getting off, but I am not going to stab anyone on an empty train. First of all, I have to be somewhere, and it could be a mess. Second, I don't want to explain why I did it to Delphini. Then she will know she is filling the hollow part of my chest without even trying.

The train slows and we get off. I let go of her hand as the door closes behind us. Delphini takes a deep breath of fresh air as we resurface. I suppose it has been a few days since she has been out. Getting a bit of enjoyment before a demon or giant lizard murders her is a small price to pay. We walk the few blocks up, and she pauses again when we stand outside the churchyard. There are a few cars parked in front, on the street. Lights outside the parish centre are on, although nothing inside to indicate it's open.

"This is a weird spot for a date."

"Because this isn't a date." I give her a weird look. Why the fuck did she think this was a date? I'm dropping her off and returning to my quarters to scrape the last five days off my skin.

She looks momentarily hurt by this information, but now isn't the time for the hard edge of me to turn blunt. We have a meeting to get to. Delphini follows, still not questioning what we are doing. Love's presence isn't with me, which is fucking infuriating. By the time we are at the doors to the basement, we are both silently seething.

From the outside, I can hear the voices of the others. The usual crowd, except for Kragnash, is here. Deg'Doriel at the top of the room, Augustine in his regular seat with Ramón on his left and Nora on his right, and the new guy. I scowl, thinking about how long I have been gone and how much trouble this will cause me. It is Augustine's fault after mating a being without their knowledge. He is lucky we do not brush paths outside of these meetings.

As I open the door, Delphini grabs my hand, a soft gasp on her lips.

"Orthia," Nora sounds like a mother whose lost child has returned. I don't understand why she worries about me. I suppose it is in her nature or something, but it is unnecessary. I have lived centuries before she was even born.

"You're late," Deg'Doriel growls, and Delphini doesn't flinch in her hold on me. She has seen a variety of monsters on the ship, but this group is incredibly unique.

"We aren't staying." I look from the demon to Augustine. "I won't return until I know that he has righted the wrong he has committed."

He is in the middle of a stupid excuse, trying to convince me his mate is fine, when his phone rings. He brushes by us and out of the room. Delphini scoffs at his behaviour and I hold back my smirk.

"So who's your friend?" Ramón asks. "She looks familiar."

The fingers wrapped around mine flinch, but I ignore it.

"I have a problem."

Deg groans, his tail flicking back and forth across the linoleum. "Let me guess-"

"She's human."

I say the words in a rush, loudly cutting off the demon. Everyone in the room looks at me. This isn't the tension I thought I would have. There isn't hunger in the air from the vampires or the demons. This isn't how this is supposed to go at all. No one is taking her away.

"For fucks sake," Deg pushes his large hand into his face.

"Who cares?" Ramón waves a giant clawed mitt through the air. "I swear I have seen you before."

Delphini lets go of my hand as the lizard moves closer, crossing her arms over her chest. She's not scared of him and something about that makes my brain freeze.

"She trusts in us."

Nora rushes me before I can process Love's admission. She wraps her big, meaty arms around me and lifts me up. Chills rush down my spine and I want to be furious that her touch has caused the usual icy feelings in me.

"Put me down." I frown at her.

"Glad you're alright." She claps my back once and then takes a step back. "And I understand why you haven't been around. I wouldn't want to let her out of my bed."

"The human has never and will never be in my bed."

That's not true. She was in my bed, lounging on the edge and allowing me to get lost in her warmth while I healed her hand. She let me help her despite how close to breaking down she was. Now she haunts my bed, and I wonder for the first time if her presence will haunt other parts of my ship.

"If you ever called your friends back," she starts, "you would know Nash and Auggie pushed through a motion to get rid of that rule on human relationships."

"I-" my thoughts stutter. "Why?"

Maybe there were pockets of mixed communities, humans and monsters living together at some point, but there are none now. I have sailed the world more times than any one being can count, and nowhere do our kinds mix in harmony. Gwenmore is the closest we get to living amongst humans with ease. I've heard that there are more cities like ours across the States, but there isn't a world like ours anywhere else.

The mixing of our worlds will surely be an end to something, but fuck knows what.

"Auggie bonded with a human like a drunken idiot," she starts to cackle, her sharp teeth and shining freckles catching in the light.

"Nora," Deg'Doriel barks, and the scent of brimstone rises in the air. "Shut your trap, and sit the fuck down."

His mate is a human? To think the holier than thou monster would fall so hard. *No, focus.* "That doesn't matter. I am not in a relationship with that human. I don't want her. Take her-"

Before I can finish my command, Love takes over me, swallowing the control I have over my body. Their presence warps my vision. There isn't enough anger in my thoughts nor blood pumping through my veins for them to be doing this, so they must be using their limited power source. They are using it for her.

"*If any harm comes to the chosen, revenge will be swift.*" The lights flicker, and I am back navigating my own body. I look around the room, again while the others show fear, Delphini looks anything but. She stares me down with such fury in her gaze it makes me think that she may have been the power source Love used to speak or that she may try to take my life.

"*Accept our gift, heart, or risk ruin.*" Their words are a threat in the back of my head, rumbling hard enough to make my knees buckle.

"Yikes," Ramón whispers loudly to the ghoul whose name I haven't bothered to learn yet. I know he isn't a threat.

"Are you staying or not?" Deg'Doriel's voice cuts through the staring match I am having with Delphini.

"I'm leaving," she says.

We all watch her walk out. The door clicks softly behind her with such finality that it makes me shudder. Problem solved. She realises I can't be her soul mate. She can't be what I want. She is leaving of her own volition. Love's presence is missing from my thoughts, though; they've gone out the door with their new plaything.

Why is there a more profound, aching sense of loss settling on my chest, then? A strong storm has taken out a light in my life. The ghost of her presence is a haunting darkness. I am alone at last, but I want to claw open my chest to make sure something else hasn't been taken from me.

"Not sure I could handle my princess walking around like that outta my sight." Ramón comments. "Can't scare the idiots away."

"Shut the fuck up, Ray." I turn and chase after Delphini.

CHAPTER ELEVEN
ORTHIA

7 Days

She is out of my sight for mere moments, but it is like icy water has been dumped over my head. My skin prickles with goosebumps. I have to grit my teeth together to keep them from chattering. Delphini is gone and my blood freezes over. All the warmth of my soul disappeared when she left me. There is no reason to claw my chest open when I know what is missing.

I must find her. This shake in my hands, this shiver that cycles up and down my spine commands my instincts to find warmth. It has me racing through the empty side streets to the train station. As much as I didn't want her on my ship, I was never far from her. It never occurred to me that this would be the consequence of her leaving.

My body is dying without her near me. I must find her. Pain sears in my muscles at the mere thought that she will go where I can't find her. My body is weak from Love's use of it, their power feeding off me during the summoning.

What if I can't catch up with her?

I push harder, every moment we have spent together in the past five days rushes through my thoughts. Every soft good morning, the way she whispered my name, the sass that coated her tongue as she called me captain. The words echo in my skull like prayers bouncing off the walls of a temple.

The doubt that leaked into my every action now floods my lungs until I am drowning. With heaving breaths, I can feel hers on my lips again. The heat of her body as her knees bent to me like she wanted me to push forward until our mouths met. The look of hope on her face when I told her we would be going out.

Delphini beats me to the train. As I step onto the empty platform, I see her leaning against a pole. I curse the gods and myself for this. She better be going back to the fucking ship. I pace up and down the platform while I wait for the next train. My fingers dig into the meat of my chest the longer we are apart.

Does she not feel this pain?

Beyond the fact that certain people believe she is dead, she is also a young woman with no phone or money. My mind spirals out of control with thoughts of her alone. This is wildly unsafe of her, and it's my fault. Does she not care about her personal safety any more? Maybe she has never cared and that is what got her killed in the first place.

The next train arrives, and I take a seat by the doors. No one else is in this car. I close my eyes and try to connect with Love. I visualise them, their eyes, their tentacles, but nothing comes to me. They remain silent, but I keep meditating, focusing on them, my anger, and the raging oceans far from the Docklands.

We are all angry tonight.

"My Love, speak with me," I whisper.

"We have given you a gift, heart, yet you throw it away." Their voice multiplies and echoes in my skull so harshly tears come to my eyes. They leak down my cheeks, but I keep them closed, trying to stay with this connection while it lasts, even if it drains me further.

"She isn't meant for us."

"She is you, but your hatred for your own kind has blinded you."

"No. I am not one of them."

"And neither is she."

Their silence is jarring and loud when they leave me again. My eyes flutter open as the tears leak from them, and I scrub them away with the sleeve of my shirt. Delphini wants to be mine, then fine. She shall be mine, and she shall be a part of the crew.

She will see the error in her ways.

My discussion with Love has taken me to my stop. The station is desolate, the overnight guard locked in their booth and reading something on a tablet. A salty breeze picks up when I step towards the dock. I don't see Delphini, and I don't want to search all the Docklands for her before going home to sleep off this horrible evening. There is a tug underneath my skin, which I know is Love guiding me to her. I follow the soft pull to a dive bar.

The Salty Dog is a locals' bar, one run by a human scumbag. It doesn't make good hunting grounds for the simple fact that everyone here knows everyone. And they know me as well. The local crazy woman obsessed with the legend of a pirate queen. If only they knew.

However, Delphini will be drawing all their attention to herself dressed as she is.

Ignoring the men smoking outside, I head in. Humid and rank, this place smells of unwashed bodies and fish rot. Some of the fishermen come here after shifts and drink away what money they do have before going right back to their boats. It's like they've never heard of bathing.

The pink dress stands out in this crowd. Delphini leans up against the bar and watches closely as a lady pours her two shots. How has she paid for these? The answer to my question sits next to her. They knock glasses together, and she downs her shot with ease, not even a flinch as the undoubtedly cheap liquor burns her senses. She makes eye contact with me the moment she swallows.

When she licks her lips, my eyes follow the peak of pink that traces the plush shape. The man next to her doesn't see it, but for a brief moment, her dark eyes turn a milky shade of white that I have seen reflected back at me before. His hand goes to her wrist and she doesn't push him away, or bristle at his touch. I step forward, intent to rip the skin from it for touching her and to drag her back to the ship and...

And I don't know what. Have a discussion like we are a couple who had a misunderstanding? As if it isn't fucked up enough, the higher power we have both pledged our second chance at life to hasn't played matchmaker? It's all so fucking ridiculous to me when I have had one mission in all this time. They said we were to bring about a new age, but why does this human factor into any of this?

Fishermen step in my way carelessly and I lose sight of Delphini. Once I have shoved past them, making sure they see the icy rage on my face for standing in my way, she is gone. I scan the bar, but there isn't a single inkling of pink left. The neon signs are shades of blue that offer no comfort.

She's not left the bar and the guy who bought her the drink isn't at the table any more either.

I'm going to kill him.

I am going to kill him for this fucking inconvenience and make Delphini watch my knife carve out his heart. She will see what I am capable of and what I will do just because I can. The pleasure of feeling his last heart beat will purely be for myself. That will prove to her that she is no match for me because I don't have any humanity left. Centuries of taking lives have warped the being I am, incapable of real love. I have been since my rebirth. The only thing inside me is a festering anger that keeps me going, keeps everything going.

And I won't give that up.

There are only so many places they could have gone. I weave through the crowd and down the small hall that has the gents and permanently closed ladies. Both are as disgusting as I imagined they would be, but empty. The third door leads to a supply closet that is so small I'm not sure even one person could stand in the small space.

The fire door outside leads to an alley that I know better than I know this bar. It's a good waypoint between the city and *The Despair* when I have fresh meat in tow. During Love's heat, as it has come to be known by the crew, it helps to keep some men alive long enough to kill them with an audience. It feels like more of a ritual, something all of us can indulge in from the safety of the ship rather than another task to complete. But there is only one reason Delphini could want to bring a man out here.

Is fucking a stranger in an alley her act of revenge after my rejection?

As I step outside and breathe in the scent of piss, it's easy to find Delphini and the man. The full moon is high in the sky and the distant street lights are enough to illuminate them. I flick my pocket knife out of my overalls and let the weight of it settle in my shaking hand. This will be done quickly. I'll leave the scum for someone else to deal with, but she needs to be taken back to the ship.

Our closeness is easing the ache, but anger races to replace it. Already, I can feel her. Even with a few feet of distance between us, her presence brings a stop to the shaking in my bones. Goosebumps spread across my arms and prickle at the back of my neck.

There is a masculine grunt and my gut recoils. Love's weight isn't wrapped around me. They can't offer me their comfort around this vile man. I am alone in this act. My breath stalls.

A clap of skin against skin echoes down the alley, followed quickly by a high-pitched gasp that has me moving closer.

Pink bleeds red under the light of the moon. Delphini's body jerks as she moves against the man. It's rained recently, but the day was dry. The puddle forming at her feet isn't water. The man slumps, and she shoves him into the trash piled up next to them. Her dress is splattered with blood and a cheap fishing knife slips from her fingers as she locks eyes with me.

"Is this what you wanted? Have I proven myself to you yet?" Her chest heaves.

My thoughts soar as my vision tunnels into the sight before me. Every part of me vibrates with an urgency I haven't ever felt for anyone but Love. Her clenched fists tremble. Her anger is palpable, like it's trying to wrap itself around me. I know that she isn't a nymph. She isn't a siren. To even think that she could be something so simple is stupid. This creature is coated in rage and blood and beauty.

Delphini is a goddess.

Every part of me wants to drop to my knees before her. Such a simple act to take a man's life, and yet so hard for most. They can't picture themselves harbouring such violence, they can't stomach the beastly pleasure of taking until their prey is dead. But she has done it as an act of devotion to me.

"Don't you see how good I can be?" she demands. "I can be as good as you. Let me prove it to you."

These feelings don't make sense and I'm frozen in this rank alley. She stumbles over to me, exhausted, causing her frame to move without her usual grace. My knife is fisted in my hand. The short blade is exposed and waiting to be soaked in blood, too.

"Who will you choose?" Love's voices thunder through me, powerful and blessedly hungry.

"Speak to me," Delphini looks down at me, casting her shadow over me like a dark promise. I want nothing more than to sink into this feeling. To forget the world outside of my Love, and now my human. This woman before me is chaos and violence and so much obsession. Her soul, her mind, her body. I want all of it.

I can see all of it now. The vision Love showed me all those centuries ago is a hazy memory, but I see her. Where she fits in our mission is clear to me. I am a ship in Love's vast ocean, but she is my centre mark. An obelisk that rises from the dark depths to keep me from straying. She is my *omphalos*.

My knife slips from my fingers.

"I..."

I am in full control of my body. Love is with her, and yet I feel like I am watching everything from outside of my body. My hand rises to cup her cheek. Delphini pants, and I know her eyes are locked with mine despite how dark it is. My thumb ghosts across her plush cheek and I feel a wetness there. Is it blood or tears?

My skin warms at our connection and I hold myself still, waiting for her to slap me away. I am so certain that she will fight me here. For as much as she may want me, I don't deserve her or the warmth of our connection after everything I have done tonight.

"Why would Love bring us together if we were not meant to be? Please, I can't be alone any more," she whispers, voice breaking. "Can't you feel it?"

"Yes, my human."

"Then why?" She sounds close to tears, her teeth grinding together to prevent them.

"Do you really wish to give yourself to me?" I counter. "I am a cruel being at my core. I will do whatever I must to raise Love from the depths. I could hurt you."

"Hurt me then, as long as you want me, hurt me."

I grab her nape and pull her lips to mine. Heat, so soft and hungry, erupts through me. She is sweet, her sharp inhaling tickling my cheek. There is the taste of blood on her, and I can't stop myself from licking it away. Delphini opens her mouth in an offering, but I pull away.

I spit the blood of the dead man back on his body.

"You are mine, now."

CHAPTER TWELVE
DELPHINI

0 DAYS

My chest constricts at her touch, at her words, her kiss.

Orthia's hand on my neck is like coming home. The adrenaline pounding through my system slows and feeling returns to my limbs. I don't know what came over me at that community centre, why I ran here of all places. I've never lost control of my anger like that before. I couldn't just shove the feelings down. They flooded my system with so much power.

I killed a stranger without a single care for his life if it meant getting what I wanted, getting Orthia to see what I will do for her. I thought I would feel sick when I did it. There wasn't a backup plan when I recklessly agreed to come out here, but he was quick enough to pull a knife on me when I told him no. The stink of cheap tequila on his breath made me gag and I'm glad he is the one I used to prove my point.

She called me hers. My eyes flutter shut as I try to remember everything about this moment. Her chapped lips on mine, the slick and foreign feel of her tongue on my lips. I want to explore more, to keep her lips on mine for the rest of eternity. Her warm hand on me is everything I never knew I needed. What will it feel like if she touches the rest of me?

"A small victory in a long war you will fight for your soulmate, sweet one."

The weight of Love's tentacles slides from me to her with such ease. They switch between us as if this is how they are meant to move through space and time. A breath shudders through me as the sensation of them leaves me. Orthia steps back once she realises what they've done. She clears her throat and looks behind me. I am dead on my feet and couldn't give a single fuck about that shit bag. The morning will come sooner than I like.

"You didn't do it right," she finally says.

I blink.

"Love still hungers. You've got a lot of fucking work ahead of you." Orthia moves around me and uses her boot to turn over the guy I stabbed like three times for her. "Did you even aim for a lung?"

For five days, I have held my tongue because why start a fight with my soulmate, who a literal god says is afraid of me? Her unimpressed tone and the annoyed look on her face now is the last straw. I can't keep doing this. I am only human.

"I wasn't fucking thinking about what part of him the damn knife was piercing. It's not something you can fucking look up online."

"You can." Orthia scoffs, "but it's not really accurate."

"Oh my god," I groan. "Why are you ruining our moment?"

She takes a deep breath; I can see her shoulders move up with the action in an almost comical way.

"I'm not- Look." She turns around and rubs a hand over her fuzzy head. "We are not experiencing the same moment right now."

"What do you mean?"

"I have been alive since before the great temples in Athens were constructed. My life has been nothing but rage since I- since Love found me at the bottom of the ocean. Destruction is all I know, even as battles have left the sea and our work slowed."

She pauses in her speech, but it says enough. Not only does my existence in her space scare her, threaten her, Orthia's carefully crafted world is crumbling around her because of me.

"Then we will build a new world together. From the rumble we will all rise. You, me, Love, the three of us can do this. You just have to let me in."

We don't speak again until we get back to the ship. Orthia tosses the dead guy over her shoulders and walks to the far edge of the dock before she dumps him into the water. I don't even flinch when his body slaps against the water.

Nargol is waiting when we get to the side of the ship with the ladder from earlier. I read the name on the side of it in the dull light, *The Princess's Despair*. Yeah, I'd agree with that. It stung the first time she rejected me, but at least that had been in private. There was any amount of hope in me that thought I could win her over to my side then. Remaining delusional, I assumed she was as shocked as I was at the time. Whole new world opened up to me and I was presented with my soulmate.

Now?

Now, her acceptance should be a weight off my shoulder, she has claimed me, kissed me, and yet it has left me off balance.

"Should I get the party started?" Nargol asks when we are on deck once again.

I have no clue what she means by party, unless it's a pity party. My body sways, and now I feel like throwing up. Stupid sea sickness. I grab onto Orthia's arm for stability and she wraps her hand around my waist. I want to melt into her touch. But I can't push this new change in her yet.

"No," she answers. "This one has a lot to learn before she's ready to fulfil her promise."

"Well, humans are delicate about these things."

Orthia and I both scowl. "What?"

"How did you know what she was?" She demands, fingers tightening around me. I need to get on solid ground again. Exhaustion is taking its toll on me. The warmth of Orthia's touch is lulling me into a state of comfort that has my eyes begging to close.

"It's hard to miss, Captain. Plus, Lagulla knew who she was before this." Nargol smirks.

"Not me any more," I say carefully, trying to hold it together.

"We got you, Del." Nargol's voice softens. "You're one of us."

"For Love's sake," Orthia grumbles. Then she says, "Gather the crew in the mess hall. We've got a new crewmate to toast to."

Nargol whistles, and the night shift crew appear out of the darkness like shadows. We all head below deck, but once we are in the safety of the solid dimension and I no longer feel sick, Orthia doesn't let go. She guides me to the front of the dining hall where there is a small dais.

Her fingers squeeze my soft side as we step up, helping me maintain balance in my exhaustion.

Around us, the crew swoops into action. There is loud splashing from the baths and tell-tale sounds of glasses being set up for drinks. I'm struggling to pay attention to any of it because of her touch. Orthia is scowling at the blood-stained dress I am wearing.

"We will order you things in the morning to wear when you aren't on shift."

I want to ask if this means she really likes me and about a hundred other things. But a glass is placed in my hand, the clear liquid sloshing around a crystal tumbler that I haven't seen in my time washing dishes. Must be for special occasions.

"Sisters," Orthia shouts over the crew.

There must be about twenty or so women and people here—each of them in various states of undress. The night crew look ready for a stealth attack, some are dressed in pyjamas, and others are simply standing around naked, still dripping from the debauchery in the bath.

"You all know Delphini, but under my instruction, you have not welcomed her as we would a new recruit, which was an error on my part." She swallows and steels her shoulders. "Love has proclaimed that she is not only one of us, but that she is to be mine."

On cue, I feel the slide of their tentacles across my skin. I suspect they are transferring between us again, but when I feel the slickness on my skin, I see the real, teal thing touching me. My pussy clenches at the memory as my skin tingles with need. I look at Orthia. Her cheeks are flushed red, and there is a soft glow coming from her again.

"She is officially an officer for *The Princess's Despair*. Treat her as you would any of your sisters. Her training begins tomorrow."

Cheer erupts through the crowd. I knock back my drink without a thought, the burning herbal taste of the gin nearly catching in my throat. I keep my face neutral to hide how much I want to flinch and only when I feel the tentacle push my jaw in her direction, do I look at Orthia.

Her gaze is all hunger and heat, and unlike every other time I have caught her staring at me over the last five days, she doesn't look away.

"From this day forward, you are mine, Delphini, and I am yours. We shall be at each other's sides for as long as we live. We shall watch the tides rise and swallow this land. We shall bring forth the glory of the new age as one."

Around us, there is more cheering, glasses knocking together in excitement, but I'm holding my breath. We have jumped from one mixed signal to another here, but I crave her attention, her approval more than I have anyone else's. She says that she is mine, but what does she really mean?

"You are my mate, my human, my wife."

She grabs me by the front of my stay and slams her mouth onto mine before the words even register. This round of cheers is explosive, and my body is alight with need. Love's tentacle curls around the two of us until our bodies are pressed together. Her palm presses into the mark on my chest as both my hands cup her face.

Her wife.

The last thing I should be thinking about is how right the word sounds. Weddings and marriage are the reason I'm here at all. Not wanting to be in one is how she found me at the bottom of the bay. I should hate that she has called me that, but my mind is swimming with how the words sound on her lips. From her, the soul mate I have been fighting for, it doesn't sound so bad. It sets my heart fluttering and giddiness actually has me smiling into this kiss.

Orthia bites my lip hard until I can taste blood again.

Instead of pulling back, this time, she thrusts her tongue into my mouth. It isn't a tongue. Her mouth parts and a slick tentacle teases my teeth. A sucker pops against the inside of my mouth and I moan. The cheering gets louder before it morphs into something more heated. The bath activities are starting again in front of us, and it's just egging me on. I twirl my tongue around hers, feeling every difference in her anatomy.

Only when I suck on it does she pull back, and I catch a glimpse of the thing between her wet, swollen lips. A small, teal tentacle that swipes away the evidence of our kiss.

"Go to your rooms, Delphini, you need your rest."

"Yes, *Captain*."

When I call her that this time, my meaning is different. There is no subtle annoyance or challenge. Pure desire to please guided me to say those words and I am rewarded with a pink flush to Orthia's cheeks and a darker hunger in her gaze.

She wants me.

Chapter Thirteen
Delphini

3 Days

It has been impossible to get a moment alone with her since she pronounced me her wife.

Aoife assigns me a new post on Wednesday morning. I am now selling the tickets for the tours, which means for eight hours a day, I am holed up in some kind of old timey ticket booth dealing with humans. She explained the role pretty basically. The one thing I have to be vigilant about is rude customers. If anyone steps out of line in any way, their ticket gets a stamp so the girls know who they can really sing to and feed off of on deck.

It's an easy job. There is a large fan to keep me cool, and every time the ship docks between tours, someone comes to check on me. They bring me water, and after finally asking Cookie about it, the kitchen stocks matcha and coconut milk. So if I need a boost in the afternoon, someone will bring me one of those. There are also an abundance of snacks brought to me.

It gives me too much time to think. My fingers twist into the fabric of my shirt until I can feel Love's mark on my chest. I miss my *Yiayia*, and I want to hear her voice, but I have been too scared to call. Instead, late at night, I pull out the wedding rings she gave me and contemplate if I will ever wear them.

I have learned more about monsters in three days than I could ever have imagined. They are all so happy to explain this uncovered world to me. Everyone wants to know about me too. What my life was like and what I plan to do after my revenge.

My gut instinct is to be hesitant with telling them anything. What if they use it against me, but every mealtime, someone new is opening up, being honest about their trauma and their healing. Nobody here is hiding away from how they got here, or if they are hoping to leave at some point.

I've thought about that realisation a lot recently. There are no secrets, no one is using the other to get a step up on the ladder or to gain favour with Orthia. They are all here because they want to be. This is their safe space, and they want me to be a part of it.

"I want to visit my *Yiayia* in Greece." I admit to my regular dinner table of Nargol, Lakelynn, and Neela. "She has always been-"

"Delphini!" Orthia barks my name from the entrance of the dining hall. "Get changed and meet me in the training room."

My body burns.

The training room in the ship is sweltering and the dagger in my hand feels like it weighs a metric fuck ton. Where there aren't blisters all over my hand, there is sweat. I am that sweaty, my hands are slick with it.

In front of me is a magic self-healing jelly dummy who the crew uses to practise stabbing. Every time I pull the long dagger I wield from him, he fixes himself like my knife was never in his guts. Orthia and I have been at this for what feels like hours.

I want to talk about this soulmate thing with her now that we both are acknowledging it. What are her expectations? I know she wants to fuck me, but how? Does she want to be touched by me like that? I have seen how she flinches away from the touch of the others. Does she want to watch Love fuck me?

"Delphini," she shouts my name as she paces behind Jelly Man. "Arms up, c'mon. Where are you aiming?"

"Lungs," I groan.

"Then why did you stab him in the stomach? Again!"

I groan and take up any form of stance I can. My fingers clench hard around the engraved hilt of the dagger and I lunge forward. The blade sinks into the jelly as easily as it did the man from Tuesday night. Its insides swirl with dark fake blood, but when I remove the blade nothing comes out. Orthia looks at the jelly and then at me.

"Good girl," she purrs, a smirk forming on her lips as she watches me pant. Her eyes don't leave mine when she says the words and it makes my cheeks heat. The words send a jolt right to my clit like her tongue had flicked across it. "Oh, that does work."

"Love," I grumble and feel their rumbling in my head.

"Did you think they wouldn't tell me about your little affliction?" She asks. The way she says affliction is aimed to humiliate me, but I have long since gotten past any sort of shame around sex. I'm game for most things as long as we're all consenting.

"A little praise and Del turns to a puddle. What a weak woman," she taunts me.

I don't get why she's doing this, but that smirk is still in place. She's not wrong. Praise from Love, from her, does turn me into a puddle. I crave those simple words from them, but I am not weak.

Orthia keeps taunting me. Panting turns ragged as my anger swells. My limbs tingle and the dagger in my fist feels lighter. Adrenaline is pumping through me, finally. I lunge for the jelly.

The blade punctures higher, but instead of the blood, a rush of bright pink swells into the stab wound. My colour glows inside the jelly and a rush of energy flows through my blood until all I can hear over the rushing in my ears is a chanting for more. I shove the blade deeper and watch the Jelly Man's insides turn pink. My breathing is ragged, but I draw the knife back and shove it in again.

As quickly as it appears, the glowing pink is sucked out of Jelly Man. With a heavy, tired grunt, I pull the dagger from his chest and it falls to the ground. My fingers shake uncontrollably, my knees give out. I can hardly suck in a full breath, let alone warn Orthia, but she is already catching me. For someone who is a few inches shorter than me and maybe half my weight, she is incredibly strong and fast.

God, I bet she fucks hard.

I'm blaming that thought wholly on how fucking exhausted I am. And how warm her touch makes me. It coats all of me until it feels as though I've been lying in the sun for hours. She steadies me from collapsing further but then takes her touch with her. Now I am just sweaty.

"Better, you even summoned a bit of your power that time."

She crosses her arms in such a way it pushes her tits up and I shamelessly stare. They are small, but that is all I know. Orthia is always dressed head to toe. I want to see all of her.

"Why are we doing this?" I ask.

"Because killing is easy, but feeding on the essence of a human is difficult. You have to be able to summon Love's power so they can draw it from the meat. The more they feed, the stronger they become. But each time they use their power in our world, it drains them and us. When we bring them here wholly, they will be able to feed as they please. They will be free."

I groan. "That's so much."

"You can do this, Delphini, as long as you take this seriously," she promises, before slowly cupping my damp cheek.

Warmth shoots through me at her touch. I want to drown in that warmth and not sweaty gym clothes. After a heartbeat, she leans into me, laying me down on the floor until she is straddling me. I smell pomegranate on her skin.

Without thinking, I run my nose against her neck to breathe in more of it. Summer days, hot sunshine, the wonders that ocean waves would wash up on the beach, the memories it pulls from me make my skin tingle and pussy throb. My lips part, ready to taste her again, ready to feel all of her, but then she pulls away.

I killed a man for her.

That's another issue altogether. It's been three days since that night. When she kissed me, that's all my mind focuses on when I think about that night. Not the stabbing, not the way the fabric of that man's shirt hindered the knife or the way he still clung to me in death. Those are like puddles compared to the flood warmth of Orthia's lips on mine and the tentacle that acts as her tongue exploring my mouth.

I want to crawl into her skin until she can't tell us apart.

"Don't think she is without needs," Love murmurs through my thoughts. *"She desires your touch, she wants to devour you."*

So why hasn't she done that? Why is it that whenever I try to talk about our relationship, she leaves the conversation? It's like she would rather walk into the sea in those moments than have a discussion about us. What is she so scared of?

She takes hold of the hand I have raised to cup her cheek with, and even as warmth explodes from the touch, a trickle of misguided fear has me flinching before she twines our fingers together.

"I can't let you fail," she continues, voice softening as her other hand strokes my plush sides. "If you can't feed Love their promised souls, they will take you instead. I've only let it happen once, Delphini. I can't let you get distracted from what's important."

"Our relationship isn't a distraction." I place my hand on her cheek, letting the warmth relax some of my shaking muscles. Orthia leans into my touch, nuzzling into my palm.

"Wife," she hums, her lips brushing across on the inside of my wrist.

I take a deep breath before seizing this moment with her. She looks at me with hunger when I pull her mouth to mine. My fingers scrap against her scalp and the short hairs as her lips part for my kiss. Orthia releases my hand so both of her can caress my body. Her tongue dives into my mouth, the suckers teasing my teeth as she takes control of the kiss.

She leans forward and rises up higher on her knees to apply more pressure to our kiss. There's hesitation when my tongue dips into her mouth. She tastes like sweat and pomegranates. The coiling feeling in my belly grows tighter at the flavour. I'm chasing the taste of it, my mind and body hungry for more of her. She shivers, but she doesn't pull away. Her fingers graze the underside of my breast. I moan against her lips and bring my hand up to cup her nape.

Orthia freezes and I pull back. Her eyes are glazed over white again, her lips glisten from our kiss, and her skin has turned a subtle shade of teal. What is Love telling her? There is a soft glow all around her, from under her clothes to behind her teeth. She blinks, her eyes clearing, and suddenly she is on me.

In a frenzy, her lips crash into mine. As our bodies collide, warmth eases every part of me. My thoughts slow, my body sings with how fucking good she feels on top of me. Her knees spread on either side of my hips and the warmth of her pussy presses into my tummy. I kiss her as hard as she does me, my hands moving to grab her hips, but she stops me.

"Know that I want you, Delphini, desire you more than the sun on my skin and the salty breeze of the sea," she groans, her hips grinding into me. "But you aren't ready for what I have planned, and when you are? I want you to beg me to fuck you."

She's off me before I can even scoff at that suggestion. I don't beg.

"Go clean up," she says. "We have an errand to run."

"Yes, *Captain*." I flutter my eyelashes at her and she blushes. I may have a thing for praise, but Orthia enjoys a bit of power exchange. "I'm washing my hair, though."

"Fine, *wife*. Nargol should have already dropped off your packages outside your room."

She walks out of the room before I can thank her again for ordering everything I needed. It was a minimal amount, basically nothing compared to my usual shopping sprees. There would be time for more frivolous shopping after I got my first paycheck. I shuddered at the thought. The wages are unfair to me, but Neela said that this was the best paying job she's ever had.

I bought the basics, mainly underwear and then most budget self-care supplies I could justify. Goodbye

Yiayia's magic cleanser, and hello five-in-one cream. *It's about being clean, Del, not about brands.*

As I drag all my boxes into my room, I reminisce about my old life. Specifically on my times in Greece. Would Orthia even want to visit Paxos? I have put together that she is Greek, but she doesn't get homesick in the way some of the crew do. We have all been cast aside by our families and our friends, and in joining our crew, we have done the same to them. But the captain never talks of home. Only life on the ship.

I rip open the boxes.

Clothes? Check. New towels? Check.

The last one must be my products. I tear it open and tip the contents out, but it's not what I ordered. They are the products I wanted, but not what ended up in my basket because they were too expensive to justify.

"She is trying." Love sounds so pleased in my head that I know it can only mean Orthia changed the order. *"We are as well."*

There are tears in my eyes when I gather everything up and get ready to shower. They did this for me. The familiar scents cling to the steam in the shower as I get to work detangling my curls. God it feels like a dream getting to do this with something so familiar. I work through my routine and feel at peace when I'm stepping out of the shower. Diffusing my hair takes longer than

I remember, but when I look in the small mirror of my bathroom, I feel more like myself than I have in ages.

Getting dressed is quick after that. I pull on a pink tennis dress and cropped, matching sweatshirt I bought on sale. The pirate uniform I have to wear for the tourists sucks the life out of me, so everything I bought is pink. I'm not worried about repping a brand or whether something looks chic enough any more. I want to look good, but I can also think about comfort. What I feel nicest in, and right now I want my pink armour back.

I slide on the pink tennis shoes that I got from the clearance outlet and stop. Am I supposed to get Orthia, or will she come to me? I haven't been to her quarters since she healed my hand. As I look down the length of the hall, most of the doors are closed. A nervousness settles in my gut. I've never felt like this before. It's an odd sort of excitement that I imagine is what picking up a first date is like.

Though, that's not what this is. It's a chore.

With that thought in mind, I square my shoulders and walk towards her door. We really need to have a talk about expectations and needs. I can do the whole platonic soulmate thing if that is what she really wants, but I have romantic needs.

I raise my hand to knock, but my knuckles don't even touch the wood before it creeps open silently. There is slick-sounding pop on the other side, followed by a low, feminine groan. That should be my sign to leave. I know exactly what those noises are. I can hear them every night coming from the bath, not just because I have experienced Love's tentacles in action. It's a slippery, hot mess.

Instead of doing what I should, though, I peer through the crack of the door into her room. Its lamp lit, and how I remember it. The screen is on the far side of the large room, the huge bed is next to it, and the raised platform is where Orthia is currently sitting. Her back is to me while she leans back in her old chair. One booted foot is placed on the desk, and the other is hidden underneath. Both of her hands are in front of her. A large tentacle pierces the floor in a soft glow of pink and wraps around her, holding her in place.

"Fuck. Love," she moans, and I swear all my blood turns to fire.

Orthia is having sex with Love. Every bone in my body is urging me to join them, but I can't. The moment she knows I am here, it will be so awkward. Fuck. Shit. I need to leave.

"Stay put, sweet one." They whisper in my ear.

I squeeze my eyes shut. Shit, this is so wrong. Does she know I am here? Would she want me to watch her?

"I want her. You know I do." Orthia moans and there is another wet pop.

"Yes. Yes," she whines. "Yes, gods, Love, stop teasing."

I should cover my ears, but instead I press my palm over my mouth to muffle my sounds. We are at the end of the hall, my back to the rest of our world, but I don't care. My focus is completely on listening to my soulmate. My clit throbs as she groans again.

"Because-" Orthia gasps and I want to swallow that noise. "I want her to beg for my touch, crave me."

Her words put a spell on me. I do crave her touch, but could I beg for it? Orthia growls something I can't make out but then something inside of me moves. I nearly double over at the sensation. It isn't painful, but my breath stalls in my throat like it is.

I reach into my panties and tears come to my eyes. No, no, this is too much. Two tentacles wrap around my fingers as I feel my wet pussy.

"Keep listening," Love commands.

My stance shifts, my forehead resting on the doorjam and I try to breathe through what's happening. I keep my hand over my mouth to keep from crying out. The suckers kiss my fingers before searching out their real target. One wiggles between my ass until there is a sucker right on my hole and the other attaches to my clit with such accuracy I bite my tongue to hold in my scream of pleasure.

This reaches a whole new level of fucked up, but that doesn't stop my hips from jerking forward. My pussy feels a slight stretch, but there's no movement from the tentacles. They are holding me open like I'm supposed to be filled by something. I can't open my eyes, I can't. If I do, I am going to cum right here in this fucking hallway.

"I want her in the baths. I want my sisters to turn her into a mess and refuse to let her finish." She pauses, and I can practically hear Love demanding that she spell out her fantasy. They want me to know every detail. Orthia groans, "Because I want her to beg for my mouth, for my tentacles."

Holy. Shit.

The suckers on my skin both bite down in unison and I cum so hard the pink shards of light are back. I hear Orthia's gasping sigh, the bitten-off 'fuck', and my knees threaten to hit the deck so hard. It's not until I hear a boot smack down on the floor that I think I should fucking run.

My heart jumps in my throat and I dart down the hallway. The tentacles slither back inside me so quickly, that if it weren't for the slick mess around my ass I would call it a hallucination. My hand is on the doorknob to my room when I hear the creak of Orthia's opening.

"Good, you're ready to go." She sounds as gruff and stern as normal. Not at all like she just came while thinking about me.

I pretend like I am closing my door and try to smile at her. This is not the time to lose my poker face. I didn't spend my whole life learning how to act like nothing was wrong for me to lose it because I got to hear my soulmate cum all over her personal tentacles.

"So where are we going?" I ask.

"This looks nice," Orthia says instead, her eyes lazily trailing over my outfit. "Sensible shoes."

"Are we going on a walk?" I leave out the dock part, reminding myself before it's too late that we are running an errand.

"No, we are going to get your old things."

Now my smile isn't fake.

Orthia buys me another metro ticket, and we take the train up to the more central part of Harbour Crest, where the buildings are new and tall and filled with luxury. It's crowded and people stare. I'm not sure if it's because of me or us. Do people recognise me from social media or from my explosive nightmare scandal? Are they staring because my small butch soulmate has her arm wrapped around me like an angry chihuahua.

"So where are we going exactly?"

"Did you not know? You just decided we'd go somewhere? What if we had to go back to Chicago?" I ask. I am astounded at this lack of a plan.

"I figured you'd have something within the city limits." She shrugs. "Again, this is something I discuss with the new recruits early on."

"Huh? And who's fault is that?"

Orthia rolls her eyes at me. "Mine, but I am trying to fix that. So where are we going?"

"I shared an apartment with my ex-fiancé. Assuming he hasn't thrown my stuff into the street yet, it's all there."

The gears in Orthia's mind start to turn and she doesn't say anything for the rest of the train ride. Her arm tightens around me though, pressing the sides of our bodies completely together.

This late at night, the receptionist is in the back office rather than manning the desk. It's too late for regular residents and too early for partygoers to be returning. We slip in easily. There was a moment when I thought my thumbprint wouldn't work on the exterior door. That Miles will have erased me for good, but the lock clicks and the door softly buzzes while we enter.

Everything goes smoothly. Even the six-digit code to enter our flat is the same. Miles is so sure and unbothered that I'm dead and nobody will come looking for me. He hasn't changed a thing. My jaw clenches as I twist the knob. He better be in.

The apartment is dark, with not a single light on. Miles isn't here. It makes more sense that he isn't. He is a bachelor again and can happily go back to his partying ways now that he's got my money.

A low whistle sounds behind me when I raise the lights fifty percent. This place is minimalist and decorated in shades of grey. Everything is shining metal or granite or leather. It's as uncomfortable as can be. I'm not sure how I lived here for six months without a touch of my own design sense.

"Make yourself at home. I can pack my stuff."

"Not," Orthia falls onto the couch and puts her dirty boots up, "a problem."

Chapter Fourteen
Orthia

10 Days

Delphini heads down the hall towards her old bedroom and I'm fucking glad she never had to share a bed with her ex. Even what little she was willing to offer up on the journey here was enough to make me hate the guy even more. This little scare tactic will be a perfect addition to her revenge.

I look around again, noting the lifeless coffee table books and shit art on the walls. I thought rich people were supposed to have taste, but I guess I'm wrong on that count. Moments tick by and this far inland it's best not to summon Love. Meditation is an option, but I don't think Del will be too long. I check the news on my phone instead. It's an odd habit I have. The dealings of humans, what they consider noteworthy, should not interest me. I can't stop my curiosity though. I scroll through the headlines and smirk at the chaos of this society. They are crumbling so easily. Greed and gluttony are truly great sins they suffer.

There is an article about Kragnash, his re-election campaign now in full swing as incumbent mayor. He is up against an older white man who looks like he commits hate crimes in his free time.

Nothing about bodies washing up or the coast guard dredging for anyone. It has happened a few times that the remains of my kills have washed ashore, but nothing comes of them. Either because of our monstrous network working behind the scenes to keep us all hidden or because the police service in Gwenmore is simply too stupid to see how the murders are similar.

At the bottom of the site is celebrity gossip. A guilty pleasure, a touch of the woman I used to be. When there was nothing but the market gossip and a temple full of women, it was all there was to do but listen and learn. It feels like I am looking at someone else's life when I think about that part of my past, the one that is full of more joy than anger.

Pinned to the top of the news site, is a story about some hotel heiress.

An heiress caught cheating, family disgraced.

Family disgraced sounds absolutely archaic, but I don't care. I open the article, click bait be damned.

Affluent and luxury influencer and heiress dropped by own family brands after sexually explicit images of her surfaced late Friday night.

I have always been one to take this sort of news with a pinch of salt. What most likely has happened is that woman did something with her own body and free will, and now she is being villainized for it. Like all click bait articles, it takes a while for the writer to get to point. They waffle on about exclusive resorts and high-end skincare, before showing a blurred out picture with the caption "NSFW".

I shouldn't have clicked.

Her face is half cut out of the shot because her curls, but I recognise the hideous dress she is wearing. The curves of her body are unmistakable to me already. Even in the grainy image, I can tell she isn't coherent. Hands grope where they shouldn't, with poorly placed peach emojis to make it safe enough to share online.

The Fields' family released a statement on Monday morning saying they have cut ties professionally and personally with their daughter, Delphini Fields. This follows eyewitness accounts of Delphini Fields fleeing the scene with her two unknown lovers.

I won't pretend to know how social media works. I have heard of influencers before, I know some of the tourists who take our tour make their living sharing their lives online. But it is not something I have engaged with beyond lurking and when searching for information. It is also a useful tool to throw off investigations into missing persons. The risk of bringing the police or questioning humans to my gangplank is too great for me to truly engage with it.

But this article makes it out that Delphini's life is over. The article ends with the announcement that her recent engagement has also ended and the unnamed fiancé, while devastated, will not be commenting on these revelations.

Fields has not responded to multiple inquiries or messages sent to her.

My blood boils.

For her and *at* her.

She hasn't responded because whoever took these pictures of Delphini killed her. If we had a proper conversation when she first awoke, I would have been able to do some research. Looked her up online to decide how we were going to handle her promise to Love.

Fuck knows what I am going to do now.

Every ounce of me is furious that a man would do such a thing to another, to so publicly shame and ruin them. This hits at something deeper in me, something darker that gnaws at my past, my own death. The tentacles beneath my skin surface and fight against my clothing for freedom.

A brush of a tentacle between my shoulders does nothing to calm me down. Love's presence with me instead of her does not lessen this fury inside of me. It is too familiar, our stories are not the same, yet we were each ruined. I resist the urge to pull up Delphini's social media, to search online. I don't need to see more of this vitriol.

I am at war with myself. Should I show her this article, or is it better she doesn't know? I know she misses having a phone. It's evident in the way she sometimes pats her sides like she is looking for the device.

She needs to know what has been done. There should be no surprises when she seeks her revenge so that when Miles begs for his life, she will revel in his weakness. I stand up and start towards her room. Delphini is on her hands and knees, with her upper half stuck under the bed. Her skirt has slid up and even though she's got matching pink booty shorts attached to this outfit, I am still getting a vision of her ass and thighs. No, this is not about how fucking hot I am for her and the shit I'm gonna share is going to hurt.

"Motherfucker," she groans, and then there is a scraping sound across the dark wood floors. "Gotcha."

She tosses a small safe onto the bed that I now see is laden with more clothes and toiletries. That is some fancy shit in that designer luggage. It doesn't matter; the task at hand is making sure my soulmate is informed.

"Delphini, I've got something you need to see," I say.

She doesn't look up from inputting the code into the safe. "What's up?"

It pops open and she's stacking a roll of cash, passports, and a jewellery box into her luggage.

"You told me you remember what happened."

She finally pauses what she's doing and looks up at me from her knees. Her eyes are wide, that all-consuming deep bronze colour is threatening to swallow me whole. And I want it to, because then I don't have to show her this. She nods her head for me to continue.

"I just saw a picture-"

"Of me," she interjects. Her voice is stern, accusatory, unlike the Delphini who speaks to me every day. It's like a punch in the gut. "I knew that they would get shared, part of the whole master plan."

"What plan?" I ask, my fingers clenched around my phone.

I don't know why I am angry at her. She has a right to her own fucking story. But I'm furious with myself as well. If I had done this right from the start. Everything would be different. We could have been different. There are people across the world who get to see her last horrid moments, and she's resigned to it.

"For Miles to get out of our sham engagement and gain access to my trust."

"Why the fuck didn't you say anything sooner?"

"Because what good would it have done?" She stands up now, and the note of anger in her voice calls to mine. "What could you possibly have done?"

"I know people, they can-"

"Can what? Erase lewd pictures from the internet? "She hurls her questions at me like she would a fist. "You say you want to help me, Orthia, then help me. I need to harness Love's power and get my revenge. What will hiding those pictures do for me now, Captain?"

With my title on her tongue, I couldn't stop myself from grabbing hold of her sweatshirt. There are tears in her eyes. Anger seeps from her pores and yet she holds onto her emotions so tightly. She's more controlled than I have ever been as she glares at me. Her breathing is harsh and warms my skin with shame.

"I gave everything up for this second chance at life, to be with my soulmate," she hisses. "And you've been cold this whole time, even when you say you want me. So don't act like seeing a glimpse of my past has changed you."

"You're right," I say, dragging her down until she is almost touching my nose. "I have been the worst possible soulmate for you. I have been cruel, and I don't know how to rectify that, Delphini. I have failed at every turn up to this point, but I will spend the rest of my days trying to make up for it if you'll let me."

When she licks her lips, she nearly touches mine. I feel the ghost of her heat on my skin and I want it. Though the words won't stop falling from my lips like the rain, I refuse to stop them now.

"You're right, seeing that photo is just a glimpse and change takes time, just like learning all the parts of you will take time. All I can promise is that even when I stumble, I am still changing for the better, for you."

She closes the distance between us. All her anger and hunger bleeds through the kiss as she grabs the side of my face. Her fingers curl into my short hair and scrape across my scalp as warmth explodes around me. I surge forward into her hold and my back bows into our embrace.

Her tongue traces my lips and she sucks the bottom one into her mouth when I refuse to open. I could push her down onto the bed behind us and show her real power, but I can't. Delphini doesn't deserve roughness. She deserves a tender love that shows her power is more than strength and anger. It's patience, understanding, and knowing when to let others in.

When her plush body presses into mine with a need for friction, I break the kiss. Her forehead rests against mine as we breathe each other in.

"I won't beg," she says, recalling my earlier promise. "That kind of play is earned."

"You're right. I haven't earned your submission yet, but will you let me show you how goddesses are honoured?" I ask. It's her choice if she wants to test the waters of our desires. This isn't a power play to show her what a dominant partner I can be. I am asking her as a priestess coming to worship at the altar of my goddess.

"Yes," she purrs, her nose tracing mine.

I push her suitcase onto the ground and gently lay my *omphalos* down on the delicate silk sheets. Her body sinks into the mattress as she relaxes and my heart warms. With one knee on the bed for balance, I lean over her. The sigh on her lips is soft, and I'm chasing it with a kiss. Her tongue dips into my mouth slowly and I let her explore. My hands trace the curves and dips of her slowly, squeezing her plush form until her hips rise for something more.

She tastes of minty toothpaste and need, but I have a promise to fulfil. I slide down her body until I can kneel between her spread thighs. The material of her dress has bunched up and the elastic shorts have ridden up to press into her pussy. Delphini leans up on her elbows to look at me. I stare at her through my lashes in awe at her beauty, at the hunger in her eyes.

"Tell me if I overstep," I murmur, kissing the stretch marks on her inner thigh and savouring the burst of warmth at our connection.

"Of course," she promises. "Can I touch you?"

I think of the first time she asked me that question. The awe for her I felt then seems immature now. It was a selfish thing that didn't take into account the full breadth of her wonder. She is vicious and hungry for revenge, yet she cares for me, for Love and I, like we were her lovers lost long ago at sea and now finally returned to her. There is intention and grace in everything she does.

"Guide me in how to worship you, my *omphalos*."

Delphini's hand brushes across my cheek. Her thumb pulls at my bottom lip until my tongue slips out and wraps around it. I draw it into my mouth and suck on it gently, just like I would her clit. Her eyes burn into me as I let go of it. Her fingers scratch against my scalp as she cups the back of my head. My skin tingles, and my clit throbs with how good this feels. A moan slips from my lips and her smile is brilliant.

Delphini guides my mouth to her covered pussy slowly, like she expects me to pull back like I have so many times before. I am not going to do that again. There will be no more confusion about how I hunger for her, desire her presence in every corner of my life. When my nose brushes against the seam of her shorts, my arms shoot out. I scoop up her thighs and press myself into her.

The phantom touch of Love's tentacles wrap around me, holding me to every part of our human we can touch. They purr in my head until it vibrates all the tension from my muscles. The smell of her musk drenches my underwear. I inhale the scent of my wife, rubbing my face against her cunt until I'm certain I have it memorised. Placing one of her thighs over my shoulder, I spread the other further apart so I can grab hold of her shorts and pull it to the side.

Delphini's pussy is hot and wet. She urges me back to her lushness and I let my tongue lead the way. The flavour of her bursts on my tongue, the suckers on it grasping at her folds to clean up every drop of her. Her arousal coats all of my senses until I believe I will drown in it. When a small tentacle wraps around my tongue, I groan.

"Fuck," Delphini moans as I suckle at her tentacle.

"You are divine," I proclaim, kissing her drenched pussy lips. "Unlike any being I have ever met, and all mine."

"Ours, heart, to worship and devour." Love whispers through my thoughts before I feel them slip to Delphini.

She gasps above me and pulls my gaze to her. Her eyes are the familiar milky white, Love is speaking to her. Are they encouraging her to command me? Her body shivers as she blinks.

"They are a devious god," she says. "Love says they will make you come, if you make me."

"Then I must rise to the call of our patron, shouldn't I?"

She grins as I seal my lips around her clit. Tentacles glide out of her pussy and grab at my fingers, holding her shorts to the side. They pull me to her until my finger is pressed inside of her.

"Is this what you need, wife? To come around my fingers?" I ask, pulling back to look at her again. If that is what she wants then I will give her my everything. I will work until my body is broken if that is what she wants.

"Yes." As she says the word, her cunt squeezes around me. There is a desperate calling in her voice now and I must answer.

"Thank you," I whisper with another kiss to her pussy. "You are such a good girl for me, wife. Lie back for me now, and let me worship this gorgeous pussy."

Her hand slips from my head as she does what I request. A slight shiver tracks down my spine at the loss of her heat, but the focus is not on my needs now. Instead, I go back to my altar, slowly stroking my finger in and out of her pussy. I listen to Delphini's moans of pleasure when I add my second finger.

As I fuck my fingers into her, my tongue flicks at her clit, teasing the hot bundle of nerves until she is moaning and bucking against my face. Her arousal drips around my fingers the more I work her up and press against that spongy spot against her walls. My cunt clenches as I try to drink up all of her. I want to devour every last drop of her blessings.

"Don't stop," she commands. "Don't stop."

I feel her body tighten and so does mine. Tentacles slip from my body and cover my pussy, latching onto my aching clit. The ghost feeling of Love's tentacles press between my thighs hard enough that I whimper into her pussy, sucking at her clit. More of my tentacles reach up to hold her thighs open for me. My free hand reaches up her body now, caressing every part of her it can reach until her fingers wrap around mine.

She stops breathing.

Then, the floodgates of her pleasure burst. Delphini's exhale is a moan that echoes around the room and my skull until there are tears in my eyes. We come together. Her pussy pulses around my fingers, and her clit twitches as I keep suckling at her, even as my hips grind back and forth with my own pleasure. Love's tentacles bind us tighter together. The three of us joined as one. Delphini moans again, and she melts into the bed. No doubt Love is purring for her now.

When she squeezes my hand, I slowly pull away from her.

"My perfect wife," I mumble, licking her folds and teasing her entrance. "The sweetest being to exist."

"Captain," she calls, and I rise to her, careful to remove my fingers from her pussy. She pulls me into a kiss, tasting her release on my tongue. "Take me home."

Chapter Fifteen
Delphini

3 Days

We clean up slowly, not worrying about the mess, but making sure our fingerprints aren't left behind on things they shouldn't be. As Orthia sweeps through Miles' room, I stuff my laptop into my suitcase and wait for her by the front door. I am happy to leave this place behind. There isn't a single memory that is worth keeping here. If I could scrub this part of my life from existence I would.

Scrubbing the people who ruined my life from existence will be enough for now.

Once she's done doing whatever she wanted to do in his room, Orthia pulls a giant marker from her pocket and writes on the pristine white walls over the couch, 'I know what you did'.

We don't speak again until we are standing on the crowded metro platform. In one hand, I have my stuffed suitcase, and in the other is her hand. With each brush of someone squeezing by us, she grips my hand a little harder, like she is chasing the warmth of our connection.

"I never would have come to Gwenmore if it weren't for that stupid engagement contact," I say.

"Something would have dragged you here," she leans on my shoulder. "Fate is cruel that way."

"You tried to fight it." I kiss the top of her head.

"Another failure on my growing list." She hums.

I huff, but don't disagree. Instead, I roll my neck to ease some of the tension in my body. The stabbing lesson worked a different kind of muscle that I'm not used to and now my body is mad at me for it.

Around us the platform eases a bit as a different train arrives and collects some of the people. It's stifling down here. I don't get how anyone can stand it. The noise and smells are enough to put me off this form of travel unless absolutely necessary.

"No, that's definitely her."

The whispered words might as well have been shouted. I glance back as subtly as I can. Behind us, taking up the whole fucking bench with their spread legs, are two men. They are finely dressed for a night out, their hairlines dotted with sweat and their eyes not capable of fully focusing.

"Take a picture."

I freeze. I can't stop my body from reacting to them, nor can I make myself stop the tears that form. My heart beats so loud it drowns out all the noise around me. There is a moment when Orthia lets go of my hand and it's replaced with the ghost of Love. They reach through the ether the best they can and wrap themselves around me, but it isn't enough I can't move.

"Hey, Delphini, right? You wanna take pictures with us? My buddies have never been with a fat-"

My chin trembles as I try to stand strong, but I am crumbling into a million pieces. I don't understand what's wrong with me. Tears slip down my cheek as the rushing sound grows and grows until it sounds like I am underwater. Suddenly, my body dips and Love takes control of me.

Love moves me onto the train and I know Orthia is standing over me, watching me, guarding me. Her petite frame overwhelms the deafening noise of the train moving and people talking too loud. All I see is her. The way her body doesn't even rock as the train jerks to a stop or sways into a turn. She is as steady as a lighthouse in a raging storm, but there is still so much ocean between us.

It's not that I see her with my eyes, but it is that Love feeds that information to my brain. They hum in a low tone that vibrates through my soul until I can't even think. My muscles loosen until I'm slumped into the plastic seat.

If Orthia is my lighthouse, then Love is a hot spring I've sunk into after a week on my feet.

They said I wouldn't feel fear again, but I do. From all the little things like spiders to the crushing weight of disappointing everyone. They were all there lurking behind a performance, a mask that I was stronger than what happened to me. It all came to the surface when those two guys spoke to me, tried to take a picture of me.

Love's phantom grip and sweeping control of me are welcome and soothing, thawing the ice that had frozen my muscles. I want to curl up under the warmth of Orthia and Love until this fear burns off of my skin. Until my tears are dry and there isn't a trace of shame left on me.

There is no place for that emotion in my life, there wasn't a place for it in my old life, but I can't stop it. I knew about the photos. This isn't the first time randoms have recognised me on the street, but something about this encounter hurts. There is a wrenching feeling in my chest that I can't get a grip on. I'm not the kind of famous person who encounters paparazzi regularly. If we were invited to an event, our pictures would ultimately be taken, but I was scandal-free and respectable in the eyes of the public.

My whole life imploded when I called out that designer, and everything since then has been trying to crush me. Those pictures were the last straw. I avoided thinking about it because I reasoned it wasn't worth the thought. I gave up that old life to be here. Why should I linger on something that is not part of the new Delphini brand?

But why am I boiling my life down to a brand? I am more than that, more than what I show people on social media. Those parts of me I keep secret that I knew would upset my family were hard kept. All my plans for the future; leaving Chicago behind to be with *Yiayia*; finding a purpose for my life, becoming more than a brand and doing something good with my life.

Those parts of me don't have to be secret, not any more.

Yet all that guilt and fear are still there. Like I've dived into the water and been refusing to surface because I'm scared of what will happen when I do. I'm scared to see the person I am when I am free to breathe and be myself.

Everything about my life has been held under a microscope, from my parents to head teachers at prep schools to my engagement to Miles. It is well documented with academic awards, sports trophies, and witty social media posts, so much information about me is public knowledge that I am not sure what part of me is performing for them and what part is real. I can't look into the world of the past me and assess myself. I'm not under the microscope and I'm so lost now. There isn't a thing about my new life that I've documented.

If it weren't for those fucking creeps, I honestly would have been a ghost. No one cares that I'm not around any more. It's liberating and terrifying. My mind can't make itself up about how to feel as these thoughts roll through my head like old workout tapes until the frame freezes on that fact again.

Who is the real me?

Orthia may have blundered through trying to tell me something I already knew would be true, but she never said, "People are looking for you; they hope you're okay."

Because nobody cares now that I am not performing for them.

I don't remember getting back to the ship. Love moves my legs, and Orthia holds onto my hand like she's worried I'll drift away. Which almost makes me cry. She tends to me like I am a wounded animal to be rescued, but she doesn't really want me. There's a physical pull between us, whether that is pure lust or some sort of soulmate magic I don't know.

The warmth radiating up my arm into my heart from her light touch is overwhelming, dizzying. It reminds me of the first time I tried the sauna with my *Yiayia*. She came to Chicago for Christmas only to complain so much about the blistering cold wind that Mom booked us a whole weekend spa. Little twelve-year-old Delphini sat on that wooden bench until she nearly passed out just to feel like she belonged.

Maybe it's blood rushing to my head from laying down. Orthia tucks me into my bed and looks down at me. Her hand cups my cheek again like it did on Tuesday night and Love slips away from me. My muscles seize as a shiver so fierce racks down my spine. They were keeping me loose, but now I am so tense I ache all over again.

"Tomorrow, we shall train, plot your revenge, and your wounds will scar."

That's not what I want though.

Revenge, yes. I want to see all four of them hanging from their toes, begging for my forgiveness. I want them to feel how I did. That confusion and violation that I felt, Miles and Audrey are going to experience that on another level. All before I channel Love's power to draw out their essence to feed my new god. It's a win for me and a win for them.

It's the scars I don't want. My skin is stitched together with stretch marks that I have taken years to come to appreciate. I love my body, and I love taking care of it in all its glory.

The internal ones that are a phantom pain, a flinch when someone touches me, a hyper-vigilance I have never needed before. Those are the scars I don't want.

My life has been one of luxury, and with that came a sense of ease because I was always taught to be cruel to get what I want.

I should have been able to be cruel to those men, too. Every instinct I had was to strike. To not take those words lying down, yet I was frozen on the spot. There was no fight or flight, I froze like a weak bit of prey. I should have turned around and shoved that phone down one of their throats to send a message.

"A pleasing thought, sweet one, but those scars will keep you safe. Your instincts are evolving, just as you have." Love's soothing voices echo in my head, bringing tears to my eyes again.

It's a terrifying and comforting thought. I am changed, irreparably.

Some things can't be changed, though. I am still filled with anger. There is blood in the water; some of it may be mine, but it's theirs as well. The people who thought they could get rid of me so easily. It is time I start taking these matters into my own hands.

Orthia is right. Tomorrow I will begin my own hunt, and I know the weakness I will target first. It's time I seized control of my revenge. I told her our relationship wasn't a distraction, and I will show her just what I can do. She will see what it is like when I hunt for the prey I have promised to feed our Love.

"Sleep in peace, my *omphalos*," she whispers.

I don't know what that means. She kisses my forehead, though, and the ghost of her lips on my skin is like a kiss from the sun. My Greek isn't perfect, but it feels sacred when she calls me by that name.

When she slips from my room though, I am bombarded with thoughts about my life. How every single thing I have ever done for it was all pointless. Love said my fate had been split into paths when we first met. My life was always going to turn up this way.

There was nothing I could have done to change that night. No amount of performing or rebelling for my parents' affection would have changed my ending. Something would have brought me here, according to Orthia, something would have happened, and I would have ended up in the water.

All that shit my parents used to spew about blood being thicker than water meant nothing to them. They saw a weakness in their blood, and rather than helping it, they had it drawn out. Since the incident, they have done nothing to find me or defend me.

When the restlessness in my head reaches my fingers, I dig through my suitcase and pull out my laptop. In only a few strokes, I set up a burner account and a VPN to fool my location settings. On muscle memory, I check my socials and my emails. Despite Orthia's efforts to keep me in the dark, I'm a regular human who needs access to the internet.

I look up every single person. I need to know everything that I've missed. Lottie has sent me a few messages. In the days following the leak of those photos, she tried to check up on me, called Miles every name under the sun and told me that even Teddy Bushwhipper was doing everything in his power to get the source of those pictures found.

The tears nearly ruin my laptop; I can't get them to stop. Whenever I type out a message to either of them, the right words won't come to me. How do I explain my current situation to them without giving away everything I have learned about the world? Instead, I send a simple message from my burner accounts and hope it doesn't end up in Lottie's spam folder.

I'm okay. You'll see.

Chapter Sixteen
Orthia

My body threatens to come apart at the seams. I am barely holding myself together. Every moment I spend with Delphini, I want to tear off her clothes and devour her. I want to consume every part of her and make her suffer so sweetly that she begs for me. She invades my every thought, but I must be patient before I push for more. I want to give her time to heal after what I saw at her old flat and after what happened on the metro.

She'll come to me when she's ready, right?

"Janet called," Aoife states, rolling her neck. "This month's donation is much appreciated. The Dallas office had an incident with the police, and they were scrambling for extra funds."

I hum along, just barely listening as I pull at a loose thread on my long sleeve. Janet is the director of donations for our charity for women, and she calls about once a month to update us on how things are. I helped a previous crew member set up this charity at the start of the twentieth century to spread our message. The Saints for Love Women's Charity is one of the oldest in the world and we have centres in almost every country.

The Princess's Despair has been their principal benefactor from the beginning. Most of that money comes from the wealth I have collected from centuries of pirating. It's more than I would ever know what to do with, so spending it to further our cause makes good use of the capital. I am the head of the damn thing in name only because every other monster I have attempted to give the title to has refused. Apparently, I am a symbol of some kind.

"When is it too soon to ask someone if they are ready for more intimacy?" I ask, but I'm not really interested in a finance report.

"They normally tell me, Captain," Aiofe says, lounging further back into the steaming bath until only her chin is above the water. "Or they come to the bath like any other crewmates."

Tourist season is officially rolling. Our boat tours are booked for every trip, and the crew works around the clock to ensure The Despair is in tip-top condition. Even now, Nargol and the night shift are replacing some ropes along sails that snapped during our evening check.

Everyone knows that staying open means money in our pockets to help tide us over when the season ends and we go back to the more challenging job of fishing.

It also means that when we aren't on shift, a good portion of the crew has taken to lounging in the bath to soothe sore muscles. A few of the sirens have taken to sleeping beneath the ship again to rejuvenate in the salty waters overnight.

"Delphini hasn't been here yet," I state.

"Only she can tell ya if she wants more," Cookie says.

Her harpy sits between her large legs, receiving a massage after nearly pulling her shoulder this afternoon. I catch a whiff of the balm they are using and grunt. They should use mine, it's better. I walk to the far side of the room and dig through the jars until I find my special reserve to use on Hamako.

Centuries at sea of watching life after life be lived to completion have given me a great appreciation for taking care of one's physical form. Balms, salves, oils, herbs; they are all things I took an interest in when I quickly realised that, unlike my compatriots, I would not get to rest amongst Love's tentacles for eternity because my life will never end. The tinctures I make are infused with a drop of Love's power to aid in healing and calming my crew.

It takes some searching to find the right jar of oil, but once I do, I toss it at Cookie, who easily catches it in her massive hand. Hamako's moan of pleasure is enough to tell me she might not be in as much pain as she let on. Cookie will pamper her anyway with the way she is wrapped around the harpy's tiniest talon.

The troll tosses the oil back to me and it's only when I'm setting it down that I slip and knock over a jar that I have long tried to forget. The one piece of that place that still exists. A jar that I should have filled with offerings to the goddess before I promised myself to her. It's never been filled with anything. When I made my promise to Love, I gave them myself– mind, body, and soul. The terracotta figure jar has sat atop many ships and shelves, but when the bath was constructed, I buried it amongst my others to finally forget about it.

Now, scattered across the tiles is a handful of pearls. The colours vary from a pure white to a deep, almost purple, brown shade. They sparkle in the low lamp light. I turn back to stare at the still-fresh mosaic on the wall that now depicts a Wolfen creature on two legs lapping at the cunt of a mermaid.

"Has someone been pearling?" I ask, staring back at the gemstone.

"Too early in the season," Aiofe says. "Why?"

I don't answer her. The tipped-over figure stares at me, and I know where these have come from. I recognise these high-quality pearls like I recognise my own fucking face. In a swoop, I pocket the pearls into my loose trousers and push my slides back on. The women in the bath stare at me as I pass by them to leave, their curious looks following me out of the door.

Since Delphini's arrival on the ship, I have been different. The crew aren't wary of the new human, but I am. That hasn't stopped me from giving her extra attention. I have rationalised with myself that it is simply because she is human. She doesn't have the predator instinct that monsters do. That's why I have spent nearly a fortnight with her in our training facilities. It's the least I can do to prepare her for this life.

Delphini is more capable than most. She trains without complaint. Even as her limbs shake and sweat drips down her neck, she will attack again. I remember her reaction that first morning when I grabbed her. It curdles in my stomach that my touch has brought that reaction to her.

She can't freeze up if the prey she hunts grabs hold of her. The four people she must kill will consider themselves untouchable. Even after the message she left, they will still believe they are predators.

She must show them they aren't.

"She is more ready than you know." Love's claim echoes around my skull.

I roll my eyes as I leave the bath. As if I can't see her potential, her strength. But now, I crave something more from her. To hear Delphini beg for my touch.

The crew have welcomed her with open arms and the sight of it makes the dead thing in my chest skip. But I crave more than the domestic intimacy of it all. The lightness she has found on my ship is important, but I want to see the darker side of Delphini again. Coated in blood and rage, demanding and begging for me all at the same time.

We are going to have a long discussion about *everything*.

I stuff my hands into my pocket and swirl the pearls between my grip. Love is absent from my thoughts, as they have been recently. Maybe that is why I am voicing concern aloud and half complete to my crew. Without them in my thoughts at all times, I can't bear the silence of it.

I'm past my anger at having to share them with her. Delphini needs Love's steady reassurance and conviction as much as I do, and as much as it pains to be without them, it causes an ache much deeper in my chest, knowing she is entirely alone.

My sandals slap across the tiled floor as I march down to her room. Normally, this late in the evening, the door is shut. My human has locked herself away for the night. It's open now.

Delphini's quarters are the same layout as most of the crews; spacious room meant to house a being of any size, and substantial en suite. The only thing I don't allow in these rooms is food. Not because I am worried about pests, but because eating meals together is an integral part of camaraderie and trust.

Her room is an odd mix of the things she bought and things she brought from her old apartment. The old quilt from a previous crew member still lay on her bed, but I see the luxury she is holding on to.

Pink silks and knits draped in her wardrobe that is now so full it doesn't close. There are a plethora of shoes lining a wall. I am not even sure when she would wear those high-heeled shoes, but she brought them. A desk tucked into the corner is now littered with makeup and...

There is also a laptop.

Where the fuck did she get that?

I don't remember that from her old place, and I am certain no one on this ship would have given her that. She is supposed to be keeping a low profile, not only has she already killed one man without a plan, but she has also started her first stage of revenge against her ex. Certain people believe that she is dead or possibly back from the dead. If she leaves a trace of her existence outside of that incident at the apartment, people will look for her.

I walk into her room and flip the laptop open. The metal case is warm to the touch, meaning she used it recently. The display screen lights up and prompts me for a password. How the fuck am I supposed to know that? The little question mark near the side that offers a hint doesn't help either.

'*Yiayia's* first product.'

That's all it says, and those words mean nothing to me when strung together. I sneer at the screen and slam the lid shut. While Delphini is polite and friendly with the crew during mealtimes, there is one crew member who seeks her out regularly.

Nargol leans against the railing and stares off into the sea. She doesn't turn around when I approach her, but there is a shift in her body, a gesture of openness.

"Captain," she smiles, the blunt ends of her tusks touching her scarred top lip. "What can I do ya for?"

"Have you seen Delphini?" I follow her gaze across the water and see her focus is on the party happening on the opposite side of the pier. When the wind picks up just right, I can hear the beat of the music.

"Not since after dinner," she frowns at that, "she seemed really shaken yesterday. Maybe she's trying to find a quiet place to meditate."

I nod. This isn't right. It's hard to not know where someone is in this crew. The pocket dimension is only so big, and with her seasickness, it isn't like she would be hiding outside of it.

"She's not in her room," I explain.

"Sure, she's around somewhere, probably doing one of her fancy face masks."

Nargol grunts but doesn't take her eyes off the party. My duty to my human and my duty to my crewmates are split as I look at my gunner. Her green skin is hidden under the cover of darkness, but I know she craves the sun. The days when we are in the open water and without a human in sight.

There are ways to hide in plain sight.

"You know, I could talk to-"

"Captain," she cuts my suggestion off. "No disrespect to your relationship with the city's mayor, but not even in the pain of death would I allow that blood traitor to give me anything. No good orc would. He's cursed."

"You deserve happiness," I counter. "Why are you letting something from a world that casts you out guide you now?"

"I could say the same damn thing to you."

It is my turn to grunt, changing the subject once more. "Fine, you're getting a week off soon. You're too pale."

She cracks a smile but doesn't say anything contrary as I take my leave. I sweep the lower decks, but there isn't any sign that Delphini is even on the ship. There is a rushing sound in my ears when I go back to my quarters. I pass by her open door and move faster until I am running. There is nothing here that would indicate she entered my quarters without asking. My room is dark, the lamp light so low it might as well not have been lit.

"Love," I growl into the emptiness, but they don't respond.

I go back to her room. Every instinct I have tells me that Delphini has left the ship. She's not here resting; she's not tucked away somewhere else to train on her own. I flip the laptop open again and pull out my phone.

Her social media is easy enough to find and pull up. A time capsule of before she was murdered, the last update she has is the morning of it. She's wearing a pink tennis dress with a matching pink sweater over the top. Her sunglasses are pulled down enough to see her coyly wink at the camera. There is a green drink next to her and she's glowing under the sunlight.

It's simple, but I can't stop watching her. It's like she fucking winked at me, like she is teasing me. Rationally, I know she isn't, which is why I click the link on her page and begin my deep dive into the person Delphini was before she joined the crew.

There is so much and yet so little information. I should have done better.

It's overwhelming to see so much surface-level information about my human. She is clearly successful at whatever she was doing for her family's business. Every charity or gala they have sponsored she was there, dressed impeccably and smiling with ease. She isn't listed on their website, but she wouldn't be if they have disowned her. Her parents have basically no social media presence. It takes me five minutes of scrolling to find an old picture of Delphini sitting with an older woman. She is not as dark as Delphini, her skin more olive-toned, but they have the same eye shape and the same smile. Both of them are holding glasses of wine with a skyline that strikes me to my core.

I know that skyline. The familiar wash of blue ocean dotted with cliffs. My vision blurs as I see it in my mind's eyes, smelling the salty air as I watch my island disappear beneath the sea. Love swallowing up the whole land mass as I wait a safe distance away on a ship I stole.

A shiver racks through my body as I read the Greek written in the caption. *My light is leaving me after a summer of sun and wine.* This must be her *Yiayia*. It only takes a few more clicks before I have the name of the product. Some pomegranate-infused clay face mask claiming to heal sun-damaged skin.

The laptop unlocks right where Delphini left off. There is an open browser with a list of organisations, most of them crossed off, along with a schedule of events at the Harbour Crest Yacht Club. Tonight, they are closed for a private event. Two weeks from now they are hosting a regatta. A few weeks after that there is a charity auction and banquet being held. I ignore those future events; they don't have any bearing on where she could be right now. Flipping through a few more tabs I see the dress code for a high-end club pulled up.

There are also reviews, pictures, surrounding bars and clubs, anything Delphini could find pulled up.

She is hunting.

I don't know which of the men she is after. Miles is the only name I know, but she said there were four of them. Maybe she doesn't know the other three? I grit my teeth. This is too dangerous. She is going to end up getting herself killed going in blind to a situation like this.

Delphini isn't ready to kill for Love yet. She hasn't been able to focus her power enough to even summon them on the practice jelly yet. If they find her and she can't do it right, it will fuck everything up. It will kill her. There will be no choice but for Love to take her as retribution. A promise is a promise, her essence would belong to them.

I will have failed both of them if she doesn't succeed.

My fingers dig into my pocket, the pearls easily crushed in my palm at the thought of her gone. Rage swells in my gut.

Where is she?

Chapter Seventeen

Orthia

2 Days

This club is nowhere near my usual hunting grounds. We are a fair distance from the water, closer to the historic district than the bay. On a Saturday night, there is a long queue wrapped around the front entrance. People dressed in their expensive clothing, smoking and shouting at one another. Most of them already smell of alcohol.

This is also not a monster-owned club. The man at the door is a human as they come, meaning I will actually have to work to get inside.

There is not a chance in this life that I will stand and wait to get into this place. I tug the sleeves of my billow top lower over my wrists while I walk around the block to get a view of the back alleyway. There are a couple of security lights, one car with blacked-out windows, and a long row of dumpsters. The car's engine is turned off, and when I shove my face up against the glass, it is empty. *Good.* I don't need some random fuck getting in the way of me dragging my human out of this place.

I scope out the back door to the club, waiting for someone to come out for a break or to take the bins out. The longer I am left standing there, the more my body demands that I move. To break down the door and cause a scene.

That would blow her cover though, put us both at risk and then I might have to kill more people than I could explain away to Deg'Doriel. This is a good operation we have going, but if I have to leave because of this, it isn't that bad, I suppose.

Delphini is worth it.

I blow out a heavy breath, my fingers running through my buzz cut. *Shit.* She really is worth it, getting kicked out of the group and uprooting our entire gig here. I'd do it for her, to keep her safe.

When the fuck did I start thinking like this?

There isn't time to examine all my feelings about Delphini Fields because the door finally opens. It takes no effort to sneak in before the door closes. The kitchen staff ignore me, not paid nearly enough to care, as I stalk through the crowded main floor. Lights flash and fake, sweet-smelling smoke swirls around the feet of crushed bodies on the dance floor. The loud music pumping through the sound system is some sort of new electric shit that makes my ears ring. It's a crush, pushing through the crowd is nearly impossible as my body shivers with every brush of these people. The bar is as crowded, and every person I look at could be a threat. I stand to the side, trying to push myself up a bit higher on the bar to see over everyone's heads.

Not a speck of pink on this fucking dance floor. Between flashes of light, the wide arc of the beams, and projections on the ceiling, I'm sure if Delphini were here, I would have seen her. Even if there was no light, I am confident I would be able to find her in this room. She is my human, my fucking *omphalos*.

"Hey, you want a drink?" the bartender shouts at me over the noise.

I give her a look, though I keep the derision to myself. That sort of energy I am saving to unleash on Delphini for running away.

"I'm looking for my girlfriend. She's like this tall, really pretty hair, pink outfit?"

Using those prescriptive words to describe someone as complex as Delphini causes a pain in my chest. She is so much more than those things. There is so much of her that I have only scratched the surface of due to...

"Stubbornness."

My eyes flutter closed as the ghost of Love's tentacles wrap around my chest and neck. The weight of them settles the rabid energy shaking through me and their voices drown out the gods awful music playing here.

"She is here, but to find her, you must prove you want her just as much as she desires you."

My outfit tonight should be proof enough that I desire Delphini. I'm here pushing through a crowd of people, feeling their icy touch with every jostle and shimmy people make, all while wearing a pair of skintight leather pants. These fucking trousers were the only thing in that costume room that would fit the dress code.

I feel fucking ridiculous in this.

The closer to the centre of the crush I get, the colder I become. There is no way to avoid the touch of so many humans. They move in practised motions with their hands raised above their heads so they can fit tighter together. It's taking all my willpower to stay focused, to not react with every snag of my shirt sleeves. I want to punch and stab each one of these fucking humans for being so close to me. Even Love's fading touch has not calmed enough to be able to cope with these cretins.

If completing this test, if finding her, is what it takes? I will do it over and over again until she is satisfied.

It's not until I think I am going to have to stab someone to get any further through the crowd that I catch a glimpse of her signature pink. Delphini dances in the middle of the room, completely surrounded by other women. They move in unison with her, bodies reacting to each sway of her hips.

This is where she is always meant to be. She is the centre of the club, the centre of this universe—a sacred beacon calling everyone to her glory.

Her gaze zeroes in on something overhead. Tucked into a dark corner, there is a raised platform roped off. She barely blinks as she watches a couple be allowed to pass the ropes.

Unceremoniously, I shove the woman in front of Delphini away.

"Delphini," I shout over the noise.

Her eyes flick to me, volleying between the VIP section and me like she can't decide where her focus should be, until she grabs the front of my shirt. In a quick twirl, she has my back pinned to her front with her hand resting on my hip. Warmth swallows me in waves as her thumb tucks into the low waist of my trousers.

"How did you find me?" she hisses in my ear, but all I can focus on is the pure warmth radiating from my hip and spreading between my legs. "I'm doing this whether you think I am ready or not."

I am not a dancer. Performing my final battle is the closest I get to keeping a beat to something, but Delphini is perfectly capable of moving my heated body against hers to match that of those around us. The music changes to something that, while just as high temp, is more sensual. The hand that is not on my hip gently touches my wrist until she has my hand placed on her neck. My fingers trace her pulse and her hold on me grows tighter until I believe she is trying to leave a mark on me.

Her grip lessens slightly, but her lips touch my jaw. The heat of her body on mine makes my skin vibrate, Love's power seeping to the surface. The markings that cover my body turn slick and tentacles writhe beneath, ready to come out and feast on whatever offerings I have for them. A thin tendril slips free of my trousers and wraps around Delphini's thumb. A shaky breath breezes over my cheek.

"You aren't the only one whose body is a temple."

"Like these fucking leather pants weren't enough to ruin me?" she taunts.

"If you want me to ruin you, my *omphalos*, you will have to beg for it."

"Later," she promises with another kiss to my jaw. "I'm not leaving without blood."

My lips brush her neck when I turn my head up towards her. "Then show me you have learned something, wife... And maybe I will reward you."

It's as if her hands pull away when her attention moves from me back to the VIPs. Her pelvis is still pressed to mine, her soft stomach moulded to my lower back, but she turns us slightly. A small group of people are leaving the section. My senses focus, and I scan each of their faces as if they could be the man Delphini is hunting tonight. They are a sloppy group, spilling their drinks as they stumble towards the direction I entered the club. The bathrooms. It's an easy guess what they will be doing in there if Miles is any indication of the crowd she used to be a part of.

My hands itch to take over, to simply kill them for her and get this over with so we can get back to the ship. Those few hours where I couldn't find her were enough. The stars, the fates, the meddling of an ancient god, whatever has tied our souls together, will stop at nothing until we are one. They do not care that I want to hear her beg, and at this point, I simply hunger for the taste of her on my tongue. We have eternity to bathe in our carnal desires.

But I have to let her do this. She has a promise to keep to our Love, this is her kill, and I shall help her finish this however she needs me to. For many, this first revenge kill is the hardest, but she has already proven more than capable of doing that part.

It's summoning Love's power I am worried about. She's only done it once in training. Will she be able to unleash her anger now that her target is personal?

Or will this be the end of her?

I snap back to attention as we start moving towards the bathrooms. Bodies continue to brush up against mine, but Delphini's hand on my hip negates it. I can almost forget they are even here with her beside me. They don't pay us any attention either as we weave through the crush.

My pulse rushes in my ears, like the steady beat of the sea against The Despair in winter. I can't hear the music any more; all there is is the thrumming of Love's hunger in my veins. She is going to do this.

I believe in Delphini.

The quiet in the bathroom is more unsettling than the horrible music being played in the club that is trying to bleed through the walls. I quickly take in the room; minimal, sleek black fixtures with as few flat surfaces as possible and two toilet stalls. One with the door open and the other with three pairs of high heels underneath.

We are recreating a scene from one of those horrible mafia movies Ramón likes. It's an overdone trope in those films, but I guess if it works, it works. Don't fix something that isn't broken, as Aiofe tells me every time I make a fuss about the ship or the pocket dimension.

I wait for my directions.

Delphini motions for me to stand by the sinks while she steps into a stall. It doesn't bother me one bit what we are about to do. I know Ramón would try to sink his claws into me if he knew my human was planning on killing a woman. But if this human hurt something that is mine? She is going to deserve every second of pain that Delphini gives her.

You don't hurt other women to gain false power over them.

The whole plan is still a mystery to me, so I busy myself by washing my hands. I stare through the mirror at her. Shadowed by the half-closed door, Delphini looks like a harbinger of death wrapped in a blush pink dress. The silky material shines in the artificial light and my thoughts are out of my control again.

They are simply on her. On sliding the hem of that shift up until I can cup her pussy in my hand, feel the centre of her warmth for the first time. How wet she will be for me as I tease her nipples until they ache. Love, the marks I will leave on her skin. The deep, circular bruises from my tentacles, once I place them on her, will never truly fade. I won't be able to stop the suckers from latching on to her any chance I can get. They will mark her as mine just as Love's has.

"Leave, I need to pee," one of the women whines.

Delphini's eyes meet mine, giving a small signal for me to stay where I am. Two thin white women slip from the stall without even pretending they need to wash their hands. One of them does the truly foul thing of licking her phone screen while the other one snickers.

They don't even question the half-closed stall door before they stumble out of the bathrooms. I roll my eyes. Bad instincts.

The one left in the stall finishes up and flushes. I step away from the sink and stand in front of the door. There's no lock, which is smart, I suppose. No club-goers can lock themselves in here to fuck or do something worse with no one able to reach them.

Doesn't mean I can't jam the thing closed with my knife. The blade slips between the frame and door above the top hinge, forming a makeshift stopper. She is utterly oblivious to my existence. She sways on her feet as she tries to wash her hands, giggling all the while. Honestly, this is concerning now.

If she dies of blood alcohol poison or shitty designer drugs, I will bring her back from whatever pit she crawls into so my *omphalos* can slay her properly.

Finally, when she turns to leave, she sees me. It says something, not only about the overindulgence of mind-altering substances, but of this woman that she is so wildly unaware of her surroundings. I can't remember a time in my life when there wasn't a level of vigilance I kept. Even as a child, I remember my mother taking me aside and telling me to always be wary of strange folk, be they gods or enemies.

Now this unknowing woman is about to meet the one true god.

She scowls at me as I cross my arms over my chest. Purposefully, I look her up and down. She wears chunky high heels, the kind that has recently come back into style, a skimpy skirt number with a matching top, and her blonde hair is loose. She's got her phone on some sort of corded leash draped over one shoulder. But that is it. She's nearly identical to the two women who left before her, yet I see ugliness in her that I didn't see in the others.

Her outfit is so tight, I know there can't be a hidden weapon on her.

"Move, bitch."

I don't respond to her. I simply look over her shoulder where Delphini rests with a hip against the sink. She is inspecting her cuticles as if she has all the time in the world. Everything about her paints a beautiful and calm picture, not at all one of rage or murder.

"Audrey Paine."

The words are barely out of Delphini's mouth and Audrey is scrambling to get past me. I throw my arm out and catch her around the waist. Curses leave her mouth like they are racing to a finish line, but I ignore them and the chill. I drag her to the far wall, away from the one visible weapon in the room and wait for Delphini's next move.

"You are supposed to be dead," Audrey whimpers. "We watched you go down. You sank like a fat fucking rock."

My hand is around her throat before I can think to stop myself. "You do not speak to her in that regard again."

"Captain." Delphini's voice when she calls my title now is dripping with sin and I want nothing more than to be done with this hunt so I may roll around in her warmth for all time. My whole body shivers and I feel the tentacles under my skin pulse with our combined excitement.

Audrey lets out crocodile tears as she nods to what I have said, even as my hand moves to the base of her throat so my palm can rest on her chest.

"Do I look dead?" Delphini asks. "I feel very much alive, but you wanted me to feel something else, didn't you? What was it you said? My memory of that night is a bit hazy."

She starts blubbering louder, and snot trickles down over her lips. If it touches me, I may have to kill her myself.

"Please, I'm sorry. I'm sorry. Miles said-he said-said that it would be easy money."

"Murder is easy money to you, Paine?" I can't keep my mouth shut, and I don't care. She hurt my human for money?

"Yes-no, no, it wasn't easy. She weighs a fuck ton," she slurs.

Before, when Delphini wasn't in my life, I wasn't an impulsive person. Now? Now, I can't even form a full thought before my body reacts. I slam my fist into this rich piece of shit's face and she crumbles to the floor, passed out.

CHAPTER EIGHTEEN
DELPHINI

13 Days

H oly shit, that was hot.

Everything about her is hot in those fucking pants, but watching her punch Audrey's lights out? That is something I will stow away in my head to daydream about endlessly until I die. But now we have a new problem on our hands.

"For fucks sake, now we have to carry her."

Orthia, with blood on her fist, gives me a look that I would call patronising on anyone else, and maybe she is trying to be like that with me. This is an unplanned outing and probably against captain's orders. I can already hear the girls whispering about how the captain is going to put me back on dish duty.

But I was tired of sitting around on the ship, hiding away in our void. My revenge is on my timeline, and each day I don't track them down, the more they will think they are better than me. I don't want them to believe they beat me.

"We don't have time for sass. Grab my knife from the door. We are taking this to the alley." Orthia drapes Audrey's arm over her shoulder and wraps her around her.

"Oh, are you just going to drag an unconscious woman through a club?"

"Yes, we are. What were you planning on doing?"

I reach up and take the short, bladed dagger from the door frame. The golden handle is longer than the steel. It looks ridiculous, but knowing Orthia, this thing will be sharp as fuck.

"Three inches, legal to carry around the city as a concealed weapon. Now, let's go before she wakes up." She urges me onward. "Last thing I want to do is give this woman the show of me punishing you before you kill her."

Heat rushes to my cheeks. I'm not against an audience on occasion, but punishment? Oh, I am definitely not letting that comment drop. What does Orthia think a punishment is? Is this a part of her need to hear me beg?

"Yes, Captain," I say before I can think harder on it.

I hand Orthia back her knife and watch her slip it into a sheath in her long, over-the-knee boots. I can't take my eyes off her legs now that I can see them in the light with complete focus. She has never worn such revealing clothes before. Sure, her shirt is still buttoned all the way to the stop, but it's thin. I can see the sports bra she has on underneath.

If I think about those trousers again, I am going to have to peel them off her muscular thighs in whatever alley she is going to drag us into.

During her performances on the ship, she wears that corset belt, but always with a heavy overcoat. Even on the days when the sun beats against the dark wood of the ship, she doesn't take that teal thing off. But this look? This is the look of a pirate queen, a woman who will ruin any man who so much as glances in her direction.

It's a wet dream.

"The door, Delphini."

She doesn't sound annoyed that I am gawking at her. I take that for the win that it is and open up the door to the bathroom. There is a small queue of people waiting outside, but none of them look like staff. I put on an apologetic smile and shoo away any concern for 'my friend'.

"She fell and hit her face. We're gonna get some ice from the kitchen." Which I hope to fucking god is the direction Orthia is leading us in, because like fuck do I know where that is.

My plan was to coerce Audrey out of the club and make her pay for a taxi to the docks. She's high enough on coke to stay awake, but drunk enough not to fight me too hard. I don't know if this is a better option yet, but I am not the one with experience in premeditated murder.

Orthia is, so I'm following her lead.

I squeeze in front of her to pull open the door for her. Not a single head looks twice at us as we walk through the kitchen. Orthia moves around the stainless-steel square like she owns the place. I follow behind her and keep my focus firmly on the floor until she is at another door. As she waits for me, she shuffles Audrey on her shoulder. As she groans and rolls her bloody head to the side, Orthia raises her eyebrows at the door. I have to shove the door to get it to open, but when I do, light floods the alley and we are off into the night. The heavy door slams closed with such a clank I jump and look around. We are utterly alone out here unless you count the rats.

"Holy shit," I whisper. "That really worked."

"Why are you whispering?" Orthia swings around like the woman in her arm isn't more than a small purse.

She drops Audrey next to the dumpster and looks at me. The faint light from behind casts her in shadows and my brain is jumping from one fantasy to the next because Orthia now looks like a 90s vampire wet dream.

Fuck.

One dance, one little fix of a soft touch from her, and I am falling apart at the seams. I can barely stand in the same room with her without craving her warmth, without desperately trying to hold myself to any standard of decorum after she told me I'd have to beg for her to touch me again. It's no surprise all it takes is a little bump and grind for me to ruin a perfect pair of panties. I am ready to burst into flames at the next brush of her against my skin. I crave it. I need it like I need air in my lungs.

It's now or never to have this conversation. It's the worst time I can think of, but I am not sure I will be able to keep my hands off her long enough once we get back to the ship.

"Do you want to have sex with me?" I blurt out.

Have I had multiple conversations with partners in the past about needs, wants, limits? Absolutely. Are any of these skills transferring over right now? No.

"Obviously, Delphini."

Audrey groans, but doesn't do much else. I tear my eyes away from Orthia to look at her, but she still passed out.

"At what point should we be concerned about that?" I point down at her.

"We can give her a few more minutes." Orthia crosses her arms over her chest and the billowy fabric makes her shoulders look even broader, more tempting. "Now, do you want to have sex with me?"

"Of course I do. I've wanted you to fuck me or for you to let me fuck you since day one. Even after you threw me in a fucking prison cell."

We are gravitating closer together. I don't know at what point during that small confession it started, but we don't stop until we are nearly chest to forearms. The storm that surrounds her engulfs me, too. Like some kind of whirlwind that is pulling us closer and closer. I look down at Orthia and there is that hunger in her eyes, just like the night in the training room.

"Ground rules?" She asks the question like we are about to have a fight and not like we are discussing bedroom preferences.

"I like being submissive for sex only," I say, taking a step closer to her until our shoes nearly touch. "My preferred safe word system is traffic lights. I don't like being gagged unless I'm drowning in pussy."

"I know you want to be praised, but do you want to be my good girl or my pretty slut?"

A shiver courses down my spine, my tentacles pulsing at the possibility of both. Orthia smirks as she flexes her biceps.

"I'm a good girl, but sometimes," I lean forward until our breath mingles and I can almost taste her. "I like being naughty, Captain."

Her eyes dip for a moment to the swooping neckline of this dress, where just the tip of my tentacle etching peaks out between my cleavage. I smile at the show she is trying to put on for me.

Then it falters for a moment. A phantom pain in my wrist and a sudden rush of feeling in my stomach make me feel like I'm falling and have me turning a bit cold. The smile drops from my lips as a sinking sensation overcomes me.

"I don't want to be yanked around. That's a hard limit."

Orthia uncrosses her arms, and brings her hand out for me to hold. My fingers slide between hers effortlessly, because they are meant to be there. It's insane to me that I have a soulmate, that I'm even alive, but I'm leaning into the illogical, the irresponsible. She is literally a centuries-old serial killer with enough trauma to topple a city, and I don't want another person besides her. I have seen her devotion in action. I want that directed at me. The way her shoulders relax when our hands meet is like the sun on her skin for the first time. It's perfect.

"I won't do that again, nor will I allow anyone else to do that to you, ever," she promises. It's hard to tell in the dark, but I know she is looking at me with brutal sincerity.

"What are your ground rules?" I ask, swallowing the lump in my throat. I am about to murder someone; I am not going to cry over our kink negotiations.

"I like to be in charge," she starts, but before she can keep going, Audrey wakes up.

"Was going on?" She moves to sit up.

"Shh," I hiss, ready to shove my designer high heel right into her mouth to keep her from talking. I need to hear all of this.

Orthia cocks her head to the side and arrogant energy rolls off of her in waves. She squeezes my hand softly before letting go and turning towards step one in my revenge plan.

"You can *earn* the rest of my rules, wife. Consider edging one of my favourite pastimes, though."

"Yeah, I know all about that, Captain," I grumble, before crouching down to face this traitor among women.

Her eyes are struggling to focus. Audrey blinks heavily and stares like she's still got sleep in her eyes. My fingers snap in front of her face and that gets her to focus quickly enough. Her nose isn't gushing blood down the front of her dress any more, but it's definitely broken. I look over my shoulder at Orthia, who shrugs at my disapproving look.

I hike the skirt of my dress up to take the dagger from the holster strapped to my thigh.

"Where the fuck did you get that?" Orthia's voice is husky and whisper-soft when she asks me that.

It's my turn to let arrogance roll off me. I smirk at my soulmate and shrug. "I took it from the closet."

"Don't put it back."

She doesn't elaborate further than that, but as I turn back to the woman I am going to murder, my lower body clenches as tentacles pulse inside me with lust. Now is definitely not the time for these feelings. Once I've scrubbed all the evidence off of my body, then we can be horny. Right now, I need to let the anger out, need to let it centre in my chest until I can feel Love's power surge through me to draw out Audrey's life force.

"Audrey." I tap the edge of my knife against her cheek and she hiccups. Tears swell along her eye line and her lip trembles. "I need answers."

"Delphini, you don't have to do this," she whimpers.

"Did you have to do what you did?" I ask. "Was drugging me fun for you? Did watching strangers assault me make you feel good?"

She doesn't answer. Heavy tears fall from her eyes and mix with the drying blood around her mouth. It's disgusting. She's scared, and I don't care because this is barely an ounce of what I felt on that night. These are the tears of someone who is being eaten alive by guilt.

No, these are tears of someone who is upset they got caught. Audrey Paine would have happily lived her whole, expensive life without giving what she did to me a second thought.

Those tears are what bring the waves of anger rushing through me. Makes my limbs lighten and makes my fingers flex around the hilt of this dagger.

"Because that is where you and I differ. I have to do this, but it won't be so bad if you talk." I rest my knifepoint on her chest. "So, tell me what you know."

"I don't know anything," she sobs, the lie falling from her lips so easily.

"That's not how it sounded when I stumbled down the stairs on that fucking boat and you said... What did you say, Audrey?"

She shakes her head at me. The anger in me draws in closer, tighter into my chest, like the ocean receding before a storm. I need my answers before the storm breaks, before the wave of my fury crashes into Audrey and I've fucked this forever.

"You said, 'the fat bitch would need an extra pill' to Miles." I remind her. "Now that sounds an awful lot like you and Miles were in cahoots together to me."

I drag the sharp blade of my dagger across her collarbone, little pebbles of blood forming in the thin cut. She whimpers some more, and maybe it finally sinks into her that I'm not fucking around because she spills her guts before I can press my knife back into her chest.

"He told me everything about the contract." The words rush out of her mouth. "The debt, the payout, the fake marriage. Miles and I were high when I suggested it.

I didn't think we'd go through with it until he got the drugs and hired the two guys. I knew how much money he'd get and I couldn't say no. It was too easy."

"Where did he find the guys?" I demand, trying to fill in the gaps of my knowledge while I'm still in control.

"They were a part of the team hired for the event, security or something."

"Names. Now."

"I don't know." she shakes her head. "I don't know. They worked for the company. Names didn't matter, I just had to make sure they got their cash at the end of the night."

"How much?" My teeth grind together. Everything in me is shouting *attack, thrust, lunge*. It doesn't matter how much she paid them. It doesn't.

But I need to know.

"What-"

"How much money did you pay those fucks to assault me?" I shout.

"Del-" Orthia steps closer behind me, but Audrey interrupts her.

"Hundred g-grand each," she whispers. "Nothing compared to what we were gonna make from your trust."

"And this is nothing compared to what you did to me," I hiss.

Her eyes go wide when she finally realises she isn't getting out of this. I'm not sure why she thought I'd let her live to begin with, but I call it the idiocy of the rich.

I shift, and the dagger sinks between her ribs, right into her lungs. Like I practised.

Love's powers rush through my arms like a great wave finally crashing into a rocky shore. My skin ripples, and the writhing and desperation of their tentacles cause goosebumps to erupt across my body. Pink light surges bright, like it did in Jelly Man. Her body illuminates subtly as Love drains her essence. Audrey's weak gasp is inaudible compared to the sound of mine.

As though my entire life is being sucked out of my chest, Love's power expels me. Heat leaves my body, and all the adrenaline that made my arms tingle and feel light is gone. I can barely hold my weight up as weakness threatens me.

It's over as soon as I slump forward, sinking the blade deeper, upwards towards her heart. The motion is second nature now after the hours of practice. It's not perfect; there is some kind of resistance, but it works. In a flash of pink light, it's done. When Love's power returns to me, it's like a slow crawl across my skin. Every invisible sucker on every phantom tentacle caresses my body until I am shaking with so much addictive power.

I could take on the world. I could keep doing this forever and ever until there isn't another soul left on this planet. Every hair on my body vibrates and sways in the wind of this dank alley. There is nothing, no one, who could stop me. This power is all-consuming.

My vision blurs as Love takes partial control of me. Something about my hands shifts, and when they grab Audrey's limp body, it's like she weighs nothing. Everything about this feels perfect, feels right. It is as if a part of me was missing before, and I am finally a whole being. Love and I control my form together as one unit. The dagger slips from her torso and the clatter of it smacking the blood-soaked pavement is the last thing I hear connected to this reality.

"You have pleased us, sweet one. A pillar has fallen, but there are three more yet to crumble before your promise is fulfilled."

Chapter Nineteen
Delphini

0 Days

Warmth coats my skin like the Greek sun in August. Every muscle in my body is lax. Not an ounce of worry or stress filters through me.

The crackling of firewood eases me out of my sleep like it did the first time I woke up in Orthia's room. My eyes adjust quickly to the low light and I recognise all the old worldly charm of Orthia's bedroom. The dark wood panelling, the screen, the four-poster bed that looks like it weighs more than the ship itself. Orthia is exactly where she was the first time as well. Her bare foot shakes as she waits for me.

It's like we are getting a do-over. A chance to have our moment.

"We have to stop meeting like this," I murmur. "Makes me look bad."

"For Love's sake," she sighs, running a hand over her scalp. "I thought you'd fucked it for a moment."

"Was that not supposed to happen?"

"Too far from the water makes it hard to summon Love. It takes more energy. When they took over you, I thought it wasn't enough. They didn't speak, and then you both dropped to the ground. I thought I lost you."

"You should know by now you aren't getting rid of me," I huff.

"I have been a horrible mentor to you," she murmurs.

Orthia comes down on the floor next to me, her knees pressed into my side as she leans over to look in my eyes. A hand slides behind my neck and grasps my nape, her warm fingers pushing at the tendons until I'm putty in her hand. She stares at me with such a calculating focus, her brown eyes more alive than ever in the firelight.

"The thought of you suffering, of no longer being in my world, broke something in me that I thought was already dead," she confesses. "For centuries, I have waited for Love to deliver you to me. I was callous and stupid to ignore you, to deny Love and you. You are my human, Delphini, my *omphalos*, and I can't bear the thought of being without you."

Heat rushes to my cheeks all the way down to my toes at her confession. I am hers. The thought sends my heart soaring, elation making tears prick in the corner of my eyes. Her apology is a sweet victory that I want to indulge in until the world ends. She is starting to change, or at least see me as changed. It's a start.

This is how we should have started.

"I want a relationship," I say bluntly. "I want the whole romance. I've never had that before, but I want it with you. I want to fall in love."

"I won't deny you those things. We can make our own romance," she promises, leaning over to press a kiss to my forehead. She stays there for a moment, savouring the warmth of our connection. My fingers brush through her short hair and she hums with contentment before pulling back.

"We need to finish our conversation, but all I can think about is ripping this dress off of you."

All the heat from the club, the feel of her in my arms, the press of her body against mine comes rushing back to me. My fingers shake as I grip on to her shirt. She doesn't budge. Her free hand wraps around mine and I feel warmth burst through the touch until I'm no longer shaking.

"Promises, promises," I tease.

A look takes over Orthia, one that's all lust and determination. Her fingers pause at my hairline, asking for permission.

"Green," I confirm.

She stays there a while, watching my breath come in shorter and shorter bursts as I wait for her to do more.

Her thumb teases the side of my scalp, the blunt nail scraping against my skin. She doesn't move to do more. My fingers flex against her shirt, trying to guide her down to me, but she doesn't move.

"I have spent centuries waiting for this, do not think I will not bask in your beauty."

"Kiss me," I demand.

"Ask me nicely, wife." She smirks.

"Will you kiss me, Captain?" I ask softly, worried that speaking too loudly now will break the spell between us.

"Until you are breathless," she promises.

Orthia leans into me slowly. Her breath tickles my lips as I wait. I close my eyes, but when I move to complete the kiss she holds me in place. Her fist clenches in my hair and holds me back. My lips part. The words to demand more are there, so are the ones to beg like she genuinely wants me to, but then her nose brushes against mine.

The touch is warm, soft, completely contrasting to the grip at the base of my scalp that tingles with heat. Even as my heart flutters with the romance of it all, my clit is throbbing and it takes everything in me to not squirm, to not make demands. I don't want our first time to be like that. This time, I will play nice.

"I want you to be a good girl for me." She whispers. "Use your safe word if I take it too far. I need you to promise me."

"I promise, Captain."

She rewards me with her lips. They press against mine with urgency, unlike the patience she claims to have. Orthia tugs at my hair until I open for her. Her tongue, her tentacle, teases my teeth before slipping into my mouth. She holds me in place as she plunders me. Suckers pop against my tongue and I moan into the sensation. I wrap my lips tighter around the muscle until I can suck on it.

Orthia's moan is like a victory call. The warmth of her touch bakes my thoughts until I can't think straight. I don't know which way is up or down, but I know that if she takes her lips from mine I might die. I breathe deeply through my nose, trying to make this kiss last longer. To feel her spit slick my lips like a fine gloss and to have her tentacle wrap around my tongue.

Her hand moves from mine, ghosting over the curves of my body until I feel her hard grip on my thigh. She takes control of me by the holster still strapped there, and I can't stop the moan that leaves my lips as she guides my leg up and straddles the other with her leather-clad ones. My softness moulds her hardened body to mine, cushions it from the harshness of the world just for this private moment. She places my raised thigh around her waist and I desperately want to grind my pussy against her until I see that pink light again.

The press of metal against my chest cools my thoughts and sends a shiver down my spine. She breaks the kiss to look at me, to wait for me to say something, but I lay there panting for air and clinging to her shirt.

That's the dagger I used to kill Audrey. It's clean, I assume, by Orthia while I was passed out. The blade is long, and the handle of it is plain, wax-sealed wood. It's a well-loved weapon and expertly taken care of by its owner.

Orthia pricks the low neckline of my dress and I finally catch on to what she wants to do. My heart flips in my chest.

"Do you trust me?"

"Green, yes, oh fuck." I thrust my chest higher in the air to make it more enticing to her.

The fine pink silk tears apart like old, cheap cotton under her knife. In one long slice it's split in half. This could have been a one-of-a-kind dress, although I couldn't give a single fuck with how Orthia is looking at me.

Like she wants to carve a place for herself inside of me.

She leans back to fully take me in, every curve of my body on display for her. Her eyes trace the sheer pink of my corset. The knife glints in the firelight, and her hands shake with how tightly she clutches the weapon.

Does she want to hurt me?

"Love has given me the greatest gift. You, Delphini."

She looks down at my body again, caressing each of my curves with the tip of her knife until I am shaking with need. The blade traces Love's mark on my abdomen in sharp swishes that nearly have my heart pounding out of my chest. I want her touch, the warmth only she can bring me, but the words stay locked in my throat. I will not beg yet. My hips roll all the same when her blade taps against my straining, covered nipples.

"I won't ruin this." In a quick flick of her wrists, she flips the dagger to hold the sharp blade in her fist.

"Yellow," I say, and she freezes immediately. "Jesus, be careful. I don't want you to cut yourself."

A soft smile breaks her hard features. Unlike all the smirking and scowling she does, this smile is precious and rare, like a pearl that can only be found in the deepest parts of the ocean. Her hand moves from my hair to brush across my cheek and down to the mark on my chest.

There is a soft pink glow at her touch and her body changes. Beneath her billow shirt and tight trousers, tentacles begin to writhe and slip from the openings of her clothes. One of them takes the blade and she shows me her palm. A patch of fine, slick teal scales cover her skin.

"My body is a temple for Love, they keep me from harm, mostly, as I keep everyone on this ship from harm. It's a special talent of mine." The tentacle tosses the dagger and she catches it by the blade. "Now, how do you feel?"

"Like if you don't fuck me, we are going to have a problem, Captain." For all the sass in my remark, when I raise my hand to touch her cheek, I hold still before making contact. "You'll tell me if it gets to be too much?"

"Yes." She leans into my touch and we sigh in unison as warmth blooms from that point. "This time, I'm going to stay dressed, but in the future, we can try more."

"No rush," I assure her. "We just have until we take over the world."

For the first time in all the weeks I've known her, Orthia laughs. It's higher pitched than her voice, reminding me again of glass beads gently knocking together in the wind. Harsh, a sound that might be grating to some, but it sets my heart ablaze with as much warmth as her touch.

She kisses me again. This time, her lips are slick and taste of pomegranate, like Love. Her tentacle tongue twirls and pops against mine as the other tentacles take that as all the invitation they need. They slip across my skin and coat me in that glorious aphrodisiac until I'm panting and moaning against her. Suckers attach to my chest and throat, marking my flesh further.

More of them appear beneath Orthia's shirt until they have pulled the garment from her trousers. As they slither around my raised thigh, a deep, echoing rumble shakes the room. Neither of us stop what we are doing.

I push my centre on Orthia's thigh and as the pressure sends me a little bit closer to that sweet pink oblivion, my insides coil. My lower stomach heats, and the tentacles inside of me pulses.

Orthia groans, breaking our kiss and looking down at my panties. They don't match the corset. They are a cheap thong I got at the last minute when I was buying underwear. It's not a fantasy I'd really thought about before, but once it's in my head, my mouth says the words.

"Cut them off, please, Captain."

It isn't exactly begging, not in my book. She doesn't think for a moment about it either. Orthia slips the blade through the front triangle and slices down through the soaked gusset of the panties. The elastic snaps back against my pussy lips so sharply I moan. Tentacles wrap around their waistband and tear until the fabric is in shreds. She stares at my pussy, her chest heaving with every ragged breath she takes.

Her hand is slow to move, ready to strike or flee if I say the word, but when her thumb slips between my folds, spreading me open and collecting my arousal, I let my eyes slip closed. I can't focus on her actions; I want to *feel*.

Warmth swirls at my core, arousal dripping down her palm. The tentacles inside me crawl against my pussy walls until they are wrapped around Orthia's thumb.

"Have you felt the pleasure only Love can give you, wife?" she asks.

My stomach swoops, "Yes."

"Do you have a secret to tell, sweet one?"

The question comes out of her mouth like a purr, a rumbling sound that tells me it isn't just her speaking. I open my eyes and see hers are milky white. Love stares at me through Orthia, and if her experience is anything like mine, I know she can still see me, feel me, and hear me. Her thumb strokes the tentacles around my pussy, sending shivers of pleasure up my spine.

I moan. "I listened to you touch yourself. Love told me to stay, I wanted to stay."

"Did you like what you heard?" They ask.

Orthia leans back until she is seated fully on my thigh. A tentacle wraps around the holster I'm still wearing and spreads me wide open, exposing my sex and tentacles for all my world to see.

"Please, I want to do all of it."

"Should I punish you for watching me?" she asks.

"Yes, Captain."

In a flash, the thumb toying with the tentacles is gone and a harsh smack lands right over my clit. My back bows, the searing heat from her touch and the sensation of the wet slap threaten to be my undoing. Orthia blinks, and her brown eyes look at me with a hunger that could ruin a person, destroy them. She pulls her hand back and only once I nod does she deliver two more slaps. My eyes blur with tears as the stinging bite turns to a raging fire of need inside of me. Her hand glistens when she raises it again and I know it's because of me. She looks at me as her tongue laps the mess from her fingers.

She hums. "I'm proud of you, wife."

I break. The words flood me with so much goodness and warmth that I need to come. I can't remember the last time someone said that to me. My body is already begging for her to do it, to make me shatter into a million pieces. The way my nipples strain against the mesh of this corset and the way my pussy is still leaking, should be enough. Any other person would see this as me being hot and ready for them.

Not Orthia, though.

No, she wants me to beg until my voice gives out. She will not give me an ounce more pleasure until she hears the words. The dagger is still in her hand. Her dry thumb is casually sweeping over the handle of it like she did my clit.

"Captain," I pout softly. I can't help myself even if I'm begging. "Fuck me, please. I need your fingers, tentacles, anything inside me. I need it."

"Is that what you think you deserve? My touch on your divine body until you come apart for me?" Her hand smooths over my stomach and up to my breast.

She cups the right one, tracing circles around my nipple while she waits for my answer.

"Ye-" My words turn into a keen as she plucks at them through the fabric. "Yes, I did so well tonight. Please!"

She pinches harder, commanding me without words to add that please onto my little speech. Her movements don't stop, so neither do I. Words pour from my lips in higher and higher pitches as she moves from my right to my left nipple. They rub against the mesh and her fingers grow wetter, like she is trying to make the slick that Love produces drip from her fingers. It makes my skin tingle and heat. If she keeps this up, I will come anyway before she even gets anything inside of me.

"Please, Orthia, please. I am begging you," I plead. "Fuck me."

She smirks, "Good girl. Was that so hard?"

There isn't time to lavish in her backhanded praise. With her hand still teasing my sore tit, she moves the handle of the knife between my legs.

"Love will restrain you," she states clearly. "Colour?"

"Green, so green, Captain."

"Breathe," Love rumbles.

I don't know why I am babbling about that, but as tentacles arise from the ether, coated in that sweet juice, I don't care. Pomegranate fills my lungs the more I gasp. Love wraps around my wrists and slips between my fingers until I can grasp them. Two other tentacles wrap around my thighs and keep them spread open. The short tentacles in my pussy slip out of me and open me up. One slithers between my ass cheeks and suctions onto my hole. A chest-deep moan falls from my lips.

"Don't cum until I say so," she commands.

My eyes threaten to roll back into my skull at the press of hot metal. The tentacles inside me provide a slight barrier. I can't feel the grip on the handle, but the pressure and overwhelming sense of fullness are there. It isn't as good as Love's tentacles. I am not sure anything will top those, but as Orthia presses harder into me, when the hilt touches my pelvis, it's close. The suckers of my tentacles are pressed into my walls, massaging the muscles to keep me loose and as she pulls back, their shiver is like a vibrator touching my goddamn soul.

The moan that rips through me is loud enough to wake the dead. Her eyes never leave mine, though. Orthia stares at me through every thrust of her knife handle into my pussy. They are practically molten with the heat in them. Her body glistens with sweat and slick, her skin changing from tan to teal in places. The shirt she wears covers most of her body from me, but it sways as she rocks against my thigh.

She's rocking against my thigh.

"Yes, Captain," I whimper. "Fuck me."

"Fuck," she hisses. "Does that turn you on, Delphini? That I'm using your soft, sweet-as-fucking-sin body to make myself come?"

I nod, the words lodged in the back of my throat. It sends a shiver down my spine and makes me clench harder around the knife. When her hand leaves my breast, I cry out. Both at the loss of warmth and in sweet relief. My mind can't decide which is better, even as the air cools the juices left behind. She leans back to look down at my pussy.

"Do you know what fucking torture it has been? Love telling me how fucking beautiful you look stuffed full, yet never showing me? They took so much pleasure in teasing me with how your pussy sounded."

"She begged us, and we denied her," they purr.

Again, I'm at a loss for words. How am I supposed to respond to that? Love flexes their tentacles around my fingers, a sweet comfort as Orthia's words have my body shaking with need.

"Goddess alive, you are taking it so well for me, Delphini. Dripping all over my fucking knife. Marking it as yours." Her hips stutter and she falls a bit harder on my thigh. A groan, full-bodied and heady like a glass of port after a big dinner, comes out of her mouth, and it is as delicious as her praise. "So fucking divine, so fucking good for us."

Her thumb presses against the side of my clit and I hold my breath. I know in my next breath I'm going to burst. My pussy clenches so hard around the dagger, I am not sure how she can still be fucking me with it. As she moves her finger, the coil inside my belly winds tighter and tighter.

"Please," I gasp. "Please let me come, Captain."

"Give it to me, wife. Because when you are done, I am going to lick your cum off this knife while I ride your thigh. And you are going to watch me."

My legs shake with how hard I have been holding back. I unclench my fingers from Love's tentacles and I breathe out. Shards of pink light burst behind my eyelids as I cum on the handle of Orthia's dagger. My pussy convulses and spasms, the tentacles inside of me vibrating and the one on my asshole adding more fullness than I have ever felt before.

"Eyes on me." Orthia's command is like the sun on a hot day. It beats down on my euphoria enough for my focus to come back to her, to us.

She grips my hip, fingers squeezing my plush sides and tucking into my tummy roll. Every part of me is basking in the warmth of it. In the intimacy of it. She didn't hesitate to touch me where others have. She grabs me as she wants, as she should, so she can drive her leather-clad pussy over my thigh. Her tongue slips from her lips and the suckers coil around the handle.

Her eyes flutter closed and I could come again from this sight. My clit throbs as I watch her. With each pop of the suckers on the dagger, I remember what they feel like on my skin. Her groans morph into something higher, lost between a whimper and moan.

"I am yours, Captain. Cum for me."

"Fuck." She tosses the knife away. "You are such a good fucking girl for me."

She falls forward, her hands on either side of my head as she grinds on my thigh. Her tongue sweeps into my open mouth and I'm met with the taste of me and pomegranates again. She thrusts her tongue against mine until she stutters. Her hip falters as her body seizes up. Orthia is quiet as she climaxes, but when a tear hits my cheek and the tentacles that were holding me still begin to move, it is so natural the way our worlds collide.

Love wraps us both in their tentacles. My arms wrap around Orthia's body until she goes limp. Her fingers weave into my hair as she kisses my face. Gentle caresses as we come down, come together again with our bodies and Love's.

"You are amazing," I whisper to her.

Her breath hitches and I pause. My fingers stop running over the fabric of her shirt as I wait for her to say something, to push me away even.

"I wasn't ready until now to receive a gift such as you, my *omphalos*. We will do whatever it takes to keep you safe and satisfied."

"All is as fated."

CHAPTER TWENTY
DELPHINI

1 Day

Apparently, keeping me safe and satisfied does not exclude me from mopping floors or working the ticket booth. I pull my pink heart sunglasses out of my hair and put them on as the summer sun beats down on me. The fan mounted in the booth is nice but mostly blows hot air around. When Orthia dropped off an iced matcha for me, she even made sure it had extra ice to keep me cool.

The last tour of the day is lining up. Families and history buffs alike queue to buy a ticket and wait for *The Princess Despair* to sail back to the dock. At least I don't have to plaster on a fake smile. The bay is calm, like usual. Love is more than satisfied at the moment, so their hunger isn't upsetting the tides.

"We still wait for three." Their rumbling voices echo in my head.

"Mm," I hum in acknowledgement, taking a sip of my iced latte.

The next person in line strolls up. My fingers hover over the number pad to type in how many tickets they will want.

"Hi, how are ya?" The guy is overdressed for this tour and the weather. His shirt is a decent material, but not well fitted. It is the dress shoes that really make him look out of place in a sea of sandals and tennis shoes. He has on loafers, with the tassels and everything. Evening shoes in the late afternoon.

Is he here about the car Orthia stole last night to drive me home in? Because if he is, it's at the bottom of the bay now. After she got me onto the boat she had some of the girls make sure that thing and Audrey never saw the light of day again. He'd be better off trying to get his insurance to cover some of the cost.

"Fine, how many tickets?"

His hand comes to rest on the ledge of the booth and he leans in a bit closer. I stay where I am, waiting and pretending this guy isn't a fucking creep. I am going to mark his ticket so Neela knows to fuck this guy up good.

"You look familiar," he says instead. "Did you go viral or something?"

"Or something." I frown. "If you aren't here to enjoy the tale of The Pirate Queen, move along." I peer out the side window in the booth and see the ship is about to dock. "The people behind you would like to get on our last tour of the day."

"One ticket." He flashes his phone over the card reader. "You are Delphini Fields, aren't you? Cause you look just like her. Figure, curls, and all. My boss has been trying to track you down for weeks now."

The ticket spits out of the printer, and I mark it with two pink heart stamps before handing it to him. Since I started working at the booth, I have used the stamp a total of three times now. Once when a dad shouted at his family and another time when a small bachelor party thought doing this tour drunk would be a great way to start their festivities. Generally, the crew are pretty tame with their melodies, but when they get the stamp they know they can really feast. Double stamp means they can absolutely go ham on this guy.

"I have other people to serve. Please wait in line to start the tour."

Completely ignoring his questioning is not the safest option; lying would have been more correct, but I need this guy out of the fucking way so he can be siren food. Also, I need to get all these people to buy their tickets so I can close up the booth, cash out, and be on board before the final tour sets sail. The last thing I want is to be further away from Orthia when I don't need to be. Plus, any extra time I can get to track down those two fucking randoms who Audrey and Miles paid off, the better. I'm running out of options other than loitering at the yacht club, waiting to see if they work another event there.

Because I can't remember the name of the security company we'd hired and the club only offers a list of approved services, it is a guessing game trying to find these guys. My emails are basically useless, just the list forwarded to the Fields event manager. It's not like employees are listed on company websites. There are a few I crossed off because I straight up called and asked to speak to accounts under the guise of being my dad's financial assistant. It's not great for a security team to give me that information, but I won't be mad about it. There are still two companies who wouldn't fork over any information to me. Client confidentiality bullshit. They know what they are doing, meaning the guys definitely work for one of those places.

The last customer buys five tickets for their family, making this final tour officially sold out, so I start my shutdown process. I turn off the exterior display board, lock up the window, and begin counting bills. Tens, twenties, and debit receipts bundled up and shoved into a bank bag, I turn off all the internal shit. Pouch in hand, I lock up the booth and turn to see Aiofe walking over to me.

Perfect.

The selkie and I have a tense relationship. Respectfully distant since that first meeting on the deck of *The*

Despair is how I describe it, but I get the impression from Nargol that is how she is with everyone. I hand the bank bag over to her without a word and we start walking towards the ship.

"What'd he do?"

"Asking the wrong questions," I say, assuming she knows about the double heart stamp on that creep's tickets. "His shoes are all wrong, too."

Aiofe nods in acknowledgement and doesn't question me further on it. I take a deep breath through my nose and breathe out through my mouth as we walk up the gangplank to the ship. Less than two minutes from solid ground to our void, sweet void. There is no reason I should get seasick in that time, but the swooping feeling always makes my knees feel unstable as we walk down the steps to the lower deck.

Orthia leads the tours across the main deck, with Joanie taking up the tail end to keep the stragglers from touching things they shouldn't. We make eye contact, my fingers flexing around my cup as she stops the group near the stairs below deck. Already I feel warmer, despite my stomach threatening to riot against me by being on the ship with her. One hand she keeps casually rested on her sword, her hip jutted out enough to make sure it's fully pointed away from the crowd. Her other rests by her side.

The side facing me.

Oh. My. God.

We are going to brush hands. I don't care what happened last night. This is going to be the hottest thing she has ever done to me, for me. I switch my cup to my other hand and wipe the condensation off my palm. I'm lost in the moment, in the vision I've created in my head. Orthia in her glorious dark teal jacket, her long sword, her sun-bleached red scarf expertly tied around her elegant neck; it's perfection.

"Delphini!" Someone shouts my name, and I turn without thinking, half a smile still on my lips.

A camera flashes and I flinch. Goosebumps erupt across my flesh and my blood turns to ice. My vision twists from my soulmate's glory to a hideous white leather couch, to people I never expected to hurt me like they did. Hands grip my arms and when I try to shake them off, I see their faces. The two men whom I have been looking for. Rage burns in my memory as I try to commit what they look like; blue eyes, brown hair, nose shape, anything. I have to remember this now: I am going to find them. My matcha slips from my fingers and spills across the main deck.

The crowd jumps back and the man with the bad loafers lowers a camera. Everyone swoops into action before I can blink the pink haze from my vision.

"Feel it, sweet one. Embrace your anger. Feed it, feed us," Love growls, their voices reverberating through my body as my fury spikes. *Attack, lunge, thrust.*

My chest heaves as I drag in ragged breaths, staring the man down. He isn't leaving this ship. I don't care what anyone says or who the fuck he is. That man is mine.

I take a step towards him, ice crunching under my boot, but Orthia's hand on mine stops me. She nods when our eyes meet, before cocking her head towards the crowd again. Aiofe and Joanie are taking the man below deck and Neela has brought the mop upstairs already. The crowd stares at us.

"He ruined our moment," I whisper.

Orthia pulls me down while also rising on her tiptoes until her lips brush against my cheek. Sweet warmth erupts from the spot and slows the rushing inside of me.

"And we shall ruin him together," she whispers before pulling away to announce. "Now, let's get on to the Captain's quarter, and then we can get back on schedule."

I pace in front of the cell. Nargol has set up a chair next to the door and watches me. I've changed out of my uniform and into my pink tennis outfit. I know it's ridiculous, but this is my shield. I need it right now. This fucker is going to tell us literally everything he knows. Orthia is going to pry it out of him in whatever fucked up way she can. I'm sure she has done this plenty of times before.

For a while, I busied myself with trying to find pictures of the men online, even ones of guys who looked remotely like them, so if I had to ask around, I could present people with a visual, but I found nothing that felt close enough. They are average white guys, but that didn't make finding a picture easier. After about twenty minutes of searching, I gave up and took up pacing.

Every once in a while, the guy throws himself against the door. Each time, the metal rings out, but doesn't shudder. Nargol slams her fist against it in response just to hopefully scare the guy because when she does it, the door rattles.

"How many pictures of me did he have?" I ask again.

His camera and his phone were both confiscated before he was tossed in the cell. It's much nicer being on this side of the door. I hope he is shitting himself in there.

"Three," Nargol picks at the end of one of her long braids. "Do you think I should get blue pieces when I redo my braids?"

"Absolutely, you'd look amazing with an aqua colour." I turn on my heels and pace away from the cell. "So when I was standing in line to get in the club, and then one of me at the booth and then on the ship."

That isn't too bad. The one at the club is a bit concerning. It's a blurry mess, I could be mistaken for anyone else with ease, but he still found me. I didn't even know he was there. If he is looking for Audrey, he shouldn't be able to connect me with her. I mean, if the fucker is a cop, it doesn't really matter. I am not letting him leave this ship. If he is working for Miles, that poses a different problem. It means he knows where I am. It also means that my message to him scared him more than I thought it had. He is doing more than taking extra boxing classes.

Miles is spending my money to protect himself.

A pink haze threatens to take over my vision. I should kill him now. Then he can't report back to Miles. I could rip him limb from limb and send pictures of that Miles. Show him what happens to people who threaten me now.

Tentacles materialise out of nothing, wrapping around my middle and stopping me from moving further. Nargol doesn't even look up from the inspection of her nail beds. There is another bang on the metal door, this one the softest one yet.

"Breathe, sweet one. Our heart will be here soon. Then we shall feast." Love flexes around me, suckers moving over my low back in a gentle massage. *"She wants his suffering as we do."*

The tip of their tentacle smooths along my spine until the haze recedes. My eyes close as I try to centre myself. I take a deep breath, but they remain holding me, touching me. A bone-deep sigh leaves me as they rub further up my back to massage my shoulders.

"Do I need to leave, or are you gonna put on a show?" Nargol asks.

One of my eyes peeks open, and she is watching us, her elbow propped on both her knees. A smirk tilts the corners of my mouth up. "No show today, babes, but when there is one, you'll get a front-row seat."

"Promises, promises," she huffs and then grins at me, her broken tusks grazing her upper lip. "So I hear things are going exceedingly well with the captain."

"Major breakthrough," I agree. "The funk I was in last week didn't help, but-"

"Del, trauma is not a funk," she interrupts. "We've all got plenty of it, we understand. And being out there," she gestures towards the door across the hall, "doesn't make it easy to deal with."

"I know, I know," I say. "Anyway, do you wanna know what a great lay the captain is or not?"

"Of course, I-"

Speak of the devil, and she will appear. Orthia storms through the door with the rest of the crew behind her. She doesn't stop until she stands before me, her hands settling on Love's tentacles rather than me. I raise an eyebrow at her.

"Is this how you greet me after a day apart?" I ask.

"What?" She frowns at me.

"Captain," Nargol interjects. "That's not what she meant."

"Aye," Aiofe agrees, walking past us towards the training room. "She's angling for a kiss."

"Is that okay?" Orthia clears her throat, her cheeks blushing a shade of red similar to her scarf. "I meant to ask how you were feeling, but your question distracted me."

"I told you I wanted romance."

"Then ask me nicely, wife," she commands. Pink still stains her cheeks, but her confidence is back now that my consent has been reiterated.

"Please, may I have a kiss, Captain?"

Her hand wraps around my nape as she drags my lips to hers in searing heat. Love's tentacle holds her touch to my skin. I grip onto the lapels of her teal jacket and open my mouth. All the anger is morphing into a different hunger now, one I will gladly feed over and over again. But Orthia pulls back after a quick nip to my bottom lip.

"Good girl," she whispers just for me to hear.

It lights up my insides. Love slips from our dimensions and returns to theirs when we part. My cheeks heat and I can't stop myself from licking my lip in the place Orthia bit down. The tender, plump flesh still tingles.

She releases me and turns around when Aiofe and Cookie drag a heavy platform with a pole in the middle of the training room. Nothing about it screams torture device until Hamako climbs on her partner's back and attaches a chain to the loop at the top. Her fingers run across the pole like it might actually be used for dancing, but there isn't much time for that kind of fun now.

Nargol and Orthia open the door to the prison cell and the guy comes bursting out. He screeches when Cookie plucks him off the ground. The troll chef is the least of his worries. In a few moments, the man is chained up, the tips of his loafers brushing the platform. His head whips around as he tries to take everything in, but I can see it on his face. It doesn't make sense what he is looking at. The size of this room when he was on a ship, the monsters staring at him with mixed interest, it's all too otherworldly for the mind to comprehend.

The bargaining begins the moment Orthia takes off her jacket and the array of knives strapped to her torso comes into view.

"I'll give you whatever you want."

Lakelynn slams her door shut, and faintly, I can hear the metal music she likes bleeding through the heavy doors. Yeah, I think he will be a screamer too.

"Who do you work for then?" I ask. "Because you aren't here for a fucking history lesson."

"Prospectus, the security company, well, I used to work there. I don't any more. Oh my god," he whimpers.

To my left, Lagulla has removed her headscarf to reveal her waist-length hair filled with snakes. The serpents hiss and stretch before settling around her shoulders. It's not like she is even looking at the guy. He can calm down. Orthia snaps her fingers in his face.

"Focus, dickhead. Why don't you work there any more?"

A knife appears in front of him, and she drags it down to the top of his trousers. Another scared sound comes out of his mouth.

"Got caught stealing shit from a client two weeks ago. Fired instantly."

"So why're you fucking around with my girl?"

The moment the words leave her mouth, my whole body starts tingling. Will I ever get tired of her public declarations?

No. I need every single one of these to get rid of the feeling of her rejection. Whenever she calls me hers or shows me her affections in front of the crew, it heals that sore spot in my chest a bit more. She is trying. Orthia may have me begging for her touch in bed, but everywhere else? She makes sure people know who I am to her. There is no questioning our bond now. She is mine, and I am hers, and we are Love's.

"Some of the guys who I used to work with asked me to check around. It was a lot of money, okay? Heard some things about her and-and- wanted me to find her." A tear slips down his cheek. "Please, I didn't know. I won't say anything, please."

I surge forward and grab his shirt. He squawks, his shoulders taking his full weight as he loses balance on his toes. He's pathetic. Any authority he had evaporated the moment he was chained up. Around us the crew lounge around and watch this man begin to blubber. Orthia has even put her knife away. It's sad to see there is no loyalty, but when money is the only thing keeping you around, why would there be?

"Names, now," I snarl.

"Pat Lovette and Darren Gross. They're big guys but basic-looking. Darren's on a fishing vacation right now. Pat only goes to three places: his apartment, the gym, and work. His next job is that fancy regatta next week. Darren isn't scheduled to work until the big shit show at the yacht club. That's everything I know, I swear," he stammers out the last of his information as quickly as possible.

More tears slip down his cheeks as I continue to stare at him. Whatever anger I felt earlier is twisted into disgust. This guy is a weasel, a conniving little predator that never stood a chance. I release him with a shake, and his head knocks against the pole softly. He doesn't deserve to live, but it won't feel good to make him suffer for being an idiot. I stand next to Orthia and look down at her slightly. Her lips are pursed like she is having the same thought I am. Love is silent, and when I focus hard to reach them, all I can sense is exasperation. There is no hunger in them for this sad meal.

"Did you look up, Delphini?" she asks, her voice soft. She is hunting for a reason to be angry, to rally Love and the crew. "Do you know what your co-workers did to her?"

The man gapes, his mouth opening and closing a few times before sputtering, "Who hasn't seen the pictures?"

Tears sting my eyelids. The pictures are something that I have resigned myself to. Because this fucker is right. Who hasn't seen the pictures? Seen the violence committed against me and claimed that I'm some fucking villain. They don't know the truth. But all the crew who are present raise their hands. They haven't looked for that image or seen it by accident. They have respected my privacy since day one, even when they weren't sure I would live much longer. A breath catches in my throat as I see them, scowls replacing their looks of boredom. Orthia grabs his chin and forces him to look at each of the women.

"You see that? Not a single one of my crew saw it. Was it necessary to do your job?"

"I'm sorry," he begs. "Please, I was just doing my job."

"So am I," Orthia says.

There is a flash of steel, and a subtle pink glow follows quickly. She pulls her knife from his stomach.

"For Love," Aiofe shouts.

The crew responds with a resounding shout and cheer. Orthia dismisses them after requesting a clean-up and someone to check on Lakelynn.

"Delphini." She uses that authoritative captain's voice of hers that makes me want to kiss her stupidly. "Come with me, we have work to do."

Chapter Twenty-One
Orthia

16 Days

I want to scratch my clothes and skin off as we walk through a crowd of people on the hottest day of the year so far. The pier is heaving with locals and tourists alike as we make our way from the public entrance of the annual Gwenmore Regatta towards the yacht club. While anyone can see the boats race from the pier, this is a privately funded event by the club. The finish line is out of view for the average person dressed in their finest linens.

Delphini looks stunning. Her sun dress is a fine blush pink colour thing with a short skirt and puffed sleeves. And crocheted panelling, it's not lace, which is different, apparently. Centuries of living and I have never been inclined to care for such differences in lady's finery. I still don't, but listening to Delphini explain the difference and why this designer dress is more appropriate for a day event than something she usually wears about the ship makes me want to learn for her. These are things she has spent a lifetime learning, and if they are still things she cares about, I shall learn all the right things.

Which is why I am dressed in a navy unitard with a flatteringly expensive cream quarter zip over the top. The sleeves of the unitard are long with loops for my thumb to go through, but the sweatshirt is sleeveless and cropped below my waist. My full lower half is basically out for the world to see. At least I am still wearing sensible shoes. The flat, pink trainers Delphini has lent me for the day match the silk scarf she gave me to wear.

"This will tie it all together." She laughed and laughed this morning when she handed the thing to me before leaving to finish getting ready.

I don't like being away from the ship during the day, let alone on a busy day, but Aiofe and the crew practically shoved us out the door. My quartermaster coyly telling me to enjoy a walk around the docks while I am out. I couldn't stop from rolling my eyes, no matter how appealing the idea is.

The wind picks up, and the scent of saltwater helps quell the anxiety that is threatening to overcome me. At the opening of the Paspawa, the pier is far enough away I can't see the ship. Delphini's fingers thread through mine as she guides us around a family in matching outfits and girls with team names printed across white shirts.

My *omphalos* is in her element. A smile on her lips and hips swaying with ease.

"She is free of expectation, of fear." Love's voice washes over me in a wave of relief. It's sweetened by the rattle of Delphini's iced drink before she takes a long sip. Her glossed lips purse around the straw and I want her. It's as simple as that. Seeing her enjoyment in something I have provided makes me want to give her more so that she may see fit to give me even an ounce of her attention, her affection.

Again, I am struck with a desire to worship her, to get on my knees and prostrate to the goddess before me. Deeper than any ocean I have swum to, I want to dive into her very being. In the same way, I crave Love's tentacles swarming around me, I want to cover myself in Delphini.

I raise the hand holding mine to my lips and kiss her knuckles. She looks at me and winks. I'm not sure what she is trying to convey or what I have done that could possibly garner that response, but for five minutes I forget my ridiculous outfit and enjoy the warmth of her touch. There will never be a day that I am not grateful she is so accepting and more stubborn than I am.

"This is really nice," I tell her with another kiss to her knuckles as we continue to make our way up the boardwalk of the pier towards the private docks.

"Sunshine, matcha, murder, what more could a girl ask for?" She giggles and I want to bottle it up. Delphini brings a lightness to our work. She doesn't shy away from the gore or the evilness of it, she just does it dressed in her bubblegum pink tennis outfit.

"I can think of several things I would ask a girl like you for."

The teasing line is hard pressed against my teeth, not as natural as my commanding tone nor as worshipful as she makes me feel. Her fingers still flex in my hand, and the smile on her lips tells me it still works.

"Later, *Captain*," she promises, deep brown eyes sparkling.

We keep talking about anything, so we appear to be another wealthy couple on a day out for the races. Delphini tells me secrets, things about members of the Gwenmore elite I had never heard before. I show her places where I have killed men throughout my long history here in Gwenmore. There is little of this city that doesn't conceal the bones of previous meals to Love.

The closer we get to the yacht club, the knot in my stomach twists tighter and tighter. I am not concerned about finding this Pat. We shall do that, and Delphini shall dispatch him with ease. My nerves screw up at how the others will see her. These used to be her people, and after the very public shaming her parents did of her, I am scared she will freeze up, or worse— I will cause a scene that alerts too much attention to us. Any number of monsters lurk within the upper echelons of Gwenmore, and anything out of the ordinary puts our secrets at risk. This is a community that I have been allowed to subtly feast on for generations, taking their wrongfully discarded sisters and turning them into warriors of the new age. Love will be brought forth with our efforts. It is only a matter of time.

We pass by security while a large group of drunkards keep them occupied. My fingers clench around Delphini's, and Love's phantom tentacles slip around our joined hands. We are a unit, three pieces of a whole now that I never want to see separated. There is no future if they are not by my side. Her eyes quickly scan the surroundings, but then they are on me again. The smile is still on her face, if a bit less anxious now.

It doesn't last.

"Phi! Oh, my goddess, Phi!" A woman screeches over the crowd, but all I see is a hand wildly waving, and suddenly, the whole club looks at us. My cheeks heat against my will even as I stare down every single person who looks at us, monster and human alike.

"Lottie?" Delphini's grip on my hand loosens and I am forced to release her as a familiar Naiad wraps her slender arms around my human.

Charlotte swings her about with too much strength to ignore. I intervene before she is the one to cause a scene here, even though I am just as pleased and shocked to see an old crewmate. I place my hand on her arm and let Love's power seep through the skin of my palm until it is scaly and slick. This only makes it worse. She gasps, pulling me in for a chilling hug as if twenty-five years haven't passed since she left the ship.

Just as they were then, her emotions are wild and unruly. Fat tears dribble down her cheek as she looks from me to Delphini and back again. Her bottom lip won't stop trembling.

"Captain, I-" she starts, choking on the words.

"Lottie, I-." Delphini tries to play off their emotional reunion, but I hear the sadness in her voice as well. She clearly had a friend in her, and this moment is essential, but people are staring at us as they walk by. I can't let her risk exposing Delphini.

"What happened to never coming back?" I ask, changing the subject and getting Charlotte detached from us.

She swipes at her tears, a weak smile on her lip. "I didn't mean to, but my mate found me."

"You know each other?" Delphini hisses. "Oh my- for fuck's sake Lottie."

She shoves the woman playfully and water splashes on her skin. It's like a vast world has opened up to Delphini now, and she has yet to categorise all the ways in which these new people respond. Confused, she jumps a little at the water but doesn't act like it's out of the ordinary.

"I was Pirate number six for five years running," she smiles, but then it crumbles. "How do you..."

"The same way you met," my human shivers and I cling on to her hand again, trying to let our warmth and bond ground her. "I'm no actress, though."

Charlotte's hand covers her mouth, her emotions coating her features like water. Her hairline dribbles onto her linen dress as it struggles to hold its solid state. I don't know how to move the conversation on or how to comfort the melting woman in front of me.

Delphini pulls her in for another hug.

"We can't change the past," Love's voice echoes through me. *"There is only the future."*

"So," I clear my throat. "You've met my mate?"

The Naiad delivers another gasp, and another chilling, bone crush hug. Even as she weeps all over us, there is something profoundly settling about calling Delphini that to someone off the ship, like admitting it to an old crewmate has fixed a small piece of my heart.

"I think I prefer being wife, if I'm honest," Delphini pulls back and smiles at me. "You did basically marry us, wife."

Is this what feeling faint is like? It's like my head has caught in a whirlpool, swirling and swirling until I don't know what way is up or down, left or right. The warmth of our connection explodes and my body is struggling to contain Love's tentacles under my skin. My face is on fire.

But nothing is as hot as the place between my legs. My pussy has transformed into some kind of fucking waterfall, my underwear suddenly so damp I am concerned it will show through this unitard Delphini has dressed me in. My thoughts are flooded with that word, of her calling me her wife. We are bound together so much deeper than that, yet the word is at the centre of my whirlpooling mind.

Her wife.

"Captain, *please please please* tell me you-"

"There was no wedding." I interrupt before Lottie gets any wetter in the face and say the most logical thing that comes to mind. "Love chose her for me."

A pout forms on her lips. "So romantic, finding your mate is amazing, right? I heard a rumour that the council has changed a rule about dating humans. I think if I hadn't found Marcus stuck in that tree, I'd have found a human."

As she rambles on about fate and destiny, I sense Delphini's focus shifting. Her gaze drifts around us, scanning the crowd. As much as we didn't want to make ourselves known before we found him, Charlotte may have alerted Pat to our presence past the security gate. With her additional height, my human can see over the crowd enough to see faces. I am stuck eyeing people's shoulders in hopes I can find anyone. Charlotte's gaze slowly drifts, following Delphini's watchful eyes, and conversation blissfully ceases.

"Charlotte, have you seen this man?"

Delphini pulls out my phone and unlocks the device. A picture of Pat is on screen in seconds, something she found on his social media after we got the next names on her list. Now that we have knocked over the first pillar of her revenge, Audrey Paine, the hunt has begun in earnest. The sooner we can be finished with it completely, the less likely the other prey will suspect us.

She looks at the picture for a long moment, then raises her fingers to her lips. It appears as though she is only blowing air through them, but a few heads turn towards us before a large man with thick black hair and arms the size of tree trunks is lumbering over to us like a dog just told he'd get a treat. Werewolves.

Before this man can get ahead of himself, I step in front of Delphini enough, so he keeps his filthy paws to himself. He will not lay a finger on my human.

"Phi! You're alive." His smiling, bubbling personality is a perfect match to Charlotte's. To prevent himself from getting into trouble, he wraps both his arms around his small mate and looks at us expectantly.

"Again," Charlotte adds with a firm nod to me, putting her mate in his place. Like me, she has always thrived on control, and it seems training a mutt is what she needs.

"It's terrifying and nice to meet you, Ma'am."

"Have you seen this guy, puppy?" She presents the phone to him.

Delphini's fingers twitch in my hand at the pet name. Her eyes are focused on Charlotte for a moment too long, one that has me questioning if their friendship was something more or that perhaps she wanted something more. What about them did she crave? Was it a masculine presence in her relationship, or was it the softer, dominating tone that Charlotte used to ask her question? She has stated before that she wants everything I can give her, that *we* can give her. But is that enough? Does my *omphalos* crave more than just Love and myself? Does she want everything *the crew* can give her as well?

"Yup, he's having a smoke at the far end of the club by the deckhands' shed, out on the dock."

"Fetch him and make sure he stays there." Charlotte issues her command coolly, and Marcus bares his fangs before he rushes away from us.

My human clears her throat and I take a deep breath, calling on Love until I can feel their tentacles coil around me. This has been a surprisingly easy venture, one aided by an unlikely source.

Charlotte starts leading the way in the direction Marcus bounded off, but Delphini stops us from following.

"This is not the best time, but was it okay I called you that?"

My breath stutters. Was it okay? I pull her down until my cheek is pressed to hers, until my lips tease the shell of her ear. "I want to hear you scream that in front of the whole crew while I make you cum. You can call me your wife forever."

"Tonight," she says, her lips warm against my skin and the heat of her touch on my waist making my knees weak. "Take me to the bath, and I'll do whatever you ask."

She pulls back to look at me. Her breath heats my lips, but I don't kiss her like I desire. If I do that now, I will drag her under the pier like a sea monster of old and fuck her senseless. Denying us now will make giving in so much more powerful later.

"Then be a good girl for me, Delphini."

Pat is a decent-sized man in real life. Tied to a chair with rotted nylon rope in his mouth, he looks downright small. Marcus stands by, patiently waiting until we are in the narrow repair building. With the sounds of the regatta happening around us and waves crashing against the mooring points, we have utter privacy. Charlotte rubs his ear and whispers something that has the werewolf's lips part.

"Do you-" She starts to ask.

"I've got this." Delphini pulls Charlotte into a final hug. "We'll get brunch soon."

More whispers are exchanged, but I don't catch them. Pat is trying to move his chair now that the big bad wolf has turned his back. I yank the man's head back by his hair and force him to stay there.

He keeps fighting, but I am much, much stronger. As he wriggles around and mumbles bullshit through the rope as the other two leave, I watch Delphini. She bounces on the balls of her feet and rolls her neck, psyching herself up for this easy kill. This isn't like invading an orcish community or tracking a human fur trapper. They have exertion and hunting. This kill is served on a silver platter to my human.

She has to summon the power, the rage, to call forth Love on the spot. There is no warm-up battle, nothing to spark the anger but herself.

It's a wonder to watch her transform. Her fists clench, her nostrils flare as her breathing becomes heavier. She truly is a goddess that I would have happily worshipped. As I would give up my life for Love, I would also for her. When she looks at me again, the fury in her gaze heats my pussy. My body and mind are finally reacting as one when I look at my *omphalos*. The craving for her that I possess is a beacon, not a distraction.

When she is ready, Delphini pulls the rope from Lovette's mouth.

"You fucking bi-"

My free hand slaps hard over his mouth and my skin crawls from the mix of saliva and chill that runs up my arm. If the tentacles that run the length of my insides could curl up any tighter, they would.

"Think before you fucking speak to her again," I sneer.

He nods, face turning red the longer I press my palm into his teeth. I push a little harder, squeezing his jaw to make sure my message is clear before I let go again.

"You are fucking dead, you stupid-" He shouts.

Delphini strikes. Her fist collides with the centre of his face and she draws back with a hiss, shaking her hand while Lovette blinks and moves his nose about.

"That looks so much easier in movies," she whines.

"Solid hit, though," I compliment her. "But we can work on strength training another time. Actually, you know who is really good at this kind of combat?"

"Aoife?"

"Cookie," I say. "Not 'cause of her massive hands. A long time ago, she used to do some underground fighting for extra cash."

"Oh my god," Pat groans. "Typical fucking women, you won't fucking shut up."

"And it doesn't seem like you will either, dickhead." Delphini scowls before presenting her hand to me. I pull a switchblade knife from under my sweater and hand it to her. Pat's face doesn't move an inch as she flicks it open. "What did you do with my money?"

"Fuck. You."

Seconds before it hits, I slap my hand over his mouth again. Delphini sinks the blade into his spread thigh and Lovette screams. His arms jerk in the restraints, but they hold tight. Sweat beads across his forehead as his body begins to shake. She waits until he's stopped groaning to speak again.

"What did you do with the hundred grand, Pattie?" She asks again.

"Slots and hookers, Atlantic City," he answers, chest heaving. He refuses to look down at his skewered leg. "Look, if you want it back, I'll find it somehow, okay? Did Johnny tell you I was working today?"

I look at Delphini, it must be the dead guy. She understands this as well, because she smirks.

"You assaulted me for a wild fucking weekend?" she asks. "You ruined my life for that?"

Her voice raises in pitch, in volume. My hand twists harder in his hair when I know what he's done. That haunting picture surfaces in my thoughts, his hands on her body. My chest tightens, tentacles pressing against my unitard to get at this fuck. To hurt him for hurting my human. The anger in me swells and swells until I have ripped the chunk of hair out. Pat squeals as the new bald spot appears on his head, blood trickling from the place where my fingernails dug in too hard.

"Did you hire that guy to watch me?" she asks next.

"No, that little bitch Miles did. I just gave him the details after that coke whore of his went missing. After the pictures got taken, I was done with those two."

"Hey," I say, grabbing his neck. "You want another dagger to the leg, maybe one a bit higher? Stop insulting such a fine profession."

Delphini runs her tongue over her teeth as she stares at Lovette. Again, right before it happens, I have the sense to slap my hand over his stupid mouth. The wet clap echoes around the building as she yanks the knife from his thigh. I force his head down to make him look at the blood pouring from his leg. For the first time, he turns a colour other than red.

"Is Miles planning something?" I demand.

"Wouldn't you like to know?" He is mocking us, in his final moments he thinks this will somehow make it easier for him.

"Does your buddy know anything about this?"

"No, took the money and ran. I haven't seen him in weeks."

When I look up at Delphini again, I can see the faint glow peeking through her chest. The grip she holds on the knife is so firm her fingers are shaking.

"Is Miles planning something?" she asks.

"Eat shit." Even as he says the words he gags.

Delphini lunges forward and the blade slips through his ribs. A perfect strike.

"He's going to kill..." Pat gasps, but doesn't finish the threat.

Pink light filters through the building and in a blink again it's gone. She has fed another soul to our patron, another pillar of her revenge has crumbled. Delphini's shoulders rise and fall quickly, her curls covering her face. I hold my breath, waiting, wondering if I am going to have to steal a boat this time to get us home safely. Her hand jerks, the distinct sound of wet meat being roughly sliced, covering up my sigh of relief. She removes the blade from Pat Lovette and stumbles back.

Her hand is covered in blood, the front of her dress is also splattered with it too. Each breath she pulls in has her chest and shoulders rising like she has swum the length of the bay. I try to call out to Love, but they are silent. I stare at my human, wondering if Love's power will overwhelm her again.

She dabs her free hand over her face and relief washes over me.

She's okay.

"You got a little." I look down at her dress and she follows.

"For Love's sake."

Chapter Twenty Two
Orthia

16 Days

Pat Lovette shouldn't be haunting me. His pathetic threat and his weak promise should not be echoing around my skull, but they do.

The ease of it all grates against my skin as I sit at my desk, locked away in my quarters after returning to the ship to peel away these new clothes. The need for comfort, the urgency to hide myself, was so strong I abandoned Delphini at the door. The silk around my throat had turned constricting, stealing my breath away. While I stare at the wall of obituaries behind my desk, my finger traces Love's mark. The swirl of tentacles around my throat keeps me in a singular piece now, instead of two.

"They know not who they are battling, heart. Do not doubt the abilities of our sweet one." Tentacles move beneath my skin, and the addictive touch of suckers on

the inside of my wrists and neck eases my thoughts, but not completely.

"It's not-" I don't know what I am going to say. My worries for Delphini are not that she is incapable. My *omphalos* has proven to be steadfast and strong, beautiful beyond measure and yet so hungry for blood that I wonder what life would be like to serve her, to bring her sacrifices to feed on. "It's not her, Love. It's me. I'm failing her at every turn because of my actions. What if next time I rip a head off instead of his hair?"

"All know the risk," they rumble. *"She has done well and should be rewarded. There is much more that will come before her revenge is complete. Take these moments."*

I purse my lips. Love goes silent, leaving me to ponder their ominous message. It now mixes with Lovette's words. Humans make everything complicated. One slip, and they could accidentally kill themselves and ruin Delphini's revenge. Is he going to try and kill her or himself?

The knock at my door reminds me of my promise, of the reward my human has earned.

Delphini blinks when I open the door, wrapped up tight in her silk robe with her curls piled on top of her head. Her eyes wander from the flush on my face to my bare throat. The exposed skin burns under her gaze and yet I want to expose more of me to her, to feel that burn cleanse some part of me that has been ruined for all time.

She licks her lips like she knows I want her to feast upon me.

I take my time to look at her, from her sandals to the gap in her robe that exposes Love's mark on her chest.

Delphini crosses her arms under her breasts. Nipples press against the stretched fabric now. "Ready? Nargol says you watch sometimes, but I've been dying to at least have a soak, so we could ignore them or watch or…"

She trails off, her finger pulling on a loose curl and twisting it around her finger as she stares at me now. That little coquettish action is my undoing. Finally, it's mine.

I grab the ties of her robe and pull her to me. Our lips meet with ease, the grin on my face keeping it from deepening. My human's desires are something that I have been dreaming of for weeks now. To see her wet and begging for me, to see how she will bend for the crew over and over again without release simply to please me.

"We are going to do so much more than watch," I promise, grabbing her hand and leading us towards the bath.

As we near the sliding doors, the sounds of pleasure grow to a steady cacophony. They bounce off the tiles and drown out any rational thought. There is a sweet song weaving through each moan and it makes me pause to look at Delphini again. Her pupils are softly dilated, the pulse at the base of her neck thumping visibly under her skin.

Still affected by the siren's song, then.

"If anything goes too far or you want to stop, tell me," I say. "The crew's trust in one another is what makes this special. It relies on everyone being honest about their desires and limits. It's a freedom that was once stolen from them."

I grab her chin with my free hand and make her look down at me.

"You give me that same freedom, Delphini." I pull her closer to my lips, let the power of the song sink into my bones and loosen me up. "I have been dreaming of you with my crew, for the chance to watch you with them."

There is no waiting, no questioning my resolve. Delphini pushes the door open, and I release her, following her like a lust-sick fool into a den of starving lionesses. The noises don't stop; the crew is too occupied with their own pleasure to stop to observe us entering. Neela sits at the edge of the water, her feet dangling in the pool while she sings loud enough to influence the room. Between her thighs, Nargol feasts on her cunt. Hamako is pressed to Cookie while the troll teases her nipples. Others lounge on chairs, content to watch through the steam while others play for their enjoyment.

My eyes connect with Aoife's, and she nods while a whimpering Joanie is spread across her lap. A resounding clap of flesh makes Delphini gasp, her fingers gripping mine again, but she moves us faster around the room.

We walk around the edge of the lounge deck towards a dry bench to set our belongings on. Her hand stops at the ties of her robe and she looks at me again.

"Are there any rules for the room?"

"Just honesty," I explain. "For you though, only I can make you come tonight. When you can no longer think straight, I want you to beg *your wife* for release."

"Fuck," she breathes. "That sounds like a challenge."

"Then make me proud, wife."

I watch her steel herself, centre herself enough to feel the pulls of Neela's song, but stay clear headed enough to remember my instruction. Her chest rises slowly, and when her eyes close, I wonder if she is speaking with Love. I am struck with the realisation that I don't want to take Love from her, or hoard them away for myself, but I want to share their link as well. I want to know what Delphini whispers to them or what prophetic words bring tears to her eyes.

My fingers take the ties of her robe and loosen the simple knot. I need to be the first to see her naked form. The swell of her breasts, dark nipples begging for attention, the stretch marks on her stomach that blend with Love's mark, the tight curls at the junction of her plush thighs, all of Delphini is imperfectly divine. I have never thought of anyone as holy, but she is.

Doused in steam and lust, she walks towards the bath with goddess-like grace.

There isn't much time to swallow the emotions clogging my throat. If there is anything I have learned in our short time together, it is that she doesn't shy away from the darkness, from the ruined. My *omphalos* shines in it, and I will go towards that light until there are no more days and the land has disappeared.

I take off my clothes and walk to the edge.

Delphini floats in the middle of the bath. Like she is the sun, the others are circling around her without getting too close. Her fingers glide across the water as she sinks deeper until it touches her hairline. With her back turned to me, it is easy to get lost in her orbit, too. It isn't until she has floated around to face me again that I feel my chest constrict.

Her eyes are soft, warmth radiating from the smile on her lips as she relaxes in the water. Everything about her is at ease and open to us all. She looks at me with nothing but joy and lust. There isn't a moment of hesitation in her gaze as she traces the bare form of my body. The softness in her features turns to hunger as she takes in all of me.

"Captain," she calls out, her voice low and breathy. Her tongue darts out to wet her bottom lip before she starts to move unconsciously back towards me.

The others turn to see me standing in all my naked glory. The mark of Love covers nearly my whole body. From my ankles to the base of my neck, tentacles are etched into my skin in swirling patterns. They hide the long-lost scars of my past and reveal that I am more monster than they have ever thought. This is the first time anyone has seen me. The mark that circles my neck burns from the attention, but I am not going to shy away from it. Not when I can see the respect and affection in the eyes of my crew mates.

I slide into the water next to Aoife, who is now alone. Joanie has left to take comfort with Saphielle. They both lounge out of the water at the far end of the pool now. The only ones left in the water are six of us.

"Ruin her," I command. "Softly."

Neela strikes first. The siren swims up behind Delphini and begins whispering in her ear. Through the steam, I can just make out her nod and the way her lips form words of agreement. Neela sinks her teeth into the spot on her neck that is softest, in a place I know will leave a bruised mark tomorrow for all to see. My legs spread wide, the water lapping at my exposed sex as they all move about.

Delphini quickly turns around to take charge of their coupling. Her mouth moulds to the siren's, but around us I can feel the zing of their song pulsing in the air, the hum of other sirens in the bath growing as they watch their sisters-in-arms.

Next to me, Aoife slips into the water like a predator. She has always been this way, dominating and in control. Watching the women before us fight for that same feeling has awoken something in her. Delphini moans, the sweet noise echoing off the tiles, when one of Neela's hands slides from her arm beneath the water. My human has lost the battle for control so easily. She rocks her hips against the hand that works her pussy open, teasing her until she cries out for more. The siren simply smiles at her, licking into her open mouth for all of us to see.

A smirk forms on my lips too as Neela turns her around again to face me. Delphini's eyes are hooded when she looks at me, but they fall closed again when Neela kneads her heavy breasts, pinching her dark nipples. My chest tightens at the vision they make together. One of Delphini's hands grabs onto Neela and pulls her mouth onto her neck again. My nipples harden to peaks in the warm air.

It has been a long while since I have truly joined to watch the crew indulge in one another. After centuries of waiting, with no way of chasing away the cold touch that all beings gave me, now watching the one whose touch I crave most indulge where I can't, makes my blood burn with need. The look of ecstasy on my *omphalos'* face as she sees me transform makes me want to cover her in my marks, to torture her with all the slick and suckers my tentacles have to offer.

They slip from my body, the soft pink light going unnoticed by those around us. The slow release of power calls forth their master. Love's tentacle slips from the ether and wraps around my waist. The slick of their skin against mine only makes my need grow. Pomegranate perfumes the air and there is a collective sigh from all of us. It's nearly Pavlovian now, how our breathing calms and our bodies relax from getting a hint of our saviour's scent. I lean into their hold and let their comfort erase any thought of the past from my mind.

"Please don't stop," Delphini whimpers, her hips still rocking even as Neela's other hand grasps her breast.

"Captain's orders," she hums, a vicious smile on her lips as she licks at Delphini's skin.

Her eyes meet mine, full lips parted as her nipples are teased beneath the water. Unconsciously, I spread my legs further apart, tentacles slipping from my pussy to splay across my inner thighs. Her mouth opens like she wants to speak or to have it filled, but Aoife stepping in front of her breaks our eye contact.

"She is wondrous and hungry," Love rumbles. Their voice vibrates down to my bones and I wrap a hand around their tentacle. *"As are you, our heart."*

"For her," I murmur, struggling to focus and stay present rather than slipping into Love. "For us."

"Has your trust in her grown to match your lust, though?"

My focus snaps back to the present as a giggle erupts.

Nargol has pulled Delphini out of the water and tossed her over her broad shoulders. My human grabs hold of the green globes of her ass while she's carried to the edge of the bath. The orc lays her down on the tiles. I can't see much from this angle, but I don't need the visual for this little play. Nargol spreads Delphini's legs apart, placing her feet on the lip of the bath. Around her the more voyeuristic members of the crew look on. Even Lakelynn takes her earbuds out and leans forward to watch.

"Now," Nargol announces loud enough for all to hear. "Human pussy is very sensitive. You have to be gentle with it."

"Uh-huh, where did you hear that one?" Aoife asks.

"From a book."

"Babes, that book I suggested is fiction," Delphini giggles and I want to bottle it up. She is free, from the sound of her voice, I could wonder if she'd ever actually harmed a fly before. There is a lightness about the tone that makes my heart flutter, the tentacles beneath my skin skitter to the surface, trying to reach for it.

"So you don't want me to be sweet on your pussy, Del?" Nargol sounds like she's pouting, completely put out but before Delphini can respond, she continues. "Guess I'll devour it whole then."

I see Nargol's head move and then my human's legs begin to shake. Her surprised moan has everyone leaning in to observe the feasting. My eyes close for a moment, savouring the sounds of pleasure around me instead. The slap of skin, the lapping of water, the gasping moans from my mate as her friend takes her closer and closer to orgasm. I listen for the change in her voice, how her breath catches and when she finally holds it. Her little tell when she's close is obvious, even to someone who has never fucked her before. I open my eyes to watch her be denied yet again.

Nargol pulls back and Delphini's back arches high up off the tiles like her orgasm has been ruined. A string of "no's" pour from her lips as green hands sooth her thighs and pull her back into the water. Delphini floats in her arms for a moment as she regains her control. Water drips down their naked bodies as they move back to the centre of the bath.

Only when Nargol moves to say something to her does Delphini react. She grabs the orc's face and smashes their lips together. Her tongue moves into the other woman's mouth like she is searching for her lost orgasm in there. Nargol moans, but pulls back, finally murmuring something to Delphini before moving to the deeper end of the bath.

Next to me, Aoife hauls Neela by the waist onto the corner of the bath. She turns the siren to the side where the steps are widest. She spreads her thighs wide open, her pussy glistening in the air. One of her feet still dips into the water, swaying softly as she waits for her next instruction.

Water splashes, a muffled moan turning all our attention to Cookie and Hamako. The troll has impaled her mate on her cock, stretching the harpy around it until she is fully seated. Cookie grunts softly, rolling her hips until she receives a sharp nip to her fingers to stop. My eyes drift back to Delphini, watching her react to their display.

She doesn't disappoint. Her fingers clench around Aoife's hold on her throat and her lips are parted again in hunger. She clenches her thighs together as she watches the other two fuck. It isn't until Hamako moans at a particularly harsh twist of her nipples that the rest of the crew snaps back into their own plans.

"You're going to thank Neela like a good girl and make her cum with your mouth, is that understood?" Aoife asks loud enough for the whole room to hear. A direction from our quartermaster is never missed, her voice strong and clear as she issues commands.

"Yes, Ma'am," my human agrees instantly. Her eyes locked on the feast before her.

"If the crew doesn't think you are doing well enough, I will punish you. Do you understand?" Aoife continues.

Delphini draws in a shaky breath, taking in the women surrounding the bath and those in the water. Her eyes lock with mine and when I nod, she winks again. From this short distance, I can feel her nerves, but there is sass in the action. Like she wants to be punished.

"Yes, Ma'am," she says, finally.

Aoife guides her slowly up the steps, arranging Delphini on her hands and knees until her face is nearly pressed into Neela's pussy and her ass is up in the air. Water laps over her calves and her legs are spaced far enough apart I can see her pussy from where I sit, too. I have a near-perfect view. Aoife stands on her other side, her skin flushed red from the heat. She smooths a hand from Delphini's shoulders to her ass, taking a fistful of that glorious part of her and exposing more of her to me.

"Begin."

The command is simple, but she is slow to respond. Delphini looks at Neela and whispers something before she begins kissing her inner thigh. She moves without urgency as she lathes kisses across the whimpering siren. Aoife doesn't display any emotion, but when she looks at me, I know she is checking in before she strikes my mate.

"Wife," my voice rings out and I can feel the room hold their breaths. "I don't think chaste thigh kisses are how you thank a sister who was so kind to you. Do you want Aoife to spank you?"

"Yes," she moans, pressing her teeth into Neela's thigh until it leaves a mark.

Neela pouts for effect more than anything, and it's all Aoife needs. Her hand cracks against Delphini's ass hard enough to force her mouth onto her pussy. Her gasp is easily muffled and drowned out by the room. Cookie thrusts into Hamako again only once Delphini has started her display of gratitude properly.

My human places one hand on Neela's thigh, spreading her even wider as she begins to lap at the siren. From here, I can't see much more than glimpses of Delphini's tongue licking up the arousal. She works with a vigour now as Neela throws her head back. The siren moans, a musical sound that makes the room grow hotter. The tentacle around my waist flexes and my insides coil tighter as desire makes my clit ache for attention, for only Delphini's attention.

"Stop teasing, Del," someone calls out, which is quickly followed by another sharp slap to her ass.

She moans into her task, moving her mouth higher up until she wraps her lips around Neela's clit. She shouts in pleasure and we all feel the rise in magic again. None of us are unaffected by it. The couple in the water have moved closer, the room's eyes torn between Cookie's thrusting and Delphini's sucking.

My eyes are stuck on her pussy though. Between her wet labia, tentacles slowly move around her. They slide through her arousal like they are teasing me. My human is wet and needy, but she hasn't given up on the challenge yet. Her mouth slows, a flash of teeth scraping against flesh has Neela whimpering.

"Del, please, I wanna-" Hamako's begging is cut off when Cookie pulls her down hard on her sex.

Aoife lands two hard smacks across each cheek until I am sure that Delphini's skin must burn from the sting. She shakes her ass as she focuses back on bringing Neela to climax. I tear my gaze from Delphini's weeping pussy to look at the other couple. Nargol stands in front of them, kissing and teasing Hamako's breasts. The harpy moans, her lover's fingers working over her clit again. I am not the only one playing games with my partner tonight then.

Cookie meets my gaze and she smirks. "The captain is watching you beg like a little whore, birdie."

Hamako shudders and colour rises in her cheeks, but she smiles. She likes that I am watching, that I am hearing her beg for my human to keep licking the pussy of her friend.

"She tastes so good, Hamako," Delphini groans. "I don't want to stop yet."

My chest aches with a deeper pleasure for my crew, my *omphalos*, my family. She is one of us, is all of ours just like we are hers. My fingers flex against Love's tentacle around me as I bathe myself in this moment.

Hamako's feathered legs shake as her lover pounds in time with Delphini's efforts. One hand holds onto her troll, the other holds Nargol to her breast. Another sharp smack has my attention drawing back to my human. Neela has stopped making sounds, her mouth open and chin pressed to her chest as she gazes down at the woman devouring her.

The tentacles around Delphini's pussy spread her open subtlety, teasing anyone who can see. They glide through her slick and suckle at her flesh while she moans into Neela. Around me there are more moans, breathy and hungry. We all want to see Neela cum across the face of the human in our crew. Aoife's hand slides down to tangle the small tentacles away from Delphini's clit. She fucks them back inside, but it only makes my wife moan louder. Neela's hips stutter against Delphini's face, and the wail she lets out when she comes pierces the bath. The room shakes with the magic of her call, more of the crew crying out in pleasure as they come with her. Nargol, Hamako, and Cookie crash into my peripheral view as they collapse in euphoric release. The troll carefully wraps her arms around her mate and the orc as she withdraws her sex.

Aoife pulls Neela back into the warmth of the bath and then does the same to Delphini. Her touch is soft yet steady as she guides my mate to me for further instruction. Delphini whispers something to her, and my quartermaster's smile is small, but honest. She kisses her forehead before returning to give Neela care.

Delphini kneels before me, her shoulders above the water. Her eyes are glassy and her lips are stained with Neela's cum. She places both her hands between my legs without touching my skin.

"Wife, can I please make you come?"

Chapter Twenty Three
Delphini

0 Days

My pussy clenches every time I look at Orthia.

The tentacles that Aoife fucked back into me suckle at my walls and it takes everything in me not to come apart at her feet now. My jaw aches, but I am hungry for more. She has barely spoken a word to me, just that short reprimand, but I need her praise.

I want Orthia to tell me how proud I have made her by pleasuring Neela, by playing with Nargol, by listening to Aoife, by not coming without her permission.

If I show her how good I am, beg her sweetly enough, she will fuck me with the teal tentacles spread across her inner thighs. My eyes trace the real ones to the ones etched across her skin. The grooves cover scars and stretch marks, circle the dusty pink of her nipples, and then finish at fine points around her collar bones, like daggers pointing to the centre of her chest. The circle of etchings around her throat make my heart ache.

I lick Neela's cum from my lips as I wait for her to answer. Her gaze burns into me and my cheeks heat. Her own skin is flushed a deep shade of red from the heat of the bath and from calling her my wife. The word came to me so easily when I spoke to Lottie, felt so right on my tongue I wanted to say it over and over again, but seeing how it affected Orthia made it all the more alluring.

"Please, wife, I want to lick your pussy." My fingers twitch as I try to hold still. One of my tentacles teases my asshole the longer I wait for her response.

Love's tentacle around Orthia slips away as she leans into me. The world falls away. All my senses hone in on her and her only. There is no one in this room, but us. Her nose brushes against mine with an explosion of warmth between us. She inhales deeply.

"I love the scent of her cum on your lips, wife," she says before whispering softly. "But I want nothing more than for you to be covered in me. It's just-"

Orthia's hand moves to her throat and she rubs the skin until she has calmed down enough to speak again. "I have not allowed the touch another, besides Love, since I-"

"You are in control, Orthia," I murmur, bringing my hand up to her cheek softly. "Tell me what you need, I want to please you."

"I know. I trust you, my *omphalos*."

Her words send fluttering through my heart as her lips press against mine, sealing them between us. The warmth that radiates from her sends vibrations of pleasure through me as my thoughts try to latch onto her promise. Trust is worth more than any proclamation of love. Loving someone is easy, loving someone will still get you hurt over and over again, but trusting them? There is no comparison in my world.

For as much as I loved my parents, I learned from a young age I could never trust them. Orthia giving me her trust is more than I could have ever asked for when I set out to make her accept me. Everything about us is falling into place and I have never known this much happiness and pleasure in all my life.

She breaks the kiss off with short pecks across my cheeks and jaw, sucking on the places Neela bit me to make sure I am marked tomorrow.

"This is about your pleasure," I mumble over the words I need to say while her tongue tickles behind my ear. "When you're ready to be done, we're done. Don't focus on finishing, just my mouth on your pussy."

"Talk to me a bit more, wife. How are you going to lick me?"

The question makes my clit throb. She's called me her wife again; she's opening herself up to this new form of pleasure while staying in control, she's asking me to talk dirty to her. One of her hands moves to hold my nape, her fingers sliding under the one loose curl at the back so she doesn't tug it by accident. She moves my face to her neck. Love's mark there is thin but the tangle of tentacles is somehow tightly woven together. An illusion to make it look like there are masses of them in such a small area. My breath shudders as I inhale, the scent of our patron leaking from her skin making my mouth water.

"I'll start kissing your thighs and tentacles softly." My lips meet the mark on her throat with reverence. I kiss around the mark to the front of her throat, hints of that addictive taste reaching my tongue. "Then I am going to lick the arousal from around your pussy." I lower my head and tease the shallow valley between her breasts with my tongue. Orthia's heart pounds in her chest as I look into her eyes again. "Once I've made sure I have had my first taste of you," I say, lip hovering over one of her hard peaks, "I'm going to suck on your clit until you're wet all over again."

Her fingers flex on my nape, urging me forward until I flick my tongue over her nipple. She gasps softly, holding my hand tighter and arching into my mouth. I suck until her hips roll beneath me. She never takes her eyes off me. Orthia looks at me with anticipation and need, her teeth sinking into her bottom lip as I gently bite down on her nipple before releasing it with a pop.

My tentacles slowly stretch my ass. Their slick glide into my hole is arousing but nowhere enough to get me off. The teases.

"Once I know you're ready for more, I'll fuck my tongue into your tight pussy and have you ride my face until you're done with me," I explain. "I'll do those steps over and over again until you tell me to stop, until the world ends and there is nothing but the ocean for as far as the eye can see."

"Then get to it, wife." She grins.

"Yes, Captain."

As her hand guides me the rest of the way down, my other hand grabs her knee and spreads it further apart. Orthia leans back into the bench and watches me. I follow the flush on her cheeks down to her pussy. The water of the bath laps at her puffy folds and the tentacles that have her spread open for me.

And I do as I told her I would. As much as I want her tentacles in my mouth, I only allow myself one teasing lick. My mouth waters for a taste of her. When I am finally at the apex of her thighs Love's aphrodisiac hits my senses. It's addictive, tart and divine all at once.

Above me, Orthia moans, and I crane my neck back to look at her through my lashes. She is glorious like this, flushed and desperate. Her hunger for me is something that I have seen glimpses of, but being under the full weight of it now only makes me crave it more. There is nothing I desire more than the taste of my captain, my wife, on my tongue.

"Fuck me," she moans when my next lick over her pussy drags my tongue across her clit. "You are so fucking gorgeous with your tongue out for me. Come here."

Her grip on my neck moves to my chin until I have to rise higher up out of the water. She looks at me, my mouth still open with my tongue teasing my bottom lip. My nipple tightens in the warm air, but it doesn't even register when Orthia spits in my mouth.

It's slow, lands right on my tongue and she holds my jaw firm enough to keep me from swallowing it. Her gaze is fully locked on my tongue, like she can't believe what she's done either.

"Such a good fucking girl, Delphini," she growls and I can't stop the smile on my face.

Orthia pulls me back to her pussy and I go straight for the kill. With her spit still on my tongue, I suck her hot clit into my mouth. My tongue rolls over the hood and she jerks up into me. My eyes close as I lose myself in the taste of her, in the way she holds my hand to her thigh. Everything I am right now is for her pleasure.

"Oh fuck," she whimpers suddenly.

I look up and Love has suctioned two tentacles to her breasts. Her back is arched into them, eyes closed like she has completely lost herself in the moment, like she is finally allowing herself this release.

"Sweet one, make her come." Love's command brings tears to my eyes, words shaking me down to my core, overwhelming all over senses I have except for the taste of pomegranate on my tongue.

With one last flick of my tongue, I let go of Orthia's clit and lick the arousal from her entrance. Her legs shake as I throw one over my shoulder, allowing her to pin me to the bench before I dip my tongue into her pussy.

"Yellow," she gasps, and I pull my mouth away from her without letting go of her. "I need to be on top, to be more in control."

"Thank you for telling me." I kiss her thigh and slowly rise from the water.

Every breath she draws in has her chest heaving. Orthia is flushed head to toe, her body taking a slightly teal hue as tentacles emerge from her skin and recede again like the tide. Her body glistens with sweat and slick and I want to lick every inch of her.

"You are my everything," she murmurs.

I lean in to kiss her, and she is already there. Her tentacle tongue sweeps into my mouth and my denied arousal surges another level higher.

I'm unsteady on my feet, my ass plugged with my tentacles and drunk off her pussy, but I make it up. Cookie hands me a large cushion from somewhere that's wide enough for Orthia's knees and me. It's only then that I remember everyone is watching us. While it doesn't bother me, it's also not something that makes me hotter. It makes me want to be even better for my soulmate.

The tile is cold when I lay down. Despite the heat of the room, goosebumps rise across my body and my ass stings from the delicious spanking Aoife gave me. Orthia kneels over my stomach, but rather than moving forward she tweaks my nipples. Her fingers tease them until the peaks ache and I am fucking delirious with a need to come. Like my tentacles are controlled by her, they move inside my ass until I am trembling.

"Please," I beg. "Please, wife, I need to come."

"Not yet," she says, massaging my breasts until I have calmed down and tears leak from my eyes again. "You've been so good for me. Just a little longer, and I'll fuck your pretty pussy in front of the whole crew."

Reminded again of the crowd, the sounds of their pleasure filter through me more like soothing music in a spa than erotic audio. My focus is wholly on my wife looking down at me.

"Ready?" I ask, swallowing my need to show her how good I can be with my mouth.

"Smack my thigh if you need to breathe," she says, sliding forward until her pussy hovers over my face.

The tentacles aren't stuck to her thighs any longer, just teasing her labia until she is dripping with slickness.

"If this is how I die, then I could not ask for a more noble send-off than suffocating on your fucking gorgeous cunt."

My hands rise to grasp her hips and I am met with tentacles. They wrap around me loosely, and that familiar tingling sensation from Love's slick makes me moan into her pussy.

The taste of her bursts on my tongue as I lick and suck at her flesh. I fuck my tongue inside of her and her tentacles do the same. My mouth opens wider as I push deeper inside of her. Thigh muffling all sound, I focus on the motions, her hips grinding on my face so her clit rubs against my nose and tentacles shaking against my hands. I suck one of her pussy tentacles into my mouth and the others latch onto my face like it's a lifeline.

I plant my feet on the floor and roll my hips in a fruitless effort to slake my own need. Every shallow breath I draw in has me inhaling more of Orthia and I have never smelled anything finer. She's overwhelming all my senses, waves of her arousal flooding my mouth. I think I am going to pass out.

But then it happens.

Her thighs clench around my head, hard, and she doubles over me without making a sound. The tentacle in my mouth curls and the ones around my face release all at once as her pussy convulses around my tongue. I suck every drop of her cum from her body I can. She jerks against my face until she has stopped clenching. My hands are released carefully, and Orthia shakily rises in her knees.

My first full inhale is laced with the scent of cum; of pomegranate and musk. Something inside of me twists when I open my eyes and see the look on her face. The sheer wonder, the tears that threaten to spill from her eyes, it makes my heart ache. She cups my cheek, damp with tears and arousal, with reverence.

Orthia's past is her own. Whatever happened is her story. I don't need her to tell me to know that what we have shared tonight has altered her perception. Despite having centuries with the crew, with women who grow and love so freely, she has kept herself apart from them. In fear of intimacy, or because she was waiting for her soulmate, it means she has denied herself.

And she trusts me with this. Given our horrible start, this is like the sun after a storm. I smile up at her as emotions clog my throat. My hand rubs across her skin, memorising the way Love's mark etches her body and traces her curves.

"You are a goddess, my *omphalos*. So much more than a broken thing like me has ever deserved. In my wildest dreams, I never imagined you would be so divine."

My chest shakes as I gasp around sobs, trying to stay quiet. Orthia swipes shaky fingers across her own cheeks and takes my head in both hands. It's awkward, but she manages to kiss my forehead. My head swims with her praise, her adoration. She has seen me worn thin and shaking with fear, and yet she sees me like I am holy.

"Are you ready for me to show you how proud of you I am? For being a good little wife for me?"

"Kiss me first," I beg. "Please."

"Anything."

The weight of her leaving me makes me whimper. The air hits my damp chest and I am reaching for her even as she positions herself between my legs. She leans over me and I chase her lips. Her lips taste of tears, but she plunders my mouth with hungry strokes of her tongue. She grabs my nape and holds me in place. I writhe against her once again, until my desire and need have taken hold of any thoughts I had.

She pulls away from me and stands tall on her knees. Arching up to see what she's doing, I watch her stroke and arrange the tentacles between her legs upwards until they form a cock shape. The suckers are pointed outwards and the tip is narrower than the base. More tentacles pull from her body and wrap around her hips like a harness.

"Holy shit," I whisper, unable to stop myself from reaching for it, too feel it under my grasp.

"Love," Orthia groans, her eyes fluttering closed when my fingers slide over them, stroking her tentacles and letting the warmth of our bond keep her arousal up. "Hold her for us."

The bath shifts and the tiles beneath me rupture into a mass of tentacles. Pink light coats everything, shines off our skin like jewels and makes me dizzy with need. My arms are quickly encompassed by Love and my hips pushed up until Orthia's tentacle cock is able to glide through the slick between my legs. Each little sucker attaches to my folds, drawing hiccupped whines from my throat. My muscles tighten like I am going to come from this alone. I have been kept on edge for what feels like hours, but I desperately don't want this to end yet.

Her eyes open again and they are milky white.

"Sweet one, you've done so well for us. You've earned your reward. Breathe."

I can't take my eyes off of her cock. Their voices purr with pride as they continue to tease me. Just like the first time they instructed me to do so, I inhale deeply, letting my muscles relax and trying to centre myself in the moment. Orthia's cock taps against my pussy.

"That's a good girl, Delphini," she says, swallowing an amount of nerves I've not seen in her before.

"Wife," I reply with urgency. "If you don't fuck me with that, I will die. Horny and unsatisfied. And that's not what you promised me."

She takes a calming breath, her mouth parting enough for me to see how the suckers on her tongue click against her teeth as she looks down at me. Her eyes dart to the crew around us, everyone lost in lust, and a smirk forms on her lips.

"Can't have that, can we, wife?"

"No we can't, Captain."

With a final look, one that fills in all the gaps, one that says 'if it's too much tell me' and 'trust me' all at once, she presses in. The tip sinks into my pussy slowly and both of us gasp, the stretch and fullness sends jolts of pleasure down to my toes until it feels like my soul is threatening to vibrate out of my feet. Orthia grabs onto my hips and drives forward in a full thrust.

"Motherfuck-" Her words are cut off. She throws her head back and groans loudly. "Love's sake, they are sucking on my clit too."

She eases out of my pussy and slowly fucks the bundle of tentacles into me. This time every sucker latches onto my walls, teasing out every ounce of pleasure my body has to offer her. It tugs at my g-spot, pushing me closer to seeing those pink shards of light. She keeps this slow pace, letting me adjust and building into the motion until her hips slap against mine so loudly, messily that it's all I can hear.

It's perfect.

This is what she needs, I can see it on her face. Giving me pleasure, keeping me satisfied is enough for her to do this act, but knowing she is receiving the pleasure she deserves from fucking me, sends me higher. It connects every part of sex between us to pleasure, keeps us anchored in the moment. Her breasts shake, nipples hard peaks, and I am desperate to have them in my mouth again.

"Perfect," she moans. "Let me worship you, wife, let me be yours."

"Forever," I nod.

Orthia gazes at my body. Her eyes can't focus on one spot. They go from my face to my slack mouth, to my heaving chest that aches to be touched again, to where her tentacles are sucking every bit of slick from my pussy. She sees the way my body moves with her thrusts and she fucks me harder, pushing us until we are screaming for release.

"A goddess, my goddess," she pants, falling over me with one arm to catch herself. She kisses my cheek, my jaw, my throat, never missing a beat in her thrusts. Pleasure and warmth crash into me over and over again like waves against a cliff and I am so close to crumbling.

"I want you to come for me, Delphini. Be my good little wife." Her teeth grit together like she is holding back and the flush on her cheeks travels down her neck.

"Come with me," I whimper. "Together, please."

"Forever," Orthia says.

Her grip on my thigh tense, as a tentacle slips from her stomach and moves to my clit. The sucker attaches to my clit and the world explodes. I scream through my climax, the over stimulation, the long denied release—it all rushes through me. My pussy clenches around the tentacles inside me and pink shards of light burst in my vision. Everything goes quiet inside of me, like I have reached a state of bliss I didn't even know was possible.

The only thing I can feel is the weight of my soulmate.

Her body lays on top of mine, heaving and stuttering. Sweat, arousal, tears, we are covered in each other and I never want to wash it away. Orthia's fingers glide over the curves of me with ease until she holds my face in her hands.

"I am so proud of you, my *omphalos*. I am so grateful for you," she breathes, pressing soft kisses to my lips between words. "Thank you."

"You are my everything." I tell her, because it's true.

She is all I have and all I want in this world.

CHAPTER TWENTY FOUR
ORTHIA

30 DAYS

I don't like this. Not one single thing about this evening seems real. I pull at the sleeve of this stupid jacket Delphini has wrapped me up in for this outing. This is firmly the last time I ever allow her to dress me up like a toy doll.

"Do not act so put out, our heart," Love soothes, phantom tentacle slipping from me to her.

I can't help but smile in a sort of agreement. They are right, she can dress me and parade me around so long as she is by my side, giving me the same heated look she is now.

"Does it make it better knowing I'm soaking my panties seeing you in black tie?" she asks.

My *omphalos* is a vision in this shade of pink. The colour burns the eyes and yet she looks softly divine. Nargol has braided her hair in long, thin strands that reach her waist. The pink in those shimmers and matches her glossed lips. Delphini is a goddess looking down upon us common monsters.

I grunt in response and adjust the black silk around my throat, making sure the knot at the side will not come undone. She sighs, recrossing her legs as the car she hired for the evening drives us back to the Harbour Crest Yacht Club. I have become far too familiar with that building.

The number of times I have been near those pretentious cretins before Delphini, I could count on one hand. And each time was on my own accord, without the need to dress up in these ridiculous and impractical clothes. Since she has come into my life, I have been thrust into a caste of society I had left behind. It's not enjoyable seeing how little it has changed, despite humanity's advancing in other places.

"Lottie's texted." She smiles, looking down at the phone I bought for her this week after much demanding. "Our names are on the list. Marcus and co. are on the look out for Darren, and Miles hasn't arrived yet."

It should be a great comfort to have one of us on hand, someone who understands the importance of what has to be done. But I need to prove to Delphini that I will not fail her. Every step I have been stumbling after her, rather than guiding her like I have done for centuries. Already,

Lottie has proved to be a much more useful asset in my human's revenge.

The shifting of silk draws my attention back to where it matters.

"Are you jealous?" Delphini asks.

I left out a breath, "That isn't- it isn't that exactly. I want to be good for you, to prove to you I am useful, too."

"I don't want you to be useful." She shrugs. "This might be shitty, but leveraging Lottie was always my end goal. She's my friend, I will keep her secrets and respect her till she has proven herself unworthy of it, but our relationship has always been business first to me."

My fists clench and the tentacles under my skin curl up in what I can only decide is shame. What am I supposed to do then?

"Our relationship isn't business, Orthia. You want to be good for me? Keep trusting me." Her voice lowers and she leans across the seat until her forehead touches my temple. "Love me like I love you."

My head nods along because there is nothing I can say to this. Tears threaten to spill as the warmth of her touch and her words sink into me. I have done nothing deserving of love, but Delphini has given me hers. For as long as it takes, I will prove to her that I can keep it safe. That I will worship her and treat her like the goddess she truly is.

The car pulls up to the club and I quickly get out to open her door before I make the mistake of trying to fill the void in conversation with nonsense. Delphini takes my offered hand and now the show begins. We walk up to the podium where a man holding a tablet is checking in guests.

"Orthia Moore," I tell him, completely ignoring his greeting to us. Every muscle in my body is begging me to check my scarf, make sure the black silk is still in place. My hands tremble as I wait for him to scroll through the stupidly long list.

"Of course, there you are and your guest..." His voice trails off as he looks at Delphini and I glare at him. He clears his throat. "Perfect, just pass through security and enjoy your evening."

I blanch at the mention of security. Why the fuck does a charity gala for rich fucks need security at check-in? Who is trying to bust into this crowd? Delphini leads us to the man and woman doing visual pat downs and bag searches. This is not something I agreed to. For a brief moment in the back of my head, I feel the rumbling of Love's presence, a touch of comfort before they slither back to her for the night we have planned.

My wife squeezes my hand hard before letting go and walking ahead of me. She already has her small clutch open and the guard lets her breeze by. I swallow hard and step up. The weight of two daggers at my side, leather harness cutting into my shoulder—

"Do you have any bags?" She asks, barely sparing me a glance.

"No."

"Have a nice night."

Once we are inside, seats are located, and then we are abandoned to head for the bar. Delphini whispers to me, "Easy peasy."

Yes, step one of a million has gone successfully, but the large reception hall is packed with people. Some wander around to look at displayed auction items while others gossip about fuck knows what. On the far side of the room is a stage set up with a podium next to it. This is going to be a fucking challenge.

My nerves are on high alert, blood pounding in my ears so hard I'm on the right course for a splitting headache. Even through two layers of clothing, every stray brush of a stranger sends a shiver down my spine. This is the last place I would ever want to be willingly.

"Teddy Bushwhipper, I have told you a thousand times, there is no-"

That pretentious sandbag.

Augustine Ravenscroft's voice stands out amongst the others who are loitering about. At his side is a plump, mousy woman about Delphini's age, holding an espresso martini with both hands while she listens to the two men in front of her have an argument about Gwenmore history. She smiles the more riled up Augustine becomes.

It shouldn't surprise me that we both abandon the bar to head towards the group, yet I am. Delphini loops her arm gracefully through Bushwhipper's and completely halts whatever rebuttal was about to spew from his lips. I shove myself in front of both of them, ignoring the gasp and instant chatter that starts behind me. A sneer settles on my lips as I prepare to enact a part of a plan that I did not expect to encounter tonight.

Another thing to add stress to this evening.

Augustine rolls his eyes at me, but a slip of the blasted sand still winds its way from his hand to hers.

"Orthia, may I introduce my mate, Joanna."

Her grip shifts on her glass and she offers me a sandless hand to shake. I ignore it. I can't handle the chill right now. Beneath the surface of my skin I can feel my tentacles writhing, begging me to let them out and fight. Any action, anything to gain some control of this situation.

"I love your work," Joanna says, pulling her hand back and tucking a loose strand of hair behind her ear. "I went through a real pirate phase when I was a kid, and my Mimi took me on your tour after I begged her for a whole school year and-."

"Is he forcing you to be here?" I ask, shoulders tensing, ready to pounce. If I am going to fight this low-down monster, I am going to make sure every grain of sand inside of him is ruined. There will be no more boogeyman.

"Oh no, I told Augustine we should go because I'm nosy."

"*Mon abeille*, the sea witch is concerned I am keeping you as some sort of prisoner," Augustine explains. "Because of the nature of our relationship."

Her eyebrows furrow for a moment, like she doesn't understand either of us any more. She opens her mouth like she wants to say something but quickly closes it. I can see the wheels in her head turning and she doesn't look at Augustine. She stares at me seriously and my teeth grit together. The plan is already there in my head. I'm going to shove this Roman bastard behind the bar and stab his chest until I find his heart.

It is only by the grace of my Love that nothing happens.

"Let me guess," Delphini says. "Life or death situation?"

"Yes," the woman blushes. "But I had a crush on Augustine for months beforehand, and, and-."

"Eh, same sitch." She smiles and holds out her hand. "Delphini Moore, new member of the secret club."

"We are not the same," I start, but my wife turns to me, and I see the flash of milky white cover her irises. A blink clears it away, yet the warning from Love is crystal.

"How would you know about our situation?" Augustine asks.

"Apparently, werewolves have excellent hearing," she answers. "And our mutual friend, Marcus, tells me your partition is paper thin." Joanna's cheeks explode with a deeper blush that goes down to the subtle neckline of her dress. What the fuck are they going on about?

"Auggie, rule number one." Teddy squeezes into our tight circle, making sure to stay clear of me. "Never dally with a werewolf around."

Augustine pinches the bridge of his nose and mutters something about letting dogs lie with their books, but I am distracted by Delphini. Her eyes scan the room. Her stance is sprung as tight as mine was a few moments ago. Gone is the easygoing, playful act to diffuse the tension. A frown graces her lips and I do my best to see over the crowd of people to where she is peering. The conversation around us moves forward, but it takes several more moments for her to relax again.

"Thought I saw him," she murmurs.

I grab hold of her hand to bring her attention back. It takes a moment for her gaze to stop scanning the room, but when she does look at me again, I can see the anger on her features. The centre of her brows is pinched together and that frown on her face puckers like she'd rather be spitting on Miles' grave than be at this party.

"Then let's hunt them down," I say.

Without a proper course, I guide us away from the group. There will be time to sort out Augustine later. The unease from earlier is rising in my gut again. Fucking Pat Lovette's threat is right there in my ear, taunting me as we search for our prey. This has to go well; she has to succeed. Nothing will prevent my *omphalos* from enacting her final revenge on the scumbags that hurt her.

Charlotte suddenly raises her hand and signals from across the room, leading us to look at the back of a man I don't know. But Delphini does. She comes to a halt in the back of the room, and power surges within her. A phantom tentacle from Love wraps itself around our joined hands and it's the only thing that keeps her from bolting across the room. I tighten my grip and use my other hand to grab her nape.

Pink braids curtain around us, blocking our view, and my lips trace her jaw until I can whisper in her ear.

"Breathe for us, wife. His hours are limited. Your time will come by night's end." My breath shudders as more of Love's tentacles wrap around us, their weight pressing us together until my back arches and my front is pressed into Delphini. Our lover's embrace is a perfect distraction, a grounding sensation that sets my skin ablaze.

"He needs to suffer." Her whisper is harsh as her fingers dig into my hips.

"And he will," I promise.

She inhales deeply, her forehead relaxing against mine as the auctioneer calls the crowd to attention. Chairs creaking and the shuffling of clothes is a muted background noise as we breathe each other in. Love's tentacles slowly recede as her power draws back. The first lot goes by quickly, numbers are shouted out quickly and then some vase is sold for ten grand.

"Next, we have a first edition set of *Jane Eyre* by Charlotte Brontë. They are in immaculate condition and do not contain the notice from the *Calcutta Review*. The starting bid is sixty."

Delphini perks up at the title, but the rise in her spirits doesn't last. On stage standing next to a small cart with a glass cloche over the top is the second man of the hour. Darren Gross. I cross my arms over my chest, letting my lower hand reach into my jacket to hold the small handle of my dagger. His tattooed hands are folding in front of him and his legs spread enough to intimidate, but it has nothing on my *omphalos*.

She rises to her full height and stares at the man. I can see when their eyes meet, how his throat contracts as he swallows. There is a sunglasses tan around his eyes that brightens further as his cheeks turn red. He doesn't move an inch from his position. My eyes shift to my human. Delphini twirls one of her braids innocently, before slowly bringing it to her throat. My skin grows hot when she slices it across her neck.

As a sinister grins spread across her face, my tongue suckles at the front of my teeth. Beneath the surface of my skin, my tentacles writhe and bubble up. I want to trace that line of her throat, want to kiss, and lick, and protect it from any possible damage. A blush rises in my cheeks as my clit pulses.

Augustine and Marcus Astor are in a bidding war for the set of books.

"Do I hear one hundred and ten?" the auctioneer calls out. "Going once..."

"One fifty." I raise my hand, and a few heads turn towards me.

I've brought attention to us. Miles knows Delphini is alive and here, but he can't leave, can he? He has tried to shun Delphini from this crowd, from a group she has belonged to her whole life. Showing an ounce of weakness now by retreating would cause too much gossip. To see his ex-fiancée on the arm of another so soon after their tragic ending must be confusing and infuriating. Not only does she live, but she has also found someone better in every way.

She exudes composure next to me, a goddess staring down at peasants, but my focus is on the moustached idiot trying to control himself. The scowl on Augustine's face threatens to dip lower than human and I smirk. Charlotte grabs hold of Marcus's hand to keep him from raising. It's the sandbag and me now.

"One sixty," he says.

"One seventy-five."

Joanna leans over to whisper something to him, and I see his eyes flash that fucked up black colour before he signals to the auctioneer he won't bid again. For now, I will take this win. Not only have I won the auction, but Joanna has also proven she has more control over that pompous fuck than I thought. Maybe I will just give the books to her if Delphini doesn't want them.

"Sold to the lovely pair at the back, please follow our attendant to finalise the sale."

She threads her hand through my arm and I walk us around the crowd. Her gaze never falters from Darren Gross on stage, but as we through tables and pass the one nearest the stage, she leans to the side.

"Good to see you, Miles."

I don't look back. I can't let myself stumble at this moment for her. But silence settles over the room as we leave. My heart soars with pride for my *omphalos*. Polite and deadly, a combination that I have never mastered, but one that Delphini wears like a second skin. Her hips brush against mine as they sway with each step we take closer to her first kill of the night.

Darren pushes the cart off stage and into a side room. We are right on his tail, which means when the door swings shut behind us and he tries to bolt, I easily grab onto his jacket and yank him back. Delphini smiles at the few other people in the room like this is a normal occurrence. Tentacles emerge from my hand, sliding into the slits of his jacket and wrapping around his thick waist to keep him from escaping. He stumbles as they cinch around him.

"Darren," Delphini smiles. "It is so good to see you again. It's been too long. How was your holiday?"

"Holiday of a lifetime." He gulps.

She hums, the fake smile still on her lips. "You're going to take a walk with me."

My limbs lock, tentacles squeezing tighter around the meat bag. She leans around him to look at me, but my face doesn't convey how much I fucking hate that idea because she winks at me. I open my mouth to protest, but she grabs hold of my hand and squeezes the tentacles. They slip back into my skin without my control.

"We don't-"

"You are going to go with her, or I am going to rip your nuts off and feed them to you," I say quietly before letting him go. "You have five minutes, and then I'll meet up with you."

"Yes, Captain," she says.

I shove Darren in the direction of a different set of doors. This building is a fucking maze. Delphini better know where the fuck she is going as she follows after him. Her hand slides onto his shoulder to make sure he doesn't try to run again. She isn't strong enough to keep him from breaking free, but I wouldn't put it past the fucker to try something.

They disappear quickly and then I turn to the accountant seated to my left. They don't blink as I walk up to them. In fact, under the bright lights in the room, I see a hint of sweat beading across their temple.

"Will this be your only purchassse for the evening?" They ask, their accent slipping in a way that I recognise they aren't human. Lamia. "Ms. Moore."

"Yes," I say, unbuttoning my jacket as I sit down. Both hilts of my daggers flash in their holsters. "And it's Captain Moore."

Their hands shake as they slide a certificate of authenticity across the table along with the bill. This is an expensive way to show up Augustine Ravenscroft, but it slowed my anger towards him for the moment. I fill out the account information required to make the transfer of one hundred and seventy-five thousand dollars.

Aoife is going to kill me in the morning.

CHAPTER TWENTY-FIVE
DELPHINI

14 Days

He doesn't even fight me. Gross follows me back through the yacht club until we are in a storage room filled with holiday decorations. Surrounded by carefully wrapped oversized Christmas ornaments and neatly folded Independence Day bunting, Darren looks resigned to his fate. Does he know I am going to kill him? It's not like Pat could have told him, since he's literally fish food. It's a relief to know that his last words were worthless, empty threats. Nobody has died without my hand plunging the knife in yet.

It's hard to work up the anger to summon Love.

Except then he scrubs his face with his hand and I see the tattoos. The hand that yanked me down the stairs until I fell, and wrenched up my dress until he could shove that hand between my legs while his buddy grabbed my chest, yank, yank, yank. The sensation of my body being pulled in so many directions makes me feel sick. Like I am on a boat instead of solid ground.

"You assaulted me." I state the facts like I am the judge presiding over a case.

"It had to happen," he replies quietly.

"What the fuck does that mean? None of it had to happen. You didn't have to say yes. You didn't have to let them do any of that."

"Yes, I did." He shudders. "Just like I am going to let this happen."

I pull up the hem of my dress enough so I can unsheathe the knife strapped to my thigh. I can't listen to this bullshit, because that's what this is. These are mind games to confuse me and distract me from piercing this fucker's heart. He deserves everything that is going to happen to him.

He swallows when he sees the blade but doesn't try to run.

"I've known about that night since I was twenty-three," he starts, tapping his forehead. "Have you ever looked death in the face?"

"Yes, obviously."

"Didn't you try to run?"

"I was drugged, Darren. Your friend Pat saw to that." I sneer. "But when I face death again, I'll put up one hell of a fucking fight."

He shrugs and nods, apathetic gestures from a man staring down the blade of a knife. "It sounds crazy, but I know this is the end of my life. There is no future I can see beyond this point. All roads I've chosen land me here in the end."

"So, you're fucking psychic? Then why did you run?" I ask, bored and annoyed with this weird conversation while Miles is out there. He could be on his way to fucking Cuba right now on his family's yacht as this man tries to convince me he saw the future.

"Instinct?" Darren shrugs again. "You can't fight fate, but my gut thought I should try."

"Fate doesn't excuse what you did. You still had a fucking choice," I seethe.

"You're right and wrong. Every choice I've made in life led me to that night. I chose to accept the money because I knew my days were numbered. I also chose to make sure Pat didn't do even more fucked up shit to you. You can only fight it so much."

"You disgust me," I hiss, advancing forward.

Darren doesn't move and that makes me angrier. I don't want to risk this dress over a physical altercation, except fuck this rotting feeling in the pit of my stomach keeps growing. I don't pity this shit bag. I don't. He deserves to spend eternity suffering. He deserves whatever hell his soul will suffer through Love's ancient powers.

"As I should."

The knife cuts through his shirt and slips between his ribs with ease. He doesn't make another sound, he can't. I've punctured his lung. My teeth grit together, my limbs shake as the power surges through them. It's a fight to get it through me, to feel the burn and see the pink glow from my chest. Darren closes his eyes, and a tear slips down his cheek. That disgusting feeling in my stomach doesn't budge as I twist the knife higher and puncture his heart.

Once the ebb of power has rushed back to me, I step to the side to make sure my dress stays clean and remove my knife. Darren Gross crumbles to the ground, dead.

Love hums in my mind, satisfied.

"Only one remains."

"What did he mean that he knew?" I ask. "H-he was human."

"Humans are profound conductors of magic, sweet one. You channel our magic even now. Sometimes, that magic can linger even once the source has left. It would seem he still possessed an amount that gave him a prophetic vision of his own death."

"God, this supernatural shit is fucked."

Love doesn't respond, but I need to get back. Not because Miles is a flight risk, but because Orthia is a fight risk. It wouldn't look good to have her tearing down every room in search of us. Whether I want to be a part of this tier of Gwenmore society or not, the last thing we need is to cause a scene that gets Darren's body discovered before we're gone for the night. I wipe the blade clean on his trousers and secure it back to my thigh holster.

The toilets next to this closet are empty, so I can quickly check my dress and wash my hands. I walk back into the small room as Orthia is about to open the door. We collide and I feel Love switch between us. It's jarring, and I'm not sure why they've done it. The pit in my stomach grows larger, and my stomach growls as if eating will fill the void.

My wife frowns. "Let's get you some food."

I don't bother to protest. Food won't fix this feeling, it never has, but something to keep my energy up for Miles would be good. We head for the main hall again. The auction hasn't progressed much further, from what I can tell. The small display of the donation goal has only increased by about ten percent. The catering staff wander around tables between each presentation, refilling drinks and dropping off new plates. Orthia leads us to our table, where Charlotte and Marcus sit with a few other people who look like they might be Marcus's family... pack?

And Teddy, of course, who looks uncharacteristically sad when we sit down again.

Orthia pulls out my chair for me before she grabs hold of the nearest server. I don't hear what she tells the guy, but he blanches enough for me to know it's a threat.

"You look good together." Teddy smiles. "I just wish I had done someth-"

"It was destiny," I interrupt him. "I'm learning to look past the first shit hand fate dealt me."

"I'll drink to that." He slides a wine glass to me and then raises his. "Fuck fate and being fucked by it."

I knock back the white wine, savouring the hints of stone fruit that grace my palette before swallowing. The uneasiness I feel lessens slightly, and when Orthia tosses her arm around the back of my chair, I relax into it. Her fingers trace the shape of my shoulder, carefully avoiding my hair so we are in constant contact. Warmth laps at my skin like waves on the beach.

"So... how did you learn about all this?" I ask after the server drops off an entire tray of hors d'oeuvres.

"My long-dead relative was a highborn druid." Teddy sighs. "Very powerful, very disliked by all. I've got the last bit of magic left in the lineage, so I am being urged to find a suitable partner to procreate with to continue the family's misguided legacy."

"I didn't mind Milson Bushwipper too much." Orthia grabs a crab cake and offers it to me, feeds it to me really because she refuses to let go of the thing. "He liked being in everyone's business, which meant he liked to know things. When I told him my grand mission, he learned to stay the fuck away lest he meet the sharp end of my blade."

"Others aren't so open." Teddy giggles over his wine glass. "But I also have a penchant for needing to know everything."

"Which is why we are great friends," I agree. "If I knew of any decent men, Teddy, I would send them your way, but I am happily living without them."

"I don't think I really fancy parenting anything, anyway. Not even a plant."

"Now, c'mon," Marcus pipes up, distracted from the bidding. "Ted, you'd be a great dad."

Teddy shivers at the thought, and the conversation moves on. I look around the room and find the back of Mile's head. I stare at his dark hair, the cut of his shoulders looking bigger than I remember. Probably padding in his suit. He bids on stupid stuff, wins a load of shit that I can only imagine will refill his family's once empty house if they haven't done that already. Vases, paintings, Persian rugs— his bill is racking up higher and higher.

He's enjoying spending my money, while I watch, unable to do anything about it. I'll never get back my trust fund, whatever is left of it, but that doesn't mean I enjoy watching it be squandered away. After bidding insanely over the value of a truly hideous balloon animal sculpture, he turns enough to look at me. I hope he felt so inclined to do so because he could feel the daggers I'm glaring at him, but he smirks. Miles looks pleased with himself and not at all scared to see me. Slapping his hand on the back of a man seated next him, he stands to leave.

Unlike Orthia, who had to secure payment early as an unknown buyer, the Bradshaws do not. They are expected to spend large sums of money, and the club knows they are good for it. Well, they are now at least. It means that when Miles gets up and leaves in the direction of the bathroom, I get up as well. Charlotte catches my eye and nods, the only bit of encouragement she can offer me right now.

This won't be the last time I see her, or Teddy, but there is a sense of finality when I look up at them to leave the table. They understand, I am on a vastly different life path now than I was three months ago, or when I first moved to Gwenmore. The openness in their expressions that I didn't know I was missing, makes it feel like I'm on a better path than I ever thought possible for myself.

Orthia rises with me. She nods, the frown on her lips is natural and determined. The set of her shoulders is tight, and I know she hates the suit I've dressed her in tonight. I am giddy to be done with it all. Not because I have struggled with the task; on contrary, I think I've become pretty damn amazing at this vigilante shit. The idea of spending eternity murdering bad people side by side with my soulmate is what I am giddy for.

The lobby to the club is quiet as we follow Miles. He doesn't head for the bathroom as expected. I wouldn't have put it past him to need a top up of whatever designer drug he is currently interested in, but instead he takes a left that leads to the private entrance of the wharf. Orthia draws the daggers from her under her jacket and I do the same. I catch the blush on her cheek as I raise the hem of my dress and she sees the thigh holster.

"I knew it was there, but seeing it..." She trails off, eyes glued to the straps until I drop my dress again.

"Later, *wife*."

Miles is halfway to the *Platinum Signal* by the time we are on the vast rows of docked yachts. Beyond the simple security lighting, there aren't any security guards around. Everyone is too focused on the charity gala to worry about non-members sneaking in.

When our engagement party was here I remember them mentioning that security does rounds regularly, but I didn't care enough at the time to really worry about it. The people who dock their massive pleasure ships here are the type of people who don't want security cameras seeing what all they get up to. What they care about is making sure outsiders aren't let in.

But we are already in. As Miles steps onto the family ship without a care in the world, we are only a few paces behind him. It's still moored, so won't be sailing off, but we are far enough away from the crowd that when I beat the shit out of him before killing him, nobody will hear us.

She takes a long moment to look around before saying, "I'll go first, make sure there are no ambushes. You have one goal. Don't get distracted. Ready?"

"Yes, Captain." I agree without question.

Now isn't the time for fuck ups. She takes her jacket off and rolls the sleeves of her shirt up to expose the marking on her arms. Already they glow a faint shade of pink, a hint of power slipping through her cool I. Orthia is ready to take on an army so I can kill my ex.

I grab her by the holster and kiss her, smearing whatever remains of my lip gloss on her mouth. She pries my mouth open and pomegranates burst on my tongue like popping candy. Her tongue tangles with mine for barely a second before she is pulling away.

"Kiss me proper when he's dead," she whispers before darting up into *The Platinum Signal.*

A heavy breath blows past my lips. I am going to do so much more than kiss her when this night is done. We are going to have the fucking party of the century, the orgy of the century. There won't be a part of Orthia that goes without my mouth on it.

Ahead of me, it's silent, so I focus on breathing when I step on to the yacht. My stomach rolls slightly, my knees wobble for a moment, but I push through. The halls are dark, and as much as I want to turn on my phone light, I don't. The element of surprise should make this easier. My free hand fumbles for the wall, and I use that to keep my balance as we hunt down Miles.

It's too maddening, and the silence breaks with every step I take across through the lower deck towards the staircase. The purse in my hand weighs twice as much. That pit in my stomach grows the longer I wander around the yacht. There are too many places for Miles to hide. I end up at the back of the lower deck, out in the open air again and staring out at the bay, and the Atlantic.

My chest glows as I look at the calm waters, feeling Love call to me, soothe me. I nearly jump out of my skin when there is a splash above me. A small, half-aborted noise rips through me. My clutch tumbles into the sea, but I don't think as I rush to the stairs that lead on to the main deck.

Orthia stands on the side, drenched while a man lies face down in the pool.

"Jesus Christ," I hiss, stepping closer.

"This deck is clear. Five guards, no guns, but they have tasers."

As she says it, I see the small holes and wires in her shirt. Blood drips down the side of her face. Tentacles slip in and out of existence as she wipes a hand over her face. She sheathes one dagger into the holster then looks me over.

"Seasick?"

"No, I'm good. I want this done. It's creepy here in the dark."

She nods but doesn't say anything else. As I pull the knife from my thigh holster, Orthia pulls the last of the taser wires from her chest. She nods to the stairs that lead up to the owner's deck and I follow behind her. I don't like it here, even when I didn't think Miles was capable of physical violence. The design is cold, pristine even, but without the touches of life around the ship, it's haunting simply by nature.

Trying to control my other reactions, the ones that are trying to fire up my instinctual response to run, is not helping me. I need that energy to focus on stabbing Miles, on harnessing the power Love has given me. A scuffle startles me and I'm blinded when lights flash on.

Miles sits on that white leather couch, watching the reflection of the TV as Orthia grapples with a massive man. Two wires are attached to her stomach, her body shaking and fighting the electric current. Tentacles squirm around her bare skin, curling in on themselves rather than strike the man. She brings her knee up into his face, but he dodges her.

"Focus, Delphini," she grunts, as the man lunges for her again.

I shouldn't be torn on what to do, but I am. She is more than capable of taking out the attacker. It's only when I see Miles stand to leave that my body finally kicks itself into gear. I adjust my hold on my dagger and follow him down the hall towards the primary suite.

Attack, thrust, lunge.

Adrenaline douses my blood with fire, and my limbs begin to tingle as I push the door up and see him standing next to the Jacuzzi. He doesn't look back at me, doesn't have an ounce of fear on his features when he finally turns to look at me. The light from the water glows across his pale features, making him look like a ghost already.

"Phi-phi, I must say I am impressed."

He grins when he looks at me. The fucker grins at me and I want to rip his teeth from his mouth. I step up onto the platform carefully until there is nothing to get in the way, not even a railing to keep us from falling off the edge. My stomach drops into my knees.

"Breathe, sweet one."

"You survived, but I guess Audrey wasn't the best at knots. Just wish I'd fucked her that night before she died." He turns his back on me as he walks towards the bow of the yacht.

"You were there?" I ask.

"No, no, but she had been staying at the apartment. She saw your message and thought changing the codes would be enough. She insisted you weren't capable of getting physical." A crash behind us interrupts him. Neither of us look back to see who has walked onto the deck. "But you've found someone who's happy to do the dirty work, I see."

"I killed Audrey," I proclaim, stepping forward and pointing my dagger at him. "And I killed those two fucks, and now I'm going to kill you."

"Are you?" He asks, twirling around to face me in the dark. "I'm not sure you could even get near me without throwing up."

"You motherfucker."

I see pink. Love's mark explodes with colour as I lunge for him. Miles catches my wrist, but we fall onto the deck in a struggle. The dagger clatters to the edge of the ship, but I can't worry about it. With both my wrists restrained I have no choice; I slam my forehead into his nose. The shock loosens his grip. He barely has a chance to grunt before I am rolling off him and towards the knife. I scoop it up and dart towards the bow. He takes a step back towards the light and I see it.

He pulls a gun on me.

"Don't bring a knife to a gun fight."

"Nice try," Orthia hisses, kicking him in the back on his knee.

Miles falls to the ground and she grabs his arm that holds the gun. In one swift motion, she breaks it and the weapon hits the deck. Miles wails into the night. My chest heaves as I step forward, knife poised to strike.

My body vibrates with power. The glow from me, from Orthia, illuminates the whole deck. Sweat dots Miles' face, his nose drips blood and his tears flow from his eyes. He's pathetic. With every step I take towards him, the rage inside of me grows. I am going to destroy him, and Love shall feast on him. He will never know peace for what he did to me. He ruined me and I am going to ruin his afterlife in turn.

Orthia grabs his hair to keep him from slumping forward, yanking his head back until he is forced to look at her blood-stained face. His broken arm falls to his side as she grabs his face with her other hand. She makes me look at me.

When I stare at them, all I see is the rage and hunger in my soulmate's gaze. She's controlling herself so I can do this, so we can do this together. For as much as I want Miles Bradshaw to rot for eternity, so does she. Orthia is keeping good on her promise to be better in a way that's violent and bloody and so fucking hot.

The final pillar of my revenge cries like a baby in the face of death. Miles looks at me with fear and I love it. I want him to fear me, to feel the inevitability that I felt that night. Wind whips at my dress and the tide begins to rise. There is a rumbling in the air.

"Ple-" he chokes on his words, pleading to me.

Orthia's tentacles lash around his throat and she forces him to look at me. His shrieks carry in the breeze, out across the bay for anyone to hear.

"Look at her," she demands. "You defaced *a goddess* and now you will pay for your crimes."

There is no speech or gloating. On shaking legs, the void in my belly threatening to implode as the waters become choppy, I grab hold of Miles' jacket. The black fabric crushes beneath my hand. I feel the padding. He isn't as strong as he wants people to believe. Miles is just as pathetic as he was when we last saw each other, using other people and a facade to create his strength. He isn't scary, he isn't stronger than me really.

"I win."

My dagger sinks into his torso, my hand shaking as he tries to breath but can't. His body jerks like he wants to run away, but instead, it just tears his insides. Love's power surges through me. Victory, revenge, it's all mine but something isn't right. Pink fills my vision, my arm burns with the force of it, but it won't stop. I can't pull my knife from his chest.

"Delphini," Orthia says my name, but I can't respond. Blood trickles over my hand and I'm mesmerised by how much it looks like tentacles slithering over my hands. It takes all of my focus to pull my gaze back to her. There is nothing but fear in her eyes now. "What's wrong?"

She is a vision in pink. I can't blink away the haze, and the longer I stare at her, the more fuzzy she becomes. Orthia isn't a human any more, replaced with a mass of tentacles, all writhing and forming the shape of what she should be. Her head bobs atop them like a small boat at sea, and I feel almost seasick watching it.

"Love, what's happening?" she demands.

Her hand grabs onto mine, and she tries to pry my fingers from the blade, anything to get me disconnected from Miles, to stop the power still surging through me. It's not working. My body is locked into this space as she shouts at me and at Love. She doesn't understand and I can't help her.

The sky erupts with lightning and the ocean quakes. A tentacle, monstrously large and teal, rips through the yacht, through Orthia's holds on me. The last thing I hear is the many voices of our patron– whisper, screeching, sobbing.

"Trust us."

CHAPTER TWENTY-SIX
DELPHINI

0 Days

Am I dead again?

Is that what this floating feeling is? I didn't fail. Love's power flowed through me like it should have, but I didn't feel the rush of energy like I had previously. There wasn't the hunger or the surge of greatness like previous times that made me feel truly invincible. I can only remember the burn of it that welded me to Miles, to the dagger I had plunged into his torso.

Orthia's fingers attempting to pry mine free.

I move my fingers to make sure they still work, that I am in control of them once again. My toes are next, then I scrunch my nose up just to test it works. My body is weightless here as I float through a dark abyss. As I exhale through my mouth, I see faint pink bubbles float above me.

"Love, what's going on?" I call out, but they don't answer.

Centering myself doesn't help. The more I practise cycling breathing to focus on myself and my energy, the more scared I get. I am trapped again in the dark, but I can't feel anything. I can't get out of this place.

What did I do wrong?

Even in the pink glowing light from our collective marks, Miles didn't die until I killed him. My promise to Love has been fulfilled as they required it be. I toppled the fourth pillar of my revenge.

"Is this enough?" A distinct and sharp voice screams.

There is another sound, wet and grotesque, before something heavy splashes around me. The void I'm in turns red, stained with whatever that was and now seeping around me. It creeps across my skin, trickling up into my body until all I see is Orthia.

Her body is drenched with something, her cheeks blotchy. A light around her explodes and my vision of her goes with it. What has she done?

I need to go to her. She has to know I'm okay, but that something is wrong. Whatever is happening isn't her fault. We did everything we were supposed to do. Love has never steered her wrong before.

Their words to me echo around the space as if by thinking back to the first time I was ever in a place like this has materialised them.

"Trust us. Join with us."

I have joined with them, I do trust Love. Why are they doing this to me? What more could they want? I try to remember more of that first as I roll to my side. Twisting and turning, my braids wrap around my body like tentacles until I am cocooned.

"STOP." Love's bellow rips through the ether. My bones ache, my teeth threaten to fall from my mouth with fear just as my tears do. I stop twisting, stop breathing, stop thinking.

My mind fractures, pink shards of light splintering across my vision until I see something new.

Orthia swimming, her body a mass of tentacles that moves with grace and destruction. Bubbles explode from her mouth, but she keeps going. She's chasing something, but I can't see what. There is nothing I can do to save her, to stop her. More tears slip down my face. I can't blink them away as I watch my soulmate's pink glow slip further and further away from the darkness.

"Please, Love, please, tell me what I need to do, and I'll do it." My words echo and reverberate around the abyss until I am drowning in the sound of it. There is no escape from the desperation in my voice, the tragedy of my new life ending so soon.

"We wait, sweet one, we wait for our heart." Love whispers, the hope in their voice chilling me to my soul. Hope is supposed to be a positive emotion, yet our

patron, our Love has only ever been sure, all knowing. Why do they need hope when they simply are?

Orthia screams. Bubbles erupt around her and the tentacles that make up her body suddenly recede. She floats in the dark waters, lifeless. Her body is mangled now, limbs not where they should be. I choke on a sob at the vision before me. The tentacles that are etched into her skin glow faintly, her soul still fighting, still chasing. But her body has given up.

"Please," I whisper, "Come to us, Orthia, find me and we can fix this together."

"Her destiny has split," Love echoes the same words they spoke to me months ago. "She must choose her new path now that she has done what she set out to do centuries ago."

"I don't understand," I cry. "We have a path. It's to bring you to our world, Love. So we can be together, rule together."

"Yes, sweet one," they purr. "*We three shall rule the tides and seas, but as you have given us your body, we have given our heart to another. As you have evolved so must she now.*"

It's not dread that unravels my braids coiling around me, though it isn't relief either. A sense of understanding and finality, anticipation as I wait for my wife, my love, my captain to make the choice I know she will make. My limbs move with ease now, as if recognition has released me from whatever was mentally blocking me.

A movement in the corner catches my eyes and I float towards it. A glimmering pink light, barely strong enough to break through the darkness, settles around a curled-up form. Tentacles wrap and twist around it, cocooning it just like I was moments ago. I fold myself over it, and something comes over me. I have to know who or what this is. I pull at the tentacles until I see what's actually there. A body takes shape, a monster I haven't seen before or heard the crew talk about. It's soft, angelic even, with teal skin and tentacles that form at odd places before fading back into the dark.

"Love?" I whisper, unsure how this could be our patron, our god. I know it is, though, in the same way that I knew Orthia was my soulmate after that first vision; something about this creature tells me this is who Love used to be.

Six eyes open at once and look at me. There is something innocent and destructive in them that calls to me. *"Would you still choose a god who used to cower?"*

The question stops me. Imagining our Love, scared and alone in this dark place cracks my open. More tears fall streak my face as I look at them anew. I cup their cheek, feeling the scars and groves under my palm. And I know the truth.

Their story has been locked away in the depths of the abyss just as they have. Mistreated and abused by primordial gods the world has forgotten, Love was locked away and forgotten, cast aside just like those they have spent eons trying to help heal. Love has given so much to the rest of us, but it is time now that she sees the light again.

"It's your turn to evolve, Love." My voice cracks as I speak to them. "You know Orthia will make the right choice just like you knew I was the one."

They lean into my touch, tentacles wrapping around my hand and slowly wrapping around my arm. *"We will be forever grateful for your trust in us, sweet one."*

I lean down further until my forehead is pressed to theirs. My body sinks into theirs, tentacles warming my skin and soothing my racing heart. There is a flash of pink light.

"We have a captain to save," I murmur, my nose brushing against their face.

Love kisses my lips for the first and last time. *"She has always been a reckless heart."*

EPILOGUE
ORTHIA

0 Days

I slap my hand across my face when something tickles me. The joints in my fingers crack with the impact of my jaw and that is how I know I am alive. I can still see the explosion, wood splintering, the choppy waters bursting as their tentacle ripped through the yacht.

Behind my eyelids, there is no pink glow, just a dark orange. I am warm and dry, except for the spot that touched my face. A part of me doesn't want to open my eyes. I don't want to return to *The Despair* with a crew who will see that I am back, but she isn't. I can't bear the emptiness that will come with it. The lightness she brings to our life will be replaced with the weight of my failure.

I don't know how, but I have failed my *omphalos* and my Love.

A tear slips from the corner of my eye, cooling my heated skin. Their words echo in my thoughts: *to forge a path unknown, you must relinquish that which isn't yours*.

I sobbed, begged them to take everything from me, so long as they wouldn't take Delphini with them. I'm not sure if they heard my cries.

"We've got to stop meeting like this."

The air is punched from my chest when I hear her voice. I open my eyes as Delphini blinks tears onto my face. Her hand cups my cheek and warmth explodes from it. My body sings with the glory of her divinity. She's still here. I raise my hand to touch her as well, to swipe the tears away from her cheek, but I stop short.

My skin is clear, speckled with hair and odd dark freckles, but I am without Love's mark. There are no scars, no tentacles. I try to call them forth, but all I feel is my tongue. The suckers latch onto my teeth, but the rest of me is human. She must see the concern on my face because Delphini hushes me.

She grabs hold of my hand and brings it to her face. Warmth grows where we are connected and I weep.

We are together. She is real and whole. My *omphalos* is still with me. My lips part as I suck in stunted breaths. There is so much I must do now, but I need to hold her in my arms. My muscles ache as I move, but I fight through the pain. She is really with me. As tightly I grip her, she holds me just as fiercely. She holds onto my nape as I bury my face in her braids. She chokes on a sob.

"I'm sorry I failed you," I say, over and over again until I am hoarse. "I will spend the rest of my days proving myself to you."

"Shh." Her hand brushes through my short buzz cut. "No, Orthia, we did it."

"No," I argue. "I ruined everything, and I thought I lost you."

"Listen to me, wife," she says, squeezing me lightly before pulling back.

I am not worthy of the title now, not after what I have done to her. She deserves so much more, someone who will follow her without getting in the way.

"We did it," she asserts again. "Love is here now."

Her eyes flash a milky white and then she transforms. Her body morphs, braids twisting into tentacles and skin slickening. Where Delphini's two brown eyes are warm, they are replaced with a set of six navy blue eyes. Her nose flattens into nothing. Her lips are as dark as the depths.

"We had to evolve and reclaim the broken parts of us," Love says. *"You gave us the strength to be here, your love did this."*

"But what about Delphini?" I ask, staring at the creature before me. A human-like torso that melds into a mass of tentacles, all of them teal. All of them covered in scars and etchings.

"I am right here." The body turns halfway back to hers, the etched teal replaced with her smooth brown skin. "I am still here, Orthia. But so is Love."

"If you had known all along, Love, why didn't you tell me?" I ask.

"You know there must always be a choice. First you accepted us, then our sweet one. We were destined to reunite, to join. Her soul is a small fragment of me that was once lost to the cosmos. But we needed our soulmate, too." They weave their fingers through mine. We are holding hands for the first time.

I have never held them like this. For as long as we have been connected, Love has never had such a human form with me. I never desired one; what I wanted was them, but now they appear before me like this. I find I crave this touch just as much.

Delphini has ruined me. Centuries of denial, of being chilled to the bone by the simple brush of another, and it only took a summer to have me craving her hands, her gentleness. And Love offers me the same. Their grip is secure enough to touch all of me yet loose enough that I could pull my hand away without effort. A gentle, supportive hold that I have known for nearly all my life.

"Truly the goddess I was always meant to worship at the altar of," I whisper, my chest aching with emotions I have never felt before.

"You are our priestess, our captain, our wife," Delphini says, smiling as Love takes over her form once again. *"Our heart."*

"Kiss me."

There is a breath, a moment where Love looks at me with wonder, with hunger, like they can't believe they will get to touch me like this. Wet lips meet mine, and I am lost in the taste of pomegranate and salt that coats their tongue. My body buzzes with energy from their slick, but when I take control of this kiss, they soften. Love's form pulls me on top of them. The tentacles that make up their lower half twist around my legs softly while their hands cup my cheek. I am immersed in their warm embrace like never before.

The god before me bows to my needs as I plunder their mouth—our first kiss. And when I pull away, a goddess stares up at me, one I will happily follow into our new age.

12 Days

Even as I shove my feet back into my boots, I don't want to leave. Tourist season is over, finally. Why the fuck should we be doing anything but relax? We should be in the bath with the rest of the crew. I should be watching my *omphalos* lick every inch of Cookie's sex while Hamako sits on her troll's face. There should be nothing but debauchery before me.

But no. It's Tuesday night. And Aoife refuses to attend another meeting in our stead. According to news reports, *The Platinum Signal* hosted a much too wild party involving drugs and fireworks that caused an almost unbelievable explosion. The family is distraught that their son is missing, but no official charges have been brought up against him or the Bradshaws. Everyone is just happy to see it all swept under the rug as an accident.

Apparently, I owe Ramón and Arlo for the body cleanup. Fuck that. I would have been happy for the shitty Gwenmore Police Department to clean up that mess.

"Do we have to go?" I ask for the tenth time this evening.

Delphini applies a coat of lip gloss in front of the vanity in our room, the whole table strewn with her beauty supplies. The high-tech and vibrant-coloured tools and palettes are a stark difference from the dark wood and neutral furnishing. But her silk pillowcases brighten the bed. The extra clothing rack we bought for her sits adjacent to the bed and acts like a pink curtain for that half of the room.

"Yes." Love answers. Through the reflection of the mirror, they wink at me. This new, playful side of them is dangerous and free, but it makes my heart race, too.

"We go for the whole meeting this time," Delphini adds quickly.

"Did you call your *yiayia* back?" I ask, changing the subject while I scrub the back of my neck, fingers digging into my one remaining mark before I tie my scarf off.

"Yes, she's demanding to see us." She turns to look at me before half morphing into Love. Tentacles float around her head, the tips kissing her neck before slipping back into Delphini's curls. The three eyes and blue skin remain in place.

"It will be good to see the start," they say.

Since they have escaped their void, Love is extremely weakened. There is no more controlling the tides or sinking islands, but there are moments when I can still feel them in my mind and can reach for them. That is enough for now as we start off on our new path into the unknown.

"Oh, wait," Delphini gasps, shoving her stool back and rushing out of our room.

She runs down the hall to her old room, which still holds quite a few of her belongings. I lean against the jamb of our door and wait for her to return. There is a moment when I think I hear a giddy, familiar laugh in my head, but it is gone as she reappears.

As she approaches, her shoulders square like she is about to fight me. Her fingers curl into a fist, but I hold my ground until she stops directly in front of me again. She stares down at me, her incredible dark eyes glowing with mischief.

"Orthia," she begins. "I have known you for a short time and for lifetimes. You are my soulmate."

"Yes, I am." I smile.

"My *yiayia* gave these to me on my eighteenth birthday, with firm instructions to only offer them to someone who understood all I could."

I think of that picture of her *yiayia* that I saw weeks ago. Will she approve of me?

Delphini raises her hand, and as her fingers unfurl, two rings appear. One is simple, a silver band engraved with filigree similar to a tree branch. Around the band, it is dotted with tiny red gemstones. Next to it, is a much larger ring, atop the silver band sits a fat red gemstone surrounded by smaller white ones. The longer I stare at them, the more I believe that they are actually rubies.

"You are my wife. And I said I wanted to be romanced, for everyone to know. Will you please wear one of these, for us?" she asks.

"Holy shit." I smirk, mimicking the phrase she says to me so often.

"Wife," she pouts, her shiny bottom lip poking out.

I raise my bare left hand and place it in front of her. "My *omphalos*, my goddess, you are my whole world. I would be honoured."

Delphini lets out a shuddering breath, and a brilliant smile creases her face as she puts the simple band on my finger. I slide the other ring onto her finger before bringing her knuckles to my lips. I trail kisses over her hand, to her wrist, and up her arm until I am pulling her down to meet my lips.

The gloss sticks my lips to her perfectly, but she pulls away much too soon for my liking.

7 Days

I miss Greece.

I miss the sun on my skin, my *omphalos* naked in the surf, and how Love shined beneath the waves. The three of us free and at peace together. A scowl forms on my lips as more memories of our vacation slip from my meditative state. It's the middle of winter and I'm bored out of my fucking mind. Aoife has taken the commercial ship and most of the crew out to sea, so there isn't much to fill my days, and I refuse to leave Delphini's side. She slips her hand into mine without even breaking the conversation she is having with Joanna. The ring on my finger shines in the cheap fluorescent lights overhead as warmth blooms from her touch.

Nora sits beside me, preventing me from meditating further on my goddess.

"So, next Friday, you, me, the humans, and a bottle of my finest-" She doesn't get farther in her proposal before Deg'Doriel storms through the doors of the basement. He has barely passed through the door before bursting into flames.

"Shut the fuck up and sit down." He barks, and I roll my eyes at him. "Don't start with me. Your little Greek escapade made the fucking news."

"Cut the shit, Deg," I grunt, but can't keep the smirk off my lips. "It's a miracle those women made it to shore after the freak storm capsized the pirate ship they were on."

Truly a miracle. Much to *Yiayia's* delight, I convinced Delphini we should spend the day on water rather than get sand in places it doesn't belong. We happened upon some merfolk who knew about a ship trafficking women. The storm that brewed when my *omphalos* heard that. The hunger that burned in her eyes. A heat settles between my legs as I think about it, my fingers squeezing hard around hers.

This meeting can't be done fast enough for my liking. Around me there is more conversation, but my focus drifts across a vast sea of more interesting things. Delphini's thick thighs wrapped around my head, her tentacles teasing my tongue with the taste of her musk.

Love's tentacles taking over her lower leg until they can slip between my legs. Suction on my clit makes me groan into the wet pussy threatening to drown me.

"Del, go."

My *omphalos* brings my knuckles to her lips with a wink.

"If you keep teasing us, our heart, we will cause a different storm."

Love's voice is soft in my ear now, the rumbling more of a purr now that they are free from their void. As their power slowly grew, this was the first ability that returned. Tears still prick at the corner of my eyes when I hear their voice again. I don't know how long it will last or how much power they still need, but for now, this is enough.

Delphini's pink silk trousers slip gracefully around her form as she stands, the matching jacket draped carefully across the back of her chair. As ever, she is a vision of grace and glory.

"This week has been trying. I've started my new role as head of the Saints for Love Charity." At the mention of her problematic week, Love morphs across half of her face. There is no flicker of lights, but I can hear the shift of people in their seats. The manifestation of a god before them makes them nervous. The tentacles of Love's hair caress Delphini's cheek in a sweet gesture, though. "So, despite how much I want to kill for these women, we are still at seven days."

She sits back down and I wrap my arm around her shoulder. Tentacles intertwine with my fingers as I press my forehead to her temple. "I am so proud of you, Delphini."

Thank You for Reading!

If you liked this book, please remember to leave a review on your preferred sites to help other readers find my work.

None of this would have been possible without the amazing help from generous and supportive people in my life. Thank you for never giving up on me.

Special shout out to-

- To Lyonne and Kassic for listening to complain and cry about this book

- To Emma and Orla for constantly being around to do sprints and cheer me on.

- To Caitlin, my developmental editor, who pushed me to make this story all it could be.

- To my beta team, I'm so sorry for all the typos, but your encouragement and kindness got me through it.

- To Bee at Nemosyne Digital for sensitive reading and giving feedback that made me cry and laugh.

- To Angie at Lunar Rose Editing Services for

taking this hot mess and making it readable.

Ash Raven is an indie author who specialises in spicy monster and alien romances that focus on plus-size and LGBTQ+ leads who get the love of a lifetime. They strive to write stories that are inclusive and real, with a touch of magic and a boat load of spice. When they are not writing, they are cuddling with their two orange cats and playing cosy video games. Born and raised in Indiana, they have been living their own insta-love romance in London, UK since 2015.

Want to know more? You can find Ash on most social media as @authorashraven or subscribe to their newsletter through the QR code below for exclusive updates, art prints, and cat pictures.